EQUINOX
ON ARRAN

Equinox on Arran

Published by The Conrad Press Ltd. in the United Kingdom 2022

Tel: +44(0)1227 472 874

www.theconradpress.com

info@theconradpress.com

ISBN 978-1-915494-24-5

Typesetting and Cover Design by: Charlotte Mouncey, www.bookstyle.co.uk

The Conrad Press logo was designed by Maria Priestley.

Printed and bound in Great Britain by Clays Ltd, Elcograf S.p.A. Equinox

EQUINOX
ON ARRAN

IAN ROBERTSON

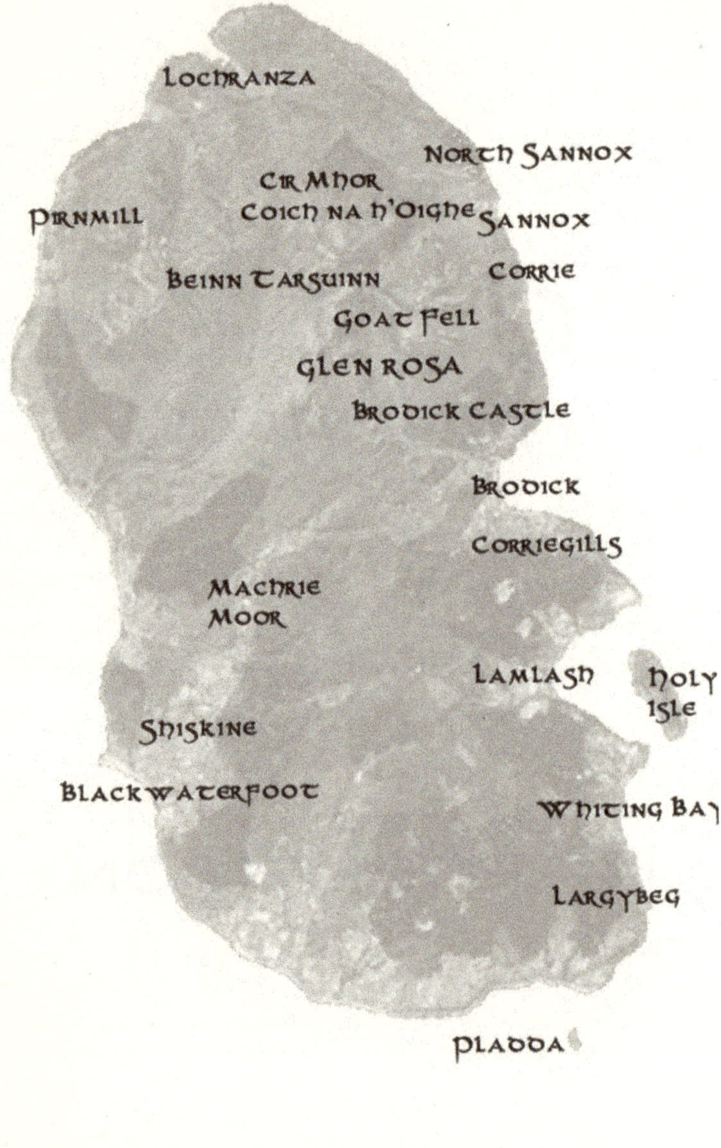
Lochranza
North Sannox
Cir Mhor
Coich na h'Oighe
Pirnmill
Sannox
Corrie
Beinn Tarsuinn
Goat Fell
Glen Rosa
Brodick Castle
Brodick
Corriegills
Machrie
Moor
Lamlash
Holy
Isle
Shiskine
Blackwaterfoot
Whiting Bay
Largybeg
Pladda

In loving memory of Jim, Effie and Ailsa,
with whom I have enjoyed many
happy memories of Arran.

Introduction to Arran

This land full of life, so peaceful and still,
with its shores and ridges, its mountains and hills,
is filled with abundance of wild fertile land,
gracefully given by nature's best hand

Goat Fell dominates Brodick's sheltered bay,
Commanding respect in its own scenic way.
Its friend, the warrior, sleeps forever at rest,
his head on Glen Rosa, his feet to the west

Look at his face. See his eyes, nose and chin,
and remember his name: Beinn Tarsuinn.
Calmly fierce and so well defined
These mountains can be so cruel or so kind.

At the foot of Goat Fell, its castle is poised
like a soldier hailing the island's loud voice.
This beauty is perennial since time began.
Forever, this is Eilean Arran.'

CHAPTER 1

21st March Equinox

Logan parked his car out of sight from the prison entrance. He didn't want to make this visit, especially on such a cold morning. He wasn't sure if he was being watched. He knew he was hated. He considered the possibility that he could be ambushed by a gangster or perhaps shot at by a sniper even though such possibilities were unlikely. Looking around carefully, he limped cautiously towards the entrance, paying attention to the icy patches on the pavement.

Wearing his tweed hat and dark rimmed glasses, he had his grandmother's olive wood walking stick which he occasionally used to support his leg injury. The layers of clothing beneath his thick winter jacket gave the false impression of him being fatter than he actually was. On this occasion he exaggerated his limp, trying to give the appearance of being an older man with a disability, all for the purpose of avoiding recognition by anyone who may know him. He signed himself in at the prison entrance and gave the prison staff custody of his walking stick.

'I'm here to see Verhoeven,' he said. 'Clive Verhoeven. He's expecting me.'

After a few minutes he was led into the inmates' meeting room. Other inmates sat at their allocated tables waiting for their family members to arrive. It had been almost twenty years since Logan had set eyes on Clive, but he recognised him immediately, sitting alone at the farthest away table in the distant corner of the room. Clive, wearing his obligatory prison clothing, didn't immediately recognise Logan until he approached the table. Clive's face had a calm expression as he tried to conceal his extreme hatred for Logan. He became sarcastically welcoming, almost grunting as he spoke with his harsh tone of voice:

'Well, at long last, the prodigal son arrives.'

Logan raised one eyebrow at this comment as he sat down. It was obvious to both men that the atmosphere was tense and that it would remain so throughout their meeting.

'I've been called many names but never been called a prodigal son,' replied Logan with a straight face.

'Yeah, Equinox,' said Clive with his increasingly sinister tone of voice. 'Apparently, it's your birthday today. I just wanted to see my son on his birthday. I hope this hasn't spoiled your birthday plans.'

'Your son's dead,' said Logan. 'And I'm not your son. But don't worry about my birthday plans. I have them sorted for later.'

'You've put on a lot of weight,' said Clive. 'You've become a fat bastard. Eating too much shit, are you? Or are you just thoroughly lazy?'

'Too much of the good life.' said Logan, almost gloating. 'No prison food where I've been.'

This comment irritated Clive.

'And glasses? You're going a bit blind, are you? Mind you, you were always shit at seeing things my way.'

'I just put them on so that I could see your beautiful face

again,' replied Logan sarcastically with a fake smile. 'Because I'd let myself forget about you for the last twenty years while I moved on with my life. Anyway, why am I here? I got a call from the prison saying you wanted to talk with me. That's the first time in twenty years. We could sit her and throw nasty comments at each other, or maybe it would be a better idea for you to just cut through the crap and tell me why you wanted to see me. And I really don't think you wanted to wish me a happy birthday.'

Clive sat there silently staring at Logan. After several seconds of awkward silence, Logan looked around the room, telling Clive:

'I've never been inside a prison before, so I don't really know how this works, but I think these meetings are only for a short time, so either you tell me now why I'm here or I'll just get up and walk away. I'll give you five seconds to start talking.'

After five seconds of tense silence, Logan made his move to stand up, stopped only by Clive's next comment:

'You think you're smarter than me, don't you?'

Logan sat back down again, then replied:

'Actually, now that you mention it. Yes. I do think I'm smarter than you. Much smarter. You've spent twenty years locked in this shit hole because of the bad things you've done while I've been outside enjoying my life, not harming people. So yes, I'm smarter than you. Definitely. What's your point?'

Clive reduced his sarcastic tone to that of being more inquisitive while changing his calm facial expression to one of spiteful hatred.

'I'm getting out of here soon. I just want to make sure you know that.'

'Wow! You wanted to tell me that? Why would I be interested?'

'You're an ungrateful little shit,' said Clive, almost spitting his words out. 'A lot of people want to kill you and I've stopped them. It's because of me that you're still alive.'

Logan remained composed at that comment, calmly replying:

'I don't owe you any gratitude for anything. The only reason you would stop anyone from killing me is because you'd rather do it yourself.'

'I was meant to get out of prison last month,' said Clive. 'It's because of you I've spent twenty years in here. And now again, because of you, I got another nine months added to my sentence. You're proud of that are you?'

'Because of me?' asked Logan. 'I'm flattered if you think I should take the credit for that, but it was your own doing. I wasn't the one who committed these crimes all these years ago. And as for the extra conviction, I'm not the one who nearly killed an innocent man with a crowbar because he supported your least favourite football team. You did that all by yourself. It just took twenty-six years for the truth to come out.'

'So, what happened?' asked Clive. 'You just decided to go to the police?'

'No, I didn't decide anything. I didn't even know you'd committed that crime.'

He looked up to the ceiling to his left, allowing himself to remember the occasion like a distant dream.

'I was eight years old. I remember that orange crowbar. It used to hang on that hook inside the garden shed to the right of the door. And I remember that day when you got rid of it. I was in the car with you. You were on your way to see someone.

I forget who, but anyway, you wrapped it in a plastic carrier bag. Wherever we were going, you stopped off at that building site where you used to meet Donnie. I think it was a Sunday because nobody was working. I wanted to play on the tipper truck, so you left me for a couple of minutes. You thought I couldn't see you. But I saw you. You put the carrier bag in between two layers of wall in that half-built house at the end of the row. I remember asking you why you were placing it there and you said something about leaving it as a present for the builders when they'd return to work the next day. I just thought that maybe the builders were your friends. I didn't know you were hiding evidence.'

'So why did you mention it to the police now?' asked Clive angrily.

'That guy, Grant Nisbet. The bloke you badly injured… that innocent football supporter… he knew it was you who'd beaten him up. When he woke up in hospital he remembered the orange crowbar. But he was so terrified of you and your gangster friends that he never named you to the police. He faked amnesia so that you wouldn't worry about him talking.'

Clive seemed surprised at this news. Logan continued:

'The police suspected you. Apparently, you were questioned about it at the time, but I was too young to know anything about that. Nisbet was so scared of you that even after he knew about you going to prison, he was scared that you'd get out some day and come after him again or come after his family. Well, he died about five years ago. I don't know why. Old age or something. But he'd already mentioned to someone about the orange crowbar. I don't know who he spoke to, but you couldn't take revenge on Nisbet after he'd died, so, whoever he'd spoken to decided it would be safe to anonymously tell the police. So, the police asked me what I knew about an orange crowbar. Quite honestly, I didn't know anything about Nisbet, and I'd forgotten about the crowbar until the police questioned me and jogged my memory. I remembered you hiding it and I remembered where. I could have given the police this information five years ago, but your additional sentence would have just been absorbed into your original one. So, I didn't tell the police anything until three months ago when I found out you were about to be released early. A few days after I spoke to them, they found that crowbar with Nisbet's blood still on it and with your fingerprints dried into the blood.'

'What were you playing at even telling the police that you remembered that? You piece of shit, you should have kept your mouth shut. Even when you were a kid I'd keep telling you to keep your mouth shut. But no. You just couldn't do it could you? You opened your big mouth. You got us arrested. Did you really think you could do that without consequences?'

Logan sighed a faint laugh at this comment.

'Consequences? The consequences have been fantastic. I'm not surrounded by criminals anymore. I don't have a criminal record anymore for something I hadn't done. The violence against me stopped. And the people whose lives you were destroying are now living happy successful lives. So, yes, I knew there would be consequences if I opened my mouth. All good consequences.'

'You knew I was on the brink of making big money,' said Clive. 'You could have been part of that. You could have been very rich now. Your brother Tommy had more sense than you. I was going to teach you and your brother about success. He listened to me, and he was learning. He's turned into more of a man than you ever did or ever will be. He still visits me. He knows what's good for him. You didn't learn anything useful.'

'What could I learn from you except pure arrogance, hatred and violence?' replied Logan. 'I learnt nothing useful from you, except that I didn't want to be like you. I still remember the times when you'd beat me up. I lost count of how many times. Even when I was just six years old, asleep in bed, your beast of a wife would grab my hair and hold my head onto the pillow while thumping me repeatedly. And my only crime was talking in my sleep because I was scared. Then you'd thump me the next day just to support her actions and keep me scared. What sort of monsters would do that to a six-year-old kid?'

'I should have hit you harder,' said Clive. 'Maybe I would have knocked more respect into you.'

Logan continued:

'When people became suspicious at my bruises, you'd order that half-brained so-called brother of mine to beat me up on your behalf so that my bruises could be blamed on two brothers fighting. And always I'd be blamed for starting the fight which I never did. Some boys admire their fathers and want to be like them when they grow up, but I always knew I wanted to be the opposite of you. That's why I made sure I never got into the habit of screaming and swearing at people, drinking heavily or starting fights. But anyway, I suppose I survived unlike these other poor kids you killed. And Lorna hated you for it, especially when she found out the truth about you.'

Clive breathed deeply, shaking with anger and shouted:

'Lorna...'

'Shh,' interrupted Logan. 'No need to shout.'

Clive paused for breath to calm his temper before speaking more quietly, but with more hatred in his tone, telling Logan:

'Lorna hated you. She respected her family, but she hated you. And from what I've been hearing, she still hates you.'

'Well, whatever. I don't care,' replied Logan. 'Lorna was never my sister and Tommy was never my brother. And he's not Tommy any more. His real name's, eh, William. But, oh, who cares? I reckon that whatever he's doing, hopefully he's not in prison like his beloved ex-dad. Anyway, I was delighted when I heard about you getting nine more months for that crowbar attack. The silly thing is, if you'd confessed to that crime twenty years ago when you were first arrested you'd be out by now. You've sat here in prison for the last twenty years and at any time you could have confessed and got a big dose of leniency for being honest and making the effort to be a changed person. But you didn't. That's your stupidity. Your loss. So, like I said, I'm smarter than you.'

'Well, I have news for you boy,' growled Clive. 'I'll be out of here in less than nine months. And you should be very worried.'

Logan rolled his eyes toward the ceiling, mocking that comment, quietly saying:

'I'm so sorry, Daddy. You seem to have mistaken me for someone who gives a shit.'

'I own you,' said Clive. 'You think you got me out of your life twenty years ago. But you didn't. I've always owned you. Your brother Tommy, and a few others, keep me updated. Even from in here I've been able to keep track of you. I've been thinking about you every day. And soon I'll be coming out. My lawyer reckons I'll be out in about six months. What a coincidence. I could be out by the next equinox: your other name.'

'I'm flattered,' said Logan sarcastically. 'So, tell me, what do you know about me?'

'You thought you could hide in a witness protection scheme.'

'I only went into witness protection until I'd heard that the mammoth guy, Billy Macfarlane died. I knew you were controlling him. With you locked away and the mammoth dead, I didn't need witness protection anymore, so I came back into view. But I liked my new Irish name, so stop congratulating yourself on being some sort of detective who could make amazing discoveries.'

'But I've always known how to find you,' said Clive. 'You call yourself an artist and you thought you could become Irish by changing your name to Pete O'Head and you thought I wouldn't find out. But Pete O'Dead sounds better.'

Logan rolled his eyes, facially mocking Clive.

'Wow! Is that the best you can do? You found my new Irish name. Any idiot can find that out. I have a website with my name all over it showing my work.'

'Pete's Paintings. I've seen them on your website. They look like shit to me.'

'Your opinion is of no importance to me,' said Logan.

'I know about Leigh. That retard you preferred to be with more than anyone else.'

Logan was expecting Leigh to be mentioned and had prepared himself for that.

'So, you think all children with Down's syndrome are retards?' asked Logan. 'Really? Is that why you…?'

'I know you have a beautiful wife,' interrupted Clive. 'And two beautiful twin daughters, aged seven years old. And your wife is a former model from Ireland. I know her name's Sonya.'

'Leave them out of this conversation,' said Logan. 'They're not your concern. I'm the one you can hate if you want to. Instead of dragging Sonya into this, try taking a look at yourself. When I was a kid I actually believed your behaviour was normal until one day someone explained to me that all your violence was just a pathetic sign of your weakness. A symptom of your failings.'

'Failings?' asked Clive. 'You're the failure in the family. Let me remind you. I know you started your own business as a taxi driver, but your company went bust. I know you started a business as a painter and decorator, but your company went bust. I know you worked as a ticket inspector on trains for a couple of years, but you got sacked because of your drink problem. Then you got a job as a car salesman which you got sacked from because you kept turning up for work late and drunk. Then you started your own business doing car washing but it went bust because your customers weren't happy with the quality of work you gave them. I could go on. Let's just say you're not successful at anything you do. You're a born loser. A worthless piece of shit.'

Logan's facial expression showed nervous anger. He clenched his fists while tensing his muscles as if to lean over the table to attack Clive.

'Uh-uh, naughty naughty,' grinned Clive sarcastically while wagging his forefinger and pointing at the CCTV cameras on the walls. 'You can't touch me in here without being arrested, and there's no proof that I'm saying anything right now, so listen to this…'

He leaned over the table to get his face closer to Logan's ear.

'… I'm going to enjoy killing you when I get out of here,'

he whispered.

He sat back smugly before leaning forward again.

'But because your big mouth got me locked away from my family, I'm going to kill your family as well if they're with you. So that's why we're having this meeting. You see, you don't know when I'm going to kill you. It might be this year. It might be in five years. I've already decided when, but you don't know when. And I will always know where you are and what you're doing, just like I've always done. So, you need to get rid of your family right now. Send them away somewhere so you'll never see them again. That way when I come after you, I'll kill you, but your family won't be harmed.'

Logan's voice trembled as he spoke, his face furious, his hands shaking as he controlled his vocal chords to speak quietly and calmly.

'Does your stupidity have any limits?' he asked. 'You've been festering in here for twenty years. You could have focused on something worthwhile like studying for a university degree. With a qualification in law, science, the arts or whatever, you could be coming out of prison so highly qualified in something that you could be earning big money in your remaining years before retiring and have a really great life. But you've decided instead to focus your hatred every day on me. Why would anyone, with half a brain, waste twenty years just thinking of someone they think is worthless? And you want me to think you're the smart one.'

He stopped talking for a few moments waiting for Clive's response but there was just an awkward silence between them. Eventually Logan started talking again, half smiling while looking at his watch.

'Actually, you haven't changed. That means you're not going to kill me. I know that. Killing me isn't going to give you anything except another prison sentence, and even you aren't that stupid. Because when I walk out of here and tell the police what you said, that'll mean that if I actually go missing again or get found dead, you'd be the first and only suspect. I know you're just telling me this to get some sort of grudge off your chest. If you…'

Clive opened his mouth to speak but Logan raised his hand, gesturing him to stay quiet.

'Don't interrupt me,' said Logan. 'It's rude. Anyway, as I was trying to say, if you really wanted to kill me, and as you said, you know where to find me, you'd just come and do it. For all your faults, you're not stupid enough to warn me that you'd come after me to kill me.'

Clive shook his head in denial at what Logan was saying. Logan added:

'And as for that weird dope-smoking wife of yours. Yeah, the one I used to call Mummy. She was always on a power trip. She used to boss you about all the time. You remember how she used to always threaten to leave you when you had an argument? But then when you hid your illegal money in her bank account and put the house in her name, she'd threaten to keep it all and just kick you out of the house when you argued. You kept boasting about how you were some sort of tough guy, but you couldn't stand up to her. The only reason she was with you was because nobody else would put up with her. And the only reason you stayed with her was because nobody else would put up with you. What's happened since? The police told me she's been released. She's as evil and screwed up as you are, so she's waiting for you like a good obedient wife. At least you're perfect for each other.'

'It's called loyalty,' growled Clive defiantly. 'Something you don't possess.'

'Well whatever it's called, you could never do anything without her involvement. And she's not going to let you involve her in anything else that's going to screw up her freedom again. She won't let you kill me.'

Clive sat there saying nothing, momentarily looking away from Logan with a slightly disturbed, sad and defeated facial expression as he thought carefully about what was being said. Logan leaned forward towards him.

'If you think you've intimidated me today, think again.'

He then slowly shook his head and made a sarcastic half-smile, quietly saying:

'So, I'm not going to send my family away, because I know you're not going to come after me, even though you might fantasise about it. I'm not going to be scared of you like I was all these years ago. You've spent twenty years inside, and you got another nine months unless your lawyer can get you out early. And then you'll be free to live happily ever after with that beast of a woman you married. And today you've had your pathetic little rant. So, if you'll excuse me, I have some birthday plans to catch up with. And chocolate cake.'

He stood up and turned his back to Clive who remained sitting there in silence. As he started to walk away he stopped, then turned around and said:

'I'm working on another project. If we ever meet again, and of course you don't actually kill me, I might be able to interview you for a job.'

Clive shook his head in defiance at Logan's smug attitude.

Logan limped out of the room and collected his grandmother's walking stick. Clive was escorted from the meeting room back to his prison cell. His brother, Donnie, was also his cellmate. Sitting on the lower bunk bed, Donnie asked:

'Well? How did it go?'

'Perfectly,' smiled Clive. 'Exactly as we rehearsed. He thinks I'm an idiot. Your plan was perfect. He thinks I'm not going to come after him. He thinks that because I told him I'll kill him, it means that I'm not going to. So, he's not going to be watching his back.'

'Otherwise he'd have been expecting you,' smiled Donnie. 'It's called negative psychology. Good. Now let's concentrate on the other business. Did he mention anything about…?'

'No. Nothing. He's clueless,' said Clive.

Meanwhile outside, Logan drove his car about two miles before parking at the roadside. He sat and closed his eyes allowing himself to drift into a daydream about his past. As so often happened, pleasant memories were mixed with bad ones, and especially so on this occasion having just met the man who had caused so much hurt in his life. After five minutes he opened his eyes. He pulled his phone from his pocket and dialled his closest friend.

'Hi Robin,' he said.

'You had the meeting?' asked Robin. 'How did it go?'

'It went well. Almost exactly as we rehearsed. He thinks I'm an idiot.'

'Good. Well done. Now get your arse over here. We have a chocolate birthday cake waiting for you.'

CHAPTER 2

Six months later: Friday September 17th

Logan opened the box which had just arrived by mail order. His new radio-controlled drone was exactly what he wanted. Almost childlike, he grinned as he pulled his new device from its box. It came also with its own carry pouch.

Behind him in his living room was his army-style camouflaged rucksack, almost fully packed. His hiking boots and camera sat beside it. Hung on the wall next to the door was a framed photograph of a mountain range at sunset. Beneath that was another framed photograph of a tawny owl in flight. On the opposite wall were numerous photographs of wild birds, each picture mounted in an oak frame.

On top of his fireplace mantelpiece was a mounted photograph of him standing leaning against the engine cowling of a Piper Cherokee light aircraft, smiling, displaying a look of satisfying self-achievement, holding his pilot headphones in his left hand. Next to that picture was a photograph of himself and Robin, both smiling and wearing their camouflaged army clothing while standing next to an armoured vehicle in a desert landscape.

He plugged his drone into the electrical mains socket to charge its battery. He then put on his old gardening jacket and went outside to his back garden to tidy away some paint pots he'd been using earlier. His garden shed was now freshly painted in preparation for the coming winter. His elderly neighbour was at the adjoining fence and spoke to him.

'Hi Logan. I thought you were going hillwalking this weekend.'

'I sure am,' replied Logan. 'I'll go to the west coast again. I'll be gone first thing in the morning.'

'I think the forecast's good for the weekend,' answered the neighbour.

'Yeah it looks good but there's a storm forecast to hit Scotland in a few days, so I'll plan to get back by Monday evening in case the ferries stop sailing. Then again, if I get stuck on Arran for a few more days that wouldn't bother me too much.'

He heard his telephone ringing and returned inside to answer it. It was Robin.

'That was five rings' said Robin jokingly. 'You normally answer in two rings. You're getting slow these days. You weren't sleeping, were you?'

Logan laughed and replied jovially:

'Nah. Just hesitating as to what fool would actually want to call me when there's a football match on telly just now. Then I realised it had to be you 'cos you hate football. Anyway, what are you up to? You must be bored if you're calling me.'

Robin had been occupying an old shed in deep forestry, originally built as an emergency shelter for forestry workers, and now partially converted into a holiday cottage. Robin and Logan had enjoyed several camping trips in previous years and had found this shed. Between them they managed to buy it, and often used it for wildlife photography projects.

Originally, it wasn't much bigger than a single garage, but Logan and Robin had been given permission to extend it into a larger workshop resembling the shape and size of a small Swiss chalet. It had no electrical power or running water, but it did have a small wood burning stove where one corner of the original shed had been built with stone. On two walls were two full length shelves which could be used for seating or for sleeping on. Outside, about ten metres away, was a small stream with clean water running past.

'I'm up at the old woodshed,' said Robin. 'Nothing's changed. At least nothing except that I got the electrics installed. Just waiting to be connected to the mains supply. And I decided to give it a name, so we can have a recognised address. I registered it with the council and I'm making a name plaque for the door.'

'Uh-oh. What name did you give it?'

'I'll tell you later. I think you'll like it. I decided it should be something silly.'

Logan smiled and nodded his head, sighing:

'Yep. I should have expected that. You're on your own? Or is Roz with you?'

'Nope. Roz is visiting her sister for a few days. It's just me and Chino here.'

Chino was Robin's five-year-old golden retriever. He continued:

'He'd say hello to you but he's too busy chewing his bone just now. No internet, no telly and no damned football. Just one man, one waggy-tailed walking mop and a guitar. Bliss!'

Logan smiled and nodded his head at the thought of such peacefulness. Robin continued talking:

'Anyway, the reason I'm calling… what are your plans? You're still going camping tomorrow? Or do you want to come here?'

'Actually, I've decided to go to Arran again.' replied Logan.

'You're going for…?'

'Yeah, well, not really expecting anything but, well, what can I say? I like the place.'

'I envy you,' said Robin. 'The boss still wants me to go to Edinburgh for a meeting on Monday. Otherwise I'd join you.'

'Alright. Anyway, for now I just want to think about getting some good wildlife close-ups. I think I'll go back into that deer feeding ground at the Punchbowl then maybe try the far end of Glen Sannox where I think I'll get some pics of lizards. Then up towards Lochranza to get some pics of the eagles if I can get close enough. If they're not in Lochranza I'll have to climb Beinn Tarsuinn again.'

'How's your knee injury?' asked Robin. 'You're good to climb hills again?'

Logan looked at his telescopic walking stick standing in the kitchen corner.

'Yeah, I haven't needed the stick for a while now. I'll chance it. Even if my knee collapses on me again, I'll manage to hobble about.'

He picked up his new drone.

'I got my new toy today. A small drone. Hopefully I can learn to fly it well enough to get some decent aerial pics.'

'Ah, so, you're a drone pilot now?' laughed Robin. 'I'll bet that's a lot less expensive than all that aeroplane flying you were doing at the flying club. Anyway, if you change your mind about Arran, I'll be up here until I go to Edinburgh on Monday. Chino will be happy to see you. Catch up later.'

Logan finished packing his rucksack and set his bedside alarm for three o'clock in the morning. He knew he would have a four-hour drive to catch the first ferry to Arran.

CHAPTER 3

Saturday September 18th. Visit to Sannox.

The following morning provided good weather for hill-walking. He was quick to get ready. Two raw eggs quickly whisked into a glass of milk with some sugar was all he would need for a quick breakfast. His white Toyota Corolla was filled with fuel and thoroughly polished. Everything he needed was packed. His army training had taught him how to be well organised and self-disciplined.

His drive was uneventful, enabling him to meet the car ferry at Ardrossan with time to spare. As he waited in the queue of cars he saw a group of police officers walking around the vehicles. They were paying particular attention to the registration plates. The ferry crossing took one hour, during which time he stayed on the upper deck looking and admiring the hills which he was eager to climb like he had done so many times before.

He had been visiting Arran almost every year since childhood, so he knew the place well. The mountain of Goat Fell was fully visible to the north of Brodick with its usual majestic dominance of scenery, almost volcano shaped, enhanced by the mountain range to its west, named 'Beinn Tarsuinn', also usually known as the 'Sleeping Warrior' due to its rugged and interesting shape resembling that of a man lying sleeping with his head resting on the west side of Glen Rosa.

At the south foot of Goat Fell was Brodick Castle. This magnificent ancient red sandstone building dates back to the early sixteenth century. Near the centre of Brodick, the large Shorehouse Hotel exterior was still painted faint yellow as it had been for decades, making it visible from several miles away on the ferry crossing. Looking towards the north coastline he could clearly see Corrie harbour, specifically noticeable by its red sandstone boulders which change their positions each year as they get moved by crashing waves in storms. The Corrie coastline is one of the best places to take pictures of seals and the occasional basking shark. There was a low mist hovering above the shoreline.

Looking to the south, the Holy Isle was clearly visible, almost uninhabited except for some Buddhist Monks. The weather was suitable for his plans to walk the hills. It wasn't uncomfortably hot for climbing, and not too cold for sitting in a swamp somewhere waiting patiently for a good photographic opportunity. The sky was overcast with occasional blue patches, offering his preferred lighting conditions for wildlife photography.

Further south he could clearly see the island of Ailsa Craig, also nicknamed 'Paddy's Milestone' with its distinctly pointed, almost bullet-shaped presence, uninhabited by humans except lighthouse keepers.

On arrival at Brodick, Logan drove off the ferry, turning right onto Shore Road and driving through Arran's small coastal town of Brodick. Very little had changed there since his first visit many years ago. The shops regularly change ownership due to so many visitors buying them because they misjudge Arran's tourist season, not fully realising the difficulties of running a shop all year in a place where the tourist season lasts for only a few months each summer.

The mini-golf area beside the road had been upgraded. The putting green next to the beach was still in the same place as it had been for decades. The grass area next to the beach restored some pleasant memories of playing with kites and small model aircraft.

He drove north around the shoreline towards the small coastal village of Corrie, stopping briefly at the red sandstone boulders at the harbour there in the hope of seeing some seals. On this day, his only glimpse of a seal was of one looking at him curiously from about fifty metres offshore. His only hope of getting a worthwhile picture would be to use his new drone.

He removed it from its pouch, switched it on, and with his mobile phone attached to its controller, he launched it. Flying it was easier than he had expected, and so he slowly flew it towards the seal, recording the video footage.

'I'm going to call you *Smiler*,' said Logan quietly as if the seal could actually hear and understand him.

However, the seal became wary of the buzzing drone and hid under the water. Logan laughed slightly, quietly pretending the seal could hear him say:

'Well, I guess that was failed effort, so I've changed your name to *Coward*.'

He flew the drone back to his car and continued driving north to the small coastal village of Sannox, the name of which originates from the Viking word *Sandvik*, meaning 'sandy bay'. He parked his car in the small parking area across the road from narrow path leading into Glen Sannox.

To prepare himself for a long trek, he wore his hiking boots, two pairs of socks to prevent foot blistering, black lightweight hiking trousers, an army-style camouflaged jacket and a hat.

His rucksack contained various items including binoculars and an empty bottle with a screw top. He carried a Swiss Army Knife in its own dedicated pouch attached to his right-side trouser belt. He'd originally planned to carry his drone in his rucksack, but he found a way to adjust the drone pouch straps to attach it to his left-side trouser belt. That way he would be able to quickly remove it from its pouch and use it without having to remove his rucksack. Otherwise too much body movement might be enough to scare away any wildlife before getting a chance to photograph it.

There was no need to carry any fluids to drink because he knew there would be plenty of natural stream water wherever he'd hike.

He started walking along the narrow path into the glen which passes the old graveyard on its left side. Many of these grave stones were leaning due to years of ground movement. The grass surrounding them was continually kept short by grazing sheep.

As he glanced at the old graves, he had a quick flashback of an earlier memory of him hiding in a graveyard somewhere on a dark night. This was a memory which had been haunting him since early childhood. In this memory, the moon wasn't quite full, but somehow it seemed to have an angry face as it looked down at him. There was a van parked nearby. He could hear people crying and shouting. The noises were mixed with the sound of a woman's voice screaming. He remembered hiding in the shadows, terrified. He then heard his father's voice. He remembered seeing another boy, slightly older than himself, running between the graves while being chased by a tall man with long straggly hair, a thick beard, and wearing a woollen hat. The man grabbed that boy and punched him before dragging him back to where he had run from. He remembered seeing a woman, with blood on her face, sitting upright, leaning against a gravestone. The colour of the blood appeared to be very dark, almost black, in the moonlight. There was a man lying on the ground. Beside him was a young girl crying. The man on the ground was moving until he was struck on the on the back of the head with some sort of stick. The woman and the girl let out a scream at that moment. The next few moments seemed like a frenzy while he watched two silhouettes of men repeatedly bludgeoning the woman and the girl with their spades. He watched as he saw the shapes of what appeared to be his father, his mother and the tall man dragging the bodies into a grave. The flashback always ended with someone's hand touching his shoulder, making him look up to see an angry face looking down at him.

He could never be sure if this flashback was from an old memory of an actual event, or from a nonsensical nightmare. As always, the flashback lasted for only a few seconds, but it was always disturbing.

He started walking again into Glen Sannox. A short distance past the graveyard was a wooden gate blocking the path which had been placed there to prevent animals from wandering out of the glen and also to prevent unauthorised vehicles from entering. Going through this wooden gate, he always felt that he was walking into genuine wilderness, seldom meeting other humans there, and always surrounded by the strong scent of natural highland vegetation and sheep droppings.

The path had by now changed from a tarmac road to a rough

stone cart-track which bent round to the left towards a flat grass plateau. From there, looking up the wild slope to his left, he could see Coich na h'Oighe: a mountain which has claimed the lives of several climbers due to its steep sides and cliff. At the bottom of its cliff sits a glacial corrie called Coire na Ciche, also known as the Devil's Punchbowl. Below the Punchbowl is an area of woodland, not visible from the glen, where the red deer gather in mornings.

To the north side of the glen is Caisteal Abhail: a taller mountain with a noticeable ragged rocky formation at the top called Coire nan Ceum: also known as the Witch's Step.

Looking ahead towards the west end of the glen is Cir Mhor which, when viewed from the glen, has a sort of alpine appearance, in some ways similar to Switzerland's famous Matterhorn.

Logan paused as he looked around from the plateau, reminiscing happy times of his previous visits to that same spot. He remembered the times he'd camped there, and the times he'd climbed the hills around him, sometimes with friends but usually by himself. He stood there in a blissful daydream state for a few minutes, enjoying the fresh air and the memories until he suddenly became disturbed at another momentary flashback: this one from his Army days.

It was a repetitive memory of him being targeted by enemy fire while being trapped beneath debris and was unable to move. His weapon had been damaged so badly that he was unable to return fire. One of his group lay badly injured behind a rock and another lay dead while Logan could do nothing to help them. His head was exposed in full view of the enemy and his only hope of survival was to rely on the camouflage provided by his hat. This flashback startled him from his dream state.

After a few moments he shook his head to waken himself from this flashback while gasping for air, having broken into a sweat. He breathed deeply to try to calm himself back to the present time, eventually enjoying again the more peaceful reality of being in Glen Sannox.

With the increasing temperature from the morning sun shining onto the landscape, and the beginning of a light breeze, the mist he'd seen from the ferry was beginning to rise slowly although it was still very dense in patches. He started walking again, following the track going past the remains of the old disused copper mine and down into the Sannox stream to his favourite rock pool. With his now sweating body, secluded, being watched only by a lone field mouse, this was his opportunity to strip off and enjoy plunging into the fresh Sannox water, soothing his panic attack, and bathing in his favourite scenery, exposing his now-visible scars and burn marks on his right shoulder. After about ten minutes, he felt calm enough to continue his trek, drying and dressing himself in his same clothing, except that with the morning temperature increasing, he decided to not wear his jacket anymore and so he packed it into the netting on the outside of his rucksack.

He continued his hike, stopping occasionally to photograph some small creatures. Spiders webs on the heather shining in the sunlight were plentiful and one fascinating colourful lizard sat motionless on a rock for long enough to enable him to take its photograph. After some time, having realised he hadn't eaten anything for several hours, he sat on the grass next to the stream and filled his screw-topped bottle with fresh water. He started to eat one of the sandwiches he had prepared earlier. As he ate, he noticed something moving in the distance. Placing his sandwich gently on the rock, he pulled his small binoculars from his pocket. Looking through them, he saw exactly what he had come for. A white stag. An albino version of the red deer which inhabit the island. There is considerable superstition and mythology surrounding the existence of a white deer on Arran, but whatever anyone's beliefs, it's a rare sight which Logan wanted to photograph.

To his delight, this was a Monarch stag, so-called due to its twelve-pointed antlers. This moment would perhaps be Logan's once-in-a-lifetime chance to take such a magnificent photograph, and certainly worthy of entering into magazines and competitions. However, he was well aware that deer are shy creatures, making it difficult to get close enough to them to take a good quality photograph. He carefully hid himself in the long bracken and pulled the drone from its pouch. Hoping that a flying buzzing object wouldn't scare the animal, he decided to fly it low level over the rough terrain so that at the first sign of the stag looking concerned, he could switch off the motors and let the drone sit silently and motionless on the ground in a position for its camera lens to stay focused on the animal. He flew the drone towards the grazing animal, watching closely on his monitor screen.

'You beautiful creature,' breathed Logan quietly. 'I'm going to call you *King*. No, actually, on second thoughts, *Majesty*. That suits you better.'

The stag was about two hundred metres away, facing west, so Logan flew his drone in a semi-circular pattern so as to make it approach the stag from behind, keeping the drone as close to the ground as possible. Each time the stag looked up,

Logan switched off the motors so that the drone would sit on the ground. Unfortunately, due to the depth of heather and bracken, whenever the drone sat on the ground, Logan couldn't see the stag through its lens. He was in no rush. He gradually flew the drone in short hops towards the animal which continued grazing peacefully, looking up only for occasional instinctive inspections of its surroundings. After about twenty minutes the stag stopped grazing. It appeared to be wary of something as it started to walk further into the glen.

'Damn.' breathed Logan to himself.

It seemed that the stag may have become wary of the drone's buzzing sound. Realising he was going to lose his opportunity of a good picture, Logan flew the drone higher so that the stag would hear the noise from above rather than from any particular direction. Hopefully the stag would then hesitate about which way to run. At worst, Logan would get a good photograph from above, and at best he might be able to get the drone in front of it, even if just for a few seconds. His method seemed to work. The stag stopped walking. Logan stopped the drone motors, making it descend quietly and rapidly to a position about ten metres ahead of the stag, recording throughout. On seeing the drone, the stag quickened its pace further into the glen, but Logan was happy enough with the picture he had achieved.

He pulled out his mobile phone and called Robin. After a few moments Robin answered, jokingly asking:

'You're missing me already? Or missing Chino? He started barking, so he must know it's you who's calling.'

'I always miss my pal Chino,' laughed Logan. 'I can hear him barking, but anyway, all's good here. I got that stag picture I wanted, and the cherry…'

'An albino?' interrupted Robin.

'Yeah, and the cherry on top of the cake… he was a Monarch. A twelve pointer.'

'Well done you. Can you send me the pic?'

Logan looked at the signal strength on his phone.

'Yeah I'll do it later when I get a stronger signal.'

At that point Logan could no longer hear the background noise of Chino barking. He had lost the phone signal. He picked up his rucksack in preparation for more hiking then flew his drone to a height of about a hundred feet to look for more wildlife. He positioned it into a hover and rotated it to make a full three hundred and sixty-degree recording of the surrounding scenery, smiling throughout at his achievement of the stag picture. Suddenly he noticed something unusual on the monitor. To the north of where he was standing, there was a blue coloured object like a large sheet on the ground next to where he knew was a dangerous old triangular-shaped mining pit. He knew the pit had steep, almost verticals sides and had become partially filled with water over the years.

'What's that?' he whispered to himself.

He flew his drone towards it for a closer inspection. As the drone neared the object, he could see what appeared to be a parachute laid out at the edge of the pit. The parachute rigging lines were tangled around its empty harness and some surrounding trees. Logan had seen many parachutes in his army days. Intrigued at such a discovery, he donned his rucksack, switched off his drone motors and walked towards the parachute, picking up his drone on the way there.

On seeing such a sight, he again experienced a flashback

from some years earlier. This flashback wasn't quite as upsetting than the previous one, but he recalled a training session at a Scottish drop zone. He had been parachuting with an old army parachute and landed badly, causing permanent injury to his left knee.

When he reached the parachute, he crouched down to inspect it more closely. It had what appeared to be Russian lettering printed on its hem.

This prompted another flashback to his army days, this time from a brief moment he experienced in Afghanistan, in a back street with graffiti on its walls, again with the sound of gunfire as he and his colleagues were shielding themselves by hiding behind an overturned car. Again, he shook his head to pull himself out of the flashback and into the present moment.

Due to the canopy's conical shape and its three-pin ripcord container, he was able to identify it as an emergency parachute rather than one used for sport skydiving. Its ripcord would certainly be metallic with three straight closing pins at one end, but it was missing. He stood there and looked around. He started thinking about the possibilities of this find. Perhaps the parachute has been there for a long time, but he always kept himself updated with local news reports from the island and he hadn't heard of any aircraft crash in the area since many years. If there had been a plane crash over Arran, it would almost certainly have been mentioned in the news, unless it had only just happened that morning. So, if this parachute had been used in an emergency, the incident must have been as recent as just a few hours ago. The harness was still fastened. Any parachutist would normally unfasten the harness and walk away, so why would the harness be fastened?

He considered that there may be an injured survivor in the vicinity, perhaps hidden in the tall bracken. He switched on his drone motors and flew the drone around the area at a height of about fifty feet, enabling him to search the area from above in case someone needed help. But he didn't see any sign of human life. He then flew the drone higher to a height of about a hundred feet to look for any sign of a crashed aircraft but could see nothing as such in any direction. Shrugging his shoulders, he left the drone hovering in position with its camera focused on him to record what he'd found. He began to pull the parachute back from the bracken. As he pulled it back, he could see through the bracken into the deep cold water of the pit. To his shocked amazement he saw a little girl, aged about three years old, partially submerged in the water. She was holding on to the parachute fabric which was being held in place only by the fact that its rigging lines had become entangled with the foliage surrounding the pit. She was trembling and whimpering in fear while losing her strength.

'Hello,' shouted Logan. 'Hold on, I'm coming down.'

He removed his rucksack and wrapped the rigging lines around a small dead tree stump to secure the parachute enough to take his weight. He held onto the lines as he scaled down towards the girl. The slope was damp and slippery, making it difficult for him to climb down without sliding. He reached the girl and pulled her out of the water.

'Can you hold onto my back?'

She was unresponsive and clearly too weak to be able to hold onto him.

With considerable difficulty, carrying her with one arm and pulling himself up with his other hand, he managed to pull her to the safety of the ground above. She was wearing what appeared to be a white party dress, slightly grubby in places, white socks, leather sandals, a child's watch on her left wrist with a unicorn picture on the watch face, and a yellow woollen cardigan. She didn't appear to be hurt except for some minor bruising and scratches on her legs. Her clothing was wet, and her entire body felt cold. She appeared confused and with a sad worried expression on her face.

'Well, hello,' said Logan softly. 'Can you tell me your name?'

The girl just looked at him. Her blank facial expression didn't change. Logan looked around, this time with more desperation as he tried to come to terms with the reality of such a bizarre discovery. There he was in a quiet glen, alone with a little girl aged about three years old, looking scared and bewildered, having been found holding onto a parachute for her life. He tried talking to her again.

'Can you tell me your name? Are you with anyone?'

Again, the girl didn't answer. She just sat on the grass and stared at him.

Logan stood up and looked around. There was no sign of anyone else in the area. He shouted:

'Help. Anyone. Can anyone hear me?'

He listened but there was no reply from anywhere.

His drone was still hovering above and recording his movements, so he flew it higher and used it to scan the area but there was no sign of anyone. He landed it next to where he now knelt beside the girl.

'Eh, I don't want to do this, but I need to get these cold wet clothes off you.'

He removed her cardigan, dress, shoes and socks, leaving her only in her underpants. He removed his camouflaged jacket from his rucksack and wrapped it around her. He then carried her a few paces away from the pit to expose her to the warm sunlight. He checked his phone but still there was no phone signal. He decided to make a video recording of his situation on his mobile phone.

'Okay, so here I am. It's just after midday here on Saturday afternoon. I'm in Glen Sannox, not far into the glen near the old copper mine. Look here what I just found.'

He pointed the camera lens towards the mining pit.

'A parachute, with what looks like Russian printing on the hem'

He scanned his phone closer to the harness.

'And look here. The parachute harness is still fastened. And over here, holding onto the parachute was this little girl. I don't know her name.'

He scanned his camera closer to her legs.

'She's cold. She's conscious. I don't think she's badly hurt but she has some scratches and bruises.'

He paused to think before continuing:

'The harness is still fastened. No parachute harness is small enough for a child this size, so, eh, it's like someone somehow, eh, looks like someone used the rigging lines to tie her into the harness. That might explain these scratches and bruising lines on her legs and arms, and maybe explain why she somehow untangled herself on the ground without actually undoing the harness. I can't call for police or an ambulance or anyone else because I've got no signal here, so I'll take her with me back to my car. I should get a phone signal there. Then I can report this find to the police. Actually, I think maybe I'd be more sensible to take her to the hospital in Lamlash for a check-up.'

He was aware that the police would have difficulty believing his story, so although he had the video footage, he wanted to present all the evidence to them. Using his military experience of packing parachutes, he was able to concertina-fold the parachute into its container. Without its ripcord to hold the container closed, he had to fasten it shut by making toggles from pieces of twig from the surrounding heather. He then bundled the girl's soaking shoes and clothes into his rucksack.

After about five minutes the girl started to cry. He tried speaking with her, but she wouldn't talk. However, she was becoming more responsive as the sun heated her. Logan could have picked her up at any point but because she seemed so traumatised and frightened, he wanted her to actually want to be picked up rather than her thinking she was being grabbed by someone who was perhaps scaring her. In its crudely packed condition, Logan was able to wear the parachute harness rather than carry it. As he put it on his back, he reached out his hand to the girl, gesturing her to stand up.

'Let's go for a walk eh? Can you tell me your name?'

He took her hand and she stood up without protest although she still seemed very bewildered.

'Do you want to walk?' he said almost jokingly because she was now barefoot due to her soaked shoes having been removed.

After a couple of minutes, he picked her up and carried her in one arm while picking up his small rucksack with his other arm. His mind was racing as he made his way back through the glen. A child in a party dress, a parachute with Russian writing but with no ripcord, all seemed too bizarre for anything he could have expected to find.

After a few minutes, the girl started talking while pointing further up the glen. Logan couldn't understand what she was saying. Her speech sounded like either Russian or perhaps one of the Eastern European languages, none of which he could understand.

'What did you say?' he asked.

Again, the girl spoke and pointed towards the western end of the glen, giving Logan the idea that there was something in that direction which she wanted to see, but taking her westward would have meant taking her in the opposite direction from his car, and certainly further away from any possibility of receiving a phone signal. He continued walking eastwards down the glen towards the coastal road, but the girl started crying. Logan stopped walking and put the girl down while he sat on a rock. Using a soft voice and his uncertain attempt at sign language, he tried to point out to the girl that they should keep moving down the glen.

'We'll go this way,' he said, smiling at her while nodding his head enthusiastically and pointing towards the coast.

'But not that way,' he said with a deeper voice while pointing up the glen, making himself look sad.

The girl started crying again, talking more rapidly to him, but he didn't understand anything she was saying. Pausing for thought, he decided that because she didn't appear to be badly injured, it would do no harm to take an exploratory detour further up the glen but not before checking it with his drone. Perhaps there was something else he needed to search for. Perhaps she was trying to tell him about someone needing help.

He switched on the drone motors and flew it higher than

before, up to about four hundred feet, and scanned slowly between the north and south sides of the glen. Through his monitor he could see the stag he'd photographed earlier, mingling with a herd of deer in the distance. There was no sign of anything involving human activity. The mist was dispersing but it was still patchy, blocking his view from some of the landscape.

After carefully scanning the glen, he turned the drone to look at the raised plateau to the south of the glen. Looking at his monitor screen he saw what appeared to be a vaguely human shape, motionless, about a mile away, near the east lip of the Devil's Punchbowl. He flew the drone as close to it as he as he could, being careful to not lose line-of-sight of it over the ridge otherwise he could lose radio contact with it. Looking at his monitor, this new find looked like a human lying either unconscious or perhaps dead.

'I have a bad feeling about this,' he whispered quietly to himself.

He landed his drone at the top of the ridge and started walking up the hill towards it. This wasn't exactly in the same direction as the girl had been pointing, but she stopped crying, prompting Logan to nod his head in the satisfaction that he was complying with her wish to venture in a direction where she wanted him to take her. She started talking more calmly to Logan, but without him understanding anything she was saying. She kept touching his watch which he always wore on his right wrist, so that gave Logan the idea that he should talk to her about numbers to keep her amused and calm.

'One o'clock, two o'clock, three o'clock…'

He didn't expect her to understand anything he was saying

but at least they were having a conversation which seemed to amuse her, and every so often he would make a fake laugh which had the desired effect of making her smile slightly.

He followed a narrow track through the heather which had been flattened by regular deer walking. From the top of the ridge, he could look back to the north and see the entire valley of Glen Sannox behind him. Looking ahead to the south was the small birch forest where the deer normally gathered in early mornings. To his right, looking up towards the Punchbowl, he couldn't yet see the human-like shape which he'd seen through the monitor, so he gently put the girl down and activated his drone once more. By standing at the top of the ridge he could be sure of staying in radio contact with the drone as he flew it towards the area about half a mile away from where he now stood. Looking through his monitor screen, he was horrified to find himself looking down at what he could identify as a human body lying spread out on top of some rocks. By positioning the drone to within just a few feet of the body, he could see that it was definitely human, with ripped clothing and disjointed limbs. Some of the bones were visible. He knew he had to take a closer look, so he parked the drone beside the body, picked up the girl and started walking towards it.

With the rough terrain and tall bracken, he was able to approach the body from such a direction that it would not be visible to the girl until they were within just a few metres from it. As he walked closer to it, he positioned the girl's face so that she couldn't see such a disturbing sight, then sat her down behind some tall bracken. As he walked towards the body to inspect it, the girl tried following him, shuffling barefoot while still wearing his jacket which was far too big for her. Its length caused her to trip as her tiny feet would get snagged in the jacket fabric.

'No. No, you stay there,' said Logan while signalling her with the palm of his hand, but she didn't seem to understand.

'I don't want you to see this,' he said, but she refused to leave his side.

There was a dead tree stump, brittle enough that an adult could easily break it, but too strong for the strength of a three-year-old child. In frustration, Logan unravelled his trouser belt then wrapped it twice around the girl's waist and fastened it gently, but tight enough that she wouldn't be able to remove it. He then unravelled one of the parachute rigging lines and with his Swiss Army Knife he cut a length of it. He tied one end of the line through the belt, and the other end around the tree stump.

'I'm sorry, but it's just for a couple of minutes. I'm coming back.'

As he walked away from her, and out of sight through the bracken, she started crying, clearly distressed at being left alone. Logan stopped to think about how to calm her. He turned around and went back to her. As soon as she saw him she stopped crying. Logan removed his watch and gave it to her to play with.

'Look,' he said as he pointed at the numbers on the watch face. 'One o'clock, two o'clock, three o'clock…'

She was calm while she played with his watch, so Logan walked away from her, continuing to count numbers loudly so that she could always hear his voice.

'Four o'clock, five o'clock, half past five…'

He spoke more loudly as he walked away from her, stopping

only when he reached the body. He looked up at the mountain of Coich na h'Oighe and its steep sides. He knew how dangerous this mountain could be, having climbed it when he was a teenager. In particular, he looked carefully at the almost-vertical south facing cliff on the north side of the Punchbowl. If the body had been inside the Punchbowl, near the cliff, the scenario would look like a climbing accident. But this body was just outside the Punchbowl rim, too far away from the cliff to have been such an accident.

He could see that the body was that of a male adult. The condition of its skin appeared to have minimal decomposition, suggesting that the man had been dead for perhaps no more than a day. The torso was split open, exposing its rib cage. The skull was split open and the jawbone was partially visible. To receive such extensive injuries would require substantial force, and the only logical reason Logan could think of was that the body must have fallen from an aircraft to have become so badly broken and partially dismembered as it crashed onto the rocks where it lay.

The corpse was wearing a ripped dark-green jacket with a blue circular patch on the right sleeve showing a logo of a bird. The jacket was stained darker near the upper chest area, possibly caused by blood. Next to the body was a green rucksack. One of its shoulder straps was wrapped around the corpse's left arm. Next to it was a small transparent polythene bag held closed by an elastic band. Its position suggested to him that it had fallen out from one of the jacket pockets on impact. He could see that inside the bag were about a dozen small white pills, each one with a triangular shaped emblem embossed into it. He picked up the small bag and placed it into his pocket. He then carefully opened the rucksack. It was damp with white powder spilling out from numerous small polythene bags inside, some of which had burst open. After a few moments, he realised he had stopped paying attention to the girl, so he started counting again for her:

'Six o'clock, seven o'clock, I'm still here, eight o'clock…'

He launched his drone and hovered it at a height of about thirty feet and used it to scan the surrounding area from above. Through his monitor he could see a metallic object about twenty metres to the west, between himself and the Punchbowl lip. Keeping the drone hovering in its present position, he walked over to the object and found what he could identify as a metal parachute ripcord cable with its 'T' shaped looped handle at one end and its three closing pins attached to the other end. He picked it up and returned to the girl while scanning his drone to the east looking for other objects. He eventually landed his drone beside where he stood. The girl was sitting peacefully on the grass, still holding his watch.

'Almost done here,' he said, smiling at her. 'Eh, what number are we at? Nine o'clock maybe?'

He returned to the corpse and with his Swiss Army Knife, he carefully cut a lock of its hair from the top of its skull and wrapped it in a paper tissue from his pocket. After placing the sample into the corpse's rucksack, he checked his phone, but as he expected, there was no signal. Like he did earlier, he started video recording himself with his arm stretched out.

'So here I am again, same day, about an hour later, and I'm at the edge of the Devil's Punchbowl. As I've shown in the other video, I already found a young girl with a parachute. Now I've found a dead body of some bloke. This guy doesn't have a parachute, but he had a ripcord lying on the ground nearby.'

He scanned his phone camera towards the body and up towards the cliff.

'This body had to fall from a great height to be in this state. But not from this cliff. It's about a hundred metres too far away. And look here at his rucksack. I don't know what's in here but it's damp and its contents are covered in white powder.'

He scanned his phone at the rucksack, and then to the ripcord he was holding in his other hand. He paused to think of what to say next while keeping the video running.

'Okay so, now I don't really know what to think but whatever I do next, I can't call anyone just yet because I don't have a phone signal and I need to get this girl to somewhere safe. I'm going to come up with a vague theory here. I need to at least try to figure out what might have happened. So, eh, um, I'll switch off for a few minutes while I think of this.'

He stopped recording while he looked around and tried to understand what may have happened. After about five minutes he began recording himself again.

'Alright, so, I've been thinking. It looks like they've both fallen from an aircraft. Maybe she was wearing a parachute but someone else pulled the ripcord for her. Eh, let's think. Eh, so, white powder. What's that? Cocaine? Heroin? I don't know how to tell but, eh…'

He stopped recording while he thought more about this situation. He stood, baffled at this mystery for about two more minutes, thinking of different scenarios which could possibly explain what was going on, occasionally nodding his head when he thought of something possible, and occasionally shaking his head when he would then discard whatever idea he'd been thinking. Eventually he resumed recording. With his arm stretched out again to focus the camera lens on his face, he began talking like a nervous news reporter.

'I think perhaps this guy fell with the girl and he pulled the ripcord for her, maybe sacrificing himself to save her. Or maybe he thought he could hold onto her harness. But if he's never done that before he wouldn't have known just how difficult it is to hold on to an opening parachute. Sport parachutes are designed and packed to open gradually over about three or four seconds. An emergency parachute is designed and packed to open as quickly as possible, so, eh, with his weight and also the weight of that rucksack he must have been holding at the time, there's no way he would have had the strength to hold on to an opening parachute in freefall.'

He focused his camera on the man's hands, zooming in to see the markings on the dark blood-stained fingers.

'Look here. I think these marks are friction burns. It looks like he's been holding on to the harness while it was yanked from his grip when the parachute opened suddenly.'

He paused once more, pointing the camera lens to the glen where he had found the girl.

'This body is about a mile from where I found the girl. An open parachute descends at about a thousand feet per minute. Before I travelled to Arran this morning, I'd already checked the weather for last night and for today. The wind was blowing easterly on the ground which means the upper wind would have veered more and been blowing sort of south easterly at about ten, maybe fifteen miles per hour. If I try to calculate this, eh, well, let's say this guy fell from an opening parachute which then drifted with the wind for about a mile when the wind was about ten miles per hour, the parachute must have drifted for a tenth of an hour. That's six minutes. Descending at about a thousand feet per minute, this parachute must have been open at about six thousand feet, or maybe about six and a half thousand feet because the ground is about five hundred feet where the girl landed. Then add the fact that it takes a couple of seconds to open fully. So, whatever happened, as far as I can figure out, they fell from an aircraft which was flying over here at about six, maybe seven thousand feet. The girl was strapped into the harness while the guy just tried holding on. He fell straight to the ground while the girl drifted a mile northward. Maybe. That's the best theory I can think of just now.'

While still recording, he picked up the corpse's rucksack with his free hand. He focused his phone camera inside it to record the white powder, damp and spilling out from the polythene bags.

'This bag seems to be full and very heavy. I'd guess about fifteen kilos. I'm guessing this white powder is some sort of illegal substance like heroin or cocaine. That's a lot of white powder and that's a lot of money to drug dealers. I've seen it in movies where a detective sticks his finger into the powder and tastes it, but I'm not going to do that. Anyway, I don't know what these drugs taste like.'

He paused for more thought, keeping the camera focused on his face.

'I didn't hear any news reports of a crashed aeroplane today, so I don't think he's the pilot of whatever aircraft he's fallen from. Therefore, I think someone else continued flying an aeroplane which didn't crash. So, somebody somewhere knows about this and almost certainly knows roughly where to look for this rucksack. If I walk away and leave this rucksack here, eh, well, someone's going to come looking for it and that'll see a lot of nasty drugs going to get distributed on the streets.'

The girl distracted him from his narrative as she appeared from the tall bracken, still holding his watch, having managed to free herself from Logan's effort of securing her to a dead tree stump. On seeing the broken body on the rocks, she stood and stared at it though not appearing to have any emotional response to what she was looking at. Logan quickly placed the ripcord into the corpse's rucksack. He organised himself in such a way that he could wear the parachute harness back-to-front so that it covered his chest. That enabled him to wear the heavy rucksack on his back and carry his own smaller lightweight rucksack with one hand.

'Come on little girl, let's go this way.'

He picked her up and carried her downhill away from the body. He started recording himself again, talking into his lens.

'If he was a really bad guy I reckon he'd have worn the harness and not cared much about a child. But if he was a good guy, why would he want to hold onto fifteen kilos of nasty drugs? Whatever's happened here, I'm taking this guy's rucksack with me to show the police. But I don't want to be caught in possession of drugs before speaking to police so I'll hide it at the foot of the glen somewhere then call the police to meet me there.'

He then lifted the girl so that she could sit on his shoulders, enabling him to quicken his pace eastwards away from the Punchbowl. His drone was folded and packed into its pouch attached to his trouser belt.

The girl spoke occasionally, but Logan couldn't understand

anything she said. He continued talking with her although he knew she wouldn't understand him, but by talking to her he hoped she would feel more at ease.

'So, what do you want to talk about eh? Politics?'

He laughed at that comment as he then told her:

'Don't worry. I'll not bore you with politics. Don't know much about the subject anyway. What else? Religion? Eh, nope, not doing that. History? Nope, I'm not good at that. Motorbikes? Ah, now that's a subject I can talk to you about. Japanese bikes, German bikes, Italian bikes, chain drive or shaft drive? Personally, I prefer shaft drive, five-speed or six-speed gearboxes, heated grips and anti-skid brakes. What's your favourite motorbike?'

The girl responded well to his voice, occasionally laughing when he laughed, although clearly having no idea of what he was talking about.

His direction took them into the woodland area east of the Punchbowl where he had camped on many occasions, often with deer grazing gently around his tent in the mornings. Knowing the deer tracks from these occasions, he knew how to walk easily in what is otherwise quite rough terrain. Within this wooded area is a small stream where he stopped for a refreshing drink, cupping his hands to collect the water for both himself and the girl as she drank from his hands. He regularly checked his phone for a signal, but always in vain.

Looking out over the sea he could see the ferry on its way eastward having set sail from Brodick. This prompted him to video record himself again, stretching out his arm to record himself with the girl in view.

'I'm just thinking here. If my theory is correct, I'm carrying a rucksack full of expensive drugs, and I'm carrying a missing child. Perhaps she's a kidnapped child who is at best valuable to her parents, and at worst, financially valuable to some criminals, perhaps for ransom. Someone may have already managed to board the previous ferry to the island and is on their way here now to look for her, and if I'm right about this rucksack containing drugs, I should assume that there are bad people on their way here to look for this. The most obvious way to get to Glen Sannox or the Punchbowl is to come through the gate at the entrance to the glen. That's the same way I came earlier, and I don't want to find myself coming face-to-face with any bad guys today, so, I'm taking this girl and the rucksack down directly into the village rather than through the glen.'

On switching off the recording, he heard the sound of a helicopter approaching from the north. Helicopters are a common sight around Scotland's north east coastal area due to the oil industry there, but not so common overhead Arran. He pulled his binoculars from his pocket to look at it as it flew over the glen. It wasn't one of the usual large commercial helicopters he'd often seen around the North Sea, but a Bell Jet Ranger: a smaller helicopter, almost certainly privately owned or privately hired. He considered that this helicopter could be part of a search and rescue mission, or it could be a criminal mission to look for drugs. As it came closer, at a height of about a thousand feet, not high enough to clear the peaks on Arran, Logan quickly ran about twenty metres into a small dip in the ground and grabbed a fallen tree branch which had some dead leaves attached to it. He placed the girl, the parachute and the dead man's rucksack onto the ground, placing the tree branch on top of the girl in an attempt to hide her. Due to his own rucksack's camouflaged colouring, he also placed it over the girl while frantically pulling some bracken over himself as he lay beside her, trying to camouflage themselves as much as possible.

'Where's the sun?' he asked himself, being wary that if the sun was in front of the binoculars, the helicopter occupants may see the reflection.

On this occasion he was looking north towards the aircraft. The sun was shining from the south through a gap in the clouds, so its reflection wouldn't be a problem. Looking through the binoculars he could see what appeared to be just one pilot at the controls and another man occupying the back seat with the rear door removed. The helicopter suddenly turned right, westward, quite abruptly, towards Coich na h'Oighe before continuing south towards Corrie. When it was out of sight, Logan looked at the terrain ahead. There were places where they could hide if the helicopter was to return but there were also larger areas where they would be exposed and would be easily spotted from above.

He pulled out his pocket knife and started cutting the parachute lines into equal lengths. He tied them together to make a square net big enough to cover himself and the girl. He then cut stems of bracken and wrapped them into the net he'd made, effectively making a camouflaged blanket to cover them both as they walked. This effort took him almost an hour. He wanted to make sure that if they had to hide again they could lay still and stay hidden in an area overgrown by bracken or heather. When the net was completely interwoven with foliage, he picked up the girl, his rucksack, the parachute and the dead man's rucksack. He continued walking, talking and laughing with the girl, while nervously looking and listening, continually scanning the sky in case the helicopter returned.

Walking was more difficult now due to the camouflaged netting wrapped around them both. Even with this camouflage, he cautiously followed a track which would keep them within just a few seconds away from tall bracken in case the helicopter would return. This track eventually followed a narrow stream within a wooded area so that, if necessary, they could hide in the trench provided by the natural stream flow. Hiding there would be better than relying entirely on his camouflage in an exposed area.

As they approached the east edge of the plateau just above Sannox village, he carried the girl north along the ridge until reaching the local graveyard which he'd walked past earlier when he entered the glen. The gravestones, the mature tree growth and the hexagonal wall surrounding the graveyard would provide them adequate cover until reaching the glen's single-track road leading to the main road where his car was parked.

He walked through the graveyard, suddenly stopping as he noticed one particular headstone carved from grey granite in the shape of a cross with Celtic engraving on it. His memory flashed back once again to that of a very brief moment. It was much the same as he had experienced earlier when he was entering the glen, and on many other previous occasions. As always happened, the memory carried extreme violence. It was a brief image of someone being beaten by an object and then being dragged into a partially dug grave. Sometimes his memory was that of a woman being killed. Sometimes it was of a man. Sometimes a child. But with every flashback he had, he always seemed to remember hiding behind the same gravestone.

He moved on, passing the famous grave of Edwin Rose: a man who was allegedly murdered near the top of Goat Fell in 1889, now lying in the graveyard under a boulder surrounded by an iron fence. Logan stopped for a rest, sitting on one of the memorial benches placed within the graveyard. He lifted the girl down from his shoulders and started video recording himself.

'Here I am in the graveyard at the entrance to Glen Sannox. I have to think about something before I go any further. The short single-track road from here to the main road is only about a hundred metres long. But what if there are people waiting there? I mean, finding a, eh, Russian or Slovenian or whatever-she-is girl with a parachute and a dead body a mile away with a parachute ripcord, and a rucksack full of what I think is a haul of hard drugs, and then a private helicopter searching the area, all together on the same day... and just four days away from the equinox. There's no way that can all be some coincidental trivia.'

He stopped talking as he heard voices. Through a gap in the headstones, he watched a group of people walking past the graveyard's wrought iron gate entrance. He was able to see that these people looked like nothing more dangerous than two couples going for a hike. After they passed, he resumed recording, but this time talking more quietly into his phone.

'I'm thinking. If I was one of the bad guys, I mean, like a drug dealer or kidnapper or something, and I knew that whatever I was looking for was in this glen area, I reckon I'd get one of my gang to stand guard at that single-track road at the glen entrance to check anyone coming or going.'

He stopped talking, looking down at the girl, still wrapped

in bracken camouflage.

'You must be getting hungry? Me too.'

At the side of the single-track road flows a small stream, deeply trenched and hidden by trees and shrubs. Logan discarded the netted camouflage on the ground in the graveyard, and carried the girl down into the trench, confident they were well hidden from anyone who may walk past. He reached the main road while still hidden in the trench. He placed the corpse's rucksack under a shrub next to the girl, taking advantage of his confidence that she wouldn't go anywhere for a few moments. He removed his watch again and gave it to her to play with.

'Just one minute. I'll be back for you.'

He climbed up the trench embankment and carefully looked onto the main road. He could not see anyone else or any other car. He dashed across the road to open his car boot, quickly removing the waterproof sheet which he always kept for protecting its interior from wet muddy shoes as he often had after hillwalking. He rushed back to where he'd left the girl who was still sitting quietly. He wrapped the waterproof sheet around the rucksack and parachute then tied it securely with a length of rigging line. He then tied some loose grass and bracken onto it for camouflage. He placed the now-waterproofed bundle inside the small tubular tunnel which runs under the main road towards the shore. In that tunnel, the rucksack and parachute could not be seen from the main road or from the single-track road. He spoke to her while also trying to use sign language:

'Almost there now. We'll go in my car. We'll go to the police and find out who you are, and everything will be okay, yeah?

But just for a few seconds you need to stay here while I get the car. I just want to get it as close to this side of the road as I can so that nobody sees you getting into it. I'll only be a minute.'

He climbed the embankment again and calmly walked to his car, started its engine and positioned it across the road to the glen entrance where he parked beside the fence just above the small tunnel. Leaving the engine running, he quickly got out and climbed over the fence to slide down to where the girl was. He carried her up the embankment.

Just then he could hear a van approaching from the north, prompting him to duck out of sight. Looking through the long grass he could see that it was black transit van. He noticed that the passenger in the front seat looked suspiciously like the man he'd seen earlier in the helicopter. The man had a determined serious facial expression, with a dark well-defined beard and a full head of short dark hair. He wore a black leather jacket with what looked like a red star embroidered into the right chest pocket. His appearance reminded Logan of a comic-book he once read which featured a character named *Badger*.

After the van passed, he picked up the girl and with one final quick check to make sure nobody was watching, he opened the rear door and put her onto the floor. The girl just stared at him, not smiling or crying, but looking rather tired.

'Sorry but you need to stay out of sight. Give me a couple of minutes and I'll sort something better for you.'

He got into the car, and with a careful U-turn, drove south to Sannox harbour which was only a few hundred metres away. The harbour is little more than a concrete platform with an inlet for small boats. He reversed his car onto the harbour. He stepped out and opened the left rear door then folded down the left rear seat. He then gently pushed the girl into the boot. He then went to the back of the car and opened the boot. Inside there was a sleeping bag, a grey waterproof jacket and a supermarket plastic carrier bag with some food he'd bought earlier.

'Just going to make you a bit more comfortable little girl. I got my sleeping bag in here. And something to eat.'

He opened a bottle of lemonade, a packet of chocolate digestive biscuits, a sealed packet with tuna sandwiches, and an apple which he started peeling with his pocket knife.

'Time for a feast eh?' he said as he gave her a slice of apple before cutting the sandwiches into small pieces for her.

'I hope you're not vegan,' he thought.

She was a slow eater but hungry enough that she ate most of the sandwich, two slices of apple and a chocolate biscuit: enough to give her some nourishment and energy after what had become almost four hours since being found. After she stopped eating, Logan unrolled the sleeping bag, folded it and laid it like a mattress on the car boot floor for her to lie on. She lay down and he wrapped her in it, using his grey jacket as a pillow for her. He watched her for about five minutes until she fell asleep. Carefully closing the boot, he placed the rear seat backs to their upright positions and loosened the parcel shelf so that it sat loosely to allow adequate ventilation to flow into the boot. He checked his phone and was relieved to see that he had a signal. He looked at the internet to find the local police station number. He called the number but there was no answer, so with his phone already in his hand he began recording himself.

'I just tried calling the police here. There's no answer, but anyway I don't think they'll believe me when I tell them everything about today, so I'm on my way to Lamlash now. I could take her to the police, but actually, as I'm driving into Lamlash from this direction, the hospital is nearer, so I'll go there first because I want someone medically qualified to check her. I can call the police from there.'

He started his car engine, connected his phone to the charger cable which was permanently plugged into the car's cigarette lighter socket, and began driving south towards Lamlash, eleven miles away. He expected the drive to be an uneventful twenty-five-minute journey, but after only two miles, as he drove through the coastal village of Corrie, he noticed the black van he'd seen earlier, parked at Corrie harbour. The van was positioned facing north, with its rear doors open. Logan looked in his rear-view mirror as he drove past, enabling him to see inside the back of the van. There were some childrens' swings immediately behind it which partially obstructed his view, but he was able to see the two men, one of whom he recognised as Badger. Both men appeared to be aged in their fifties, both wearing black combat-style trousers and leather jackets. Logan could now see that Badger was of quite a stalky build. The other man was also stalky but not so tall, and of more unshaven facial appearance with a shaved head.

'I'm going to call you *Gremlin*,' thought Logan.

Badger was holding a long thin object wrapped in a green cloth. At first glance, Logan considered it to be a fishing rod as would be a normal site at the harbour, but the unusual circumstances of that morning forced Logan to be suspicious that the object may have been a weapon such as a rifle or shotgun. Gremlin was also holding an object of similar resemblance, but he pushed it into the van out of sight when he saw Logan's car driving past. Logan calmly continued driving at the same speed in the hope that he hadn't attracted any unwelcome attention to himself.

He continued south along the coastal road. After about three miles, three identical looking cars drove past him in quick succession, each car driving too fast for the narrow winding coastal road. Each car had a male driver, all in their forties or fifties age group.

He continued his way to the coastal town of Lamlash which sits in a bay about three miles south of Brodick. The bay view is dominated by the Holy Isle which sits about a mile offshore and provides significant shelter to the sea water in the bay. As Logan drove into the north end of the village, he turned left into the War Memorial Hospital there. As he drove into its car park, he saw a large dark blue car which was parked facing the hospital building. It was occupied by two men who appeared to be watching the entrance.

'Why would two men sit in a car and watch a hospital entrance?' muttered Logan to himself.

The man in the driver's seat was about forty years old, clean shaven and wearing an earring in his left ear. The man in the passenger seat was more difficult to see, especially as he was in a more reclined seat position, almost slouched. He had a scruffy appearance with long straggly hair. As per Logan's habit of creating nicknames for people, he instantly decided the driver's name could be *Earlobe* and the passenger should be named *Sloucher*. He was concerned that if he would leave the car park immediately, such action may look suspicious to the two men, so he parked his car just three spaces further along from them. The girl was quiet, apparently still sleeping, so Logan reckoned that the least suspicious thing he could do would be to walk into the hospital entrance alone, collect a piece of paper and then leave, making it look like he was collecting a doctor's prescription for something.

He looked into his glove compartment and ripped out a page from the car instruction manual, folded it and placed it into his back trouser pocket. He calmly walked across the car park to the reception area, making it look like he knew where he was going. About a minute later, he came out and walked back to his car while visibly holding the same piece of paper which he pretended to read before folding it and placing it back into his pocket. While trying hard to not look at the other car, he managed to glance at its registration plate. He then repeatedly whispered to himself its registration number until he was able to write it down. He then slowly drove away while the girl slept peacefully in his car boot. Having failed to take the girl into the hospital, he decided that his next course of action should be to take her to the police station and explain his experiences.

He drove through the village towards its south end where the police station is positioned almost opposite the academy. As he approached the station, he noticed a grey Mercedes car parked on the opposite side of the road. A solitary man was standing on the roadside next to that car while calmly smoking a cigarette. He looked to be in his late forties. He was wearing sunglasses and a beige suede jacket. He had a large tattoo of a spider's web on the left side of his neck. His jacket was unzipped open. Logan caught a very short glimpse of a bulge inside his jacket of what seemed to have the shape of a pistol being carried in a shoulder holster. Concerned about this, Logan didn't stop.

'Why would someone wear shades when it's dull and overcast?' he thought as he turned his car around.

As per old habits, Logan nicknamed him *Shades*.

'Shades for a shady character who wears shades when it's not sunny,' he thought. 'And why is he staking out a police station with a gun under his armpit?'

Logan turned his car around and drove back into Lamlash. When he drove past the same Mercedes he read its registration plate and, as before, he repeatedly whispered it to himself to hold it in his memory until he eventually stopped at the waterfront green area almost directly opposite the local supermarket. He wrote the registration on the same piece of paper. He slid his seat back to reach the left rear seat to look into the car boot. The girl was still sleeping. He got out of his car and switched on his phone camera.

'Well, here I am in Lamlash. I still don't know what's going on but, eh, there are some suspicious looking characters staking out the hospital and an unpleasant looking guy staking out the police station. I think he's armed. I don't know what to do next but at least the girl's safe for now and sleeping in my car. But I need to get her some fresh clothes and more food.'

He walked across to the shop where he picked up a small shopping basket and started filling it with various items which would be simple to eat: fruit juice, bread, soft cheese, bananas, tinned peas, chocolate biscuits, and some vacuum-packed salmon slices. From the non-food section he bought a roll of tinfoil, some paper tissues and some paper cups. On his way to the check-out he noticed some childrens' toys for sale. He picked up a small cuddly cat, and next to it was a small plastic unicorn. He placed them in the basket.

A few seconds later, Shades walked into the shop to buy cigarettes. Not wanting to be seen buying anything for a child, Logan discretely removed the toys from his basket and hid them on a shelf behind some tinned vegetables. Shades now had his jacket zipped up, but with just enough bulge under his left armpit which Logan could again recognise as being the approximate cushioned shape of a pistol. Although Shades spoke to the shop assistant in English, the music being played in the shop prevented Logan from identifying his accent. After only a couple of minutes, Shades left the shop, enabling Logan to collect the two toys he'd hidden and purchase them with the rest of his goods.

Shades drove north into Lamlash, leaving the road space empty outside the police station. This was Logan's chance to drive back there. He decided to enter alone rather than be seen carrying the girl, but when he tried to enter its main door, the police station was locked. On knocking the door, nobody answered. Logan returned to his car by which time the girl had woken, so Logan spoke to her through the folded down rear seat.

'Hi. I hope you slept well. I got something for you.'

He gave her the toys which she immediately started to cuddle. Having failed to contact the police, he decided that his next course of action should be to contact emergency services. That would connect him with a switchboard on the mainland and enable him to explain his situation. He tried to call them but when a voice answered, the quality of the line was so bad that he couldn't understand anything which was being said. He could vaguely hear multiple conversations, suggesting to him that there had been some major fault in the line. He tried calling Robin who was out walking with his dog, Chino, next to a waterfall in the Perthshire hills. The waterfall was making so much noise that Robin couldn't hear his phone ringing. Eventually Robin's voicemail answered so Logan spoke:

'Robin, I need you to answer. I got myself into something serious here. I really don't know what's going on. Can you call me back when you get this? It's as if, well, you know, it's like it's... you know... it's started. Maybe. Except it's too weird to understand.

He disconnected the call and looked at the girl. She was trying to wriggle out of the folded sleeping bag.

'Okay, I'm going to try the hospital one more time and if I can't get you in there, I'll buy you some new clothes, yeah?'

The girl replied but Logan couldn't understand her. She seemed to be talking about her new toys. Logan drove back to the hospital. Twenty minutes had passed since the previous occasion. He was hoping that the mysterious dark blue car from earlier would be gone by now. As a precaution, instead of driving to the hospital, he drove along the shore road only a few hundred yards away.

He knew there was a lodge house immediately east of the hospital, separated from the hospital grounds by a small woodland area with large mature trees. He drove into the driveway of that house and parked on its bend which is well hidden by the trees. There was no need to give the girl his watch this time while he left the car because she had her two new toys to keep her amused.

He walked carefully through the woodland until he could see into the hospital car park. He could see both the grey Mercedes and the dark blue car parked there. It was difficult to see if the

Mercedes was occupied because of its darkened side windows. The two cars were parked a few spaces away from each other. He could see the men, Earlobe and Sloucher, in the dark blue car as he had done earlier. As before, they were sitting as if watching and waiting for someone.

After about two minutes another car approached the car park. The approaching car was a smaller light green coloured hatchback. The two men in the blue car suddenly appeared more alert. It was being driven by a woman aged approximately thirty years old. She stepped out of her car and removed her five-year-old daughter from the rear seat. As she began walking with her daughter towards the hospital entrance, Earlobe and Sloucher both stepped out of their car. Initially, their movements looked like they were going to intercept the woman. But after only a couple of seconds Sloucher stopped. He turned to Earlobe and shook his head as if to signal he'd made a mistake. They both returned to their car and stood beside it as they lit their cigarettes. The woman hadn't noticed them.

Logan crawled on his belly around the trees to get as close to the men as he could, hoping he could record them speaking to each other. As he got closer he could hear them speak but he couldn't understand anything they were saying except that they seemed to have Russian or Eastern European accents. Keeping his head beneath the tall grass, he raised his phone just enough that the camera lens could record their actions which he could see only through his phone screen. As the men finished their cigarettes, Earlobe opened his jacket to place his cigarette packet into the inside pocket. This movement briefly exposed what Logan could see through his screen as another pistol in a shoulder holster. He crawled back through the grass towards the woodland area until he could safely stand and walk without being seen. On returning to his car, the girl had managed to push her way forward from the boot into the rear seat.

'No,' said Logan shaking his head. 'You need to stay hidden.'

He ushered her back into the boot and drove towards the shore, but instead of turning right, he turned left along the road leading north from Lamlash to a parking area at Kerr's Port which looks over the bay towards the north end of the Holy Isle. He knew this point was normally isolated. That would give him a chance to open the boot from outside and actually talk more to the girl in an attempt to understand her. She was still wearing his jacket from when he found her in the glen.

'Uh, I really need to get you new clothes urgently,' he said.

He called Robin again. This time Robin, being in a quieter spot away from the waterfall, could hear his phone.

'Hi Logie, how's Arran?'

'Rob, did you get my voicemail?'

Robin looked at his phone.

'Ah, oops, sorry mate, I just see now that you left a message. Sorry, didn't hear the phone. You're missing us?'

'Yeah, I mean, long story, listen, I need some help here. I got myself caught up in something. I can tell you but, eh, I need a translator. I remember you told me about your friend, the one who, eh, I think she's Croatian or Slovenian or something. The one who can speak about three or four languages and one of them is Russian. Can you give me her number?'

Robin grinned at this.

'Ah. You got yourself caught up in… uh-oh, you've met a Polish tourist and she's got big boobs and a nice…'

'No,' interrupted Logan. 'No, it's a bit more, I mean a lot

more serious than that. Do you have her number? Like right now? It's sort of urgent.'

'Okay,' said Robin, 'Her name's Anna and she's Croatian. Lives in Zagreb. What's going on? Eh, this isn't the start of…?'

'To be honest I'm not sure. Hopefully your friend Anna can help me figure that out. You got her number?'

Robin was concerned. He knew Logan well enough to know he was genuinely worried about something.

'I'll text her number to you in next few seconds. She's a clever woman and speaks several languages but she's not so great at understanding English when it's being spoken with a Scottish accent, especially over the phone, so speak slowly to her. But give me a clue. I'm curious. What's bothering you so much that you need an interpreter?'

'I'll tell you when I can. Hopefully when I speak with Anna I'll find out more. Then I can call you back.'

'Okay, talk later. Sending you her number now. Speak slowly to her.'

Within a few seconds Logan received Robin's text message containing Anna's phone number. He called the number and after five rings Anna answered.

'Pozdrav,' said Anna as if she was expecting a call from a friend.

Logan spoke slowly:

'Anna. My name is Logan. I am a friend of Robin. I believe you both worked together two years ago.'

'Yes,' said Anna in her strong Croatian accent. 'Is Robin okay? Is there problem?'

'Yeah Robin's fine. He gave me your number. I need your help. Are you good to talk for two or three minutes?'

'Yes, how can I help you?'

'Well, it's complicated. I have found a little girl. She's lost, and she speaks a language I don't understand. I think maybe Russian or something. I don't know anything about her. I am trying to figure out the best way to help her. Can you talk to her? Ask her name and where her parents are? Ask her why she was in the place where I found her. And anything else she can tell you. I have an internet signal. It's not a strong signal but it might be enough to use video chat, so you can actually see her.'

'Of course, I will try. I speak Croatian, Russian, Slovenian, Polish and Czech. Actually, a lot of words are the same or similar. But I can hardly hear you. Give me two minutes. I will use my earphones to do this, so I will hear better. I will call you back.'

Less than a minute later she called back on video chat. Logan could clearly see the face of a slim attractive woman with striking features, dark hair, dark eyebrows, tanned skin, and large brown eyes.

'I can see why Robin likes working with you,' he thought silently to himself.

'Can you hear me?' asked Anna.

'Yes. You can hear me better now?' asked Logan.

'Slightly better than before but the signal quality is not great. Let me speak with the girl. I will try for you.'

He positioned his phone in front of the girl so that she and Anna could see each other. Anna began speaking, saying 'Hello' in different languages:

'Pozdrav, Zivijo, Dobry den.'

Logan watched and listened but became nervous as he saw a grey car approaching from the village. He wasn't sure if it was the same grey Mercedes he'd seen earlier, but under the circumstances, he regarded every car with suspicion. This particular one stopped about a hundred metres away. He watched the car carefully, noticing the driver sitting watching in his direction.

Anna was successful in getting the girl to talk. It seemed that the girl was more interested in telling Anna about her toys than actually saying anything useful, but Anna persevered and switched the subject matter between the toys and personal information. After about four minutes Anna called for Logan to speak, interrupting him as he had become engrossed in watching the other car.

'Logan, Logan, are you there? Logan?'

Logan snapped out of his trance-like state of watching the Mercedes, and quickly picked up the phone.

'Sorry Anna. I was just watching, uh, never mind, I didn't understand what was being said. What can you tell me?'

'She seems confused, so I really don't know much about what she was saying. For sure she's partly Polish, but I don't think that's her first language. She's definitely not Croatian. I tried speaking Polish to her and I asked her name. I think it's Heidi. I'm not sure if that's her name or the name of her favourite doll.'

'Heidi. Okay good, that's a start. What else did she tell you?'

'I asked about her parents. Either she didn't understand me, or she doesn't know where they are. I can't make out everything she's saying. It's like she's trying to speak two languages, but I'm struggling to recognise her accent.'

'Okay, so That narrows it down a bit. Did she say anything else?'

'Yes, something about her falling. She said a big fall a long way. And there was a man with her I think. I asked her about the man. She couldn't tell me much. I asked if he's her dad and she said yes. But then she said no. Then yes again. Then I asked if he's her uncle, and she said yes, then no. I think she mentioned the name Mikhail and Pyotr, both Russian names, but I couldn't hear her clearly. The signal is terrible and she's too young to speak properly. Then she just wanted to show me her toy cat.'

'Okay thanks for that, Anna. You've given me something to work on.'

'I'm curious,' said Anna. 'You say you found her?'

'Yeah, alone in the hills. Miles from anywhere. I don't know if someone's trying to kidnap her or rescue her, but for now I just need to get her to somewhere safe.'

'Can you take her to a police station?' asked Anna.

'No. I tried that but it's not possible.'

Anna's facial expression changed as if she suddenly realised something relevant. She glanced away from her phone camera for a few moments.

'What is it?' asked Logan.

'Oh, perhaps nothing,' she replied. 'Call me back if you need any more help.'

They both ended the conversation. Logan tried to call Robin again to explain what was going on, but Robin's phone was busy, so Logan sent him a text saying:

'*I'm going to Brodick. I'll call you in about twenty minutes.*'

He asked the girl:

'Heidi? Are you Heidi?'

The girl didn't smile. She sat playing with her toy cat stroking its head. After a few seconds, without looking at him, she nodded her head slowly, acknowledging that her name was Heidi.

'Right then Heidi, let's go to Brodick and I'll buy you some clothes.'

The grey Mercedes was still parked in its position further along the road. Logan placed the folded sleeping bag around Heidi in the car boot and folded back the rear seats to keep her hidden. He calmly drove south towards Lamlash and as he passed the parked car, he recognised it as the same one he'd seen earlier. He could see Shades sitting at the wheel, still wearing dark glasses. Logan placed his phone onto his dashboard and recorded himself again.

'I just passed the same grey Mercedes I saw at the police station and at the hospital. The driver was just sitting there. He was wearing dark glasses, so I couldn't see his eyes. I don't know if he was sleeping or watching me. Whatever he was doing, I made sure he couldn't see the girl. Oh, yeah, her name is Heidi. At least, that's what I think for now. I'm concerned that whoever these people are, they're possibly looking for her. And I can't help thinking that they've noticed me.'

He checked his rear-view mirror to make sure he wasn't being followed.

'They've seen my car a few times now, so I need to assume that I've been noticed. Hopefully they'll not do anything until they consider me as a target. Shit! I think I might have become a target. Anyway, so long as I don't do anything stupid and keep the gir… I mean, Heidi, out of sight, we should be safe. Oh, I think the dead guy up at the Punchbowl… I think his name was Mikhail or Pyotr.'

He switched the camera function off and drove up the hill

towards Brodick. On the other side of the hill which slopes down towards Brodick, he pulled into the parking area viewpoint on his left and parked his car into the farthest south west corner. This parking spot is one of the best viewpoints on the island for seeing the entire mountain range of Goat Fell and the Sleeping Warrior. He'd often stopped here on previous visits, always hoping to take that perfect photograph of the mountain range with a cloudless sky. On this occasion he stopped to empty his filling bladder. He encouraged Heidi to do the same as he carried her to the hidden wilderness behind the mature growth of trees and shrubs which surrounded the small worn-out track leading away from the parking area.

'Pee time,' he joked as he helped Heidi by holding her in position to keep her balance while she urinated.

'I don't quite know how to do this properly,' said Logan, 'But I need to somehow get you washed or showered or find some other way to get you cleaned up.'

On their way back to the car, through the bushes, he noticed the grey Mercedes driving past the parking area on its way towards Brodick. Again, he could clearly see Shades driving it. He placed Heidi back into the car boot.

'I want to buy you clothes but actually I think the priority should be to get you off the island as soon as possible. We can take the next ferry. Then we can go to get help on the mainland.'

He drove into Brodick and pulled into the harbour area to see if there was a ferry timetable on display. Ahead of him were some cars parked as they waited to board the ferry. Two men were walking between the cars, talking to the drivers. He couldn't hear what was being said, but they were checking inside most of the cars. He opened his window to try to hear what was being said but the noise of a nearby bus engine ticking over was dominating the sound. After seeing four cars being searched, he decided it would be best if he left that area before he was noticed. He turned his car away from the harbour area and continued driving into Brodick. Despite knowing that Heidi wouldn't understand him, he spoke to her:

'I've changed my mind about taking that ferry. Whoever these people are, I think they're looking for you. They'll be expecting to find a little girl. Maybe I should try to make you look like a boy.'

He drove into the supermarket car park.

'You stay here,' he whispered. 'Shh! Quiet.'

He put his forefinger onto his lips to gesture to her to stay quiet. She nodded her head and repeated the gesture as if she understood. He went into the supermarket and bought a jar of coffee granules. When he returned to the car, Heidi was still sitting quietly in the car boot. Further along the road was a large shop next to the mini golf where he knew he could buy outdoor camping and hiking equipment, including some children's clothes. He was able to park in the shop car park, between other cars.

'I have to leave you again Heidi, but just for a few minutes.'

He entered the shop and immediately looked for children's clothes, but he didn't know what size of clothes to buy. Most of their clothing stock was too big for Heidi but would at least give her something to wear and stay warm for later if he couldn't get her to somewhere indoors. He picked up a pair of trousers which could be rolled up at the ankles, a small jacket which could be rolled up at the sleeves, a sweatshirt, three children's T-shirts, a pair of shoes, some socks and underpants. He was careful to choose masculine style boy's clothing. He placed them on the counter for the teller to add up. She was wearing her name badge: 'Katy'.

'It's good to be back here on Arran again,' he said.

Katy smiled as she replied:

'I remember you. I think you were on the island about four weeks ago. You're here for some hillwalking?'

'Yeah. Actually, I remember you too. I tend to visit Arran often. And yes. I'm here for some hillwalking and photography. Eh, is it my imagination or are there not so many tourists this season? Maybe I'm just not noticing them. Normally when I come here, the island is full of English or Scottish tourists, but today I'm hearing more foreign accents around the place. Are you noticing that?'

'Actually, yes,' she said. 'I think more foreign visitors this month. They sound Eastern European. Maybe Polish. I can't tell. I only learned basic French at school, so I don't know for sure. We've already had a few in today but they're not buying much, just sort of looking around.'

'Looking around? Not buying things?'

Katy just smiled and shrugged her shoulders as she finished placing the clothes into a paper carrier bag. Logan paid for the clothes and returned to his car. He tried calling the police station again but, as before, he didn't receive a response. He folded down the back seats and spoke to Heidi:

'Hi Heidi, I got some clothes for you. Let's go somewhere. Let's get you fed and dressed then we'll figure out what to do next.'

He drove onto the shore road and turned left. Ahead of him

on the same side of the road he saw two police officers: one male and one female, walking in the same direction as he'd been driving.

'At last,' he said to himself, as he pulled over and parked his car.

He opened his door to go to speak with them. Just then, he noticed Shades standing across the road, still wearing his beige jacket and sunglasses even though the sky was even more overcast than before. His left arm was positioned at his side, hiding the shape of his gun. He was standing still, looking like he was studying a folded map which he held in his right hand. Logan could see that he was glancing over the map, pretending to study it while he was actually watching the two police officers. Logan sat back into his car again, hoping that Shades hadn't noticed him. He watched Shades keeping pace with the officers while continuing to look at his map. Logan made a short video recording of this through the car windscreen. Just then his phone rang. It was Robin calling him. He was sitting on a small wooden chair inside the woodshed.

'Hi mate, you alright?' asked Robin. 'Sorry. I see I missed your call. The boss called me wanting to talk about stuff. Bad timing. Anyway, Anna told me something about you finding a little girl?'

'Yeah. It's all a bit weird. I think her name's Heidi. She looks like she's about three years old. I think she's either been kidnapped, or else someone is trying to kidnap her. I found her up in Glen Sannox past the old copper mine.'

'So, you've reported this to the police?'

'Eh, not exactly. There's more. I found her still tangled up with a parachute in that old qua...'

'What the…?' interrupted Robin.

'Yep. And a dead guy about a mile away with a ripcord.'

'F… what? Wait. Did I hear you right?'

'Yeah you heard me. I found him up at Devil's Punchbowl. And it doesn't stop there. There's a presence of something sinister going on. Like organised gangsters. They're carrying guns, watching the police station and the hospital and, well, I can't actually take her to the hospital for a check-up or go to the police without her being seen.'

Robin stood up and shook his head as if to shake off the disbelief like he was shaking off water.

'So, let me get this straight. You're on Arran, with a three-year-old girl who speaks one of Anna's languages, and it looks like she jumped out of an aeroplane, and there are armed baddies looking for her?'

'That's what it looks like.'

'And her name's Heidi?'

'I think so.'

'And the dead guy you found. You're sure he was dead?'

'I didn't check his pulse, but I could see inside his skull where his brain used to be.'

Robin paused at this thought as he tried to process what he was hearing.

'Did he have any identification on him?'

'Not sure. I didn't search him. I didn't want to contaminate evidence. He had a rucksack full of expensive-looking stuff.'

'Drugs?'

'Yeah, I think heroin or cocaine. White powdery stuff, about fifteen kilos of it.'

'Wow! And equinox is…'

'Four days away.'

'Could this be…?'

'I don't know. It's not what I was ever expecting to find,' said Logan.

Robin sat down again, thinking about what he'd been told.

'Seems like you got yourself caught up in some serious shit there,' he said. 'So, you have the girl with you, but please don't tell me you also have a rucksack full of drugs.'

'No that's hidden. There's no way I'd be walking about with that on my back. It's hidden away until I can get the police involved.'

'You haven't spoken to the police yet?'

'I can't contact them,' said Logan. 'And actually, I think maybe there's no point in going to the police unless it's Geordie and his team.'

'So, what are you going to do now?

'Well, I have a sort of theory that if I do so much as tell the police where the body and the drugs are, all that'll happen is that the police will go there, and the gangsters will follow them with guns. You remember our army days when we were looking for a mobster who was using a child for ransom?'

'Oh yes,' said Robin. 'In fact, my mind was already going in the same direction.'

'Okay, good. Well, I think you'll agree I should get the girl off the island and go to the mainland police. I can show them the video footage of what I've found. Once they see that, they'll want to send some back-up. Having said that, I still want to try to get a sort of quiet chat with the police here. I'd like to warn them about what's going on and let them know they're being watched and followed. I just need to find a way to do that without being seen.'

Robin knew how well Logan could cope when faced with a crisis. He knew Logan would always try to do the right thing and risk his own life if necessary to do that.

'Do you want me to contact Geordie?' asked Robin.

'Eh… yeah… eh… no. Not yet. Maybe I got this a bit wrong. Let me try to figure out more from here.'

'I think I need to come over to Arran,' said Robin. 'I could be there on the late ferry tonight. Is there somewhere you could go until then? Somewhere safe and discrete?'

'No. Stay put,' said Logan. 'Besides I thought you said you have a meeting with the boss in Edinburgh.'

'I can fake sickness or something.'

'I might need your help, but my priority just now is to make sure Heidi is safe. Preferably I want to get her off the island. I'll call you. But meantime can you check if there's anything in the news or internet which might help to explain some of this?'

'Yeah sure. On the case now.'

'Thanks mate. I gotta go. I'll call you later.'

Logan slipped his phone back into his pocket. He started the car engine then checked back at young Heidi who was starting to become restless in his car boot. Even though the rear seat backs were folded partially down, she was becoming uncomfortable and cramped. She was trying to push forward to sit in the rear seats which would have made her visible to Shades across the road. Logan quickly got out of his car and walked around to the pavement side. He opened the back door and gently ushered Heidi backwards into the boot.

'Just a few more minutes,' he whispered to her. 'We'll go somewhere else then you can come out of there.'

He clicked the rear seat backs into their upright positions, but Heidi started to cry, so he quickly closed the rear door, and walked around to the driver's door while trying to make it look like he had done nothing more than merely check that his doors had been shut properly. He jumped back into the driver's seat and drove, immediately making a U-turn to avoid passing Shades.

He drove through Brodick towards Lamlash again while Heidi's crying seemed to get louder. Clearly, she was distressed more so now than she had been since being found. Logan's immediate intention at that point was to find some way to comfort her, so he turned left up the Corriegills road which is just a few hundred yards up the hill after leaving Brodick. At the end of the road he switched off his engine and let Heidi out, initially allowing her to sit on the rear seats as she had been trying to do. Being a no-through road, there was little risk of being seen by any passers-by. As soon as Heidi was out of the confined space of his car boot she stopped crying. Logan sat with her and tried to think of anything he could do or say to calm her.

'Here,' he said softly as he offered her some fruit juice and a small piece of bread with some cheese on it. 'All that crying must have made you hungry eh?'

She wasn't interested in eating anything. She just wanted to see what was happening around her. Logan switched on his video camera again and made a short video of her sitting there.

'Give me a big smile Heidi. Say cheese, or, eh, something. Anything.'

Heidi wasn't initially caring about what he was doing, until he played back the video footage to her while he tried to speak with an enthusiastic cheerful voice.

'Look Heidi. This is you. Yes you, sitting in the back seat. Great fun eh?'

Heidi smiled when she saw herself on the camera screen. She grabbed the phone from him. It was like she'd never seen a video of herself before.

'Okay,' said Logan. 'We'll do some more?'

She seemed to understand his gestures, letting him take charge of the phone again, watching his every move as he switched it on. He focused the lens on himself and Heidi while talking into it.

'Well, here's the latest update on today's saga. The people who I think are gangsters seem to be all over the place. They're watching the hospital, watching the police station, and just a few minutes ago I saw one of them following two police officers in Brodick. And I daren't try calling the police because either they won't believe me, or if they do, they might get followed if they try to meet with me anywhere. I'm taking some time out for a few minutes to give Heidi some attention and give myself a chance to think about my next move. I'd take her for a walk somewhere, but I think she's tired. I can't take her anywhere public.'

He stopped recording and again played the video to show to Heidi. She smiled as she watched it. She pointed at the screen and said a few words, but Logan couldn't understand her. When the video clip ended, he recorded himself again.

'I'd take the next ferry out, but it looks like there are suspicious looking people checking cars at the ferry port. I can see they're not police officers, and not ferry staff either. They weren't wearing their usual yellow high visibility jackets. Just menacing looking characters checking cars. I don't know if they're looking for Heidi. If they're doing that with the Brodick ferry, the chances are they'll be doing it at the Lochranza ferry as well. So, I'm sort of stuck here, and I really don't know what to do next other than to visit Lochranza to check the situation there.'

He switched his camera off. As before, Heidi wanted to see the recording, so he played it back to her, letting her hold the camera.

After half an hour she was more settled, enabling Logan to re-arrange the car boot and spread out his sleeping bag and clothes for her to lie on. He picked some wild flowers from the roadside and placed them around the boot interior to try to make her feel more at ease.

'Look at this,' he said, showing her what he'd done. 'You have your own little den here, a comfortable bed, a couple of toys, some flowers. But I can't give you the camera to play with. Sorry, but I need that too much.'

Heidi willingly crawled into the car boot. Logan returned the seat backs to their upright positions.

'Let's go to Lochranza.'

He started the car and set off for the fifteen-mile drive. About three miles north of Sannox village is a small car parking area on the left side of the road. This was Logan's favourite spot for re-filling any bottles with drinking water because of the convenience of the fast-flowing stream with its taste being so rich of fresh highland vegetation. He spent five minutes there filling his bottles while Heidi dozed peacefully in the car boot. Thereafter, as he continued his drive to Lochranza, he didn't pass any cars.

On that road, the red deer often venture close to the roadside, especially at night, requiring drivers to be vigilant. In Lochranza around dawn, the deer can often be seen walking around the village and in the gardens.

One of the first buildings seen when driving into Lochranza is the Arran distillery which was founded in nineteen-ninety-five. Perhaps the most prominent feature in the village is its ruinous remains of Lochranza castle which was originally built in the thirteenth century. The castle sits on a plateau of land which partially shelters the bay so well that there is very little water flow other than tidal changes, resulting in a very noticeable odour of fermenting seaweed when the tide is out.

At the north-west end of Lochranza is the small harbour where a ferry sails regularly to Claonaig on the Mull of Kintyre. It's not possible to drive towards the harbour without being seen, so Logan drove onto the grassy plateau to the east side of the ancient castle ruin where he parked his car in a position where it couldn't be seen from the harbour.

He stepped out of his car and laid down on his stomach next to the east castle wall, taking advantage of the fact that the grassy area was occupied by grazing sheep which helped to keep him hidden so long as he'd lay flat on the ground. Through his binoculars he could see one slim man standing alone at the small harbour. Parked along on the same side of the road was a red camper van with sign writing on its side which Logan was unable to read from where he was watching. Standing on the roadside and leaning against this van was another man with a shorter, fatter physique. The two men occasionally signalled to each other like they were using some sort of sign language.

Two cars were already waiting for the small ferry which was approaching from less than a mile away. About two minutes later, another car drove to the harbour and parked behind the first two. The slim man immediately spoke to the driver who then stepped out and opened his car boot, presenting its interior for inspection.

'Ugh. There's no point in trying to escape on THAT ferry,' muttered Logan to himself.

He carefully belly-crawled back to his car where he sat on the grass and leant back against the driver's door.

'Think, think, think.' he muttered to himself.

Pulling his phone from his pocket, he recorded himself again.

'Update. I'm in Lochranza. I was hoping to get off the island from here, but just like in Brodick, the cars are being checked by someone before they board the ferry. I need to think of something else. Heidi's asleep. She's okay for now.'

He stopped recording and sat in his car. Despite his dilemma, there was something peaceful about being sat in his car beside Lochranza Castle, but several hours had already passed since the moment he'd found Heidi, and the afternoon was turning into early evening. He knew he needed to contact the police somehow. He started his car and set off towards Brodick.

When he arrived in Brodick, he parked his car in the car park beside the shop where he'd bought some clothes earlier. He sat and watched people walking along the shore road. Most of them were visitors and tourists, blissfully unaware of what was happening. The crazy golf area was still open and had some people playing there. Logan recognised Katy sitting at a table on the patio area just outside the shop where she worked. She was talking to a teenage boy who was working at the crazy golf. Logan stepped out of his car and walked over to her.

'Hi, eh, Katy? I think your name badge said Katy?'

Katy smiled and replied:

'Yes. Hi Logan.'

'Eh, how did you know my na…?'

'I saw your name on your credit card earlier,' smiled Katy.

The teenage boy looked at Katy with a subtle mischievous smile which Katy tried to ignore.

'Ah, yes, of course,' smiled Logan. 'Eh, sorry to pester you about this, but I have a favour to ask.'

'Sure, how can I help?'

'I need to contact the police about something. But it has to be very discrete. It seems there's nobody at the police station. The only phone number I have for them doesn't work. Do you have any other local police number?'

'I'll check,' said Katy as she took out her mobile phone from her handbag.

She took a minute to search the number to dial, before telling Logan:

'I only have one number for the station here. I'll try it for you.'

After less than a minute, she put her phone down, saying:

'That's strange. There's no ring tone. It's like the line's dead.'

'Oh well, thanks for trying.' replied Logan.

'Wait. If it's urgent you might find one of the officers swimming at the Auchrannie. There's a police woman who I think teaches kids to swim there in the evenings, but I don't know if she'll be there tonight.'

'Eh, okay thanks. Do you know her name?'

'Yeah PC Reynolds.'

The teenage boy displayed a slightly embarrassed grin as he looked away.

'What's so amusing?' asked Logan, almost mimicking the same smile.

'Well, she's only been working here a few months,' said Katy, 'and already she has a lot of admirers. Especially from some teenage boys. Especially this one here.'

Gesturing a mischievous glance at the boy, she added:

'Some local boys here almost want to get arrested.'

Logan laughed, saying:

'It's a pity the local boys don't know where she lives, otherwise they could just ask her out instead of getting arrested.'

'Oh, I know where she lives,' replied the boy as he grinned.

Katy rolled her eyes, expecting the boy to say something embarrassing.

'She's up at Hillview Place somewhere. But I don't think she'd fancy a seventeen-year-old like me.'

'And your girlfriend wouldn't dare let you go near her,' joked Katy.

'Never underestimate yourself,' laughed Logan. 'Anyway thanks. I'll check out the swimming pool, and, eh, I'll maybe try to get arrested.'

Logan considered that PC Reynolds might be the same police officer he'd seen earlier being followed by Shades. He asked:

'Actually, I think I've seen her. Is she the dark-haired woman with the, eh, the white car?'

'Yes, dark hair,' smiled the teenage boy. 'But she drives a red car.'

Logan smiled and nodded as he walked away. Katy shouted after him:

'You're coming back to the shop tomorrow?'

Logan stopped walking for a moment as he looked back at her.

'Okay, I'll try.'

The teenage boy smiled discretely at Katy, whispering:

'I think you like him.'

Logan walk away, pretending to not notice the fact that he was being watched admiringly by Katy. But more importantly, having failed to contact the police, he now had some new information about a local police officer who he could try to contact discretely. He knew her name was Reynolds. He knew she was an attractive woman with a red car, and he knew the street where she lived. At least now he should be able to find at least one police officer and report to her about what was going on.

He returned to his car, briefly looking through the rear seats into the boot compartment. Heidi was calm. She played with her toys while he drove the short distance to the Auchrannie resort. He knew it well, having often visited it due to its combination of being a quality hotel with timeshare lodges, quality restaurants and a swimming pool. It was founded in nineteen-eighty-eight in its discrete location on the north end of Brodick, surrounded by attractive wilderness. He often swam there when visiting the island, especially after one of his many ascents of Goat Fell. He walked into the reception area at the swimming pool.

'Hi, eh, can you tell me the pool times please, like, when it's open to the public, and when there are swimming lessons?'

'Of course, here's our timetable,' replied the receptionist as she handed him a leaflet.

'We don't really organise lessons, although a few volunteers come in occasionally to teach others to swim, but there's no actual timetable for that.'

Behind reception was a wall mounted television showing live camera footage of the pool. Logan could see that there were only about twelve people using the pool at that moment, all adults, none of whom were being given swimming lessons.

'Okay thanks.'

He returned to his car and again spoke into his phone camera, saying:

'I'm back in Brodick. Heidi's still with me. I'm going to try to contact the police without being seen. That might mean that I'll be speaking to an off-duty officer if I can find her. I've been given the name and approximate address of one, so I'm going to try to find her house now, and if she's not being watched or followed by anyone, hopefully I'll be able to speak with her and hopefully she'll believe what I'll tell her. Okay, Miss PC Reynolds, let's hope you're at home.'

He stopped recording and started driving. Hillview Place is on the south side of Brodick. Already knowing the streets of Brodick, he drove and parked his car at the west end of the street. He could see several cars parked there, including two red ones. One of these was a rather old looking Mini Cooper and the other was a red Renault Megane. At the far end of the road was a council van parked facing towards him. About half way along the street was the grey Mercedes he'd been seeing. He focused his binoculars on it, enabling him to see its registration which confirmed to him that it was the same car. But there was no sign of its driver, Shades. It was parked approximately mid-way between the two red cars which were parked about six houses apart.

With Heidi in a calm state, he reckoned it would be safe to leave her for a few minutes while he walked along the street towards these cars while also trying to discretely look into windows and gardens to find any clues to indicate which house Reynolds lived in. He saw some childrens' toys and scooters in one garden, making that house an unlikely choice. As he walked along he could smell the occasional meal being prepared. As he walked past the Mercedes he could see Shades' beige jacket and a folded map on the passenger seat. On walking past the council van at the far end of the street, he paused to look around and think about what to do next, carefully looking at the houses to try to figure out which one could be occupied by Reynolds.

After about a minute, he started to walk back towards the houses adjacent to where the Mercedes was parked. At that moment, he saw Shades appearing from the side garden of the house where the Megane was parked. Logan hid himself behind the council van and watched Shades from through its windows. Shades, still wearing his sunglasses, was now wearing a dark-green hiking jacket. On his right sleeve he had a blue circular patch with a bird logo sewn onto it, identical to the one on the corpse at the Punchbowl. Logan recognised the noticeable tattoo of a spider's web on the left side of his neck.

'That's him for sure,' he thought.

Shades walked from the side of the house to the front door and rang the doorbell while repeatedly looking over both shoulders towards both ends of the street as if he was wary of being seen. After about thirty seconds the door opened, and Shades entered the house.

'Is that PC Reynold's house?' thought Logan.

He walked back to his car to fetch his drone. He changed its battery as the first battery was almost depleted. Various thoughts passed through Logan's mind. Each thought convinced him more that he should fly the drone and position it so that its camera would let him see inside the house. He daren't risk Shades noticing that he was being spied on. But what if Shades would see the drone and come running out, armed and dangerous, looking for the drone pilot? If Shades found Logan, he'd find Heidi.

After careful consideration, Logan created the idea that he should park his car in another street, in this case, in Springbank Terrace which is the next parallel street to the north. From there he would still be in range to fly the drone, but of course he wouldn't want anyone seeing the drone departing from, or returning to, his car. Before moving his car, he walked over to the west end of Hillview Place where there were some shrubs across the road at Brathwick Place. Checking that nobody could see him, he switched on his drone so that it was ready for action. He then discretely dropped it behind some bushes. He drove round to Springbank Terrace and parked his car at the street entrance so that he could maintain line-of-sight signal strength to the drone as it lay hidden in shrubs. If Shades would see the drone and come running out of the house to follow the it, Logan would fly it in the opposite direction from where he was parked, southbound to Brathwick Terrace. If necessary, he could land it or crash it into the trees there. Protecting Heidi was more important than worrying about retrieving his drone.

He attached his phone to the drone controller. Seeing clearly though the drone camera, he carefully flew it over the roof tops, slightly below the north side of the roof apex to keep it out of sight from the street until he was certain it was over the correct house. Taking the drone into the hover, he made it climb to about fifty feet above the rooftops, high enough that its gentle buzzing noise wouldn't be heard from indoors. Positioning the camera onto the house where he'd seen Shades, he slowly reversed the drone northward while pointing its camera at the windows.

To his dismay, he couldn't see inside. The daylight reflection from the windows was too much to see through them. Worried that the drone could be seen from inside the house, he positioned it back onto the rooftop then hovered it above the roof gutter looking for a landing area on the ground in the back garden. There was a small bushy conifer tree there, about five feet tall. That would provide a near-perfect cover for hiding a small drone. As quickly and as carefully as he could, he landed the drone onto the ground behind that tree. From there he was able to then slowly hover it into position where its camera could see through the tree branches into the house. This manoeuver took Logan about two minutes to get the position perfect. He could see into the living room where Shades was talking to someone who was out of view from the camera.

Shades was still wearing his sunglasses. His body language appeared to be somewhat argumentative and menacing as he occasionally pointed at the blue circular patch on his right sleeve as if he was talking about it for some reason. Logan kept the drone hovering in the same position for nearly ten minutes, carefully watching and recording the event, wishing he could hear what was being said. Eventually the other person made a move across the living room. Logan recognised her as the officer he'd seen earlier, but this time seeing her face more clearly and with her long hair untied.

'PC Reynolds,' thought Logan. 'Now I see why the guys

fancy you.'

She moved towards the window, but Shades grabbed her arm as if to stop her, momentarily looking out of the window as he did so. Still holding her arm, Shades rapidly moved towards the back door. Knowing that the door would be open in the next few seconds, Logan descended the drone quickly onto the ground and switched off its motors, hoping it would be adequately hidden behind the tree. It landed clumsily, slightly tilted as it rested on an exposed tree root. In that position, the drone camera remained pointing at the back-door step, just enough to see if the door was open or shut, but not enough to see above knee height. The door opened and remained open for about thirty seconds. As Shades stood outside the back-door, only the lower part of his legs and shoes could be seen by the drone's camera. It seemed that Shades was standing there motionless while perhaps looking at something.

Logan was expecting Shades to see the drone sitting there, and so he positioned his fingers on the controller in preparation for a rapid ascent in the event of seeing Shades' feet walking towards it. After a few moments, Shades went back into the house and closed the door.

Logan activated the drone's motors again and slowly took it back into a hover. He yawed the drone around to look for any reason as to why Shades had come outside to look at something. Pointing the drone camera eastwards towards the back-road access, he could a man and a woman walking away with young girl. There was nothing suspicious looking about them. They appeared to be aged around their early thirties and possibly be the parents of the young girl with them. The little girl looked to be about three years old, and with similar appearance to

Heidi. That might have explained why Shades was so interested in what was happening as the family walked past.

By yawing the drone round a few more degrees, Logan could see two teenage boys watching it with interest. They had been walking past with their bicycles and had stopped to look at it. Logan was concerned that they may attempt to enter the garden to play with it. Such an action would likely alert Shades that he had been spied upon. With that concern, Logan decided to abort the session, immediately applying power to lift the drone and fly it to a position out of sight from the boys as quickly as possible. He flew it to a height of about two hundred feet then scanned the surroundings to locate a suitably hidden landing area. As he scanned the area, he could see through the drone camera that the boys had moved on, so he scanned again at the house. At that moment the front door opened. Reynolds and Shades were leaving the house.

'Don't look up,' whispered Logan to himself. 'Just don't.'

From the drone position being directly above, Reynolds walked with Shades as he continuously and menacingly kept one hand on her right shoulder. His sunglasses still covered his eyes. He drove away in his Mercedes. Reynolds drove away in her red Megane. Keeping the drone in the hover, Logan was able to watch where they were going as they both drove north through Brodick. When both cars were out of sight, he flew the drone back to his car, comfortable that there was nobody around at that time to see him. He calculated that he still had about ten minutes charge remaining on the drone battery.

Having failed to speak with Reynolds, he tried again to call the Lamlash police station but there was no ring tone other than a few unusual clicking noises. He opened his car boot to check on Heidi. She was awake.

'Hello Heidi. I hope you had a nice sleep. Are you thirsty? You want some juice?'

He poured some orange juice for her which she drank. Then his phone rang with Robin's name appearing on the screen.

'Hi Robin.'

'Logie, how are you getting on? How's your situation now?'

Robin was sitting in the woodshed surrounded by wild forestry.

'Not making much progress here,' said Logan. 'Have you seen anything in the news?'

'Not much,' replied Robin. 'But you should hear this. Anna called me a few minutes ago. She says there was a kidnapping of a little girl in Moscow about two months ago. Her name, if it's the same girl, is Iskra Mikhailovca. Anna sent me a picture of her which she found on the internet. I'm forwarding that to you now. That girl's dad is, or was, some sort of politician and his name is Vlad Mikhailov. He went missing about a month earlier. Anna says the news is a bit vague as to what might have happened. Some people think the girl was kidnapped for ransom. Others say she was just kidnapped to make the family disappear. Apparently, their government isn't saying much about it.'

Logan remembered Anna telling him that Heidi had mentioned the name 'Mikhail' when they spoke. He turned to Heidi, and asked her:

'Iskra? Is your name Iskra?'

Heidi didn't respond.

'She doesn't seem to know that name,' said Logan.

'Maybe her kidnappers named her Heidi two months ago

to avoid detection or something, and at her age, two months is a long time. Maybe she now thinks her name is Heidi. I just sent you the picture that Anna sent me. Check your mail.'

'Okay, stay on the line. I'm checking.'

Logan opened his email and looked at the attachment which Robin had sent. It was a poor-quality grainy picture of a young girl of similar appearance to Heidi but with longer hair. He showed the picture to her.

'Is this you?' he asked, pointing to the girl in the picture.

Heidi looked at the picture, but she didn't respond. She was more interested in looking out of the car window at a blackbird foraging on the grass.

'I can't be sure if that's her,' he said. 'It looks a bit like her but the picture's too fuzzy.'

'Mate, I think you're out of your depth on this. You've been a soldier working for an infantry. Teamwork. But you're trying to do this by yourself. And whether you like it or not, you're not only a rescuer but now you're also a sort of kidnapper. If you can't get the local police involved, then you have to call emergency services and get the mainland police.'

'I know. I already tried calling them. I'll try again.'

Logan disconnected the call. He asked the girl again:

'Are you Heidi? Or Iskra?'

She didn't respond.

'Alright. I'll keep calling you Heidi.'

He tried again to call the Lamlash police station, but as before, there was no audible tone. He decided that now his best course of action would be to try again to call emergency services. After a few rings he heard someone answer. Logan had prepared himself to ask for the police, fully expecting that he'd be transferred to a mainland police authority to which he could explain his predicament.

'Hello.'

'Police please,' replied Logan.

'Hello.'

'Police please. I need to speak to police please,' said Logan.

'Hello. Who is it this time?'

As Logan listened, he could hear what sounded like several conversations between people although he couldn't make out what was being said. He stayed on hold for about thirty seconds until the call was cut off.

This immediately raised Logan's suspicion that somehow the emergency services switchboard line had been tampered with, perhaps for the purpose of criminals blocking or intercepting conversations as he had experienced during one of his army operations overseas. Considering this, he ushered Heidi back into the car boot and drove to the Post Office almost directly across the road from Brodick Green.

At the side of the Post Office was one of the green telephone junction boxes. He could see paint scratchings and markings on the door which indicated that it had possibly been forced open. He turned his car around to drive north to the corner of Shore Road and Knowe Road where he stopped to check the two junction boxes there. They also had similar markings, indicating that they had been tampered with. He now became concerned that, if someone was illegally intercepting landline phone calls, perhaps they were also intercepting cell phone conversations. Perhaps his calls to Robin or Anna had been intercepted. He paused for a few moments to think about how the situation was developing. He called Robin and told him:

'I think pan squawk code seven six.'

Robin understood this as the partial international aviation code for urgency with loss of communication. This was Logan's way of declaring his need for help without further use of the telephone or any radio equipment.

'Understood,' replied Robin as he ended the call.

Logan switched his phone to flight mode and began recording himself again.

'Okay, so here's the latest update. I failed at calling the police or emergency services. It looks like someone's been tampering with the junction boxes on the streets of Brodick. If I'm right about that, I reckon someone's either blocking communications or maybe listening to conversations on landlines on the island. Perhaps they have the technology to intercept cell phones too. They might have even heard me talking to Robin and Anna earlier. If that's the case, they'll know I have Heidi. I can still carry some hope that they won't be able to trace what car I'm driving, or can they?'

He paused to think.

'Actually, if they have control of the police and can trace my phone number, they'll be able to trace my name, address and… oh bugger! I think from that they can get my car registration number. So, I need to change car. Ugh, dammit.'

He stopped recording. Earlier in the day he could drive past anyone suspicious and they wouldn't pay any attention to his car, but now the possibility existed that driving his car anywhere was no longer a safe option. He had to make the precautionary assumption that criminals were looking for his car and would know his registration plate.

He considered his options. Abandoning his car somewhere

would mean he would have to walk everywhere, and that would take Heidi into public view. Stealing a car would certainly attract attention when the owner would report it, and almost certainly have him being caught quickly on an island with so few roads. Stealing another car's registration plates would have the same attention seeking effect. Buying a car would provide a safer option.

Reluctantly, he switched on his phone again to get an internet signal, quickly browsing for inexpensive used cars being sold locally. There wasn't much choice but there was a Ford Fusion being sold for eighteen hundred pounds in the small village of Blackwaterfoot on the south west coast of the island. He made a screenshot of the various pictures of the advertisement from the website then switched his phone back to flight mode.

Negotiating a bargain when buying a second-hand car sometimes works for a small percentage of the value but trying to barter would be chancing his luck and possibly result in a refusal. For that reason, he decided to buy the car with minimum fuss. He checked his wallet. He had three hundred pounds cash, one bank debit card and one credit card. From each card he knew he could withdraw a maximum of five hundred pounds per day from a cash machine, but that would leave him five hundred pounds short for which he'd have to wait until the following morning to withdraw. As a temporary precaution, his immediate priority should be to remove his registration plates. He knew there was a secluded dusty parking area at the top end of the Corriegills road beside where he'd been earlier. He knew about the small business there which dealt with old cars. He knew he could find a car there which wouldn't be used for the rest of the evening.

From where he was parked in Knowe Road, he didn't regard it safe enough to drive even the short distance through Brodick to Corriegills. He would need to steal someone's registration plates before driving anywhere. Leaving Heidi in the car for a few minutes, he took out his Swiss Army Knife and walked into the shrubs and trees at the roadside. On the other side of these trees were some houses, one of which had its white Hyundai car parked at the side garden, out of sight from any other neighbouring houses. He carefully skirted around the side of the garden. Using his screwdriver attachment, he quickly removed both front and rear registration plates.

'I'm only borrowing them,' he whispered as if the car could hear him and understand.

'I'll return them in about half an hour before anyone notices.'

He rushed back to his own car and swiftly swapped the plates before driving towards North Corriegills. When he arrived at the top end of Corriegills road, as expected and as he'd noticed on previous occasions, there were about a dozen cars parked there. One particular car had a flat tyre and was covered in dry dust, indicating that it hadn't been used for several months.

'You'll do nicely,' he said quietly as he parked beside it.

He quickly changed the registration plates, continually and nervously looking around in case anyone would see him. With the plates swapped, his next task was to return to Brodick's Knowe Road to replace the Hyundai's plates before the owner would notice them missing. With that mission accomplished, he could now drive his car confidently without worrying about being identified by his new temporary car registration. Someone would eventually notice that the car in Corriegills had no registration plates, but it would be wouldn't likely be noticed until the following day at the earliest.

He went to the cash machine at the bank opposite the putting green. He managed to withdraw five hundred pounds from each card, still leaving him short for the car purchase. He would have to return after midnight to be able to withdraw any more. Heidi was getting restless and was trying to crawl through to the rear seats. Logan looked at his watch.

'It's getting late. For a little girl like you it must be almost your bed time.'

He looked at the overcast sky.

'It'll be dark soon. Let's go camping, but not in a campsite. Too many people there. We'll find a quiet spot. And, I think you're getting hungry again.'

He opened the roll of tinfoil he'd bought and ripped off a length about the size of a large dinner plate then laid it flat on the front passenger seat. He unpacked the salmon slices and placed them onto the tinfoil. He then opened the tin of peas from which he emptied the juice onto the ground and placed the peas onto the tinfoil around the salmon. After carefully wrapping the tinfoil into a sort of ball around the food he opened his car bonnet and wedged the tinfoil ball into the exhaust manifold.

'Exquisite cuisine will be ready in twenty minutes Madam,' he joked with a fake posh voice.

He drove his car northwards and parked it across the road opposite the sawmill at the north of Brodick Bay, making sure that his car was hidden behind dense shrubbery. He knew that in the later part of summer, Arran was always abundant with berries growing on the bushes there. Blueberries, brambles and raspberries were easy to find throughout the island, but brambles were awkward to collect due to their thorned branches. Wild raspberries were usually rather small, but on this stretch of shoreline he knew he could pick the larger species of wild yellow raspberry. At this location they usually grew as large as any he'd seen in any shop. He picked enough of these yellow raspberries to fill two of the paper cups he'd bought earlier. He gave a raspberry to Heidi which she ate, seemingly enjoying it.

'That's our breakfast for tomorrow morning,' he said as he sat back into his car.

He continued driving towards Sannox. On passing through the village he noticed the Mercedes parked opposite the Glen Sannox entrance. Various thoughts came to mind. Why was it there? He considered the possibility that one of his earlier phone calls with Robin could have been intercepted, in which case, someone listening may now be looking for the dead body up at the Devil's Punchbowl and hoping to find the drug-filled rucksack. Perhaps that person would be Shades, or someone being followed by Shades.

Logan didn't stop driving. He continued north up the hill then turned right towards the popular coastal camping area at North Sannox. He knew he shouldn't enter the campsite because almost certainly there would be other campers there who would see him with Heidi.

The road towards the campsite crosses a small bridge over a narrow stream which flows into the sea. He knew that immediately before that bridge he could park his car and walk down a narrow track which leads along the south bank of the stream towards the coast into a well-hidden area which would unlikely be occupied by other campers. Ramblers and walkers often used that track, but more so during daytime than at dusk.

He let Heidi out of the car. With the confinement of her being kept hidden for most of the day, her clothes were soaked with urine as were his clothes and sleeping bag which she had been sleeping on.

'Ah,' said Logan. 'Okay, It's not your fault. We'll get you all cleaned up.'

He removed the ball of tinfoil from the car engine and put it into his rucksack which he wore as he carried Heidi to the stream. He carefully undressed her in preparation for a wash.

'Eh, I don't really want to do this,' he said as he completely undressed her. 'But it has to be done. You need to get all your clothes off and get into the water.'

He also stripped off down to his underpants and carried her into the stream where he forced himself to laugh and splash the water playfully so that she would enjoy the experience. The water wasn't deep, so he knelt down and held her such that her shoulders were beneath the water surface. After a few moments Heidi began splashing with her hands, enjoying herself, playing a sort of game of splashing with Logan. He took advantage of this game by allowing her hair and face to get wet, giving him the opportunity to wipe out some mud which was still in her hair from when he first found her in the mining pit. He also enjoyed the refreshing bathe for himself.

After five minutes he put Heidi onto the grass next to the stream and used his shirt as a towel to dry her. He dressed her in a fresh pair of underpants and one of the T-shirts he'd bought earlier. She stood there patiently while he put all her soiled clothes into the stream and washed them as much as he could in the absence any soap or detergent. He found some tree branches which were ideally placed to hang the wet clothes. Wringing as much water from them as he could, he reckoned they'd be dry by morning. The sleeping bag was slightly damp due to the urine, but it was almost waterproof, so he wiped it clean with the now-damp shirt which he'd used as a towel. He dried and dressed himself.

Although overcast and getting dark, the air temperature was mild. Much to Logan's delight, there was a slight breeze to keep the midges away. Arran is notorious for midges which will bite relentlessly, especially in overgrown areas, requiring campers to be completely covered in clothing or wear strong midge repellent cream or spray. Each bite is harmless but having hundreds of midges biting is at best annoying and at worst can drive people crazy with extreme itching. Some of the world's toughest special forces commandos who have served time in dangerous tropical jungles have struggled to cope with Scotland's west coast midges.

'Midges can't fly faster than four miles per hour,' he said to Heidi as he was thinking of anything to say to amuse her. 'And I reckon that breeze is about five miles per hour. Perfect.'

He produced the ball of tinfoil which was still hot from the exhaust manifold and unwrapped it onto a flat stone. He cheerfully announced:

'Dinner is served Madam, and welcome to the Sannox Ritz.'

The two slices of salmon and the peas were very welcome after such an unusual day. They had been cooked to perfection by the exhaust manifold heat. Having no cutlery, they ate with their fingers. Heidi was hungry enough that she ate without needing to be coaxed.

'I'm glad you're not a fussy eater,' laughed Logan.

After eating, he pitched his tent. With the sleeping bag dry, he made a bed layout for Heidi by padding the groundsheet with layers of clothing to make it more comfortable for her. Heidi seemed to enjoy being in the tent.

'I'll just be outside,' he said as he zipped the tent closed.

He returned to the stream to wash the shirt he'd used as a towel before draping it over the same branch as the other clothes. He sat at the water's edge and listened to the faint peaceful noise of the sea waves lapping the shoreline. At last now he had some time for himself to think more carefully about the day's events and to create a plan for the following day. One option would be to stay in hiding for several days, but with the value of whatever was in that hidden rucksack, possibly worth a seven-figure sum of money, anyone looking for it wouldn't likely stop searching. This would be especially so if Heidi was being held for some sort of major political or financial ransom. Getting her off the island was certainly the most favourable option.

Having already seen nine suspicious characters: Shades, Earlobe, Sloucher, Gremlin and Badger, plus the two men searching cars at the Lochranza ferry, and the other two at the Brodick ferry, he tried to make sense of the day's events: a girl with a parachute, a dead body a mile away with a ripcord, a rucksack filled with an unidentified substance, nine ominous-looking men, guns, a black transit van, a red camper van, a grey Mercedes, a dark blue car, a helicopter, police being followed, a stake out at the hospital and at the police station, a young girl going mysteriously missing from Russia and a missing Russian politician named Mikhail.

If he would hand Heidi over to the local police, and the

criminals were to find out, there would be little to stop an organised armed siege to recapture her, killing anyone who would dare try to protect her.

All things considered, he reckoned the safest option would be to avoid any confrontation between the police and whoever these mystery people were. Asking Robin to call the police from the mainland could be a dangerous idea, but Robin may have already done that. Whatever happens, there was a distinct possibility that Logan would have to stay on the island with Heidi for a few more days. In the belief that his car with the stolen registration plates would eventually, perhaps very soon, get noticed, his idea to buy another car the next day seemed to be the best option for a short-term solution to stay inconspicuous until he could create a plan of action.

Thereafter what would be the plan? He still wouldn't be able to drive a car onto either of the ferries without it being searched. He couldn't think of any boats which he'd be able to rent, borrow or even steal, especially as he had no experience of sailing. And with no airstrips or light aircraft on the island there was no way he could fly anywhere. If the entire event was somehow connected to politics it may be best to ask for military involvement, but then again, politics tend to involve politicians. His opinion of British politicians was to regard them as similar to the lowest form of humanity, very likely to willingly sacrifice a child's life to support a cover-up for a hint political gain if any such pressure would be placed upon them from anywhere. His negative feelings about politicians were magnified by some of his army experiences.

While thinking all this through, Logan could feel his energy fading due to the fatigue of what had now become a long tiring day. Twilight had ended, leaving them in the comforting darkness of the coastal woodland. He opened the tent zip to check on Heidi. He could see she that was sleeping.

'I'll be out here,' he whispered, as he closed the tent zip.

He covered himself with his jacket. In less than twenty seconds he drifted into a light and troubled sleep.

CHAPTER 4

Sunday September 19th

Logan woke every hour through the night, each time checking on Heidi and each time being satisfied that she was sleeping peacefully. As daylight was nearing, Logan was keen to start the day, but being so early, there was no point in doing anything or going anywhere. There was nothing he could do for now except wait until it was late enough for him to venture out to buy that car he'd seen advertised. Driving a car on Arran would be less conspicuous during daytime than driving on quiet roads at dawn. With this in mind, he tried forcing himself back to sleep. Even just a few short power naps would be advantageous, especially as he predicted another day of chaos. Eventually, he could hear Heidi talking. He unzipped the tent. She was standing up, talking to her toy cat.

'Well hello young lady,' he said with a smile. 'I hope… no actually, I KNOW you slept well.'

Opening the zip fully, he beckoned her to come out.

'Eh, ah, I think maybe we should get your toilet arrangements sorted first, okay? You want to pee?'

He encouraged her to follow him to a nearby bush, where, as before, he held her to keep her balanced and steady while she emptied her bladder onto the grass.

'Good girl. Now we can have breakfast.'

He produced the two the paper cups which he'd filled with the yellow raspberries. Heidi slowly ate them while being more fascinated at watching Logan taking the tent down. It was almost eight o'clock: late enough to feel more confident at driving anywhere without being too conspicuous. He looked into the bag of clothes he'd bought for her while trying to invent a plan of action.

'I need to make you look like a boy,' he said.

He dressed her in the new clothes which he had deliberately chosen for her to appear boyish. Trainers, denim trousers, a dark brown jacket and hat. With his Swiss Army Knife he cut one of the tent guy ropes into two short lengths to tie her hair up so it could be tucked securely beneath her hat. Looking at her dressed like this, he reckoned she looked like she was about two years older.

'It's not yet quite good enough,' he said as he looked at her. Despite wearing boy's clothing, she still had a distinct girl's face. Her big blue eyes were very noticeable. He pulled the jar of dried coffee granules from the shopping bag and poured some of them into his now-empty paper cup. He dipped the cup into the stream to mix some water with the granules which he then stirred with his finger until they dissolved, becoming a weak coffee solution.

'I'm no make-up artist,' he joked. 'I can do camouflage, but I've never done a sex change on a three-year-old.'

He carefully smeared the coffee onto Heidi's face, neck and hands to make her skin look more tanned. He then mixed more coffee granules into the cup to make the solution slightly darker. He smeared this darker solution onto her lower jaw, drawing a line which bent upwards towards her ears. The extra darkness of this line was just enough to give the appearance of a different shaped and more masculine jaw line. He also applied some of this slightly darker solution on her cheeks immediately below her eyes and down each side of her nose, giving the illusion of her face and nose being bigger, and therefore making her eyes look smaller. He added more granules to further darken the solution, smearing it on her eyebrows. Finally, he removed her hat and rubbed this solution into her blonde hair. He placed the hat back on her head, satisfied that he'd converted the appearance of a cute three-year-old untanned blonde-haired girl to that of a five-year-old tanned dark-haired boy.

'Okay, now we can go for a drive,' he said as he collected the now-dry clothes which had been draped over the tree branch all night.

The clouds were scattered with large areas of blue sky being visible. He switched his phone camera on to speak into it, making sure it was still set to flight mode to prevent it from being traced.

'Hello again. It's now day two of this, eh, weird situation. We camped here last night in North Sannox. And looking at the sky, I think it's going to be a nice day. I'm on my way now to Brodick with Heidi to get more money from the cash machine. I'm a bit worried that someone could have traced my calls and might be looking for my car, so we're going to Blackwaterfoot to buy an old car. I've tried to disguise Heidi's appearance. More updates later perhaps.'

He stopped recording and led Heidi back to his car where he plugged his phone into the car charger. Without coaxing, Heidi crawled over the rear seats into the car boot.

'Let's go to Brodick,' he said as he started the engine.

He arrived in Brodick and stopped again at the cash machine to withdraw more cash. He then turned the car northwards to drive to Blackwaterfoot. He didn't know the exact address of where to find the car he wanted to buy, but Blackwaterfoot isn't a big place. The angles from which the car photographs had been taken showed the coastline which Logan recognised as being on the north side of the village.

He drove into Blackwaterfoot, passing the Kinloch Hotel on his left where the road bends to the right over a small bridge. He continued driving along the road to the north where he stopped his car at the edge of the village. He took out his drone and checked that it still had a few minutes of battery power available. He then flew it into a hover at a height of about a hundred feet. He scanned the houses to look for any cars parked near them. It didn't take long for him to find what appeared to be the only blue Ford Fusion in the village, parked outside a house at Harbour View.

Within five minutes he was at the house. The registration plate on the car matched that of the pictures in the advertisement. He parked his own car out of sight from the house, leaving Heidi hidden. With his cash in his pocket, he rang the doorbell. An elderly lady answered the door.

'Hello,' said Logan. 'I'm sorry I didn't call you to warn you I was coming, but I saw your car was for sale. Is it still available?'

Her speech was quiet and slow as she spoke.

'Oh, yes,' she said. 'Wait 'til I find the keys.'

She left Logan standing at the door while she went back inside. After a minute, she returned to the door with two keys on a small keyring.

‘I stopped driving a couple of years ago, and my husband can’t drive any more. Kenneth had a stroke last month.’

She unlocked the car and let Logan sit inside. It was in good condition both inside and out. He reached for the bonnet lever to open it and see the engine. He was desperate to buy this car and wasn’t too worried if it was in poor condition. But he had to check that it had sufficient oil and coolant. Satisfied that the engine looked good, he closed the bonnet then sat into the driver’s seat and started the engine. It started at the first turn of the key.

‘I like it,’ he said. ‘How much do you want for it?’

‘Oh,’ said the lady. ‘I forget how much we were asking. My daughter took care of the advertising. I can’t remember how much she said.’

In some other situations Logan would have tried to barter the price down, but he believed that to try to negotiate a price reduction with an elderly lady who appeared physically and mentally vulnerable would be unethical. Perhaps more importantly, doing so would perhaps provoke her daughter to make adverse comments to other locals, resulting in him receiving unwelcome attention at a time when he needed to remain discrete.

‘Actually,’ began Logan. ‘I remember the advert said eighteen hundred pounds. I can give you that now.’

‘Oh, I don’t know if that’s too much,’ she said. ‘I think we just want to sell it. How much do you want to pay?’

‘It’s fine,’ said Logan. ‘The advert says eighteen hundred pounds and that’s the money I would like to pay you. If you have the paperwork I can take it away now.’

‘Oh lovely,’ she said. ‘Come on in.’

Logan followed her into her living room. On the settee was her husband, Kenneth, sitting in his pyjamas. The lady spoke to him:

'This young man wants to buy the car.'

Kenneth nodded his head and smiled on the right side of his face.

'Do you want a cup of tea?' she asked Logan.

'Eh, no, but thanks.'

The lady looked in their sideboard for the registration document, while asking Logan:

You're here on holiday?'

'Yes, here, eh, with my, eh, son.'

Logan looked around the living room. Kenneth was looking out of the window at the back garden which was well kept. On the sideboard there was a picture of a fair-haired woman. The lady found the registration document.

'Here it is,' she said as she gave it to him.

Logan looked at the part declaring the owner's name: Kenneth Gorman.

'What's your name?'

'Logan. But don't worry about writing my name on the form. I can fill that in later.'

'Lovely name,' said the lady. 'I'm Chrissie. Are you sure you don't want a cup of tea?'

'No, but thanks. I, eh, I have my, eh, son who's eager to do a lot of things today. I'll just sign this document and be on my way.'

Chrissie had to help her husband to sign his name on the form. Logan gave her the eighteen hundred pounds. He was concerned that their daughter would perhaps recognise the car being driven by a stranger, so he asked:

'Does your daughter live on the island?'

Chrissie picked up the picture on the sideboard and gave it to Logan to hold.

'Yes. This is our Alison. She lives in Lamlash, working at the hospital there.'

'Good,' said Logan. 'Will you tell her you sold the car? I wouldn't want her to get all worried if she sees your car being driven by me and thinks I've stolen it.'

'Oh yes,' said Chrissie. 'She calls us every day. We'll let her know.'

Logan took the registration document and left the house. His next task was to hide his Toyota Corolla.

He drove around the corner. Heidi had crawled out of the boot and into the rear seats, curiously looking out of the windows. He parked his newly-bought Fusion and got into the Toyota which he then drove onto the coastal road towards the Shiskine golf course beside Blackwaterfoot. Across the road from the golf course entrance was a small parking area next to a beach. This was an inconspicuous place although not quite as well hidden as he would have liked. He parked in what he believed would be its most discrete corner.

'Okay Heidi. We're going for a short walk. You look more like a boy now, so let's go.'

He took her hand and started walking towards the Ford he'd just bought. The walk was only for two minutes and he was confident that nobody was watching them. He opened the back door of the Ford and she climbed inside. He let her sit in the rear seats for the short drive to where the Toyota was parked. With nobody looking, he quickly replaced its registration plates. His Toyota was now legal again, parked with its correct plates, and he now had a Ford which was legally owned but not yet registered in his name.

He transferred all the food and belongings from the Toyota into the Ford, including the contents of its glove compartment. He made a new den for Heidi in the Ford's boot, but this time he left the rear seats folded down so that she wouldn't feel trapped or that she was being ignored. His next task was to return the stolen registration plates onto the old car at the top of Corriegills Road before anyone would notice them missing.

Within half an hour, he'd completed that task. At last, he had accomplished his mission to switch vehicles, eventually legally, without raising suspicion. Buying a second-hand car had always been a straightforward task but this time it felt like a massive achievement. His next task was to try to find a way of getting Heidi off the island.

He drove back to the ferry terminal in Brodick, parking at the small petrol filling station there next to the tourist information office. He filled the Ford tank with petrol while looking around for anyone suspicious. Heidi was by now sitting in the rear car seat in her boyish clothes and small dark baseball hat. Logan paid for the petrol and started the engine when a police car drove into the harbour area and parked. He could see it was being driven by the police officer he'd seen walking with Reynolds on the previous day. The officer walked into the ferry terminal. Logan moved his car to a more inconspicuous spot around the back of the filling station. He ushered Heidi through the folded rear seats into the car boot and then pushed the seats backs to their upright positions.

He pulled his small rucksack from the back seat, placing just one strap over his left shoulder. He had an old paper map of Arran which he pulled out and held, making himself look as if he was studying it as he walked slowly towards the police car. After a couple of minutes, the officer returned, giving Logan the opportunity to speak with him while pretending the meeting hadn't been planned.

'Sorry to pester you,' he said. 'I'm waiting for the next ferry, but, eh, I wasn't going to mention this. I think it's just my imagination, but now that I've just walked past a police officer, maybe I can get something off my chest before I get the next ferry home.'

The officer seemed interested.

'You can tell me.'

'Well, eh, I've been coming to Arran all my life, but this time I've noticed a lot of foreign voices going around. Much more than normal, and a few of these people look like suspicious characters. Maybe just my imagination, but anyway I made a note of some registration numbers of their cars. Maybe you should check them out. It's probably nothing, but I'll leave it in your capable hands.'

He gave the officer the slip of paper on which he had written the registration of Shades' grey Mercedes, Earlobe's blue car and Badger's black van. The officer looked at the paper.

'Wait a minute, I'll check now.'

He activated his police car computer while sitting in the driver's seat and leaving his door open so that he could continue talking with Logan. Within two minutes he started to look concerned.

'What exactly were these people doing?' he asked.

'Nothing really. But yesterday evening I saw you and your

colleague walking past the putting green and that guy in the Mercedes, well, it looked like he was watching you. Actually, well, maybe not so much you, but your female colleague. I mean, she's not bad looking, but it didn't look like he was watching her because he fancied her. It just looked a bit weird that's all. Anyway, you can check him out. I'll leave that with you.'

He paused for thought, trying to find a way of probing for more information.

'Actually, I tried calling the police station yesterday about this. But I couldn't get through. I think there's something wrong with the phone line.'

'Yes, I know. There was a major fault on several phone lines yesterday. Nobody could contact us at the station until late evening. The telephone engineers eventually managed to fix the problem.'

'Oh. Okay. I mean, good. I haven't heard of any actual crime happening on the island that we need to be aware of is there?'

'Nothing significant,' replied the officer. 'But I'd like you to tell me more about this guy. Can you describe him?'

Logan had to be careful of what to say, although this was his chance to actually tell a police officer what was going on without fear of being listened to by anyone else through a corrupted phone line.

'Well, he has dark hair, maybe in his late-forties or early fifties. He smokes cigarettes and wears sunglasses even when it's not very bright. He sometimes wears a beige jacket. Other times a dark-green jacket.'

'Okay,' said the officer. 'I'll look into it.'

Logan walked into the ferry terminal as if to buy a ticket for the next ferry. He watched the officer from inside the building, through its glass doors. As soon as he saw the officer driving away he returned to his car. Heidi was sitting patiently in the rear seat. The next ferry departure was in three hours, but still with the concerning possibility that someone may start searching the departing cars like they had been doing on the previous day. Even if nobody was searching cars at the ferry terminal, he couldn't be sure if anyone would be doing so on the ferry. He looked at Heidi sitting on the back seat.

'If you won't stay hidden, at least you have to be safe and legal, so I need to buy you a child seat.'

He started the engine and drove the short distance to the shop beside the mini-golf. Taking Heidi by the hand, he walked in, immediately being recognised by Katy who welcomed him with her usual smile.

'You can't stay away?' she joked.

Looking at Heidi, she was initially uncertain if she was seeing a boy or a girl. Logan noticed this.

'It's a bit of a long story,' he said. 'But for now, I need a child seat.'

Katy went through to the back store, returning a minute later with a new child seat, still wrapped in protective film. While paying for it Logan asked her:

'You remember I asked you about all these Russian sounding accents around here?'

Katy nodded her head.

'I've just asked the police so now I need to ask you something. Is there anything suspicious going on that you've noticed in the last couple of days?'

'There's something happening in Sannox,' she said. 'I don't

really know what it is, but some people arrived this morning on their way there to do something religious I think. They bought a few things in here for camping.'

'Russian accents?' asked Logan.

'A mixture of accents,' she replied. 'I think maybe Polish, German or Dutch. I think they're part of some strange religious cult.'

'Cult?' asked Logan.

'I heard them talking about being part of a gathering, but I didn't hear exactly what they call themselves. Spirit bummers or something like that. I wasn't really listening much.'

'Spirit bummers,' laughed Logan. 'I've known some weird people in my time and that name sums them up quite well.'

He took Heidi back to the car and secured the new car seat in place. With Heidi's fake boyish appearance, Logan was confident nobody would recognise her. He wanted to go to Sannox to see for himself who these people were. Could this be just a coincidence that people were visiting Sannox to be part of some religious activity, or was this activity all somehow connected to the mystery he was trying to solve? Although he wanted to visit Glen Sannox, it would be too risky to take Heidi. If people were coming to Arran for some religious or spiritual activity, it would be more likely that they would wish to be around the standing stones at Machrie Moor on the west side of the island, four miles north of Blackwaterfoot. The stone circle there is believed to be more than three and a half thousand years old, magnificently made of tall sandstones set in desolate moorland about a mile walk from the road.

There is a small stone circle on the hillside above Sannox village although its history is uncertain. There is some debate about whether the stones there are the remains of a circle which was placed there for religious reasons or perhaps they are just the remains of some old building. There are a few more standing stones set on the north side of Sannox village, believed to be the remains of a stone circle which was demolished in the nineteenth century: hardly a place for a religious cult journey.

He drove north but only as far as Corrie harbour. There were two families picnicking on the sand in its small walled harbour area. He parked his car next to the swings. He helped Heidi to get out of the car while making sure she continued wearing her baseball hat to maintain her new boyish appearance. The sun was shining brightly with clear blue sky above, so Logan put on his sunglasses. He then placed the smaller sunglasses on Heidi, not so much for sun protection but to help with her disguise.

'We look like brothers now,' he joked.

She wanted to sit on the first swing, so he lifted her onto it. He placed her hands on the swing chains and made sure she was holding them firmly.

'Hold on tight,' he said as he pushed her gently.

While Heidi enjoyed this, Logan scanned the area to look for anyone suspicious.

A young girl of similar age walked up from the sandy area. She was perhaps a year older than Heidi, with blonde hair and light un-tanned skin. She was wearing sandals and a pink knee-length dress. She was holding a small mermaid doll which she had been playing with at the water's edge. She wanted to play on the other swing. Able to do so herself without help, she climbed onto the swing and started moving her legs to begin the swinging motion with her doll placed on her lap. Her parents sat nearby, watching her from their beach picnic, always able to maintain visual contact with her. Logan continued to gently push Heidi to and fro. Heidi was in no rush for him to stop, and Logan enjoyed the feeling of doing something entertaining for her while he could have some time to think about what to do next.

After a few minutes, he noticed a red transit van driving from the north. He recognised it as the one he'd seen at Lochranza. Just then the young girl on the next swing accidentally dropped her mermaid doll onto the ground. Logan stopped pushing Heidi and stepped over to the other swing to pick up the doll.

The van entered the small harbour area and parked alongside Logan's car. It was an old van with a considerable amount of rust around the left front wheel area. Its paint was so faded that its original bright red colour had become a dull, dirty looking shade of red. Painted on its side was the website name: www.spiritbeamer.com. Beneath that was an email address saying: *jasper@spiritbeamer.com*. Logan stared at the signage on the van. He recognised the term *Spiritbeamer* from previous years.

'Oh no! Ugh! Okay, this'll be interesting,' he thought to himself. 'Not bummer, but beamer. I should have realised.'

He gave the mermaid doll back to the young girl. Two men stepped out from the van. He recognised them as the two men he'd seen at Lochranza. One of them was in his mid-forties. He was slim, medium height, with dark curly hair and short facial hair. He had quite pointed features, almost like 'elf' shaped ears and a twist at the end of his nose. He wore a loosely-knitted multi-coloured woollen hat. His companion looked slightly younger and much fatter. The two men spoke to each other, almost whispering and most definitely focusing their attention towards Logan who was still standing behind the young girl's swing. Heidi, still looking like a boy, sat content waiting to be pushed again. In Logan's mind he applied his usual habit of nick-naming of the two men.

'One of you must be Jasper,' he thought. 'I guess that's you with the hideous hat. No point in giving you a nickname. And eh, I think the other one should be called *Flabby*.'

The two men walked towards the swings, immediately making Logan feel uneasy. The young girl's parents were watching from the sandy area. Convinced of imminent trouble, Logan positioned himself between the two children and the men.

'What do you guys want,' he shouted, loudly enough to make sure he was attracting the attention of the two families on the sand.

Flabby suddenly quickened his step into a brief sprint running to the left side of Logan to position himself behind the two girls, while Jasper quickened his pace to move to Logan's right side, positioning himself in front of the girls. It became obvious that it wasn't Heidi they were interested in. They were more interested in the young blonde girl on the swing next to where Logan was standing. Jasper looked at the girl, briefly trying to grab hold of her arm while Logan pushed him away as the girl looked on. The girl's parents, seeing what was happening rapidly ran towards the swings.

The girl's mother screamed:

'Ruby!'

'Get away from us,' shouted Logan as he raised his arms with fists clenched, positioning himself more closely to the girl to protect her from Flabby who was standing behind her. Jasper spoke quietly to Logan, but his words were drowned out by the girl's father shouting:

'Hey, asshole, get away from her.'

The girl's mother screamed again. Jasper shook his head at Flabby, indicating that this girl was not who they were looking for, and both men returned to their car. Having seen what Logan believed was a kidnap attempt, he considered tackling the men, but his priority was to stay with the two girls until the men drove away. The young girl's parents were shaken by what they had seen. The mother, physically trembling, started to use her mobile phone. Heidi, still sitting on her swing, seemed unaffected by what had just happened. Logan spoke to the young girl's parents:

'Do you know these guys? Have you seen them before?'

'No,' said the father as he picked up his daughter from the swing.

The parents from the other family also rushed towards them to offer support.

'I've called for the police,' said Ruby's mother. 'I'm talking to them now. Did you see their registration plate?'

Logan was reluctant to say anything. He considered that it was actually Heidi who they were looking for.

'No, I didn't see the van registration.'

Logan had now found himself in a new dilemma. He was wary of going to the police due to the uncertainty of what was going on. But now there had been what appeared to be an attempted kidnapping, witnessed by four other adults. The police had been called, and these same witnesses would have to tell the police about the presence of Logan with a full description of him and Heidi, who, for now, looked like a boy. On a positive note though, these kidnappers would now identify

Logan, his car and Heidi, in her disguise, as being a parent and child of no interest to them.

'Ask for PC Reynolds,' said Logan. 'You're still talking to police now?'

Ruby's mother nodded while she continued speaking on the phone.

'Make sure you ask for PC Reynolds to speak with us. Actually, let me speak. Let me use your phone.'

She passed the phone to him.

'Hi. Is that the police or am I talking to the main emergency switchboard?'

'This is the Arran police,' replied the male voice.

'Okay,' said Logan. 'Whatever you do, make sure it's PC Reynolds in the Arran police who deals with this. Nobody else.'

'Alright Sir, but can you give me a reason why you ask for her?'

Logan paused for thought before answering.

'Yes. There's a young girl here and, well, I'll pass you back to the girl's mother who will talk with you. But PC Reynolds is the best person to deal with this situation.'

Logan passed the phone back to the woman. Ruby's parents detected something suspicious in Logan's behaviour.

'You know something you're not telling us, don't you?' asked the girl's father.

'Yes, but not enough to know how to explain except that I don't think your daughter's in any danger. I think these guys are looking for another child.'

Ruby gave her mermaid doll to Heidi to play with.

'This is your daughter?' asked Ruby's father.

This comment concerned Logan. His attempt at disguising

Heidi as a boy had failed. However, it seemed that she was disguised enough to avoid recognition.

'Eh, well, no. I'm looking after her temporarily. This is why I want to speak with PC Reynolds. I think she might be able…'

Logan stopped talking as Ruby's mother's mobile phone started ringing. She answered.

'Hello this is PC Reynolds from Arran police.'

Ruby's mother passed the phone to Logan.

'Hello is that PC Reynolds?'

'Yes, can you confirm your exact location?'

'Yes, Corrie harbour. How soon will you be here?'

'I'm already just a few minutes away. I was in the area. I'll be there in about three minutes.'

Logan handed the phone back to Ruby's mother.

'Are you here on holiday?' he asked.

'Yes, staying in a self-catering lodge in Lamlash. We come here every year. But this? This is… disturbing. What about you?'

'I'm just here for a few days,' said Logan. 'I also come here often, and yes, it's disturbing.'

Looking to the south they could see the police car approaching. Its blue light was flashing but on the quiet road there was no need for a siren. The car pulled in to the harbour area. Logan recognised Reynolds. She was alone. The five adults grouped together as Reynolds pulled out her notebook.

'I need to speak with you privately,' said Logan. 'When you finish talking to these good people, I'll be over there on the wall.'

Reynolds spoke with the two couples while Logan took Heidi by the hand and sat her down on the small wall leading to where the large sandstones were piled on top of each other. Eventually Reynolds came over to him while the other adults packed away their picnic items into their cars.

'You want to speak with me privately?' she asked.

'Yes,' said Logan. 'But I'm not sure where to start. Maybe... just maybe I got this all wrong, so let me ask you. In the last forty-eight hours has anyone reported a missing child on the island?'

'No. But before we talk more, do you have any identification on you so that I can actually know who I'm talking to?'

Logan showed her his driving licence, telling her:

'I tend to get called by my middle name, Logan. But my first name is Craig.'

'Craig Logan Lockhart. I recognise that name. And how do you know my name?'

'I was trying to contact... uh... I can explain later. More urgently, that guy you were with yesterday... the guy who was in your house. He wears dark glasses all the time and drives a grey Mercedes. Who is he?'

PC Reynolds looked disturbed by this.

'Have you been spying on me?'

'Not intentionally. I came to your house yesterday to talk to you about what I'm just about to tell you, but I don't trust that guy. So, I didn't ring your doorbell. Who is he?'

'Actually, I don't think that's any of your business.'

Logan pulled out his mobile phone and selected pictures from its photo album.

'I saw him stalking you on Brodick's Shore Road yesterday about half past four while you and your colleague were walking northbound past Alexander's shop. He was standing across the road watching you and then following you. A bit creepy looking.'

'He's a journalist,' said Reynolds. 'He was looking for some information on some local knowledge. But more urgently I need to deal with what just happened here a few minutes ago.'

'You should see this video recording,' said Logan.

He showed her the recording he'd made of her and her colleague being watched. Reynolds frowned as she watched it.

'This looks like you were the one following me to make a video of someone following me. Why were you also following me?'

'I wasn't following you. I was just driving and saw two police officers. I was getting out of my car to talk with you both when I noticed that guy with the shades… I mean, sunglasses. I'd seen him earlier watching the police station from across the road. Then later at your place.'

Reynolds remained calm but looked concerned.

'So why are you asking me about a missing child?'

Logan selected his video file from his phone.

'My battery is almost empty,' he said. 'Only two percent but I'll show you what I can.'

He showed her the video of Heidi holding onto the parachute for her life as she was gradually sinking into the quarry pit.

'A child drowning in the old mining pit in Glen Sannox. Wearing a party dress. There was nobody with her. What was she doing there? And what's with the Russian parachute?'

Reynolds looked at the screen with a surprised and horrified facial expression, asking:

'Glen Sannox?'

'Yes.'

'Who sent you that video?'

'Nobody. I recorded it myself.'

'How long ago?'

'Yesterday. Early afternoon.'

'Where's the girl now?'

'Sitting next to you.'

Reynolds looked at Heidi, suddenly realising she wasn't a boy.

'The battery is almost finished so I'll just flick through quickly. Look at this. I made this video yesterday as well. That's a dead body up at the Devil's Punchbowl. Let me just fast forward this and I'll show you…'

The screen went blank. The battery was out of charge.

'Anyway, I can show you more of this later. I've been calling her Heidi, but I'm not convinced of that being her real name. She's maybe Polish or from some other Eastern European country. Or maybe Russian. I really don't know for sure except that, having been coming to Arran for years, I've never heard a Russian or Eastern European accent here until yesterday. Now the place is full of them. Ask Katy in the shop next to the mini golf. I think you know her. She's noticed it as well. And weird people arriving this morning.'

Reynolds pulled her mobile phone from her pocket.

'I really think that's a bad idea. I think your calls are being listened to,' said Logan.

'Why do you think that?' she asked.

'Because when I called emergency services I could hear multiple conversations.'

'We know there was a fault in the lines all day yesterday, but it's been repaired,' said Reynolds.

'I'm ex-army. I don't know enough about electronics and computers and stuff like that to know exactly how it's done, but I've been in situations when criminals have managed to intercept phones.'

Reynolds wasn't convinced at what Logan was telling her. They sat in silence for a few moments while Heidi walked towards the swing she was on earlier. Logan followed her to once again lift her onto it, again making sure she was grabbing the chains before gently pushing her. Reynolds stood up and moved towards them both to continue the conversation. Logan spoke quietly:

'You've never met me before, so I can't expect you to trust everything I'm telling you, so let me help you. During your police training there was a difficult case just over twenty years ago. It became referred to as the Equinox Enquiry. You'd have been far too young to have joined the police back then, but I know the police still talk about it now.'

'I know about it,' said Reynolds.

'You can find it on the internet. Or you can find it through official police archives.'

Reynolds stared at Logan for several moments, eventually widening her eyes as she realised who she was talking to.

'Craig... Lockha... you're really... the boy? You're the... Equinox Boy?'

Logan nodded his head.

'And that guy...Verhoof...Verho...'

'Verhoeven,' said Logan.

'Yes. Verhoeven. He was convicted again a few months ago and received an extended prison sentence because... of you.'

Again, Logan nodded his head.

'So, you think there's a connection to…'

'I'm certain of it. And as you will know, the Verhoevens had a nasty habit of organising child murder and child kidnappings. They liked Arran and had a weird fixation about the equinox which is only three days away. Although I admit, a few things still don't make sense.'

'These men today… have you seen them before?'

'No. But I think they were after Heidi here. You perhaps haven't noticed, but I've darkened her skin and hair. She actually has very pale skin and blonde hair. I think these guys thought that young Ruby was Heidi, until they saw her closely.'

Just then Ruby's parents waved as they peeped their car horn and drove away, followed also by the other family who had been there.

'How's your internet signal?' asked Logan.

'Good. My signal is good.'

'Search this. The website on the side of the van was spiritbeamer dot com.'

Reynolds tapped that into her phone. It showed a website which she showed to Logan while she scrolled through it. The main theme of the site appeared to be about promoting spirituality. It seemed to be a small organisation being run by a man named Jasper who had some delusional belief in himself as being some sort of spiritual guru offering to perform ceremonies for various spiritual events. Logan recognised Jasper from the website pictures.

'Jasper was one of the two men we met just now. And that fat one who was with him had that drug-glazed look about his eyes. I think he'd been smoking something quite potent. I reckon if he'd stood upwind of me, my nose would have detected something illegal.'

Reynolds began scrolling through the website pages.

'What do you make of this?' she asked.

'Tree hugging weirdos if you ask me. Look at that. What's that picture?'

He pointed at a picture of four bent tree branches tied together in a sort of arched shape and stuck into the ground.

'Look at the caption,' he said as he read it aloud:

'*This is the womb of Mother Earth and above is Father Sky.*'

'It's four twigs in a field. Keep scrolling. Let's see what other nonsense is in here.'

The next page showed what looked like a domed tent in a field. Its outer skin was made from a black plastic membrane. The title of the page said: *'Sweat Lodges'*.

Logan read the script beneath the picture:

'*This is an ancient Native American Indian tradition…*'

Logan joked with Reynolds:

'So ancient Native American Indians had plastic sheeting on their wigwams, did they?'

He continued reading:

'I am your ceremonial leader, blah, blah, blah. *It's traditional to bring a gift to your ceremonial leader,* blah-blah. *You should bring gifts of… tobacco.* Wait, what? Tobacco? I thought these sweat lodge traditions meant bringing a lump of wood to keep the fire going.'

Reynolds scrolled further.

'Oh, wait,' said Logan. 'Scroll back a bit. Look there.'

He read out loud again:

'*We enjoy being naked in these sweat lodge ceremonies. This is best for purification of the soul,* blah, blah…'

He paused as he saw the next line which Reynolds read out loudly:

'*... and children are welcome.*'

They looked at each other in stunned surprise.

'Have we missed something here?' asked Logan. 'Like, maybe there's an 'adults only' session where everyone gets their kit off, and maybe there's a family session where they just wear swimming costumes or something.'

They scrolled through the website again. But they found nothing to contradict what they had read.

'Ah, look here,' said Logan as he pointed to the screen. 'It says here:

'*Some people don't like getting naked in front of strangers. These are the sort of people who would take a shower with their clothes on.*'

They scrolled down further to a link saying: '*Manhood ceremonies*'.

Clicking on it, they were directed to another page which, as before, Logan read aloud:

'*Boys can't become men until they are guided by a leader. Their fathers often wrongly think they can teach their sons to become men, but the truth is that a boy cannot become a man until he has taken part in our manhood ceremony.*'

He shook his head at what he'd read, commenting:

'Well, that's a massive insult to so many parents who work so hard to support a family while teaching their sons things like how to swim, camp, catch fish, repair cars, repair bikes, polish shoes, do school homework, write CVs, prepare for job interviews, and a huge insult to all the scout leaders and teachers out there. Let's see the next page and find out what this arsehole thinks he can do to turn boys into men.'

Reynolds scrolled though the website until she found the page with the 'manhood ceremony' pictures. Most were of people standing in a field drinking, but two pictures were of men dancing around a fire, wearing nothing but some tree branches wrapped around their waists. Logan recognised Flabby in one of the pictures. He looked at Reynolds.

'What's happening here? A Russian, or Eastern European child who isn't reported missing, found half drowned next to a Russian parachute, a dead body up at the Punchbowl, a rucksack full of what I think is cocaine, an attempted kidnapping five minutes ago, Russian sounding mafia type guys going about with guns, and now this looks like a group of paedophiles.'

Reynolds' eyes widened.

'What did you just say about a rucksack full of cocaine and people with guns?'

'Oh, yeah I hadn't got to that bit yet. The dead guy had a rucksack full of white powder and that other guy… the one you say is a journalist… has a gun under his left armpit. And I think some other guys with accents are carrying assault rifles.'

'I'll need to look into that, but meantime I need to call this in. Can you take us to where you found that body?' she asked.

Logan shook his head.

'Think about it,' he said. 'Organised criminals with guns watching police and watching the island. They even had a helicopter up there yesterday looking down on Glen Sannox.'

'I… I saw that helicopter yesterday,' said Reynolds.

'Yeah, well, whoever these people are know there's a dead body and a valuable rucksack to be found, so if they see police searching the area for anything, you'll be followed in the hope that you'll lead them to what they're looking for. Maybe they'll see you from a distance. Maybe from a helicopter. And whichever police officer finds that rucksack won't have more than a couple of minutes life expectancy.'

'The rucksack's still with the body?'

'No. I took it and hid it. But maybe there's something else up there that I didn't find. Any police going to check should be as inconspicuous as possible and perhaps also be armed. I can fetch the rucksack later and bring it to you, but not while I still have the girl.'

Reynolds looked at Heidi. She knew she should carry out police work by initiating a search of the area. She couldn't be certain as to how believable his story was, but her instinct was telling her that he was genuinely concerned for her safety.

Logan pointed again at her phone screen. The website mentioned a woman named Kleo with an invitation to click a link to her own website. Reynolds let Logan click on it. Reading through the pages, it was clear that this woman was interested in Buddhism, claiming to be very involved and educated in the subject although the text on the pages didn't always agree. Logan started ridiculing what he was reading:

'Look here. It says how she's been practicing and teaching Buddhism for twenty years, but on the next page she talks about her friend who she's known for just twelve years, and that her friend has taught her everything she knows about Buddhism. How can that be possible? Maybe she needs a maths teacher.'

Reynolds was lost for words. As a police officer she had been trained to look for unacceptable practices on the internet but had never seen anything so ridiculous. They continued scrolling. There was some mention of women's group meetings in various places, although no mention of anything happening on Arran.

'At least there's no mention of kids getting naked or bringing gifts of tobacco or whatever,' said Logan. 'I'd like to go back into the glen and look around the place where I found Heidi. Maybe there's something I'm missing. I can get that rucksack and bring it to you. Whatever I do, I'd have to be alone so that I'd look like just another hillwalker. But you'd be recognised if your journalist friend is involved with this. They know you're a police officer. You shouldn't come. Or any of your colleagues. Preferably perhaps you should call for back-up support. And by that, I mean armed back-up.

Reynolds made screenshots of the website they'd been looking at. She approached Heidi and knelt down to speak to her.

'Hello Heidi. Is that your name?'

Heidi stared back at her and smiled. After a few moments she said a few words but neither Reynolds or Logan could understand her. Reynolds checked her phone and noticed that she had two missed calls from the police station.

'I need to call the station,' she said.

'Okay. Be careful. It's possible that someone is listening in.'

She spoke briefly on the phone while Logan guided Heidi back to the car and secured her into her car seat.

'We need to get Social Services involved here,' said Reynolds.

Logan looked at her, slightly impatiently.

'We're looking at some sort of organised crime here and a child's life. I'm ex-army. I'm trained to recognise baddies and kick ass if I have to. You're police. You're also trained to recognise baddies and kick ass if you have to. I've worked undercover operations. Maybe you have too. Social workers are trained to follow rules. Rules written by people in offices who haven't a clue about what they're dealing with. This isn't the time or place for that. Anyway, how quickly could you get social services here. Are they even on the island?'

'It's not that straightforward,' said Reynolds. 'We can't just be vigilantes and do what we want.'

'Alright, so, let's say you're the parent of a child who's been kidnapped from you, and you find out about a mafia style organisation with drugs and guns trying to find her and harm her. Or get her naked in a wigwam thing being organised by a delusional guru, likely connected to the Verhoevens who are notorious for kidnapping and killing children. You see your child though two crystal balls. One lets you see that your child is safe in the hands of two people who been through a tough selection process and been trained into full time jobs to do whatever it takes to protect the innocent. The other one lets you see your child through going to a social worker who has done no police training, no combat training, who only knows how to follow some bureaucratic rules even if these rules don't fit the circumstances which, for now, don't make sense. And for what it's worth, the few social workers I've known over the years are also doing drugs. So, it's your child. Who would be your choice?'

Reynolds stood looking at Heidi, saying nothing as she pondered over what Logan had just said. He added:

'You've never met me until now, so I don't expect you to trust me after just a few minutes. But instead of taking her to social services, maybe you know someone more discrete on the island who you know you can trust.'

'You mentioned Katy at the shop,' said Reynolds. 'How do you know her?'

'I've met her before on previous visits to the island. She served me a couple of times yesterday and today. She's the one who told me your name… and the fact that you have a fan club of teenage boys.'

Reynolds expressed a slight embarrassed smile.

'I have to get back to Brodick,' she said. 'Can you follow me? We need to talk more.'

'Of course. But let's talk somewhere private. Not at the police station and definitely not at your house.'

Reynolds thought for a moment while she looked at Heidi.

'I know somewhere safe where we can go. Follow me.'

Both cars set south towards Brodick. After passing the golf course, they turned right into Knowe Road and parked at a house beyond the entrance of the Ormidale Hotel. Reynolds stepped out of her police car while Logan, having parked directly behind her, wound down his window so they could speak to each other.

'Wait here,' she said. 'I need to check something first. The people here are expecting me.'

'Stop,' said Logan. 'Did you phone them to tell them we were coming here with a missing child? Someone could have been listening in.'

Reynolds rolled her eyes.

'Sure,' she replied sarcastically. 'I told them I was being followed by a psychopathic serial killer who's kidnapped a child from the Russian mafia and asked if we could come for tea.'

Logan let out a slight embarrassed laugh.

'Okay. Sorry for doubting you.'

'These people know me,' she said. 'They think this is just a social call, so if someone's listened in, that's all they'll have heard. Relax. I haven't explained to them what you told me. I'll do that now but I'm not sure how they'll react. Wait here.'

She went towards the front door, out of sight from where Logan was parked. After about five minutes she returned.

'Come with me. And bring the girl.'

Logan took Heidi into the house. As they entered, they were welcomed by a gentle looking middle-aged couple.

'You've met Katy in the shop,' said Reynolds. 'Now meet her parents, Sandra and Eric. They've agreed to look after Heidi while we do some work on this.'

Logan glanced at the hallway wall next to where he was standing. Hanging on the wall was a picture frame containing a collection of family photographs. Two of these photographs were of Katy and her parents. He glanced through the living room door and could see a marble fireplace on the opposite wall. On it was a photograph of Katy hugging a small dog. The way Katy's parents were reacting to this situation and the impression made by the cheerful looking photographs gave Logan a comfortable feeling that this was the home of a mentally stable and trustworthy family. Their dog approached Logan with her tail wagging.

'Meet Sheena,' said Sandra.

Logan patted Sheena, while asking Reynolds:

'How much have you told them?'

'She's a missing child who hasn't been reported missing?' asked Sandra.

'Yes, something like that,' replied Logan. 'And until myself and Miss Reyn... eh, I mean, PC Reynolds here, can figure out more, it's absolutely essential that she stays out of sight and not mentioned to anyone. Not in any telephone call, and especially not to the police.'

Eric asked Reynolds:

'Can you tell us a bit more?'

Reynolds' phone started ringing at that moment.

'I would if I could,' she replied as she answered her phone.

Sandra stepped forward and knelt down to take a closer look at Heidi.

'Well, we're planning to stay in for the rest of the day now.'

'If required can you keep her overnight?' asked Logan.

'Yes of course.'

'And does Katy still live here?'

'Sometimes. She has an apartment just a few minutes away but it's still being renovated.'

'Good, but please don't phone Katy about this. We don't know who's listening to phone calls. I'll go to the shop now and tell her myself.'

Reynolds ended her phone call.

'That call was about was an incident at the shop where Katy works. Sounds like that guy Jasper's been shoplifting. Maybe you'd like to follow me?'

'My pleasure,' said Logan.

He drove behind Reynolds to the shop. There was Katy and another shop colleague named Mary. Katy smiled warily at Logan when she saw Reynolds following him in.

'You've… met the attractive police officer?' asked Katy with a tone of voice which indicated a hint of disappointment.

'Purely police work,' said Logan. 'I'll let you speak with her first about the shoplifting. Then I need to talk to you privately about something.'

Katy explained to them both about how a man fitting Jasper's description had been attempting some shoplifting.

'It wasn't very much,' said Katy. 'We both saw him. He was lifting small children's toys and tried walking out with them. I thought maybe he'd just got distracted and forgotten to pay, but when Mary here asked if he'd paid, he knew he'd been caught. So rather than say something like: 'Oops sorry, I was daydreaming,' and then pay, he just said: 'God provides' and walked out.'

Logan walked out to the car park to see if he could recognise Jasper, Flabby, or the red van, but they were nowhere in sight. Reynolds followed him out. Just then Reynolds' colleague walked into the shop. He and Logan recognised each other from their earlier meeting at the ferry terminal. He approached Logan and Reynolds. He appeared to be surprised at seeing Logan.

'The three of us need to talk,' said Logan.

'We should do this back at the station,' said the officer.

'Eh. No,' said Logan. 'This shop serves good coffee. Let's talk here. I'll buy the coffee. What's your name?'

'Kyle,' said the officer. PC… oh… call me Paul. Paul Kyle.'

'Okay. I'm Logan.'

'And my name's Joyce Reynolds, but you probably knew that bit already.'

The three of them sat down and spoke.

Logan explained to Reynolds and Kyle as much as he could, including the information he'd been told about the missing Russian politician and his kidnapped daughter. Reynolds confirmed to Kyle that she'd seen a few seconds of the video footage on Logan's phone which showed Heidi holding on to the parachute. Kyle listened intently.

'Where's the rucksack now?' asked Kyle. 'The rucksack with the white powder which you think is full of drugs.'

'I hid it,' said Logan. 'I'll get it to you.'

He stood up.

'Give me a minute,' he said as he walked over to the cash point. Katy was busy opening a packet of loose change for the till while the shop manager stood behind her re-packing a toy into its cardboard box. Logan asked him:

'Sorry but can we borrow Katy for a few minutes? We'd like her help with something.'

'Yeah sure.'

Katy followed Logan and sat down at the table with Reynolds and Kyle.

'Katy, please tell these two police officers what you told me about these weird people going to Sannox. And anything else you can think of.'

'Oh them? There were people coming off the ferry last night and today. They've been buying a few things. They all seem a bit weird like new-age hippies or something. Scruffy clothes with all sorts of weird pictures painted on them. They're not the usual hillwalking people which you normally see here. And there are others who are wearing clothes like, well, trousers and jackets. I mean, like clothes someone would wear in an office. Not the sort of clothes people would wear to go into the hills. Actually, just about an hour ago two of them asked me if I was going to some Spirit meeting.'

'Spirit meeting?' asked Kyle.

'Some sort of religious thing. Apparently, it's happening

somewhere in Sannox over the next few days. I heard someone talk about it earlier this morning. I thought I heard them call it Spirit bummer.'

'Spiritbeamer,' said Logan. 'That's what was written on the side of that red van. And actually, I've heard that term before.'

'Tell us,' said Kyle.

'Ugh, well, it was more than twenty years ago. There was a woman in East Kilbride who was into all sorts of weird stuff and, well, it's a long story, but anyway, she set up a small group of weirdos who called themselves Spiritbeamers, but there were only a handful of them. She was married to a violent drug dealer who had a lot of nasty friends.'

He looked at Reynolds, telling her:

'Verhoeven.'

Reynolds understood who he was talking about. Kyle didn't recognise the name.

Kyle asked Katy:

'Do you know exactly where this event is happening in Sannox? Someone's house or garden? In the glen? On the beach? The campsite?'

'I think it's in the glen,' replied Katy. 'Do you think that's where you'll find that guy who was trying to steal stuff?'

Logan shrugged his shoulders.

'Maybe. But there's something you need to know.'

Katy looked concerned.

'I'm listening.'

Reynolds and Kyle nodded their heads, gesturing to Logan that he should tell Katy about Heidi.

'Katy, we don't really know what's going on. But you remember yesterday I was in here buying boy's clothes?'

Katy nodded, with a concerned slight frown.

'Well these clothes were for a little girl who I found alone in the hills. We, I mean, I…'

He paused as he quickly glanced at Reynolds and Kyle who both again nodded in approval of what they expected him to say next.

'… we believe she was kidnapped but we don't know more than that. And we think people are trying to kidnap her again. That's why I was trying to disguise her as a boy. She almost never talks. I've been calling her Heidi because I think that's her name. Well actually no. That's the name she responds to. I think maybe her name is Iskra. Iskra Mikhailovca the daughter of a missing politician. A Russian politician.'

Katy's eyes widened in awe at what she was hearing. She'd lived on Arran for most of her life. Arran had always been a peaceful place and well distanced from the idea of such a crime. Kyle started scrolling through his mobile phone. Logan continued:

'I think someone is tapping into the phone network here, so this can't be discussed to anyone, especially by phone, and especially not to the police station.'

'So, where is the girl now?' asked Katy.

'Your parents are looking after her,' replied Reynolds.

Katy looked even more surprised as she looked at Reynolds and Kyle.

'Why are my parents involved?' asked Katy.

'Because I know your parents can be trusted,' replied Reynolds. 'They're very discrete people and they don't own a guest house, so they don't have strangers staying with them. We think there may be some people connected to what's going on who are visiting the island and perhaps staying in guest houses. We don't know yet.'

'Found it,' said Kyle as he showed his phone screen to Reynolds.

'Vlad Mikhailov. He went mysteriously missing about three months ago. Then his daughter vanished a few weeks later.'

There was an unclear picture of Vlad standing with a young girl of similar appearance to Heidi.

'That could be her,' said Reynolds. 'Very difficult to say for sure.'

'I need to meet these people,' said Logan. 'Heidi, or whatever her name is, will be safe where she is. I should go to Sannox to find these spirit people and find out more about them. Only these two characters, Jasper and his flabby friend, saw me, but I was wearing dark glasses. If I change my clothes, wear a hat and shave off my beard, I can go there without being recognised.'

'You'll need a tattoo,' said Katy. 'Most of these people who have been coming into the shop have tattoos.'

'Shit, I hate tattoos. Never wanted one.'

'I can paint one on you back at the house later this evening.'

'What with? Make-up? Paint?' asked Logan.

'Henna. There's a shop on the way home. The woman there sells henna.'

Reynolds stood up and went to the back of the shop.

'You're good at artwork?' asked Logan.

'Not really. But some of these people who have been coming into the shop have some really awful tattoos which look like they were drawn by a drunk five-year-old.'

Logan pulled money from his pocket and gave it to Katy.

'Alright. I'll take you up on your offer. Buy that henna.

And a small brush or whatever you need. I'll go buy myself a disposable razor. I hadn't planned on having a shave. Can you make your way home now? I'll be with you shortly.'

'Oh, well, I don't finish until later.'

Reynolds returned and sat down at the table.

'I've just spoken to your manager saying we need you to take the rest of the day off to help us look for that guy who you called us about.'

'You want me to come with you and look for him?'

'No, but that's what we told your manager. We want you to go home now to your parents and meet Heidi.'

'And prepare yourself to paint tattoos on me,' said Logan.

Katy left the shop while Logan, Reynolds and Kyle continued talking.

'I'm trying to invent a plan,' said Logan. 'I'll go to Sannox. I'll look around the spot where I found Heidi in case there's something I missed. And if I can find anyone there, I can pretend I'm into spiritual stuff. Just maybe I'll find out something useful. Then I can talk with you both later.'

Kyle seemed uncomfortable at this this idea.

'Maybe you should leave this to police,' he said.

'I am,' said Logan. 'That's why I'm just going for a walk in the hills as far as you're concerned.'

'You say you'll pretend to be into spiritual stuff,' said Kyle. 'But if you're going to be surrounded by people who are knowledgeable about spiritual activities, they'll know you're pretending.'

Logan grinned.

'That's the easy part. I've met so many weirdos throughout my life and I've seen them trying to do all sorts of stuff.

They hug trees. They chant. They talk to their imaginary spirit guides which they think are hovering over their shoulders. They claim to see colours and hear music from the skies. They believe in fortune tellers. They believe anything. And it's like a competition for them, all trying to prove that they're more special than the next person. So, if I go there and tell them I can communicate with jellyfish or some pink elephant spirit that I invented, they'll claim they can do the same just to have equal or better spirit skills than me. And whatever they start pretending, they'll start believing.'

He stood up to leave.

'I'd give you my phone number but my phone's out of charge, so if you need me I'll be in Glen Sannox or at Katy's parent's house.'

The three of them walked out of the shop. As Logan started his car, he noticed Sloucher standing across the road with his gaze fixed on Reynolds and Kyle. Logan sat and watched. Sloucher hadn't noticed him. As Reynolds and Kyle drove away, Sloucher seemed to be sending a text message to someone. Logan pondered about what was happening. He considered that perhaps the attempted shoplifting just a set-up to provoke a staff member to call the police to enable criminals to keep track of police activity.

After sending a text message on his phone, Sloucher walked towards the harbour. When he was out of sight, Logan went to the supermarket and bought a packet of disposable razors and a can of shaving gel. He then made his way to Katy's parents' house. By the time he arrived at the house, Katy was already there. She answered the door.

'This must be the Brodick tattoo parlour?' he joked.

'Yes, henna and brush ready but no needles.'

Eric directed Logan to the upstairs bathroom where he shaved his beard. After a few minutes he came back downstairs. Heidi was sitting on the sofa with Sandra, enjoying a bowl of ice cream and watching a childrens' cartoon on television.

'Come into the kitchen,' said Katy. 'Tell me what tattoo you want.'

'I don't know. What sort of tattoos did these characters have when they came to your shop?'

'I didn't look too closely. I think one had a woman's face. One had a flowery pattern. Another had a sort of ribbon intertwined with a tree. Two of them had pictures of wolves.'

'And back at the shop you said you weren't good at artwork?'

'Nope. Absolutely not. I didn't take art at school.'

'In that case, maybe instead of painting a picture, maybe it's best to write some words somewhere. Peace. Love. Om Shanti. Something like that. Can you do it in a sort of fancy script?'

'Sure, but where?'

'On my neck? Yeah, around my neck just visible above my shirt collar.'

He removed his shirt to enable Katy easier access to his neck. She couldn't help noticing that his physique was well toned, typical of someone who regularly trained at hard physical exercise.

'You're some sort of detective?' she asked.

'Ah, eh, no. I'm between jobs just now. I'm ex-army and a few other things, but I have a reputation for helping police investigate bad stuff.'

Katy proceeded to paint the henna around Logan's neck.

'What does 'Om Shanti' mean?' she asked.

'It means peace. It's a Buddhist thing. And if you say it three times it means peace in the three dimensions of body, speech and mind. The funny thing is, I've been to Thailand which is a Buddhist society and I've never heard anyone say it there. The only time I've ever seen it or heard it is by weird people over here… you know the ones who go about promoting stuff like peace, love and brown bread, but are actually arrogant pains in the arse.'

Katy smiled at this.

'If you want I can write 'Om Shanti' three times?'

'No thanks. I want to look a bit weird. Not fanatical. And not too knowledgeable about this stuff either. I want them to think they can bullshit me. That way they're more likely to talk.'

Katy finished her artwork on Logan's neck.

"That's you done. You're all weird now. And not too knowledgeable. Let it dry for a few minutes then rinse the excess off.'

Logan looked his face and neck in the mirror.

'Actually, no offence,' he said. 'but if they detect this is a fake tattoo, it would be better for me to admit that it's just henna. So maybe you should put some squiggly patterns on the backs of my hands too. Then it's obvious it's henna, so they won't think of me as trying to fake something.'

Katy looked on the internet on her phone to find pictures of henna patterns which she copied to paint intricate designs on his hands.

'I hope this stuff washes off easily when all this is over,' said Logan. 'Before I go, can I look at a computer? There's a website I need to look at.'

Katy brought her laptop into the kitchen. Logan typed in 'spiritbeamer.com' and once again looked at Jasper's website.

He showed it to Katy. He then clicked onto Kleo's website. He noticed on her pages that she had made comments about the various meetings she'd been organising, each one including the words: 'bring food to share.'

'Nothing wrong with that,' he said. 'If she's with Jasper at the glen I just need to do a bit of food shopping to share with whoever I meet.'

'I'm coming with you,' said Katy.

'You mean to the shops for food?'

'Yes, and also to Sannox.'

'No, you can't come to Sannox, we don't know what we're dealing with.'

'If you go alone they might realise you're snooping around. If I'm with you, we'll look like a happy couple enjoying ourselves. And some of them have already met me and invited me to come along.'

Logan stood silent and thought about this for what seemed like a long silence.

'I need them to think I'm the same as them,' he said. 'And that might mean that I want them to think I enjoy seeing naked kids in a wigwam. If anyone there recognises you, perhaps tomorrow they'll tell people they saw you there, and even just by being there, people will think that you were part of whatever is going on. That's a reputation you don't want on this island. You have to live here. I don't. Maybe I got this wrong. Maybe these people are just a bit weird and harmless. Maybe tomorrow you can come with me. But right now, I have to do this by myself.'

He changed his shirt and wore his camouflaged jacket which he hadn't been wearing during his confrontation with Jasper and Flabby. He returned to the supermarket to buy food to share as he had read on the website. He filled his shopping basket with crisps, oranges, bananas, chocolate bars, cereal bars, two loaves of sliced brown bread, bottles of fruit juice, margarine, sliced cheese and a packet of disposable cutlery. He loaded his shopping into his small rucksack in the back of his car. Satisfied that he was prepared, he set off north-bound towards Sannox. However, as he was driving north out of Brodick he noticed Reynolds standing at the front of the old primary school on the left side of the road, uniquely marked by its blue coloured statue of William Alexander Anthony Archibald Douglas-Hamilton: a man who held many titles throughout his life, one such title being the eleventh Earl of Arran. He died in Paris in the nineteenth century and was buried in Lanarkshire but was later exhumed and re-buried on Arran fifty-eight years later.

Reynolds had changed out of her police uniform and into her casual denim jeans and dark grey shirt. Logan pulled the car over. She opened the passenger door and sat in.

'I didn't want to be seen in uniform. I brought you a present.'

She gave him a large envelope with a polythene bag inside it.

'We confiscated these from a holiday maker two weeks ago. Normally we discard them, but on this occasion, we were keeping them as evidence. You might need these if you're meeting people in the drug scene.'

Logan looked inside the bag which contained a dozen cannabis joints.

'I'm glad they're already made,' he said. 'I've never actually rolled a joint. I've seen it done many times but never actually done it myself.'

'This is only a fraction of what we found on the guy two weeks ago. If you don't have to use them we'd like them back.'

'Thanks. Shit! Does this mean I'm now a drug dealer?'

'Good luck,' said Reynolds as she stepped out of his car.

Logan drove away. On arriving at Sannox he saw some cars parked on the rough ground opposite the entrance to the glen. He noticed the rusty red van which had been driven by Jasper. He decided it would be a bad idea to park his car there in case Jasper and Flabby would recognise it from earlier, so for the sake of a few more seconds driving, he drove to the golf course just a short distance further north. As he arrived at the golf course, there were only three other cars parked there, presumably owned by golfers. With his phone battery depleted, there was no point in him taking his drone as he wouldn't be able to see anything through its camera. He knew he could enter the glen from the golf course and walk towards the mining pit without being seen because that direction would keep him north of the Sannox stream where its trees would keep him out of sight from the main camping area.

Carrying his small rucksack on his back, now partially filled with food, he struggled to squeeze his sleeping bag into it. He tied his tent to the rucksack's outer straps and walked to the pit.

The fence surrounding it was in a poor state of repair due to the overgrowth and weathering over the years. He placed his rucksack on the ground and rummaged around the area looking for any clues. Perhaps Heidi had been carrying something important which Logan hadn't noticed when he found her. As per his military training, he walked circles around the area, each time expanding the radius of the circles. While doing so, through the trees, he could see numerous tents pitched on the flatter short grassy area south of the stream.

After thoroughly searching around the area, he admitted defeat to himself and decided to give up searching for anything, especially as he had no idea of what he was expecting to find. He knew there was a small wooden bridge further along the stream, so he picked up his rucksack and made his way towards it in order to cross over the water towards the camping area. As he approached the bridge, he noticed what looked like some litter on the ground next to some rapid flowing water. He walked over to the patch of ground. He counted about twenty cigarette butts. Not commercially produced filter tipped, but roll-up cigarettes. They had been smoked such that their butts were very short, typical of when people smoke cannabis joints. He picked one up and held it directly beneath his nostrils. His suspicions were confirmed. Someone had been smoking a lot of cannabis. There were no other clues indicating that anyone else had been there recently.

He walked over the bridge towards the campers. As he approached them, he counted eight tents and about twenty people, ranging in age groups from early twenties to late fifties. He recognised Jasper from earlier. Sitting on the grass close to him was the woman he recognised as Kleo from Jasper's website link. Two young boys aged about four or five years old were playing with a football. Logan pulled out his camouflaged bush hat from his rucksack while again recalling the incident from his army days when he relied on its camouflage to stay alive. Blinking himself back to the present moment he quietly spoke to the hat:

'You saved me once before. Maybe you'll do the same again.'

He placed it on his head. As he approached the group of

campers, two of the men there welcomed him.

'Hi there, you're coming to join us?'

'Sure, why not?' replied Logan, hoping to be able to start a conversation. 'I hope you don't mind me inviting myself.'

'What's your name?' asked the man. 'I'm Matt.'

'Hi Matt. I'm Logan. I've been coming here for years, but usually just on my own. It's nice to actually find some company for a change.'

'You're here for the induction?' asked Matt.

Logan had no idea what he was talking about. He could have tried pretending he knew about an induction, but it would become obvious very quickly that he didn't know. Hopefully someone would explain to him.

'Induction? Eh, I'm not sure. I knew there was a spiritual event happening here, but don't know more than that. I've been camping up at the top of the glen. Not sure if you know it. It's called the Saddle because of its shape. I was going to camp there tonight but I thought I'd come down and see what's going on. But I don't want to disturb your event.'

'The more the merrier,' said Matt. 'Come. I'll introduce you to the organisers.'

Matt led him to Jasper.

'This is Jasper the organiser. Well, Jasper and Kleo are both organisers. Jasper, this is Logan. He's come to join us.'

Jasper smiled at Logan, not recognising him from their earlier meeting at Corrie harbour.

'Welcome Logan,' he said as he closed his eyes and stretched out his open hand with its palm facing Logan. 'I can feel the energy from you,' he said calmly. 'The spirits will like you. Pitch your tent wherever you like then come and join in.'

Logan had seen this 'feeling-energy-with-the-hand' behaviour on a few previous occasions although he could never understand it. He pitched his tent, carefully placing it away from the other tents and closer to the glen entrance to minimise the chances of being seen when he'd leave during the night. From his rucksack he pulled out the carrier bag of food and emptied the envelope of rolled cannabis joints into his jacket pocket. When he walked back to the others, most of them were already sitting on the grass, some on blankets, around a lively camp fire. Some were already smoking cannabis while others drank wine. Various foods were being shared around: cheese, bread, crisps, various dips, and what appeared to be cake. Logan placed his food onto the ground.

'I brought some food,' he said.

He realised the sales receipt from the shop had fallen from his carrier bag onto the ground. It had the date which, if anyone had noticed, would have contradicted his lie about having been camping at the top end of the glen. He quickly crumpled it into a small ball and threw it onto the camp fire. The atmosphere was cheerful and welcoming as some of the others introduced themselves to him. Despite Logan's sceptical opinion about the contents of Jasper's website, and his opinion of his earlier display of behaviour at Corrie, Jasper seemed to be pleasant, polite and quite mild mannered.

Sitting quietly and slightly distant from the group was the man Logan had nicknamed Flabby. He appeared to be less willing to engage in socialising with anyone and more content to drink beer while sitting gazing at his own feet. More importantly, Flabby didn't recognise Logan from earlier.

Kleo had been standing talking to three of the group,

positioned just out of earshot from the others. She was tall, slim with blonde hair which had stripes of blue dye on some of the strands. Jasper beckoned Logan to follow him as they walked towards her. As they neared Kleo, Logan detected that she had a Flemish accent.

'Kleo, meet Logan. He's come down from the hills to be with us.'

The three people she had been talking to immediately greeted Logan welcomingly, introducing themselves as Aileen, Colin and Claire.

'Oh my God, you're limping,' said Claire. 'Are you hurt?'

'No, I'm fine,' replied Logan. 'I have a knee injury from a long time ago. I limp sometimes but I'm used to it.'

Kleo smiled at him in a way which Logan recognised as the sort of fake pretentious smile which someone gives when they pretend they're happy to see someone while secretly being annoyed at having someone else becoming the centre of attention. As quickly as she could, Kleo started talking again to the other three about Buddhism. As Logan listened to her, it quickly became obvious that she was much less educated on the subject than she wanted the others to believe. Despite having detected a hint of an unwelcome feeling, Logan wanted to talk with Kleo to find out more about what was going on. To do that, he'd have to think of a way to make her want to talk to him. Kleo was enjoying the fact that she had an audience listening to her talk, so Logan seized the opportunity to declare himself a willing student.

'This is great. I mean, this is why I'm here,' he said enthusiastically. 'I'm just starting out as a follower of Buddhism, and no matter what I read or hear about it, I want to learn more.'

Kleo's attitude towards him changed immediately to that of a more welcoming style.

'You've come to the right place,' she said.

'Have you been to the Holy Isle yet?' asked Logan. 'I want to go there maybe later this week. I heard it's owned and run by Buddhists. It's on my list of things I want to do this week.'

'I've heard they're cruel to animals there,' said Aileen.

'Yeah, I heard that too,' said Claire. 'Apparently when the animals die they just get left lying there like they're worthless. Nobody bothers to bury them.'

Logan already knew about this. The Buddhists on the Holy Isle have a long-standing reputation for having much respect for animals and nature. They let the animals there roam about freely until they die of natural causes, after which their carcasses are left to the wilderness of nature as would happen anywhere void of humans. However, sometimes visitors to the Holy Isle don't realise this, and therefore apply uneducated criticism against the people living there. This wasn't the moment for Logan to explain this. Instead, this was his opportunity to fake ignorance and observe the group's conversation. Kleo, faced with what she could see as the majority of the small group disapproving of such apparent callousness towards animals, agreed with them.

'Eh, no,' she said. 'That's a terrible way to treat animals. I've always said that. Anyway, we don't have time to go there with what we've already planned. I don't want to see dead animals.'

Colin glanced at Logan and discretely raised an eyebrow.

Just then, Jasper invited everyone to sit with him around the fire. Logan sat with them. Jasper started speaking to everyone:

'I've made a labyrinth over there.'

He pointed to a small circle about two metres in diameter, made from a dozen small rocks.

'Before you go to sleep tonight you can deposit your thoughts onto the labyrinth to help you sleep more peacefully.'

Flabby raised his hand with a lit cannabis joint which he'd been smoking, slurring his words as he spoke:

'I'll sleep peacefully with this little baby tonight.'

The group responded with some light laughter at his comment, prompting almost all of them to produce cannabis leaf. Matt started rolling a cigarette, mixing cannabis leaf into the tobacco.

'You want some?' he asked.

'Thanks,' said Logan. 'But I'm good. I got plenty here in my pocket.'

'Good quality?' asked Jasper.

'Not bad,' said Logan as he produced a joint from his jacket pocket. 'Here, try this.'

Jasper gratefully accepted the joint and started to smoke it.

'Not bad,' he said.

Logan had never smoked cannabis and had no intention of ever doing so, but this wasn't the time to say that.

'You're coming to the Spiritbeamer gathering on Wednesday?' asked Jasper.

'Eh, yeah I suppose so. If you guys are going to be there. Tell me more.'

'Wait for tomorrow,' said Jasper. 'I'll tell you more then. But if you want to buy anything, bring some cash.'

Logan decided to not ask any more questions in case he raised suspicion that he was on a fact-finding quest. He listened to Jasper talking to the group about the things mentioned in his website. In particular he spoke about the 'womb of Mother Earth' and the sweat lodge meetings. One of the women in the group asked for more information about the sweat lodge, to which Jasper explained:

'It's a ceremony like the Native American traditions. Everybody gets naked for purification of the soul. We smoke to send our thoughts and gratitude to the spirits above, and we explore our inner peace. It's the perfect way to lead us towards the equinox. I'm going to organise the sweat lodge tomorrow.'

'Will it be big enough for all of us?' asked Matt.

'Yes, easily. And we're expecting more people tomorrow, so we'll keep it going for maybe a few hours, so people can come and go as they please.'

Logan became curious at this. He decided to invent a quick lie to answer a niggling thought:

'I have a couple of friends who told me they'll be coming to the island tomorrow. They eh, they help me get this stuff.'

He produced another cannabis joint.

'I think they'd want to take part, but they've got two kids with them. Is there an age limit?'

'Anyone can come,' said Jasper. 'It's just natural like the way of the Native Americans. It's a spiritual ceremony so there's no age limit.'

Logan raised his thumb in pretence approval with this. He looked around and was surprised that nobody else seemed to find this unacceptable. Jasper continued speaking:

'On Tuesday night there will be many more of us so we're probably going to have a manhood ceremony. None of you boys have really become men yet until you do this, so I'll be offering that ceremony. But there will be more of us, so we'll do that at the North Sannox campsite.'

The group continued talking about various subjects while Kleo quietly counted the people forming whichever opinions they expressed, each time making sure she agreed with the majority of the group, and each time saying so with a pretentious authoritative tone of voice. Logan noticed how she often contradicted herself, proving that she actually knew very little about what she was saying. However, her audience were under so much influence of whatever they'd been drinking and smoking that they didn't notice the contradictions, enabling her to enjoy what had become little more than her personal power trip. Logan suspected that although Jasper's website gave the impression of him being the event organiser, it was Kleo who craved the limelight.

But that wasn't important. His reason for being there was to try to find out about any connection between this event, Heidi, the human corpse at the Punchbowl or with anything else sinister which may be happening on the island. His experiences with narcissists had taught him that many of them enjoyed talking about themselves so much that they'd often reveal their personal secrets. If there was any connection between these people and the situation with young Heidi, Kleo would be the most likely person to mention something. So long as Logan spoke or asked questions in such a way as to make Kleo think he was enhancing her popularity, he could provoke her to enhance her display of self-appointed expertise. Eventually she would likely mention something useful.

More people joined the gathering and sat around the fire. Once again, the group conversation moved towards the subject of the animals on the Holy Isle, but this time the majority formed the opinion of approval about the way the animals there were being treated. Kleo stood up as if she was going to her tent for something. She started speaking, with much emphasis in her voice.

'Yes, I think it's a wonderful idea that these animals are left alone. I've always said that. There should be more of that in this world. That's why I want to see the Holy Isle one day. I hope they can use the Holy Isle as a sanctuary to save these poor grey squirrels. Has anyone seen where Jasper went?'

As she had done earlier, by forming what she believed was the strongest opinion in agreement with the group's majority, she had achieved another little power trip while Logan had achieved confirmation of his suspicions about her delusional narcissistic mind-set.

He didn't understand what she meant about the grey squirrels, and none of what had been said could confirm any connection to Heidi, but it enabled Logan to achieve a better understanding of Kleo, and her habit of switching quickly between opinions. This should enable him to figure out a way of extracting knowledge from her. He gave her one of the cannabis joints from his pocket.

'I'm going for a walk,' he said. 'I'm going to try to figure out what my totem is.'

Kleo smiled and nodded her head to acknowledge her approval of his stated intention as he stood up and walked away. He sat on a tuft of heather about twenty metres away and placed an unlit joint into his mouth, pretending he was going to smoke it. He sat for about ten minutes while the group continued talking. Eventually Kleo walked over and sat opposite him on a granite boulder. She was smoking the cannabis joint which he'd given her. She read the henna tattoo on his neck:

'Om-Shanti. Mister Peace Man. Have you discovered what your totem is yet?'

Logan was pleased that she'd noticed and approved of the writing Katy had drawn on his neck.

'Om-Shanti. No, I haven't figured my totem yet. I think I need more time. And maybe some more of this weed.'

He had a mental flashback to a previous army operation when he was pretending to be a gun dealer to find information about a suspected terrorist organisation. He had been sitting on a wall in a ruined building while talking to a gang of four men. They were all armed with machine guns, all intending to kill him unless he could convince them that he wasn't military personnel. Now he was using a similar method of acting to pretend to be a former drug dealer. He started talking slowly and told her:

'I used to grow this stuff. Lots of it. Like, seriously lots of it. But some friends got caught in the next village. I figured out I'd be next, so I got rid of everything. It took me exactly one hour to destroy five years investment.'

Kleo appeared sympathetic. She believed his story. He continued, smiling as he spoke:

'The daft thing is, after destroying everything… I mean tens of thousands of pounds, and not just green stuff if you know what I mean...'

Kleo smiled a bit more at that comment. Logan continued:

'… I expected the police to break down my door, so I cleaned the house with strong disinfectant and bleach in case they were going to bring sniffer dogs. The place had never been so spotless. And I made sure there wasn't anything there to incriminate me. Nothing. I threw away my phone. My list of phone numbers. Everything gone. Not even one joint. And then I sat and watched telly. All day. Then all next day. And the next. And the police didn't come. I was never a suspect. Tens of thousands of pounds thrown away.'

'You never started again?' asked Kleo.

'No. I always had the idea that I would, but somehow I never did. Maybe I found Buddhism at a good time. Or maybe this is just a stop-gap for me until I start something new. I don't know.'

'You'll be here on Wednesday?'

'Yeah I think so. Tell me about Wednesday.'

'More people are sailing over to Arran for a big gathering. We're expecting maybe a thousand Spiritbeamers. Maybe two thousand. Maybe more. We're going to have a big party on Brodick beach. We're celebrating the spirit of the equinox. Hopefully the locals will join in. The more the better.'

Logan could feel the hairs on his arms standing when he heard the words 'equinox' and 'spiritbeamer'. Hearing these terms was enough to convince him of his suspicions that part of his childhood from over twenty years ago had now reappeared as he had expected, but not in a way which he could fully understand. His thoughts drifted into distant memories while Kleo sat and smoked. She asked him:

'Do you know about the equinox spirit?'

'Yes. I mean, no.'

Kleo started to explain to him:

'The equinox happens…'

Her voice seemed to fade as Logan let his memory drift back to his early childhood. He remembered events from his troubled home life and hearing the word 'spiritbeamer' on several occasions, but it was a subject which he never paid much attention to. After a few minutes he pulled himself from his trance state of memories, realising that Kleo had stopped talking and was waiting for his response.

'Oh. Sorry. I was listening, but I got carried away. I should try to get more of these things.'

He again held up his unlit joint.

'There will be plenty,' said Kleo.

This was Logan's chance to ask more direct questions. Something big was about to happen on Arran, and Kleo was obviously involved and willing to tell him about it.

'This sounds like a fantastic party,' he said enthusiastically. 'It must have taken a long time to organise it.'

'We've been holding smaller events, mostly garden parties, around the country for two years,' said Kleo. 'We've been building interest and finding people who needed to change their way of experiencing the spirit world. We knew we'd have a big festival like this one, but we needed a sponsor to help organise and pay for a few things. We didn't get that call until two weeks ago. And it's going to be so wonderful.'

'But eh, won't the police get a bit, eh, upset if Brodick fills up with people having a party on the beach doing weed?'

Kleo shrugged her shoulders.

'What can they do?' she asked. 'We'll just be on big peaceful party. I'm sure two thousand of us will be able to explain to the police that they have better things to do.'

'Ah yeah, but there's one thing I learned a long time ago

when I was, eh, you know, growing stuff. Small towns in places like, well, places like here, tend to have vigilantes. And the Arran population... well, I don't know what their thoughts are on all this. Maybe it would be best to have that big party somewhere else a bit more, eh, well, hidden.'

Kleo was becoming increasingly influenced by the cannabis she was smoking and the alcohol she was drinking. She was having difficulty focusing her eyes on Logan.

'This is the problem we had in Findhorn,' she said. 'The place is lovely, full of spiritual people, but not so broad-minded. Whereas Arran is a popular place and easy to get to from Glasgow. The people living around Glasgow like to come here to escape the pressures of city life. This could be the new Amsterdam. A place for spiritual and social freedom. And it starts now. Amsterdam is too expensive for people to travel to every weekend. But coming here is easy.'

Logan was horrified at what she was saying. She and Jasper were trying to establish Arran as a regular illegal narcotics meeting place. Instead of people coming to Arran to improve their physical and mental health by enjoying the outdoor lifestyle, Arran would become a place filled with drug dealers, drug buyers and associated crime. He already had too much experience witnessing similar events around the world and the devastation caused by such activities. Most visitors to Arran, especially families with young children, would not want involvement with drugs. If Arran would be given a reputation as being some sort of venue for drug dealing, not only would this have a devastating effect on peoples' lives, but it would seriously damage the tourism trade upon which Arran's economy depends heavily. Arran receives over three million visitors per year, and that figure would decrease massively if it was to lose its well-established appeal. Logan continued questioning:

'So, tell me more about this big party. It sounds like fun.'

Kleo was starting to wave her arms around like she was pretending to be some sort of dancer.

'People from all over the country will be there,' she said. 'We'll be feeling the spiritual presence in each of us. We will all be free spirits. We'll all be Spiritbeamers'

She removed her almost-finished joint from her mouth, offering it to Logan.

'There will be more of this if you want some. Much more. One of Jasper's friends is bringing his boat to shore.'

'Onto Brodick beach?' asked Logan.

Kleo was so much under the influence of drugs that she was almost unable to answer as she adopted a new pose, sitting with her legs crossed in the lotus meditation position with her arms extended out, her eyes closed, and her head bowed forward. Having spent time in Thailand, Logan could identify that she was merely pretending to meditate rather than actually know what she was doing, especially in her drugged condition. He wanted to interrupt her to continue questioning but he would have needed to do so in a way which would make her feel admired rather than ridiculed.

'I wish I could meditate properly,' he said.

This was enough to distract Kleo from her meditation pose as she placed her feet onto the ground.

'We can teach you,' she said.

'You can give me some guidance later perhaps,' he replied as he tried to steer the conversation back towards the beach party and the boat she'd just mentioned.

‘Whenever I need guidance I speak to my Indian spirit guide,’ she said, looking skywards. ‘We’re all under the watchful eye of the deer, the hawk and the bear.’

Logan realised he would struggle to get any more information from her until she would return to a condition of more sobriety. For now, all he could do was let her speak whatever nonsense she would while he pretended to be impressed. Kleo spoke more:

‘My Indian spirit guide is always just above me, always available when I want guidance on anything. Anything at all. The spirits told me to organise this event on Arran. It’s the perfect place. And Jasper can carry out his ceremonies here too.’

She adopted her meditation pose again, bowing her head with her eyes closed. Within a few seconds she fell asleep in that position. Logan could do no more. He looked over towards the others around the camp fire. He noticed Colin was standing, collecting his lightweight jacket as if he was about to leave. Colin glanced over at Logan as if he wanted to talk to him before leaving. Logan stood up and started walking towards the group so as to intercept Colin.

‘You’ve had enough?’ asked Logan.

Colin raised his left eyebrow as he spoke, rolling his eyes towards the group.

‘We both have something in common,’ he said. ‘We both came hillwalking and we both stumbled into a group of barking mad freaks.’

Logan smiled. Colin continued:

‘I thought they were decent people at first. I thought they were just a bunch of friendly harmless campers, but I don’t want to be involved with them or what they’re planning. I’m out of here.'

'Did they tell you what they're planning?' asked Logan.

'Yeah a cult group are going to arrive in Brodick for a big party and weird stuff. And that guy Jasper wants kids to get naked in a wigwam sauna thing. And while Jasper's talking all this bullshit, the rest of them are too spaced out to recognise he's an arse.'

'Did they, or anyone, mention anything about a little girl gone missing?' asked Logan.

'N… no. A child's missing?'

'Just something I heard. No worries. Probably nothing. But something about a boat. Did they mention a boat?'

'Yeah something about Noah's Ark bringing supplies of some sort. I'm guessing drugs. And something about squirrels. Oh also, they're planning some sort of protest to stop the ferry sailing, but I didn't catch what that was all about. I need to get back to work, so I'll be catching the morning ferry before any protest takes place.'

'Ferry? The Brodick ferry or the Lochranza one?'

'The protest is planned for Brodick,' replied Colin. 'But I don't know any more than that except it's planned for Wednesday.'

'And squirrels?' asked Logan.

'Yeah. Someone's bringing squirrels apparently. I don't know if they're talking about cute fluffy animals, or maybe it's a code for something.'

Logan looked back at Kleo as she sat, still in the meditation pose, but now with Jasper sitting next to her in the same pose.

'As for that weird witchy woman,' added Colin. 'I've never heard a woman spew out so much crap. She claims to be an expert at Buddhism. Her real name is Paula, but she changed her name to Cleopatra because she thinks of herself as some sort of powerful woman. She hasn't grasped that the queen of the Pharaohs had no connection to Buddhism. But she spells her name with a 'K' just to be a bit more special than the original Cleopatra. Totally lost the plot. I'm getting away from these idiots now. And so should you.'

He turned to walk away.

'I'd come with you,' said Logan. 'But I already pitched my tent and I'm getting tired. Take care.'

Colin walked away. Logan strolled over to the fire to join the rest of the group there. All of them were either drunk or under the influence of various narcotics.

'All looking forward to the beach party on Wednesday?' he asked.

Nobody in group responded with anything more than just a smile. Logan sat awkwardly trying to think of the next question he could ask. Flabby started talking:

'You want to buy some stuff at the party?'

'Maybe,' replied Logan. 'If the quality meets the price.'

Logan detected that Flabby was wary of him. Kleo had woken and was being helped by Jasper to walk towards the group. They could hear what was being said.

'I'd rather buy stuff before Wednesday rather than wait,' said Logan. 'Otherwise I'll be at the end of the queue.'

'Just tell me exactly what you want,' said Jasper. 'One of us here will make sure you get it.'

'Cool,' replied Logan. 'Let me know more when the time's right. I'm off to bed. I want to get up these hills at sunrise.'

He pointed to the hillside immediately south of the glen.

'That's the favourite feeding ground for the deer on the island. That's where to find them at sunrise. That's where I'll be, so I need some sleep. Peaceful dreams everyone.'

He went into his tent. Some of the group remained sitting around the camp fire. He tried listening to what they were saying but he could barely make out anything as their voices were muffled by the sound of the light breeze blowing against his tent. He stayed awake until everyone eventually went to their own tents, at which point he quietly crept outside towards Kleo and Jasper's tent.

He could hear them talking to each other, but they didn't mention anything of any significance until after ten minutes when he heard Kleo mentioning North Sannox. This caught his attention. He'd already heard Jasper mentioning some sort of manhood ceremony there, but it sounded like Kleo was talking about some other activity taking place. Gradually their conversation faded to silence, presumably because they were falling asleep. Logan returned to his tent. He tried forcing himself to sleep on the basis that he wanted to pack up and leave first thing at sunrise as he'd told them he would.

CHAPTER 5

Monday September 20th

Logan awoke before sunrise. Despite having pitched his tent on a patch of uneven ground, he had slept surprisingly well. None of the other campers had woken yet. He left his tent and walked down to the Sannox stream to bathe in one of the rock pools there for a morning wash before starting the day. He tried to assess what he was dealing with. A missing child, mafia style characters on the island, and an event which would involve a significant drug deal being planned for Wednesday with so many people that the police would be out-numbered to be able to deal with it. He had been given the impression that copious amounts of various types of drugs would be available to buy before the event. He was also curious about three things: the mention of a boat named Noah's Ark, a protest to stop the ferry sailing and the mention of North Sannox, just a few minutes away.

He walked down to the glen entrance, once again passing the graveyard. He checked that the rucksack which he'd hidden on Saturday was still hidden in the tunnel at the end of the narrow lane. Having made contact and gained the trust of the police, he believed this would be an opportune moment to collect it and place it into the back of his car which was still parked at the golf club car park.

At least now he had more evidence to offer the police. But with dangerous criminals on the island, he regarded the carrying of a rucksack full of expensive drugs to be too risky. So, without moving it, he removed the folded tissue with the hair sample which he'd snipped from the body at the Punchbowl. He placed it into his hip pocket. Heidi would likely still be sleeping at Katy's house, so rather than rush into Brodick before the island awoke, it made more sense for him to spend this quiet time looking around the camping area at North Sannox. Whoever was there would likely be involved in whatever was being planned.

He put the folded tissue with the hair sample into his car's glove compartment then drove to North Sannox, again turning right into the hidden track as he had done with Heidi on Saturday night. He parked his car at the same hidden spot as he had done previously and then walked over the bridge into the main camping area. There were already a few tents there, but more interestingly, there was a black van parked near the shoreline at the north east corner of the site next to the start of the coastal track which leads northwards towards Lochranza. Logan immediately recognised the van as the one he'd seen being occupied by Badger and Gremlin.

There was a small tent pitched at the back of the van. Logan couldn't see anything else of any suspicion. He walked along the north side of the camping area towards the start of the coastal path which leads north along the shore. He walked past the van, hoping the occupants would be sleeping, but as he entered the path, he heard a man's voice shouting:

'You there. Stop.'

Logan stopped and turned around. Standing there were the

two men he'd identified as Badger and Gremlin.

'That path's forbidden to the public,' shouted Badger.

This was the first time Logan had heard Badger speak. He identified his accent as Eastern European.

'Oh. Eh, okay. Why's that? I've walked here before.'

'Not today. There's a nature conservation project happening here. Nobody's allowed on that path until the scientists finish their work.'

Badger's accent could have possibly been Slovenian or Lithuanian. More importantly, Logan knew he was lying. Any conservation project would have been mentioned in the local press which Logan had been reading prior to his visit to the island. And he knew the path. It's not possible to disturb nature if walkers stay on it. There was dense forestry to one side. On the other side the land sloped rapidly into deep seawater. He also knew that whenever the authorities close off land on Arran for any type of conservation project they are usually good at placing appropriate signage. Logan decided that to argue could be dangerous.

'Sorry,' he said. 'I didn't know about that. How long will it be closed for?'

'Until the weekend,' replied Badger.

Logan left the camping area but as soon as he was out of sight he changed his direction and walked onto the rough ground to intercept the coastal track without being seen. On reaching the edge of the track, he walked parallel to it while staying hidden in the woodland. Eventually, he noticed a small pile of stones, like a small cairn, on the coastal edge of the track. They looked like they had been placed there to mark something. He walked over to them for closer inspection while looking around, but he could see nothing else suspicious. He walked further along for about thirty metres and found another small pile of stones, but again, there was nothing else suspicious. As he continued walking, he noticed a pile of stones approximately every thirty metres. It's normal to see cairns marking mountain pathways but it was unusual to see regular piles of stones along an established coastal track.

He stood on the path's rocky edge, looking down into the deep water. The centuries of water lapping the rocky coastline there had created a sort of trough dug into the rock, creating an overhang. At that moment, he heard male voices coming from the campsite area. He rushed back into the forestry and hid in a dip behind a tree root. He quickly grabbed some long grass to pull over himself for extra camouflage. He felt something stinging his hand. To his horror he had disturbed a wasp's nest. It was just a small hole in the ground but with several wasps coming out to defend themselves. Within a few seconds, one wasp had stung him on the neck. Another on his right ear. He could feel multiple stings on both arms and on his face. The two men were now so close to him that he daren't stand up or he'd be seen, but he also knew how dangerous a swarm of wasps could be. With his right hand he pulled his camouflaged hat from his pocket and squeezed it tightly into the hole to stop the wasps from leaving the nest while he used his left hand to grab the few wasps which were still buzzing around him, squashing them as he grabbed them while trying to minimise any visible movement.

'Thanks again Hat,' he whispered quietly.

As the men walked closer, he could again identify them as Badger and Gremlin. Badger was carrying a long fishing rod with a large hook dangling from its end. They stopped several times as they slowly made their way along the path, but Logan couldn't see what they were doing until they stopped at the pile of stones nearest to where he was hiding. He heard them speaking to each other in English, giving him reason to believe that they were of different nationalities. Badger prodded his fishing rod into the sea and hooked what appeared to be a small piece of floating driftwood which he pulled out of the water. Tied to that driftwood was a thin fishing line which he pulled, eventually pulling out a heavier rope. He pulled on the heavier rope until it became taut.

'Yes, coke's good,' he said as he released the line and dropped the driftwood back into the water.

The two men walked further along the track. Logan could hear the wasps buzzing in their nest, currently blocked by his hat. He knew that if he would unblock their entrance they would swarm around him, so when he stood up he made sure his hat stayed firmly in place by placing his wallet on top of it. Leaving his hat blocking the hole, he walked cautiously towards the woodland edge, just enough to be able to see the two men stopping at another pile of stones about thirty metres further along. Again, he saw Badger using his fishing rod to hook what appeared to be another small piece of driftwood wrapped in seaweed and attached to a thin line. As before, Logan noticed him pulling the line enough until he could feel the weight of whatever was tied to it under the water.

'Yeah, it's good,' said Badger, as he released the line and dropped the driftwood.

The two men continued walking northward. Logan had seen enough. Whatever was happening, items, presumably drugs, were being hidden under the water along the side of path. As the men walked around the bend in the path, Logan seized the opportunity to walk towards the water's edge where Badger had dropped in the first piece of driftwood. He knew it would be too risky to try to pull out whatever was under the water, but he was hopeful he would be able to reach out and grab the driftwood while it was so close to the land so that he could somehow lodge it into the rocky edge and more easily reach it later.

He laid himself flat on his stomach, reaching out and occasionally touching the piece of wood with his fingertips as it bobbed about in the waves. He eventually managed to grab hold of it, at which moment he heard the men's voices returning. He knew that if he would stand up to run back into the forestry he'd be seen, and it would take too long for him to crawl back to the forestry on his stomach. With the sun not yet fully risen, he could already see the silhouettes of the men walking towards him as they approached the path's bend, but it was still too dark for them to see Logan in his flat position in the dark. Logan's only chance to stay hidden was to remain flat on his stomach and let himself slide into the water.

The pathway edge was steep enough that he easily positioned himself in the water beneath the rocky overhang without being seen from the path. The men walked past, unaware of Logan's presence. When he was confident that they had walked around the next bend, out of sight, Logan pulled himself out of the water, still clutching the driftwood.

He stood at the water's edge soaked, cold, and in a lot of pain caused by the wasp stings which had become aggravated due to the salty water. He pulled at the attached fishing line which pulled up the heavier rope attached beneath. After pulling about five metres of rope, he could feel that something heavy was at its end. He estimated that it weighed about twenty kilograms. As it neared the surface he could see that it was a black hard-shell suitcase wrapped in watertight clear plastic film. He pulled it onto the path. He was able to untie the film easily and open the case. It was tightly packed with a dozen plastic watertight bags. He opened one of them to find that it had been packed with numerous smaller transparent watertight bags, most of which were wrapped in black adhesive tape and containing a substance of white powder.

'Too many bags of poison,' he whispered to himself.

A few of them had red tape around them. Logan removed two of the polythene bags and closed the case with the ratchet straps. He lowered it back into the water carefully to avoid making an audible splash.

Now cold and soaking, he picked up a stone from the small pile and went back into the woods to retrieve his wallet, quickly replacing it with the stone to keep his hat weighted down to block the wasps' nest. He knew the wasps would eventually manage to escape but he'd be well away from them before they could swarm him.

When he arrived at his car, he bathed in the fresh water stream to rinse the salt water from his hair and clothes before changing into his dry clothes and shoes. The sun was rising. Shops would be opening soon, and he was feeling hungry.

He drove to the supermarket in Brodick to buy a sandwich. The early morning ferry had arrived, and the traffic flowed from the ferry terminal into Brodick's Shore Road. With the expectation of more visitors travelling to the island for the

Spiritbeamer event, he was curious to see what sort of people would be arriving from the ferry. He parked his car in front of the mini-golf and stood by it while eating his sandwich and casually watching the cars and pedestrians go past. The wind was becoming noticeably stronger from the west. The right side of his face was badly swollen due to the wasp stings. His right eye was almost closed and badly bruised, giving him the appearance of having been in a fight.

He noticed a maroon coloured motorcycle coming from the terminal. One of his habits was looking at passing motorcycles, often identifying their make and model. This particular one caught his attention. It was a Honda Goldwing. He watched intently. As the motorcycle came closer, he noticed the rider was wearing the same style of helmet and jacket as Robin normally wore when motorcycling. Closer again, Logan could see a sticker on the windscreen which he recognised. It was Robin's motorcycle. Logan stepped out onto the road, waving to attract attention. Robin saw him and pulled over. He parked the bike onto its side-stand and removed his helmet.

'Robin!' exclaimed Logan. 'I thought you had to be in Edinburgh today.'

'I promised the boss I'd have that meeting next week. He was okay about it. I figured you could use some help, By the state of your face it seems I'm right about that. What happened to you?'

'My face is okay. A few wasps gave me some cosmetic surgery about an hour ago. I'll live. I had to switch the phone off and anyway, it's out of battery power and the car charger doesn't work. Why did you bring the bike? I'd have expected you to bring the car so that you could bring Chino.'

'It was Roz's idea that I bring my bike here. Her parents are looking after Chino. She knew if I drove my bike here you'd notice me 'cos you're always looking at motorbikes or looking at the sky for aeroplanes. I just didn't think you'd see me the first minute after driving off the ferry. So, tell me, what's going on that you couldn't tell me on the phone?'

'Verhoeven,' said Logan.

'But... he's still in priso...'

'Spiritbeamers,' interrupted Logan.

Robin frowned while he tried to understand what Logan was talking about.

'I heard people talking about spirit stuff on the ferry,' said Robin. 'They were talking about a big celebration, but I didn't hear everything they were saying.'

'Uh, eh, well, what was the last thing I told you? I'm starting to lose track.'

'You found a little girl. Possible a little Russian girl, a dead body in the hills, and suspicious people in the area. And Anna said there's a Russian politician's daughter gone missing. So, just a normal day eh? And then your phone stopped.'

'Ah, yeah okay. Well, the girl's still a mystery and I think it's best to get her off the island for her safety. But someone's checking the cars going on the ferry. And I think the phones are being intercepted. That's why I had to switch off.'

He pointed towards Brodick beach.

'There's a big party being planned here on the beach for Wednesday.'

'And Wednesday is...'

'Yeah. Equinox. Hundreds... maybe a couple of thousand idiots, tree-hugging weirdos, witchy people, drug dealers and I think maybe some paedophiles. You know, delightful people who we both have so much patience for, all trying to transform the island into a paradise resort for drug dealers.'

'Seriously?'

Logan raised his eyebrows and nodded, adding:

'And almost certainly it's Verhoeven's old project. You remember that undercover operation we did in Algeria? The guys with the guns buried in suitcases waiting for the delivery truck?'

'How could I forget that?'

'Well, the same thing's happening here except the cases are under water at North Sannox and the delivery truck's some sort of ark or boat or something.'

He produced one of the polythene bags from his pocket.

'And this is what's being delivered. Lots of it.'

Robin held the bag and inspected it closely.

'If that's what it looks like, this bag's worth a lot of money,' he said.

'Yeah, and while all this is going on, nobody's reported a little missing girl. There has to be a connection to her, but I can't find it.'

'I noticed the police were at Ardrossan watching cars as they boarded the ferry,' said Robin. 'But they didn't bother me or the other motorbikes. They seemed more interested in the cars with foreign registration plates. What's that all about? Anyway, you say there's going to be a beach party on Wednesday? I checked the weather forecast with Roz last night. The forecast says there's going to be a hurricane here on Wednesday.'

'Yeah I know. I was only planning to be here until tomorrow morning. Can you look at the weather on your phone? I'd like to get an update. Can you find a satellite picture and synoptic chart?'

Robin found these and showed them to Logan.

'Hurricane-force winds forecast until Wednesday evening,' commented Logan.

'These spirit people didn't plan their beach party very well. They couldn't have checked the forecast,' said Robin.

'Or maybe they did,' said Logan as he looked at the sky. 'They're using a boat or something which they're calling 'Noah's Ark'. Maybe it's been planned for stormy weather. Just like the original Noah's Ark.'

He expanded the weather picture on Robin's phone to look more closely at it.

'It's difficult to forecast weather more than a week in advance unless it's extremely stormy weather,' he said.

He pointed at the synoptic chart on the phone screen.

'Look at these isobar lines all packed together in a tight circle. The closer the lines are together, the stronger the wind is. That's what pilots call a 'zebra's arse'. The wind blows anti-clockwise around it. And the way that zebra's arse is approaching, it's going to pass down the west coast. That's going to put a storm all over Scotland. The west coast is going to take a battering. And that storm's extreme enough that it could have been forecast as far back as two weeks or so. Arran will get north-westerly winds. Brodick's sort of sheltered from the wind from that direction because of the hills, so it probably won't be too bad here. But a few miles further east over the sea is going to be horrendous. For sure the ferries will stop sailing. So, these organisers have planned for a mass gathering of weirdos who will come here for a beach party to celebrate or worship the equinox, and from what I heard, the event is being financed by a sponsor since about two weeks ago. The organisers don't care about the storm. The ferry will stop sailing but they want to make sure of that by organising some sort of protest in Brodick.'

'Where's the girl now?' asked Robin.

'She's safe with a local family. But I don't think it's safe for her to stay here. I really want to get her off this island.'

'So, what are your plans?'

'Park your bike here and come with me,' said Logan. 'I want you to meet someone.'

Logan opened the front passenger door of his newly bought Ford Fusion.

'This is your car?'

'Oh yeah I forgot to mention, I've become a two-car type of guy.'

Logan drove Robin to Katy's parents' house. Katy answered the door.

'Morning Katy. Hope I'm not too early. Meet my friend, Robin. He's come to help us out here.'

Katy looked at the swollen condition of his face.

'Shit, what happened?'

'Just some wasps. I'm alright. Just not very handsome just now.'

'Come in. Heidi's having some breakfast just now. You want a coffee?'

'No thanks. I just came to say hello. How's she doing?'

'She's not spoken much and the few words she's said are in whatever her language is. We don't know what she's trying to say to us, but she seems happy enough.'

'You're working at the shop later?'

'Nope,' said Katy. 'It's my day off today.'

She led them through to the lounge where Heidi was sitting on the sofa and watching a children's television programme.

'Did you find any more information last night?'

'Actually yes,' said Logan. 'I'm just about to go to the police about it. Have you heard any rumours of any big outdoor event happening this week, maybe in Brodick, maybe on Wednesday?'

'Yes. I went back to the shop yesterday after I painted your neck. More strange people came in talking about Spirit bum… I mean… beamers, I think. There's to be a big beach party in Brodick. And something in Sannox. Did you go there last night?'

'Yeah, but I didn't find out any more about Heidi. Can your parents keep her here for a bit longer?'

Robin was busy texting on his phone as Sandra walked into the kitchen having heard the conversation.

'It's no problem keeping her here,' she said. 'She's no trouble. But I'm worried that nobody's reported her missing. And what happened to your face? Do you need to go to hospital?'

'It's okay,' smiled Logan. 'It looks worse than it is.'

Logan turned to Robin:

'Let's go. We're running out of time and there's someone else I want you to meet.'

Logan and Robin left the house. Logan removed the folded tissue with the hair sample from the glove compartment and placed it into his hip pocket. Robin, having been quiet for a few minutes, began looking mischievously at Logan. With half a smile, he asked:

'What's the story with Katy? She's rather cute.'

'Nothing's happening,' laughed Logan. 'She's been serving

me in the shop. It's coincidence that the police officer I've been dealing with suggested to leave Heidi with Katy's parents. And now I want you to meet that police officer. Hopefully she's still at home before starting her duty. She's, well, she's also good looking. And with my face the way it is just now, I think she'd rather look at you.'

He drove to Reynolds' house. She saw Logan through her living room window as he walked towards her front door. She signalled to him to walk round to the back garden. She was waiting for him at the back door, wearing her dressing gown.

'I don't want the neighbours seeing me like this,' she said as she looked closely at his face. 'But… what happened to you? Who did this to you?'

'Don't worry about me. I'm okay now. This is Robin. We go back a long way. We served our army time together. He's come over to help out.'

'How did you get on last night?' she asked. 'Looks like you got into a fight?'

'Yeah you could say that, but with a swarm of wasps. I'm fine.'

'Did you find out anything interesting?' asked Reynolds.

'Yes, but nothing about Heidi. At least, maybe not. I can't make the connection. But Arran's just about to be bombarded by thousands of tree-hugging cult members who are on a mission to turn the island into Scotland's drug capital.'

'Thousands?' asked Reynolds with a worried look on her face.

'Yes. I heard two thousand. Maybe more. They're coming here to take part in a massive beach party in Brodick on Wednesday. I met with Kleo and Jasper. Seems they're the organisers for the spiritual stuff but I don't think they fully realise what they're involved with. I think they're being guided by nastier people higher up. We need to…'

'Stop,' said Reynolds abruptly. 'I need you to do something.'

'Go ahead, what do you want me to do?'

'Actually, I need you to just stop,' she said. 'I understand you're trying to help, but you need to do nothing now. I need you to stop.'

'Yesterday you were happy for me to help you. Now you don't want me to. What's going on?'

'I can't discuss this with you but I… I need you to do nothing. You're not authorised to carry out a police investigation and if it comes out that I'm encouraging you, we can all be in serious trouble.'

Robin and Logan both sensed the awkwardness in her voice. Robin decided to break through the awkwardness by asking her:

'The body up at the Devil's Punchbowl. Has anyone been up there to look for it?'

'Yes,' she said. 'Two of my colleagues went there yesterday evening just before dusk to avoid being seen. They went to the Punchbowl from Corrie to avoid going through Glen Sannox, but they found nothing except a dead deer. It wasn't a human body.'

'Okay,' said Robin. 'So, you won't… I mean, will the police object to me going hillwalking there today or tomorrow to look around? If, as you say, there's nothing there other than a dead deer, then there's nothing there of any interest to the police so I wouldn't be interfering with a police investigation.'

'No, you're right,' she said. 'I can't stop you doing that.'

Logan produced the two polythene bags which he'd taken

from the case hidden in the sea at North Sannox. Robin, standing to the side of Reynolds, gave him eye contact and quickly nodded his head, signalling to him to give Reynolds the bags.

'I found this,' he said as he handed the bags to her. 'There's much more of it being guarded by armed gangsters at North Sannox.'

He then gave her the folded tissue with the hair sample.

'I don't know how easy it or how long it takes to get a DNA test done, but the owner of this hair was lying sunbathing on some rocks at the Punchbowl, with his skull resembling a soft-boiled broken egg. It's not from a dead deer.'

He removed the small packet of white pills from his pocket.

'I also found them next to the body. I think they fell out of his pocket on impact. I don't know what they are. But deer don't walk about with bags of pills. Maybe you can get them analysed. I didn't check inside the dead guy's pockets.'

Logan and Robin left the house, leaving Reynolds with a worried expression on her face as she stood in her dressing gown looking at the bags and pills she was holding.

'Do you think she's being silenced?' asked Logan. 'Or just nervous? Yesterday she was wanting me to help. Today she doesn't. What's going on?'

'She knows she's out of her depth,' said Robin. 'And she doesn't know you very well, so she doesn't know how far she can trust you. Especially if officers didn't find the body where you told them to look. And you're right about her being good looking.'

'Why can't they find that body? I told them exactly where to look. The guy didn't just get up and walk away.'

'In that case, you want to come with me now to look for a dead body at the Punchbowl?'

'Been there, done that. I know what I saw, and it wasn't a dead deer. And, my knee's playing up again. I didn't take the walking stick on this trip because I didn't think I'd need it.'

He crouched down and looked at his face in the car's wing mirror.

'What does my face look like to you?' he asked.

'Never beautiful,' joked Robin.

'Yeah but, does it look like I've been stung by wasps or does it look like I've been in a fight?'

'If you want my honest opinion, it looks like someone's beaten the crap out of you.'

'Yeah, good. I think I can use that. Let's go.'

Logan drove Robin back to his motorbike.

'I need to get back to Glen Sannox,' said Logan. 'If you're going to the Punchbowl via the glen, I don't think we should be seen together so I'll give you a head start. I need to go and visit Katy and Heidi again.'

'Logie, wait. You're okay? It's one thing finding a child on a hillside, but seems you're turning yourself into a detective again.'

'Yeah she's just a little girl who needs help.'

'No, I'm not worried about the girl. I'm worried about you taking on dangerous criminals.'

'Been there, done it already,' joked Logan.

'Yeah but we did that with military backing, military intelligence, and military authority. But now you're a one-man band. Or two-man if you count me in.'

'I took on the Glasgow mafia when I was fourteen and these vermin are still behind bars.'

'But you didn't have a choice then,' said Robin. 'You were a terrified kid backed into a corner. Now you can walk away from this. I'll help you get Heidi off the island. Then you can hand her over to the mainland police, tell them what you know and let them deal with this. This isn't Glasgow mafia. Verhoeven maybe but not the others. It can't be. Not this time.'

Logan didn't hesitate with his reply:

'One thing I learned from childhood was how Police officers are trained to understand criminals. Police have rules which they have to comply with. I also learned, well, we both know, how criminals think and how they plan things. And how they can trick the police. Criminals don't have rules. They're somehow born bad. And we're running out of time, especially if there's a storm brewing which will stop the ferries.'

Robin bowed his head and closed his eyes as his memory took him to his own troubled childhood.

'Yeah, I hear you,' he said quietly as he stepped out of the car.

He opened his rear motorbike pannier where he'd placed his helmet.

'Are these campers in the glen in the usual camping area? I'll need to avoid them when I go to the Punchbowl.'

'You're going there now?' asked Logan.

'Not yet. I need to make a call. Don't worry. If anyone's listening in to phone conversations, they won't get any information from this one. It's just someone I said I'd call. You go and do whatever you're planning. Then come back here and we'll get Heidi off this island. And quite frankly, I think you need to vanish too.'

'If you go to the Punchbowl from Sannox, go through the graveyard rather than going from the glen,' said Logan. 'When you get onto the plateau, follow the trees where we used to camp and keep going up to the Punchbowl lip. The body's at the far end of these trees almost in line with them. Maybe a bit to the north. But it's well hidden, smashed onto the rocks there. I could only find it from above with my drone.'

'Can I use that?' asked Robin.

'Of course, but it's out of battery charge. It's in the back of the car but it'll take ages to charge.'

'Did you go through the graveyard?' asked Robin.

'Eh, yeah.'

Robin stared at Logan trying to get eye contact with him, but Logan kept his gaze focused on his steering wheel, deliberately avoiding eye contact.

Hesitantly, Robin asked:

'Di… did you…?'

'Yes.'

'Sorry, I wasn't trying to…'

'It's not your fault,' said Logan. 'It's in my head somewhere. I still see myself as a kid hiding behind that gravestone watching that family being beaten to death, but then it all stops. And I know we're against the clock on that. But I can't make magic happen.'

'We still have about three months,' said Robin. 'I know you can achieve a lot in three months. It's just weird that things are happening now. It's like someone's got the timing wrong.'

'The timing's right. We're almost at equinox,' replied Logan.

They both felt an awkward silence. Logan felt compelled to change the subject as quickly as possible to stay focused on their more immediate situation.

'I lost my hat. Do you have anything in your bike I can wear on my head? A baseball cap or something? I gave mine to the wasps.'

'I don't have a hat. Sorry. Why do you need one?'

'Just thinking ahead, for my head,' smiled Logan. 'I'll buy one along the road. I need to buy a couple of things anyway.'

At that moment Robin received a text on his phone.

'Ah. A new plan. Three hours,' he said. 'Get your arse onto Brodick Green in three hours. And bring Heidi. We'll get her off this island.'

'You have a plan?' asked Logan.

'No. Yes. Maybe. Three hours.'

Logan rushed to the shops and bought an electric hair trimmer, a new blue jacket and a bush hat before driving to Katy's parents' house. Katy opened the door to him.

'Sorry Katy, I need another favour. These fake tattoos you gave me yesterday. They got a bit washed off by accident. Any chance you can let me use your bathroom? Then I need you to quickly re-do these tattoos again.'

Logan quickly gave himself a haircut with his new electric trimmer. Within minutes, he was once again sitting in the kitchen with Katy who started writing the same words over the now-faded henna tattoos from the previous day.

'Are your parents still here?'

'They're in the house somewhere,' she said as she started smiling.'

She laughed slightly.

'What's the joke?' asked Logan. 'Tell me.'

'Well, they saw you walking along the road and eh, I think they eh, I think that they're thinking that you… me are… em… well, they're not wanting to disturb us.'

Logan responded with a slightly embarrassed smile.

'Ah. Understood. Well, right now I'm in a bit of a rush. I'll be back in a couple of hours if that's acceptable to you. And okay with your parents?'

Katy gave him a shy smile.

'Okay with all of us.'

He quickly looked into the back room where Katy's parents were sitting with Heidi. They were showing her how to draw shapes with coloured crayons. Both parents gave him an approving smile.

'I'm not being rude, but I need to rush. I'll be back in a couple of hours.'

He left the house and drove to Sannox. He parked his car at the golf club as he'd done before. He walked into the glen wearing his new hat covering his haircut. More tents had been pitched since he was last there, with perhaps another hundred people. As he approached them, Kleo and Jasper were sitting around the now-smouldering remains of the previous night's camp fire. They were sitting on folding chairs beside Matt and two others. Kleo was talking to a young boy of about four years old, trying to explain something to him. The others were sitting relaxed while talking to each other. With Logan's swollen face and his change of clothing, they didn't immediately recognise him. He walked over to Kleo and Jasper.

'Hi again.'

'Logan?' gasped Kleo. 'What happened? When we saw you were gone we thought you'd gone hillwalking.'

'I did,' said Logan. 'But I got into a bit of an argument, and I lost the argument.'

He hoped his next comment would provoke a reaction, so he paused for a few seconds to allow time for the young boy, no longer being spoken to by Kleo, to skip away to play.

'At least I didn't get arrested for it, but I didn't feel like continuing the walk as planned. Anyway, enough about me. How are things here? I hope you didn't think I was being rude by leaving you all so early.'

Matt and Jasper were visibly concerned about what he'd just said.

Kleo started speaking:

'We had a wonderful time last night and this morni…'

'Wait,' interrupted Matt with a concerned look on his face. He then leant over from his chair and asked with an almost panicking voice:

'You got into a fight? Did you… did anyone report this to the police?'

Jasper also appeared concerned at the idea of police involvement. He positioned his hands on the chair arm rests as if he was about to stand up.

'Ha! No,' laughed Logan. 'My argument was with a swarm of wasps. I, eh, broke into their nest by mistake. And they got ever so pissed off at me. Look, they got the back of my neck as well, and up my arms.'

He pulled up his sleeves showing three stings on the back of his left wrist and two on his right arm.'

Matt was visibly relieved at this answer. Realising that Logan's comment about getting into an argument was just a joke, he sighed as he sat back into his chair again. Jasper also resumed his relaxed position on his chair. Kleo continued talking:

'More people are coming today, so if you're here tonight it'll be more fun. And plenty more to smoke if you want.'

'You're lucky it was just wasp stings,' said Jasper. 'One of our friends was bitten by a snake on Friday. An adder. He had to go to hospital.'

Logan considered that this may have been the reason why, when he had tried taking Heidi to hospital on Saturday, he'd seen the blue car which was occupied by Earlobe and Sloucher. Perhaps they weren't specifically looking for Heidi, in which case, it further mystifies any connection between these people and a little girl found alone in a glen.

'How is he now?' asked Logan. 'I know a baby adder gives a worse bite than an adult snake. The adults have the experience and ability to control their venom, but the babies give the full punch. I got bitten myself some years ago but thankfully it was by an adult snake, so it wasn't too bad.'

'Yeah they kept him in for observation and he got discharged the next day. He felt like shit for the day but he's fine.'

'Are you in pain?' asked Jasper. 'Looks like you took a battering. Maybe you should take some of this.'

Jasper offered him a joint.

'Thanks, but I still have some.'

Just then, Badger appeared from behind one of the tents. He signalled to Jasper to talk with him. He didn't appear to recognise Logan from his earlier encounter at North Sannox. Jasper walked over to him and the two men walked away from the tents talking quietly together. Logan was concerned that although his swollen face and change of clothes should make him difficult to recognise, it was possible that Badger would have noticed and remembered the henna tattoos on his neck. He discretely zipped up his jacket and lifted his collar to hide the tattoos.

'I've been thinking. This party on Wednesday. What do I

need to bring?'

'Bring some food and drink to share,' said Kleo.

'N… no. Not for food. I mean how much cash to buy more of these things?'

He pulled a cannabis joint from his pocket to show her what he was meaning.

'And when would be the best time to buy anything? Who do I pay?'

'Oh, don't worry about that,' said Kleo. 'Bring as much cash as you want tomorrow. There will be more than enough of whatever you want to buy. Then on Wednesday we're going to gather at about six o'clock in the evening.'

'Good. Eh, last night when you were talking to me, you got a bit sleepy, so maybe you don't remember this, but you started to tell me something about Noah's Ark. Is that the name of the bar where we meet up?'

'Oh, that. You're not supposed to know about it. But anyway, it's a boat which will bring us all we want. Depending on how close it can get to the shore, some of us will need to wade out to it, or maybe swim a bit. Can you swim? You'd be very useful if you can swim.'

Logan had an abundance of memories from some of his swimming experiences. He'd been a competitive swimmer in some of his earlier years, specialising in butterfly stroke and winning awards for his army unit.

'No, I can't swim very well,' he lied. 'Never been a good swimmer. My left leg's badly injured from many years ago which makes swimming too difficult.'

Matt pointed to Badger.

'Come here tomorrow afternoon,' he said. 'He'll be here. Tell him what you want and how much of it. He's the man we pay for the Ark. If he's not here, come and see me.'

Kleo nodded in agreement with Matt.

'I don't know how much I want to buy yet,' said Logan. 'Can I pay someone on Wednesday at the beach?'

'We… they… need to know how much to load onto the Ark,' said Matt. 'So, all the money should be paid by tomorrow night or Tuesday at the latest.'

Again, Kleo nodded in agreement.

Logan tried to think of what else to say which would give him more information without arousing suspicion that he was somehow spying on them.

Logan was determined to find more information, so he decided to question them about the weather forecast.

'Are you sure Wednesday is the best time for the party? It looks like that storm will stop the ferries sailing and then pass in the evening, but it might be later. The forecast looks better for Thursday. Maybe more people would want to come to the island on Thursday. But I'm no expert on weather forecasting.'

'Wednesday is the equinox,' said Kleo. 'We can only have the party then.'

'But we need the cash by tomorrow evening, so we can get the Ark prepared before the stormy weather.' said Matt. 'And don't worry about the ferry sailings.'

There was an awkward silence between Kleo and Matt, making Logan suspicious that there was something significant which they weren't willing to tell him. Jasper and Badger were still talking privately a few metres away. Logan became increasingly concerned that Badger may have recognised him. He needed to make an excuse to leave.

‘I need to go to the bank to get more cash out. I can do that later. But right now, my poor ageing bladder’s screaming at me. I drank too much stream water this morning.’

If he had walked towards the glen entrance people would know he was leaving, so he walked towards the trees at the Sannox stream. From where he was standing, he knew he had to walk uncomfortably close to where Badger and Jasper were standing. Badger looked at him in a way which concerned Logan that perhaps he’d recognised him from that morning’s encounter despite the swollen face, the hat and the new jacket.

Through his peripheral vision he could see Badger starting to move towards his direction as if to confront him. Knowing that some of the campers had already noticed Logan’s limp and had heard him mention his knee injury, he used that as a reason to force himself to stumble on uneven ground, falling face down as if by accident, making sure his head made contact with the ground. He picked himself up in a way which made his head slide on the grass just enough for his hat to fall off and expose his haircut. He stood up, brushed himself down, and replaced the hat back onto his head. Badger, Kleo and Jasper had seen the entire incident. Badger didn’t recognise him with his haircut and disfigured face. And nobody else in the glen had previously seen him without a hat, so nobody could notice that he’d cut his hair since they had seen him on the previous day.

‘You okay?’ asked Jasper.

‘Yeah just clumsy. I got a buggered knee joint from a bad fall some years ago. It does that sometimes.’

Logan, noticing that Badger was no longer interested in him, continued his way towards the Sannox stream. When he was confidently hidden from sight by the trees there, he made his way behind the growth towards the golf club. As soon as he reached his car, he drove back to Katy's parents' house.

'You're back sooner than I expected,' smiled Katy.

'Katy, I need to take Heidi out for a bit, so I'd like to try to make her look more like a boy. Can you come with us? I don't know where we're going but I have a feeling I might need you.'

Within ten minutes they were in the car as planned. Katy sat in the back with Heidi, now wearing trousers, boots, a blue jacket and a white woollen hat. Logan drove to Brodick Green where he'd arranged to meet Robin. He switched off the engine and turned to speak to Katy:

'I'm taking her off the island. Robin, the guy you met with me today… he's helping me. We arranged to meet here. In fact, he should be here any minute now.

Katy spoke with a concerned tone:

'This plan to get her off the island. You're putting her on that fishing boat, aren't you? It doesn't look very safe.'

'What fishing boat?'

'That ancient looking thing which was anchored off the far side of the ferry terminal earlier today.'

'I don't know anything about a fishing boat. I don't know what Robin's planned but whatever it is, it'll be reliable.'

'You trust him enough for that?'

'Oh yes. I've seen how he plans things, and yes, I trust him completely. If you want to come to the mainland with us then that'll be good, or if you'd rather not get any more involved, that's up to you. Either way, I'm coming back tomorrow but Heidi will stay on the mainland. I know some people there who I can trust.'

After waiting for five minutes, Robin arrived and parked

his motorbike next to Logan's car. He placed his helmet into the rear pannier from which he removed a plastic carrier bag. He got into Logan's front passenger seat. Looking at Logan's haircut, Robin raised his eyebrows while trying to think of something funny to say.

'I'm an amateur hairdresser,' joked Logan.

'Okay. Whatever. But for now, the timing's perfect. Follow me.'

They walked the short distance from Brodick Green northward, parallel to the golf course, and across the small wooden bridge towards an area of pebbled beach. The tide was out. Within two minutes, Logan noticed a small red aeroplane arriving from the north. As it descended towards the bay, Logan recognised it as a Kitfox: a two-seat home-built aircraft. On realising what he was seeing, he turned to Robin with a surprised and concerned look, simply asking:

'Really?'

'Yep.'

'But…'

'She knows what she's doing. After all, you taught her.'

Logan stood in shocked but pleasant surprise. The aircraft landed, almost hovering in the strong wind, onto the wet but firm compacted pebbled ground, and came to a halt almost immediately. The pilot switched off the engine and stepped out. It was Roz. Logan had taught her to fly three years earlier. She had bought a share in the aircraft about six months later.

'Robin told me my flying instructor needed some help,' she said as she looked horrified at the swollen condition of his face.

'What happe…'

'Wasps,' interrupted Logan. 'It looks worse than it is. But, I can't believe you're crazy enough to fly here in this weather. You flew across the water in that? I hope you had plenty of altitude.'

'I did what you taught me. Get high, stay in gliding range of land. Except I cheated. I came via the Cumbrae Islands and the Isle of Bute. Less water to worry about. I flew into Prestwick last night and just waited for Robin to send me a text that he'd met with you. It's quite a strong westerly wind up there above two thousand feet. It took me a while to get here. I should be quick going back. I remember you telling me about how you always wanted to land an aeroplane in Glen Rosa. I flew over it and I saw that patch of land you spoke about. But I also remember you telling me it was too rough to land on. So, here we are.'

'Can you take a passenger?' asked Logan as he pointed to Heidi.

'That's why I'm here,' said Roz. 'I even managed to borrow an infant lifejacket from the flying school.'

She looked at Katy standing holding Heidi's hand, then added:

'Maybe you should be the one taking a passenger. Or two passengers. So, do you want to fly her? You can go speak to Geordie. I can go back on the ferry.'

Logan paused for thought before answering, while Roz started to make a phone call.

'Fly it to Prestwick,' said Roz. 'Lynn drove to Prestwick this morning because she wants to help. I'm calling her to pick you up when you arrive. She can drive you wherever you need to go.'

'Oh shit, no!' exclaimed Logan. 'I'm not sure, but I think someone's managed to intercept local phone conversations. If you call her from here, don't mention anything except that it's just yourself. Actually, don't call from here at all. I'll figure something out when I get there.'

'In that case take my phone,' said Roz. 'Pin number is five three five three. You'll see Lynn's number in the contacts list. She's expecting me to return and she said she'll pick me up.'

Turning to Katy, she asked:

'You fancy a flying lesson? You can trust him. He's a professionally qualified pilot. He even taught me.'

Katy was initially apprehensive at the thought of going flying in such a small aircraft, yet also excited at the idea. Logan wasn't sure about this. Roz explained to Katy:

'I could have brought a bigger plane. A four-seater. But I knew the beach here would be too short. That's why I brought this one. It can take-off and land in shorter distances, especially in these windy conditions.'

'Katy, I don't want you getting more involved,' said Logan. 'You and your parents have helped enough already. Go home. I'll be back tomorrow.'

'I'm coming with you,' said Katy. 'I'm already too deeply involved.'

'No, really. We're still not sure what we're…'

'Stop arguing,' interrupted Robin. 'People saw this aeroplane landing here. In a few minutes there could be a crowd of curious faces rushing from the golf course to take a closer look.'

Logan looked around nervously, noticing a middle-aged man watching from the golf course.

'We're being watched,' he said.

'Don't worry about him,' said Robin. 'Just take the plane and get out of here. If Katy's involved, then do her a favour and get her off this island. You both need to speak to Geordie because Katy's seen the faces of people coming into her shop, so perhaps she has some valuable information for him. Go. Now.'

'And that upper wind's getting stronger,' added Roz. 'You've got half a tank of fuel, so your weight will be okay for an almost vertical take-off in this wind. But go now before that wind goes over the limit. It's turbulent until you get above four thousand feet.'

Katy glanced at Logan as she shrugged her shoulders at him.

'It's not negotiable,' she said as she was being helped into the aircraft by Roz.

Realising his argument had been defeated, Logan placed the infant life jacket on Heidi before placing her onto Katy's lap.

'I even got her a child's headset,' said Roz. 'It'll protect her little ears from the noise.'

Logan gave Roz his mobile phone and both sets of his car keys.

'Take this. The phone's out of battery charge. Charge it and look at the videos I made. That way you'll get a better idea of what I've been dealing with. Its pin number is easy. Four three two one. And my Toyota is parked hidden just opposite the Shiskine golf club shop. I need to get back before the storm. Have either of you spoken with police about any of this?'

Roz and Robin both shook their heads.

'Keep it that way. I'll contact Lynn as soon as I can. If for any reason I can't get in touch with Lynn, I'll go straight to Geordie.'

Robin produced a bottle of whisky from his carrier bag. and gave it to Logan.

'When you see Geordie, give him this bottle of the best from Arran's distillery.'

Logan gave Roz the keys to both cars. He then closed the aircraft door and started the engine. Within two minutes the aircraft was airborne, heading north.

Robin and Roz walked back to the car, but in silence as they both tried to think of what best to do next. They stood at the car just looking at their surroundings for about five minutes.

'What have we just got ourselves involved with?' asked Roz.

'Organised crime.' said Robin. 'I think the Verhoevens, the equinox, and maybe Russian politics. I'll tell you the rest later.'

Logan flew north, climbing to five thousand feet to get above the turbulence created by the wind flowing past the mountainous terrain. He flew over Corrie, then steered over the plateau towards the Devil's Punchbowl to see if he could still spot the dead body he'd found on Saturday, but with the rough terrain of boulders and rocks, picking out a body wearing dark-green clothing in a dark shadowy rocky area was more difficult than seeing it as he had done from a drone at a much lower level on a brighter day. He could vaguely pick out a shape on the rocks, but he couldn't be certain if he was looking at the body of a human, a deer or an optical illusion in the shadows. Descending or circling to take a closer look would have been foolish as the westerly wind blowing over Coich na h'Oighe would create a dangerous turbulent downdraught. The Kitfox, with its eighty-horsepower engine, would struggle to maintain height. Also, flying lower or changing direction would attract unwanted attention.

His flight direction took him over Sannox bay from where he could see the campers in the glen and in the campsite at North Sannox. More tents had been pitched since he had last been there. He could see the black van of Badger and Gremlin, still positioned in the same place, guarding walkers from entering the North Sannox coastal path. There was a small boat which he hadn't noticed before, positioned near the shoreline around the coastal bend north of Sannox bay.

'Noah's Ark?' thought Logan.

He kept his heading steady as he pointed the aircraft towards the Isle of Bute, then Cumbrae, at all times making sure he was within gliding range of land: a standard practice as a precaution in case the engine should fail or lose power. The increasingly strong wind at five thousand feet would have made it impossible for him to turn back to Arran should such an event happen. Katy sat there quietly enjoying the view. She'd been living with her parents on Arran for most of her life but had never seen the landscape from the air. Heidi was more interested in looking at the colouring book she'd been given by Katy's parents.

'Do you want a flying lesson?' asked Logan.

Katy smiled and shook her head. She was enjoying the flight, but she wasn't confident at actually taking the controls.

'Just show me what you're doing,' she replied.

'Put your hand on the stick,' said Logan. 'Don't worry, I'll keep hold of the controls from this side and show you what's going on. Just use small slow movements. Stick forward slightly, see how the nose drops down a bit below the horizon and more land comes into view in front of us.'

He pointed at the airspeed indicator.

'We're doing about a hundred miles per hour, but now we're diving slightly, sort of like going downhill, so our speed increases.'

He moved the control column backwards.

'Now when I move it back, the nose comes up above the horizon, so we can't see so much land in front of us, and our airspeed decreases.'

He returned the control column to its neutral position.

'There. Now we're flying level again.'

He moved the control column slightly to the left.

'See now, if I move it to the left, the left wing goes down so we're leaning to the left side but when I do that, its nose wants to move in the opposite direction, so I have to help it with a bit of left rudder by pushing my left foot forward slightly. Now the aircraft turns left. When it's established in the turn, all I have to do is centralise the stick to maintain a constant bank angle. But the nose drops slightly in a turn, so I have to apply some back pressure on the stick to stop us from descending.'

Katy put her right hand on the control column.

'Are you sure I should do this?' she asked nervously.

'Go ahead. You have control. Just make it small slow movements, you'll be fine.'

Katy moved the control column and gently moved it in various directions, but the atmospheric turbulence buffeted the aircraft in ways which contradicted her control movements, confusing her as to what she was actually doing with the aircraft.

'You can afford to make the movements bigger,' said Logan.

She took his advice and moved the control column forward, but did so more abruptly, causing her to feel a falling sensation in her stomach. She quickly released her grip.

'I think you should fly it,' she said nervously.

Logan grinned as he resumed control.

'Don't worry,' he said. 'It takes a while to actually get the feel of it.'

From overhead Cumbrae, Logan steered the aircraft more southward across to the mainland, then along the coast to

Prestwick Airport where the wind was strengthening across the runway.

Katy was nervous at the increasing gusts as they descended on final approach. She noticed that Logan didn't seem to be concerned. She commented nervously, secretly seeking assurance:

'I didn't know an aeroplane this size could cope with strong winds.'

'Strange thing about aeroplanes,' replied Logan. 'Some of them are easier to land in windy conditions than on a calm day.'

He landed the aircraft gently on the main runway, then taxied to one of the hangars.

'Welcome to Prestwick,' he said as he switched the engine off.

He started to help Katy out of the aircraft until he noticed two engineers walking past the hangar.

'Do me a favour,' he said. 'Keep Heidi out of sight for a few minutes because this aircraft isn't actually certified to carry more than two people. I'll push it into the hangar then we'll leave without being seen.'

The hangar door was partially open, enough for him to easily push the aircraft into it. As they walked outside though the back of the hangar, Logan picked up Heidi and walked towards the exit point of the airport. Once outside, he used Roz's phone and called Lynn. She answered promptly, believing it was Roz calling her as she'd expected:

'Hi Sis, did you find him?'

'Lynn. Hi. It's me, Logan. Yes, she found me, but she gave me her phone because mine's out of charge.'

'Are you alright?' she asked. 'We were all worried about you. Robin seemed a bit vague about what was going on.'

'Yeah, I'm good. We're all good. Roz is getting the next ferry back. At least I think that's what she's doing. But I'm at the airport. I flew Roz's plane to Prestwick. Can you pick me up?'

'Of course. I can be there in twenty minutes. Just outside the flying club?'

'Yes please. And can you bring a child seat for a three-year -old? Buy one if you need to on the way here. I left the other one in my car because I didn't realise I was going flying. I'll pay you. And also, don't phone Robin. We think the phones are being intercepted. I'll tell you everything when you get here.'

Lynn arrived. She was slim and attractive with long red hair. Her appearance was strikingly noticeable. Katy suspected that her hair had been dyed.

'You like red-heads?' she joked.

Logan smiled, closed his eyes briefly and shook his head.

'She's too much like family to me. She's Roz's sister. More like a sort of cousin to me.'

'Good,' whispered Katy to herself.

Lynn stepped out of her car, looking concerned at Logan's face.

'What's going on? And what happened to…'

'Wasps. I'm fine. Meet Katy. And Heidi. I don't want to be rude, but we're sort of rushing here. Can you take us somewhere to get something to eat? We're all hungry. I'll tell you what I know, and then we need to take a train to Glasgow.'

Lynn drove them to a nearby cafe. Katy took Roz's phone from Logan to exchange phone numbers while she amused Heidi with her colouring book. Logan explained everything to Lynn. After spending thirty minutes there, Logan looked at his watch.

'The ferry will be arriving soon. You need to go get Roz. Can you drop us off at the railway station in Irvine?'

'How about I just take you to the station at the Ardrossan ferry terminal?' asked Lynn. 'If you're going to Glasgow the train leaves from there.'

'No. Not with Heidi here. If people are looking for her they might be watching the ferry. Please take us to Irvine then go meet Roz when the ferry arrives. Here, take her phone and give it back to her.'

'My number's in there,' said Katy.

Lynn drove them to the railway station at Irvine where Logan, Katy and Heidi caught the next train to Glasgow. Katy carried Heidi into the train while Logan carried her new car seat.

'Can I borrow your phone?' asked Logan.

Katy gave him her phone.

At his office, Detective Superintendent George Buchanan, was sitting at his desk. His friends and colleagues called him Geordie, a name which he encouraged. His telephone rang. It was the girl from the switchboard.

'Geordie there's a man wanting to speak with you. He says it's urgent.'

Geordie sighed as he continued looking through paperwork.

'This will be the fourth urgent call from someone today. Did he say what it's about?'

'I asked him. He refused to say.'

'Well, can you tell him I'm not available. Can you pass his call to someone else?'

'Sir.'

Geordie continued studying his paperwork until twenty

seconds later when his phone rang again.

'Sir, the caller says he can only speak with you. He says it's very urgent and his name's Logan.'

Geordie immediately stopped what he was doing and sat to attention. Speaking with a sense of enthusiasm he replied:

'Oh, eh, Logan? Okay, yes. I'll take the call. Put him through.'

She connected the call.

'Logan,' said Geordie. 'How are you?'

'I'm good thanks. But I found myself caught up in a situation. It's eh, you know, it's, well it's… it's weirder than anything right now. Can you meet me in Glasgow Central in twenty-five minutes? I'm on the train coming from Irvine.'

'I'll be there. Can you give me a clue about what's going on?'

With a half serious yet half sarcastic voice, Logan told him:

'Big drugs deal, I mean massive drugs deal with a planned protest, a dead body and a missing child. You know me. Just another average day. Oh, and maybe connected to Russian politics, so possibly Soviet mafia instead of Glasgow mafia. I've been upgraded.'

Geordie didn't believe him. This sounded just like Logan's typical sense of humour.

'Okay, good. But tell me, what's really bothering you?'

'I just told you,' said Logan.

Geordie's smile faded as he realised Logan was being serious.

'You're back in the military?'

'No. I just went hillwalking on Arran. It's all happening there. I'm convinced Verhoeven is involved.'

Geordie gasped as the hairs on his arms stood on end.

'Arran. Oh. Really? But the timing… right, okay… wow!'

He looked at the clock.

'Glasgow Central. Twenty-five minutes. I'll be there.'

Geordie put the phone down and sat quietly for a few moments to compose his thoughts. He picked up his office phone and started pressing in some numbers but then hesitated and cancelled the call. He sat for a minute to ponder over what Logan had told him. He looked at the calendar on his office wall and paid attention to the date being just two days away from the autumn equinox. He made a call from his personal mobile phone.

A middle-aged lady answered. Recognising her caller, she jokingly answered:

'Glasgow home for handsome police officers, how may I be of assistance?'

'Janice…' replied Geordie.

Janice instantly recognised the serious tone in Geordie's voice.

'Uh-oh. You're going to be late tonight?' she asked.

'Janice, I don't know. But I might bring back a house guest if that's okay with you. It's Logan. I'm going to meet him, and I think he's, well… he's got himself caught up in something, but I don't know the details yet.'

Janice raised her eyebrows, looking out of the living-room window, asking:

'Is this…?'

'Arran,' interrupted Geordie. 'He says it's happening now.'

Janice froze at hearing this. After a few moments she said:

'I'll prepare the spare bedroom.'

Geordie ended the call and immediately put on his jacket which was hanging on the clothes hook in his office. He was already in his plain clothes. He walked into the next office where two of his colleagues were sitting looking at computer data.

'Davy. We got something about to happen. I'm going to meet someone. Call the drugs team. Actually, on second thoughts, call Roland directly. Tell him to get ready to re-open the Equinox Enquiry.'

He left his office and drove to Glasgow Central station. After a few minutes he could see Logan walking along the platform carrying the child seat, followed by Katy and Heidi. Geordie and Logan hadn't met for about three years, so Geordie misunderstood the situation.

'I see congratulations are in order,' he said as he smiled at Katy and Heidi.

'Ah-ha, eh, no not quite. Meet Katy and Heidi. I got lots of explaining to do.'

'Arran?' asked Geordie.

'Yeah. Can we go somewhere quiet?'

'Come on. Let's go back to my office.'

Logan decided to say nothing about the events in the car in case the information would distract Geordie from his safe driving. Engaging in small talk was more appropriate for the short drive. Geordie drove them to the police station and led them to his office there. Logan and Katy sat in the two chairs in front of his desk while Heidi sat on Katy's lap. Logan gave him the bottle of whisky.

'A present from Arran,' he said. 'One of the best whiskies.'

He then gave his explanation of events to Geordie who relayed everything to another police department from his phone. Heidi was becoming restless. Logan looked at his watch.

'I need to go shopping while we have time.'

Just then, Katy's phone rang.

'It's my mum. Shall I tell her where we are?'

Geordie heard her ask that question and while still talking on his phone he stretched out his arm and waved his hand, shaking his head, signalling to her to not answer the call. Katy let it ring until it stopped. After two minutes, Geordie ended his phone conversation.

'Katy, I'd rather you didn't tell anyone where you are just now. As Logan says, we don't know if phones are being intercepted. If you talk to your parents, maybe you can just tell them you're still on the island somewhere, maybe at a friend's house, and that you might stay overnight?'

Katy smiled at Logan.

'One guess what they'll be thinking,' she said with a mischievous smile.

'Playing Cupid?' asked Logan, also smiling awkwardly.

'I need to speak with someone,' said Geordie. 'Help yourself to the coffee machine. I'll be back in a few minutes.'

He left the office. Katy and Logan focused their attention on Heidi as they tried to keep her amused. After what felt like thirty minutes, Katy looked at her watch.

'Is that the time? He's been gone for ages.'

Logan looked at his watch.

'He must be busy.'

Just then a middle-aged grey-haired woman walked cautiously into the office.

'Logan?' she asked smiling.

'Janice!' exclaimed Logan.

Janice was Geordie's wife. They threw out their arms and hugged each other.

'Geordie called me saying you could use some help.'

She looked at Katy and Heidi.

Logan started to introduce them.

'I know,' said Janice. 'You're Katy from Arran and this little girl here must be Heidi. Geordie told me just now.'

Just then, Geordie walked in.

'Okay, so, Logan, Katy, did you make plans about where you're staying tonight?'

'Not yet,' replied Logan.

'Good. You're all staying with us,' said Janice.

Turning to Katy she added:

'We don't stay far from here.'

Logan looked again at his watch.

'I need to go shopping before the shops close. I can catch up with you all later.'

'I'll take you shopping,' said Geordie. 'You'll need someone to drive you. Come on.'

Janice waved her car keys at Katy.

'In that case I can take you two girls shopping for some clothes for the little one.'

She picked up the child car-seat and led Katy and Heidi away.

About three hours later, Logan and Geordie arrived at the house. Janice had prepared a meal for all of them. On the living room wall was a photograph of Geordie and Janice at the helm of a large catamaran.

'You're still into sailing?' asked Logan.

'I never stopped,' said Geordie. 'But I sold my last boat. Looking for another one. Maybe next year.'

'I hope to learn sailing next year,' said Logan. 'When I can find the spare time.'

Janice walked through from the dining room.

'Katy's giving Heidi a bath. The little girl's been saying a few words, but I can't make out what she's saying.'

Checking that Katy wasn't within listening distance, she whispered:

'I didn't tell her anything about… anything. She hasn't asked anything.'

'Thanks,' said Logan. 'I'll tell her when the time's right.'

Katy came downstairs from the bathroom carrying Heidi who was wrapped in a large towel.

'I put her clothes in the washing as soon as we got here. They should be dry by now,' said Janice.

Katy spoke to Logan:

'My parents called. They say the police visited them. PC Kyle and some other officer. They're looking for you. I told them we're staying with friends in Whiting Bay until tomorrow.'

Logan looked at Geordie.

'Don't worry,' said Geordie. 'Heidi can stay here while you go back to Arran.'

They sat at the table and enjoyed the casserole prepared by Janice while Heidi slowly ate a small portion of fish fingers. Logan was well aware that Geordie and Janice usually avoided any conversation about police work when they were at home or with friends, so most of the conversation was about Katy, Arran, a few mutual friends, and sailing yachts.

After the meal, Heidi was noticeably tired, so Janice led her to a small spare room where a bed had been prepared for her. Then the four adults sat in the lounge and chatted while enjoying some of Geordie's wine. The conversation changed through different subjects until Katy plucked up the courage to ask:

'How do you both know Logan?'

There were a few moments of awkward silence as Janice looked slightly worriedly at both Geordie and Logan, almost dreading which one of them would be the first to answer that question.

'We go back some years,' said Logan. 'Geordie helped me with a situation when I was a teenager. Back in those days there were some, eh, let's just say, some nasty people surrounding my life at the time. Fortunately, Geordie here was the man who was put in charge of a police operation to put these people behind bars where they belong. I'll spare you the details for now. Janice used to be in the police too and she was part of the operation.'

'I was put in charge of the enquiry,' added Geordie. 'But it was Logan who did all the detective work even though he was still a schoolboy. We've stayed in touch since.'

Janice was relieved at that answer. She knew the full truth was more harrowing. She tried to think of anything she could say to change the subject as quickly as possible.

'I've made up a room for you both,' she said. 'There are plenty of spare towels in the cupboard upstairs, and there's plenty of hot water. If you get hungry during the night just help yourselves to anything you can find in the kitchen.'

Logan noticed Katy was starting to look tired.

'You go get some sleep. We need to catch the early ferry before the storm starts. I need to speak to Geordie here a bit more.'

Katy and Janice both left the lounge as Geordie stared at Logan, reluctantly saying:

‘We’re running out of time.’

‘I know,’ said Logan. ‘I know, I know, I know. We’ve been running out of time for twenty years, six months, sixteen days, and…’

He looked at his watch.

‘… twenty-one hours. I really know. And I’ve tried. Every day I’ve tried.’

‘Are your nightmares still happening?’ asked Geordie.

‘Yes. Not as much nowadays, but yes.’

‘Katy doesn’t know?’

‘No. I’ve briefly met Katy on previous visits to Arran, so we’ve recognised each other for some years, but we only just started to get to know each other at the weekend. And I’ve already dragged her into flying an aeroplane to smuggle and hide what we think may be a kidnapped child, possibly wanted by Russian mafia or a major drugs gang who are mixed up with a group of spaced out spirit weirdos set up by Verhoeven. I think that’s already more than enough for her to deal with just now.’

‘Tell me more about these people you met in the glen.’

‘They’re some sort of cult calling themselves Spiritbeamers. And that, well, that term is screaming at me that it has to be connected to the Verhoevens.’

‘How so?’ asked Geordie.

‘Because Margaret Verhoeven had set up a small group of bizarre people long before she was arrested. I can explain more at a later stage, but for now, it seems to be too much to be a coincidence.’

‘You think Margaret’s set this up at Sannox?’

‘Maybe partly. She’s not clever enough to set everything up

by herself, but somehow, she manages to find weirdos. I'd heard that she was released from prison about two years ago. That would give her enough time to find plenty weirdos.'

'But Heidi? And Russian politics?' asked Geordie.

'I know. That bit doesn't make sense.'

They spoke for another four hours while Janice, Katy and Heidi were absent. At one point, Logan went to the upstairs bathroom during which time he checked on Katy. She'd left the bedroom door open just enough for him to look in. Seeing that she was already sleeping, he then checked on Heidi who was also sleeping peacefully in the next bedroom.

'The calm before the storm,' he thought to himself.

He returned to the lounge to continue talking to Geordie who was looking through archived computer files of known criminals.

'Janice showed Katy these pictures while we were shopping,' said Geordie. 'But she didn't recognise any of these people.'

He then looked sternly at Logan, thinking carefully before asking:

'Would it help if you speak with him again?'

'I met him six months ago,' said Logan. 'And it was because he was the one who wanted to meet. I think if I invite myself to speak with him again it'll just get him suspicious. I'd rather deal with what we already have.'

'It's dangerous.'

'I know who I can trust now,' said Logan. 'I can do this. As far as Verhoeven is concerned, I'm out of the picture. He told me he was using Tommy to spy on me. So, he's told me what he wants me to know. I think it's best to let him think he's in control.'

'We've nothing to attach the name Tommy to what's happening on Arran, have we?'

'No. But that doesn't surprise me. He's always enjoyed the idea of owning Tommy and he relies on Tommy being stupid and easily manipulated. He wouldn't dare trust him with a serious plan which requires intelligence.'

'Whatever we do, we're going to be opening a hornet's nest.'

'It's already open,' replied Logan with his eyes half shut. 'And they'll be swarming Brodick's beach on Wednesday night.'

He closed his eyes. Geordie could see that he was exhausted. He decided to stop talking as he watched Logan drift into a troubled sleep.

CHAPTER 6

Tuesday September 21st

When Logan awoke the following morning, he was slightly confused as to where he was. He eventually realised he'd slept on the sofa in Geordie's lounge. Katy was sitting opposite watching him.

'Morning,' she said, smiling. 'I didn't want to waken you, but I made some coffee.'

Logan sat up, blinking his eyes to try to waken more. He gratefully accepted the mug of hot coffee she presented to him. He pulled away the thin blanket which had been covering him.

'I got up for a drink of water and saw you sleeping. I thought you'd sleep better with, well, I had a spare blanket in my room,' said Katy.

'What time is it?' he asked.

'Eight o'clock.'

'Ugh. Okay. I guess we missed the first ferry. Where's Heidi?'

On hearing Logan and Katy talking, Geordie and Janice walked in from the kitchen where they'd been having some breakfast.

'Heidi's awake,' said Janice. 'She slept well. We didn't want to waken you, but now you're awake, breakfast's ready.'

'I've just checked the weather forecast,' said Geordie. 'And I called the ferry company. It seems that storm will arrive a bit later than expected. The ferries should run today, but they think the last two will be cancelled. The sooner you get there the better. I'll drive you to the harbour.'

Logan asked Katy to borrow her phone. He sent a text message to Roz:

'*Roz. Are you still on Arran, or back on the mainland?*'

Roz immediately replied by text:

'*I came back to mainland on the ferry last night. Lynn picked me up.*'

Logan replied:

'*Good. If you managed to charge my phone, can you send the videos and pics from my phone ASAP?*'

Roz replied:

'*No. I've charged your phone, but these videos are too long to send. Tell me what ferry you'll be taking. I'll go to Ardrossan and meet you there to swap phones.*'

Geordie drove Katy and Logan to Ardrossan where the ferry was already docked. They met with Roz. She gave Logan his phone, now fully charged and he gave Roz her phone.

'I saw the videos,' she said. 'They were too long to send, but also I thought it best to not send them in case anyone was hacking into your email.'

They noticed police standing watching people as they boarded. A few police officers were paying attention to the cars which were boarding.

'What's going on?' asked Logan.

'Some nature lover apparently thinks it's a good idea to release breeding pairs of grey squirrels to the island,' said Geordie. 'And someone else is apparently trying to catch them and take them off the island.'

'Grey squirrels would cause a lot of harm to the wildlife there,' said Roz.

'That's why the police are checking cars,' said Geordie.

'Hmm. Coincidence? Or some sort of decoy?' asked Logan.

'I only found out after you called last night,' said Geordie. 'I'll look into it more.'

Roz and Geordie left while Katy and Logan, having bought their tickets, boarded the ferry. They immediately went into the forward lounge, hoping to get the most comfortable seats.

'I thought you went shopping yesterday with Geordie,' said Katy. 'You didn't buy anything?'

'Oh that. Yes, I bought some things, but I couldn't collect them. They'll get delivered.'

Within minutes, the ferry was filled with passengers, mostly back-packers, many of whom appeared to be in their twenties. There was a noticeable stench of body odour from several of them.

'Phew,' said Logan jokingly. 'Seems we're on a boat full of stinky people.'

'Do you think they're going to that Spiritbeamer party?' asked Katy.

'Almost certainly.'

A group of six women and five men sat opposite them as the ferry set sail for the hour's crossing. Logan whispered to Katy:

'I need to start a conversation with these people. Bear with me.'

He looked at one of the women. She had a scruffy appearance with long matted hair and well-worn outdoor clothing. She appeared to be either drunk or under the influence of some drug she'd been taking.

'You're all going to the Spiritbeamers?' asked Logan.

'Yes,' said the woman. 'You as well?'

'Yeah probably. But I don't have the exact details, like what time it starts and exactly where it'll be.'

'Brodick beach,' she said. 'I think it starts tomorrow afternoon and goes on all night.'

'It might get stormy,' said Logan. 'Have you seen the weather forecast?'

'Ha! Yes. Stormy. Who cares? The spirits don't care, and we don't care, do we?'

The rest of her friends joined in at this point.

'We're the ones who are making the storm happen,' said one of the group.

'This is exciting. We're changing Arran. We're changing Scotland. We're telling the politicians where to stick their rules. We're free spirits, and we don't have rules.'

'Amen,' said the oldest of the group.

Katy looked at Logan, curious as to what information he was trying to extract from these people.

'So exactly what's the agenda for tonight and tomorrow?' she asked.

'We're starting with a dance party on the beach,' said one.

'And we're getting to be truly in touch with our inner selves. Music. Dancing. Speaking to the spirit of the equinox. That'll start in the afternoon. And we'll be there all night.'

'How do you speak to spirits?' asked Logan.

'We can give you something to help with that,' said the one of the men. 'You know what I mean?'

'Yeah, I think so,' said Logan. 'I heard Noah's Ark will be there.'

'Yeah,' said the man. 'You got the message. Good.'

'But there's to be a protest as well?' asked Logan.

'Yes, after the beach party we're going to be protesting against… against…'

'Capitalism,' said the first woman.

'… yes, capitalism,' said the man. '… and to support human rights.'

Logan and Katy looked at each other, facially acknowledging that these people didn't actually know what they were planning to protest about.

'What human rights?' asked Logan.

'All human rights,' said one of the other men. 'We need all basic human rights to be granted.'

'We want to teach children the beauty of life,' said the first woman. 'We want more freedom to be given to children in schools, so they can experience inner spirituality. Legalise all drugs.'

'What's your views on that?' asked the first man.

Logan was horrified yet not surprised at what he was hearing. He'd been involved in similar arguments over the years and felt compelled to say something.

'What are my views on that?' asked Logan as he tried to compose something to say which would be meaningful without being too offensive. 'Well, I'm a believer in the concept of live and let live but, well, I'm no scientist, but there's plenty of scientific research to say bad stuff about drugs, especially in young children.'

'Cannabis,' said one of the group. 'It needs to be given in schools.'

'You all know what the amygdala is?' asked Logan.

None of them answered. Four of the group shook their heads.

'Okay, so, it's a tiny blob in the middle of your brain. It's about the size of a pin head. I've actually seen one when I studied a dissected brain once. Anyway, there are two of them, joined together by a band of nerves and they process all emotions. Anger, sadness, happiness, love, hate, guilt and so on. When it gets overloaded with emotion it gets confused. That's what happens when people cry at a movie's happy ending or laugh when they're terrified. You've all cried a bit at a happy ending yeah?'

Five of the group smiled and nodded.

'Well, smoking cannabis puts a chemical into the brain which shrinks the amygdala permanently, so emotions become permanently overloaded. So, when people feel sad or depressed, the chemical makes them feel a bit happier, giving them the false impression that it's a good fix, but then it takes its toll on the other emotions.'

'The older man started shaking his head in denial at what Logan was saying. Logan continued talking:

'With your emotions being turned back-to-front, you start to like people who you previously couldn't stand, and you start to dislike people who are your best friends. And you start to feel depressed when you should be happy, so you smoke weed to make you happy, and so on. It's a vicious circle. And while that's going on, your brain is trying to figure out things like why you suddenly don't like your friends so much, and so it invents an idea that your friends are conspiring something behind your back, so you get paranoid… and that's just one of the effects.'

The group looked at him angrily, wishing he'd stop talking,

but he continued:

'So, rather than mess about with chemicals, I rather just find other ways of staying happy.'

Two of the women stood up and walked away. They didn't want to hear what Logan was saying. This was exactly the reaction Logan was expecting. He continued:

'It's worse in kids because their brains aren't fully developed. Same reason I drink alcohol but won't give a bottle of whisky to a five-year-old. Or give a packet of cigarettes to a six-year-old.'

'That's nonsense,' said the first man. 'Where did you learn such crap?'

'The army,' replied Logan. 'I was trained in this stuff by professionals who know what they're talking about.'

'Well, we know our rights,' said the second man loudly. 'And we're going to honour our rights.'

'I'm not trying to deny you any rights,' replied Logan. 'But you asked for my thoughts which are based on what I've been taught, so I gave them to you. But maybe you can change my mind.'

'Well we're going to change your mind on that tomorrow,' said the first man. 'The new Arran will change everyone's minds.'

Logan discretely tapped Katy's toes with his foot and asked her:

'You want to take part in a protest?'

Katy knew he was bluffing and that he wanted her play along with him.

'Sure, why not? It sounds like fun.'

'Come on. Let's go upper deck. We'll get some fresh air.'

They went upstairs. The upper deck was packed full of

people, mostly with a similar style of appearance as the people they'd been talking to. Many were smoking, and the smell of cannabis was strong, sometimes overwhelming.

'Look,' said Logan. 'Half of them are already drunk, stoned, wasted, spaced out and, well, we're not even half way across the water.'

He pointed to two young men sitting on the floor, partially smiling with their eyes half shut and unable to focus on anything.

'That's not weed they're smoking,' he said. 'They've taken something stronger. Look at the needle marks on their arms. And this is what they want to turn Arran into. And they want to sell their poison to local kids. I've seen this in other places, but never anywhere near Arran.'

Katy was horrified at what she was seeing. Until now her life had been well protected from exposure to such activities.

'I don't want to see this on Arran,' she said quietly. 'How many are on this boat? Three hundred maybe? How many already came over this morning? And how many more will arrive on the next ferry this afternoon?'

Her phone rang.

'It's my mum.'

She spoke to her mother for a couple of minutes while Logan looked around. A man of similar age to Logan was standing watching the crowd with a facial expression suggesting that he was unimpressed at what he was seeing. He was wearing a brown waterproof jacket. Logan wanted to know his name. He approached the man and asked him:

'Danny? Are you Danny? We went to school together?'

'No,' said the man. 'Not me. My name's Adam.'

'Oh, sorry,' said Logan. 'You look like an old friend of mine.'

Just then, Katy finished the call with her mother.

'Mum says the police have been round again. They're looking for you. And mum says they're not being so friendly. I didn't tell her where we are.'

'Don't worry. I'll talk with the police later.'

The ferry docked at Brodick. As Logan looked down from the back of the ferry he could see Robin standing at the wishing well next to the small bridge at the harbour entrance. They walked off the ferry and made their way towards Robin who told them:

'Roz drove your Toyota back here. Both cars are parked over there across from the mini golf.'

'You've been hillwalking?' asked Logan. 'Did you go to the Punchbowl?'

'Not yet,' said Robin. 'I decided to charge your drone before going up there in case there's something else worth finding. But charging its batteries took longer than I'd planned, by which time it was getting dark. I'll go today. What are your plans?'

'I don't know yet.'

'Well, while I was waiting for the batteries to charge, I decided to enquire about the hotel and guest house bookings on the island. They're all fully booked up because of this Spiritbeamer thing.'

'That's not surprising,' said Logan.

'True. But, it seems that most of the bookings happened at the last minute. For what seems to be a big event with so many people, almost nobody had booked accommodation in advance.'

'That doesn't make sense,' said Katy. 'They claim to be

celebrating a date which happens every year and can't be changed, so why would they make their bookings at the minute?'

They walked to Logan's Ford Fusion. During the short walk Logan explained to Robin the events which took place in Glasgow. As they reached the car, Katy spoke:

'Do you two need me for anything just now?'

'No. I'll drive you home if you want,' said Logan.

'No, it's okay. I'll go straight to the shop. You two guys do whatever you need to do. Guys' stuff, right?'

She turned to Logan.

'You'll visit me later?'

'I'll try come get you before the shop shuts,' said Logan. 'If I'm late, I'll come to your parents' house. And if police ask you anything, just tell them the truth.'

'Come to my apartment,' said Katy. 'I already sent you a text with my address. I'll be there after work.'

She walked the short distance to the shop and spoke to her manager.

'I'm back now. The excitement's over.'

He was welcoming, telling her:

'I know you were helping the police with something. That's all I need to know. Besides, we've not been too busy although something's happening today. Lots of strange people. Actually, some of them are quite smelly. They've been coming in here all morning. I wish we sold deodorant.'

Two hours later, Kyle entered the shop and went straight to Katy as she was re-arranging one of the shelves.

'Katy, where's Logan?'

'I don't know. I haven't seen him since this morning.'

'Where's the child?'

'Glasgow. Logan took her to a stay with a friend in Glasgow.'

'Eh? But, why is she not on the island? What right did Logan have to take her away?'

'Because he found her, and nobody reported her missing. And after two days she still hadn't been reported missing. Except, obviously she was. She's in safe hands.'

'This is a police matter,' said Kyle. 'He had no right to just take the law into his own hands like that. And you could have notified us that he was taking her away. How did he get off the island? We were watching the ferries. We didn't see him get on.'

Katy shrugged her shoulders and told him:

'Oh, he flew away. But anyway, it's still a police matter. He took Heidi and handed her over to Glasgow police. She's safe.'

Kyle sighed and looked away. Katy continued:

'What would you have done if she was still here? Taken her home and looked after her? Adopted her? Handed her over to Social Services even though you don't have the resources here? I know that because the only social workers on the island are all friends of mine and none of them are here this week except Jenny Grey and she's off sick just now.'

Katy discretely pointed with her eyes to a group of customers in the shop. They were of the same scruffy appearance as the ones she'd seen on the ferry.

'You have bigger problems happening here. This island is filling up with drugs and drug dealers. And really bizarre people. Tomorrow there's going to be some big druggie celebration on the beach. Hundreds of people. Maybe two thousand of them. They'll be trying to buy, sell and distribute an awful lot of drugs around the island. And then a big protest about something, but the protesters don't actually know or even care what they'll be protesting about…'

She looked at her watch before continuing:

'… and it's probably already too late for you to get police back-up because the ferry will stop sailing soon and almost certainly not start again until tomorrow evening or maybe the following morning. Whatever's going on here, Logan has taken a missing child to safety.'

'Will you see Logan again?' asked Kyle.

Katy paused for thought, looking at the floor to avoid eye contact.

'I… I hope, eh, I think so. I don't know. I think I'll see him later.'

Kyle looked around the shop at the customers. He noticed some of them had a glazed look in their eyes. As two of them browsed past him he could smell the cannabis smoke which had been absorbed into their clothes, and their stained or missing teeth and poor skin condition also indicated their activity around various other types of illegal drugs.

'That's your problem there,' said Katy. 'Not Logan. And not Heidi. And there are more of these problems arriving later. Hundreds more. And they want to destroy the way of life we have on Arran. How many police officers do you have here?'

Kyle went silent as watched the customers carefully. Katy lowered her voice to a whisper, leaning her face towards him so nobody would hear her speak:

'Talk to them and ask them about the Noah's Ark.'

'Noah's… Ar…?'

'Shh!' interrupted Katy as she put her finger to her lips. 'Find the right moment. Maybe you should wait until you're out of uniform. Or better still, let me do it. Stand there quietly and listen to this.'

Katy spoke to the two customers standing in front of the till. One was a young man in his early twenties with long greasy hair. He was wearing a T-shirt with a picture of Bob Marley on the front. The other was older and in his mid-thirties, with shorter hair which was dyed orange on one side. He was wearing a denim jacket which was heavily decorated with enamel badges.

'You guys are here for the Spiritbeamer event?' asked Katy.

'Yeah sure are. You coming to join in?' asked the older man.

'Maybe.'

The two men looked at Kyle standing there in his police uniform.

'Don't worry about him,' she said as she faked a laugh. 'He's one of us.'

The men smiled.

'Cool,' said the younger man. 'So, get out of that ridiculous uniform and join the fun.'

'I want to be there when Noah's Ark arrives,' said Katy. 'And then later go to the protest.'

Again, they looked at Kyle.

'Don't worry about me,' said Kyle as he realised his best option now was to play along with Katy. 'I'll be out of uniform by then.'

'In that case, come along to the beach tomorrow afternoon.' said the older man.'

'Just do me a favour,' said Kyle. 'I need to tell the police to not worry about anything. So just tell me what I want to hear. I mean about the protest. When I get the call about a protest,

I just need to say that it's all peaceful. No damaging property or anything like that. Will that protest be on the beach?'

The older man smiled menacingly.

'It's an offshore protest,' he said confidently. 'So, you can't get more peaceful than that.'

'Otherwise there'd be too many police here,' laughed the younger man, clearly teasing Kyle.

Kyle smiled and nodded, concerned that any badly worded remark could possibly provoke unnecessary trouble.

'Okay, good,' he said. 'That's all I needed to hear. Enjoy the party. Maybe I'll see you all there.'

The two men left. Katy and Kyle stood looking at each other for a few moments trying to think more deeply about what these men had said.

'What was that about an ark?' asked Kyle.

'It's some sort of boat which will be carrying an awful lot of illegal dangerous drugs which they want to sell. They want to get locals involved, including kids, but I don't know where it's coming from.'

Kyle looked puzzled as he confided his thoughts to Katy:

'The storm's forecast to be fierce tonight and most of tomorrow. Maybe the whole event will be called off until the weather eases.'

Katy shook her head quietly as she opened a small cardboard box next to the till.

'What are you not telling me?' asked Kyle. 'You're holding something back.'

'Think about it. What better time to use Arran for a crime scene? And I mean a serious crime scene. You're going to be thoroughly out-numbered and the weather's going to stop the ferry sailing which means you won't be able to get police back-up from the mainland. And what was that he said about an offshore protest?'

Kyle left the shop. Meantime, Adam, the man Logan had noticed on the ferry, had made his way to Glen Sannox. As he entered the glen, he started walking around the tents without being questioned by anyone. He saw Kleo and Jasper sitting with a group of people around a small fire which was almost extinguished as the embers smouldered. Sitting behind the group was Sloucher. Kleo was sitting in her meditational lotus position with her eyes shut and the backs of her wrists resting on her knees.

Adam had seen her do this on previous occasions. He knew that she had no idea about how to meditate. On the grass next to her was a small drum. He'd often seen her drumming this instrument while pretending to enter some sort of meditational trance state in her attempt to demonstrate her faked spiritual abilities. Jasper was gently strumming a guitar when he saw Adam walking towards the group. Annoyed at Adam's presence, he stopped strumming. Adam approaching Kleo and stretched out his hand to tap her on the shoulder.

'Don't disturb her,' said one of the women in the group. 'Can't you see she's meditating?'

'She's not,' replied Adam as he shook her right arm.

Jasper dropped his guitar as he ran aggressively towards Adam.

Kleo immediately opened her eyes.

'Told you so,' said Adam sarcastically. 'Deep meditation my arse. We need to talk, and we need to do it now.'

'You can't do that,' said Jasper, positioning himself

uncomfortably close to Adam. 'You can't just come here and...'

'Shut it!' shouted Adam, 'Shut your mouth before I shut it for you.'

Meanwhile, in Sannox village, Robin was talking to a married couple living in one of its houses:

'I want to take pictures of the coastline from the hill up there.'

He pointed to their back garden:

'I could take the long way around the glen, but it would save me a lot of walking if I could be allowed to climb up from your garden.'

He presented them with a bottle of good quality French wine. Within minutes he was climbing up the steep cliff-like vertical slope in their back garden on his way to the Devil's Punchbowl.

At the same time, Logan was sitting quietly on the bonnet of his car at Sannox's small harbour. There were already several cars parked there, making it easy for him to stay there without being noticed. The road along Sannox village was occupied by about fifty cars parked on the grass verge.

He looked up at the clouds and noticed that the upper wind was increasing from the south west although Sannox bay was still sheltered. Looking over to the bay, he remembered Cod Rock: a little-known large boulder submerged offshore from the sandy bay. Some years earlier he recalled being able to borrow a rowing boat and venture out to fish for cod which often gathered around that rock. Few people know the exact location of the rock as it never becomes visible, even in low tide.

He let himself drift into a dream state as he remembered the previous years when he enjoyed watching the massive basking sharks swimming close to the shore. In this relaxed state, he looked at the water towards the sandy beach where a solitary seagull was floating on the water surface very close to a clump of floating seaweed near to where he knew Cod Rock was submerged. Nothing seemed suspicious until he noticed that the seagull seemed to be drifting southward while the seaweed remained in its position.

He collected a handful of pebbles from where he stood and placed them at approximate equal distances along the harbour edge before returning to his car. He crouched down and watched the seagull as it continued to drift slowly southward. He aligned himself such that, when he closed one eye, the first pebble he laid down was exactly in line between his eye and the clump of floating seaweed. He watched the seagull as it drifted towards his alignment with the second pebble. Gradually, the seagull drifted towards his alignment with the third pebble, and then towards the fourth one. After about a minute the seagull had drifted almost thirty metres from when Logan first noticed it, but the floating seaweed hadn't moved.

With this observation, the seaweed had to be anchored in its position. This activated his suspicion as to why a clump of seaweed was being anchored at Cod Rock. He concluded that the seaweed was being used as a marker for something hidden under the water.

He walked along the coastline towards the sandy bay. He noticed the blue car of Earlobe and Sloucher parked beside what had now become a substantial collection of other cars parked almost opposite the glen entrance. He continued walking over the standing stones across the mouth of the Sannox stream as it flowed into the sea. As he walked along the sand on the north of the bay, he could take a closer look at the seaweed, giving him a more realistic perspective of its position and distance in relation to the shore. He continued walking along the sandy bay to the lookout point at the north east, giving him a clearer picture of the coastline to the north of Sannox. He sat there on the grass for about twenty minutes thinking of possibilities. He knew there were drugs being hidden under the water at North Sannox, so why would there be anything else hidden at Cod Rock?

While he sat there, a small white boat speedboat with two engines arrived from the north, slowly towing a similar-sized wooden boat. The wooden boat had what appeared to be a green tent on it. It had no outboard engine. The speedboat pulled the wooden boat to within five metres from the anchored seaweed.

Logan laid down flat on the grass to stay hidden while watching through his binoculars. He could see just one man on the speedboat and after a few moments was able to recognise him as Badger. The wooden boat didn't have an occupant. On its side he could see the words 'Noah's Ark' painted on its bow. Badger threw a small anchor overboard then untied the tow rope which also had an anchor attached to its end. He dropped it overboard to anchor the wooden boat independently in its position. He then used a long pole with a hook to catch the floating seaweed and pull it out of the water. It was attached to a thin line which he then tied to some netting which dangled from the side of Noah's Ark.

Minutes later, Logan saw Adam running through Sannox village and into a white car which he then drove southward. Seconds later, he saw Sloucher running into his blue car which Logan had walked past earlier. Sloucher started his car and sped off southward.

Logan scanned his binoculars again towards the white speedboat. Badger was standing, also looking through binoculars, watching the same action. Just then there was a break in the clouds which enabled the sun to shine for a few moments. Concerned that the sun's reflection would make his binocular lenses shine brightly, Logan put them down behind the long grass and continued watching the boats with his naked eyes.

After the blue car was out of sight, Badger pointed his binoculars to the sandy bay and towards where Logan was. Logan flattened himself more into the long grass and shuffled backwards slightly to keep himself hidden. He lay there for several minutes knowing that if he would return to the sandy bay, or to his car, he'd be seen and perhaps be recognised by Badger.

Eventually, Badger pulled his anchor from the water and started the speedboat's engines. He steered the boat northward around the coast towards North Sannox, leaving Noah's Ark anchored in position near Cod Rock.

As soon as the speedboat was out of sight, Logan made his way back towards his car. He saw a few people walking along the coastline, but he didn't recognise any of them.

Meanwhile, Robin had reached the edge of the Devil's Punchbowl. With help from Logan's drone, he found the dead deer which the police had found on Sunday evening, but he couldn't see the human body which Logan had been adamant he'd seen. The deer was a young stag lying on its right side: an unusual find for several reasons. A legal hunter would more likely shoot a mature deer and remove it from the scene immediately. A young adult is unlikely to have died of natural causes, and to find a deer in an area of stones and rocks rather than on grazing ground is unlikely.

He looked more closely at it to try to analyse its possible cause of death. As he stepped across the rocks for closer inspection, he noticed darkened blood stains on the rocks in front of its head, indicating that the animal had been dragged backwards while bleeding. He also noticed darkened blood stains on the rocks to the side of its body. Its condition looked like it hadn't been dead for more than a couple of days. As he looked more closely he could see some sort of mess beneath its body which looked like its carcass had been split open.

He grabbed its head and rolled its body towards him. As the deer's carcass rolled over, to his horror, Robin could see the broken remains of a human, exactly as Logan had described. He could also see two bullet wounds on the deer's right side indicating that it had been shot through the heart. The human remains had been partially covered by stones, and the deer was small enough for just one person to be able to carry it or drag it to this position, yet big enough to cover and hide the remains of the human corpse.

Robin's memory flashed back to a time when he and his army unit had stumbled across a massacre in the desert. Two children had been murdered and their bodies had been hidden by a donkey which had been killed and dragged over their bodies. The stench of rotting corpses was overwhelming, but visually it was difficult to detect the children's remains. Anyone finding such a scene would believe that they'd found nothing more than the rotting carcass of a large dead animal. In such a remote landscape there would be no reason for anyone to want to move the animal.

This similar situation at the Punchbowl could keep the

human remains hidden until winter when there would be no hillwalkers. The combination of both corpses decomposing would supply enough nutrition to be absorbed into the ground to encourage more grass growth. That would make it possible that by the following summer, the human corpse would become permanently hidden.

Robin carefully checked the pockets of the dead man. The right outer pocket was buttoned closed. Robin unfastened the button and removed a passport which was wrapped in a small polythene bag. Without opening the bag, he placed it into his own pocket. The left outer pocket contained a pair of badly damaged sunglasses.

Meantime, Logan had returned to his car at Sannox harbour. He sat in his car for almost half an hour thinking about his next plan. He then drove north to the glen entrance and reversed into the narrow single-track road leading into the glen. Keeping his engine running he stepped out. As quickly as he could, he climbed over the small fence and slid down the slope to where he had hidden the parachute and the corpse's rucksack. He pulled them out from the small tunnel and put them into the car boot, then drove southbound to Brodick. He stopped briefly at the shop to talk with Katy.

'How are you getting on?' she asked.

'Slowly,' replied Logan. 'Something's not making sense and I can't figure it out. Has anyone been looking for me?'

'PC Kyle was in looking for you about an hour ago.'

'In that case I should go and find him.'

'Want to catch up later?' she asked. 'I'll be at my own place after work. You remember the address?'

'Yeah, alright, but I might be a bit late. I have a lot to do.'

He left the shop and drove south to Lamlash. As he drove into the village he noticed a larger boat anchored offshore to the south side of Lamlash Old Pier. It looked like an old fishing boat in a poor state of repair. There had been some significant restrictions of commercial fishing around the Arran coastline for several years, and particularly so in the water between Lamlash and the Holy Isle, so he was immediately suspicious at the sight of an old fishing trawler. He remembered Katy mentioning an old fishing boat which she'd seen near Brodick harbour. He stopped at the Old Pier to look more closely through his binoculars. It had been partially decorated with bunting made of small triangular multi-coloured flags. On the side of the boat were large capital letters, painted orange, saying: 'SAY NO SAY YES'. The letters appeared to have been scribbled carelessly with a paintbrush. Some of the paint had run down the sides of the hull from each letter. On deck, he could see Gremlin.

He used his mobile phone to make a snapshot of the boat before then switching off his flight mode to check the internet again for a weather forecast. In particular, he looked at the synoptic charts. The forecast cyclone had moved south as expected. He knew he had much work to do but he needed to do it before the storm took its grip on the island. Looking over towards the village he could see Shades, still wearing sunglasses, in his parked Mercedes, positioned discretely behind the small car park next to the Old Pier.

Logan drove to the police station. He was greeted by a police officer he hadn't yet met.

'I need to speak to PC Kyle please. Is he here?' asked Logan. 'Or PC Reynolds. My name's Logan.'

The officer's facial expression displayed his recognition of Logan's name.

'Just one minute, Sir.'

Kyle had been sitting just around the corner and had heard Logan talk. He immediately invited Logan to come to the interview room and asked the other officer to call Reynolds.

'Joyce will be here in a few minutes,' he said. 'Would you like a coffee while we wait?'

'Sure. Why not?'

The two men sipped their coffee at the interview table. Logan looked again at the synoptic chart on his phone app, concerned about when the winds will reach gale force.

'Katy says you flew the girl off the island.' said Kyle.

'That's correct.'

'So, where is she?'

'I handed her over to the mainland police. She's safe. Much safer there than she is here. I'm guessing nobody's reported her missing yet?'

'So which police station did you go to?'

'Glasgow. I took her…'

His sentence was interrupted by Reynolds as she entered the room. She hadn't expected to see Logan there.

'Logan tells me he flew off the island yesterday.' said Kyle,

Reynolds looked at Logan suspiciously.

'What… where's the little girl?'

Logan looked more impatiently at his watch, saying:

'Don't worry about the girl just now. She's in safe hands. But you have more immediate problems. Did you see that old rickety fishing boat in Lamlash Bay?'

'Yes, I saw it,' said Kyle. 'What do you know about it?'

'Not much except I think that's the protest boat, but nobody seems to know what the planned protest is about.'

'The skipper invited one of our officers onto it about an hour ago,' said Reynolds. 'It's being prepared for a birthday party for when the storm passes.'

'A birthday party?'

'Apparently so,' said Kyle. 'When I heard earlier about a planned protest I thought it was going to be a campaign about a proposed fish farm.'

'What fish farm?' asked Logan.

Kyle answered:

'There was a planning application made to start a new fish farm in Lamlash Bay but there were various reasons why the application was rejected. One of the many reasons it was rejected was that fish farming would cause a nuisance to recreational boating in the bay area. I was worried that there was going to be some sort of vandalism being planned against some of the privately-owned boats in the bay. But it seems now it's just a party being planned for tomorrow night. A party for protestants… members of the Orange Lodge. That's what caused the confusion. Someone's misheard something being said. It seems someone confused the word protestant with protester, so the rumour spread that there's an actual protest about something.'

'Who told you it was a party for protestants?'

'The skipper.'

Logan sat with his elbow on the table as he rested his chin into his hand thinking about what he'd just heard while slowly shaking his head in disbelief.

'You two… where are you from?' asked Logan. 'I can tell you both have Scottish accents, but where were you brought up?'

‘Thurso,’ said Reynolds. ‘Why do you ask?’

‘Morayshire,’ said Kyle. ‘Near Inverness.’

‘Ah yes, I know Thurso,’ said Logan enthusiastically. ‘I lived near Wick for a while. Beautiful area. Happy memories. Anyway, the point I was going to make is this: Neither of you were brought up being surrounded by sectarianism. I was. Even at five years old when walking to school I’d get strangers asking me if I was a Catholic or a Protestant, even though I’d no idea what the words meant. And in the areas around Glasgow, Manchester and Belfast there are these marches organised by the Orange Lodge. I never got interested enough in the subject to care much about what these people are trying to achieve. All I know is that it’s about Protestant superiority over Catholics and it’s based upon some historical event which happened hundreds of years ago. Something which nobody I know with half a brain actually cares about nowadays.’

Reynolds and Kyle had heard of this subject but were intrigued to hear what Logan was saying. Logan continued:

‘They don’t organise parties. They organise marches to intimidate people, and always in daytime. The point of these marches is that they want to be seen in public. They wouldn’t do that from a boat anchored offshore at night.’

‘But apparently this isn’t a protest,’ said Reynolds. ‘Just a party on a boat.’

‘Did the skipper actually invite a police officer on board?’ asked Logan. ‘Or did your police officer ask to look inside the boat?’

Kyle and Reynolds looked at each other, neither knowing how to answer that question.

Logan continued:

‘Did the police officer actually know the skipper?’

Again, Kyle and Reynolds didn't know the answer to that, prompting Logan to add:

'Why would anyone invite a police officer onto an old fishing boat which is being prepared for a birthday party, except to somehow disarm any suspicion by showing that there's nothing dodgy going on? At least not yet. And why would anyone plan a party on a boat at the start of a vicious storm? Any boat skipper would know the weather forecast. And what's the slogan painted on the side all about? Say no, say yes.'

Kyle and Reynolds listened carefully as Logan added:

'The people I met on the ferry told me they were going to a protest, but they had different ideas as to what they'd be protesting about.'

Reynolds deviated from the subject at that moment, asking:

'Where did you find the two packets of powder you gave me?'

'In a suitcase hidden under the water on the coastal track between the North Sannox camping ground and Lochranza. Did you find out what's in them?'

'We got the lab results back this morning. Cocaine was in the all-black packet and crystal meth in the packet with the red tape.'

'Expensive stuff.' said Logan.

'These two small packets have more street value than what I can earn in two years,' said Kyle.

'Well, there's plenty more where that came from but it's being guarded. What about the pills?'

'They're concerning us much more,' said Reynolds. 'We sent them across to the mainland for analysis and got a quick result. They're all nasty pills made from dangerous chemicals and some of them contain lethal doses of cyanide.'

'Cy… cyanide?' asked Logan.

'Yes. Cyanide. There were fourteen pills in that bag and five of them contained enough cyanide to guarantee almost immediate death to anyone swallowing just one pill. Anyone accepting these pills will be playing Russian Roulette with their lives. We need to get a public warning out in case there are more.'

'But for now, let's talk about the girl,' said Kyle. 'How do we contact the person who is looking after her?'

'Honestly, I don't know,' said Logan. 'I handed her over to the police in Glasgow then came back here. I don't know exactly where she is now except that she's safe.'

'And that leads me to my next question,' said Reynolds. 'Why did you come back here?'

'Various reasons,' said Logan. 'Firstly, my car's here. Secondly, my best friend is still on the island. He's gone to the Punchbowl to look for the dead body which I know is there, and by that, I mean the human body. And the third reason, the same reason I always use when I come here… I like the place.'

He looked at his watch again.

'I have to go. I'm going to take a chance of switching my phone on again but still assuming that the lines are being intercepted. Take out your notepads. I'm going to give you my phone number. And please give me yours. Both of you.'

'Where are you going?' asked Kyle.

'Oh, I don't know,' replied Logan. 'Maybe go hillwalking and catch up with Robin to help him find that body.'

'Why do I get the feeling you're not going hillwalking? Why do I think you're planning something else?' asked Kyle.

'Because I am,' replied Logan. 'If I find anything I'll tell you.'

Reynolds wrote her number on a piece of notepaper and gave it to Logan.

'I don't normally give this number out,' she said.

Logan entered her number into his phone, jokingly saying:

'Don't worry. I promise to not become your telephone stalker. Now, follow me to my car. I have a present for you.'

They walked out to his car. He looked around carefully to make sure nobody was watching. He opened its boot and gave Kyle the rucksack. He gave Reynolds the parachute.

'I've not tried looking inside the rucksack any more than I could already see. I didn't want to contaminate evidence.'

He left the police station and drove north. His phone rang, prompting him to pull over to answer it. It was Robin.

'Hi,' said Robin. 'I couldn't call you from the hills but I'm down again on my way to Brodick. Fancy going for something to eat?'

'Sure,' said Logan. 'Where?'

'How about your favourite chocolate cake shop in about twenty minutes?'

Logan looked again at the clouds as the wind seemed to be strengthening.

'Chocolate cake. How can I say no? But it'll have to be a quick snack.'

Logan drove north towards Brodick. He stopped at the shop briefly to talk to Katy.

'I spoke to Kyle and Reynolds,' he said. 'Anything new you can tell me before I meet Robin?'

'Not much. Just more weird people. And I heard something about a vicious fight somewhere around Brodick.'

'Fight?'

'I didn't see it. I just heard something about two guys getting into a fight over a bashed car. Where's Robin?'

'On his way to the castle. We're meeting there in a few minutes.'

'He can stay at my parents' house,' said Katy. 'As he said today, all the hotels and guest houses are full. I already spoke to them when they came to the shop earlier. They want to help.'

'Okay, thanks. I'll tell him.'

With a hint of shyness in her mannerisms, Katy also added:

'You can stay at my place if you want.'

'Eh… thanks. Actually… yes. I'll take you up on that. But like I said, I might be late.'

'I'll make sure I'm home when you get there.'

Logan left the shop and drove to Brodick Castle. Its exact history is uncertain, but it's believed to have been occupied by Vikings. It experienced various battles and ownerships over the years, eventually being rebuilt in the sixteenth century by the Dukes of Hamilton, then extended again in the nineteenth century. In the twentieth century it was given some restoration work which revealed a hidden dungeon built within its thick walls. As is the case with so many ancient buildings, this one carries some superstition of ghosts.

It's surrounded by a well-preserved luscious botanical garden which is filled with an abundance of trees and plants. Various tropical species thrive there due to Arran's mild climate.

Many of the island's visitors sail to Arran for no other reason but to visit the castle and its garden. Logan had spent much time visiting this site. His personal favourite part of the garden was its wooden Bavarian Summer House: a wooden structure built in the nineteenth century and beautifully decorated inside by thousands of pine cones covering its walls and ceiling.

He parked his car at the castle car park next to Robin's motorbike and made his way to the coffee shop. Two small ornamental cannons decorated either side of the door entrance as they had done for decades. As Robin knew, this was Logan's favourite place where he could buy a snack and some chocolate cake, then eat it outside the front of the castle which looks down the steep grassy slope into a mature woodland garden which stretches down towards Brodick bay. Often when he ate there, small birds would land on his table wanting to be fed crumbs.

As he walked towards the castle shop, Robin was already sitting at one of the small round tables outside with two plates, each with a large slice of chocolate cake.

'The waitress is bringing the coffee in a minute,' said Robin. 'We timed it nicely before the shop closes for bad weather. How are you getting on?'

'Ugh, slowly,' said Logan. 'You found the body?'

'Yes, exactly where you said it would be.'

Robin produced his phone and showed Logan the video clip he'd taken as he walked around the corpse, clearly showing the dead deer placed on top of it. He pulled a piece of rolled tissue paper from his jacket pocket and gave it to Logan who then unravelled it. Inside it were two copper-jacketed bullets.

'These were inside the deer,' said Robin.

Logan looked closely at them, saying:

'Nine-millimetre round-nose full metal jacket pistol bullets. Highly illegal for hunting.'

'And look at this,' said Robin.

He produced the passport he'd found.

'His name is, or was, Gerry,' said Robin. 'Assuming this is his passport. Gerry Philip Munro.'

Logan looked at the passport.

'That doesn't sound like a foreign name, so maybe he's not Heidi's dad like I was thinking.'

'He's already well hidden by the way he's been smashed into the rocks,' said Robin. 'And that deer… it reminds me of these poor kids' bodies being covered by that donkey in the desert.'

'I'll never forget that,' said Logan. 'And that corpse at the Punchbowl is difficult to see. Anyone just walking past that area won't see it because of the way it's been smashed into these rocks. And very few hillwalkers climb Coich na h'Oighe because it's the one of the most dangerous places to climb on the island. With winter almost here, almost certainly, nobody would have found that body until next summer at the earliest. So why go to the trouble of hiding him?'

'I'm guessing someone wants him hidden permanently,' suggested Robin. 'Presumably because someone wants people to think that he's still alive.'

'He was carrying cyanide pills,' said Logan.

'Cyanide?'

'Yep. The police analysed that packet I found next to him. It looked like it had fallen out of his pocket. A few pills of illegal drugs and some identical looking pills containing cyanide.'

'But still no connection to the other things that are going on?' asked Robin.

'No. Except I can't help thinking that these spirit people are being used as a decoy. And they're so stupid they'll trust anyone who waves a cannabis leaf at them.'

'Did you speak to Geordie yet since you got back?'

'No. Not yet.'

'What do you think I should do now?' asked Robin. 'I could go to the police with these pictures. But maybe best to leave it hidden for a few more hours until we hear from Geordie.'

'Agreed. And we're running out of time. I need to go.'

Logan finished his last bite of chocolate cake before telling Robin:

'Go to Katy's parents' house. They're expecting you.'

They walked down to the car park together. Logan followed Robin's motorbike to the exit gates where Robin turned right to go towards Brodick. Logan turned left, immediately noticing that the Noah's Ark was being towed into Brodick bay by the same speedboat boat he'd seen at Cod Rock. It was being towed closely enough to the shore that he could again recognise Badger steering it. Logan didn't stop driving. He made his way towards the campsite at North Sannox.

Two days earlier, the site was almost empty, but now it was full of tents, camper vans and cars. The black van was still there although it had been moved a few metres closer to the coastal path. A waist-high rope had been attached to two poles and placed across the path entrance. Four men stood at the rope as if to guard the path against anyone trying to walk along it. He didn't recognise any of them.

Various small campfires had been set up around the campsite although the wind was increasing and making it difficult to control them. He stepped out of his car to speak to a group of campers walking past.

'Hi there,' he said. 'What's the score? Do I just park and camp anywhere or do I have to check in with someone?'

One of the women answered:

'Just camp wherever you like. Nobody tells us where to camp.'

Her friend was staggering beside her, speaking with a slow drunk-like voice. She mumbled:

'Nobody tells us what to do, so camp where you like. Say yes, say no, to anything you like, Brother.'

This was the first time Logan had heard any reference to the slogan on the side of the fishing boat, further contradicting what had been said about it being used for a party rather than for a protest. In an attempt to get more information, he faked a laugh, asking:

'Ah, you're going to the protest too? I want to take part in that, but I don't know where to go.'

'Brodick,' said the first woman. 'After the beach party. Someone will guide us.'

Logan walked with them for a short distance hoping they would tell him more, but he didn't want them to suspect him as being too inquisitive. He changed the subject towards the rope blocking the coastal path.

'What's behind the rope?' he asked.

The first woman answered:

'The sea's going to get rough with the wind so it's not safe to walk along that path. That's why they've blocked it off.'

'Alright, sounds sensible,' said Logan. 'So, what's the protest actually about?'

'It's about whatever you want,' said the drunk woman, as she struggled to focus her eyes on him.

She moved her head left and right, being able to look at his face but she was unable to give him eye contact while her speech became increasingly slurred:

'Just say no or yes, to, em…'

At that point she lost her balance and fell to the ground, causing her to laugh almost uncontrollably. Logan had heard enough. He went back to his car and returned to Brodick where he could see that Noah's Ark had been anchored about two hundred metres offshore at the north of the bay.

'Perfect,' he muttered to himself.

Meanwhile, in Lamlash, Kyle and Reynolds had been called to visit the hospital.

In Brodick, Katy continued working in the shop. The last ferry had arrived, and several hundred people disembarked. Robin had gone to visit Katy's parents. The time passed, and Katy eventually finished her work. She went to her parents' house where Robin was sitting with them. The four of them sat around the kitchen table discussing the various events which were taking place. Both Katy and Robin placed their phones on the table, both eagerly waiting for Logan to call or send a text message. As time passed, the wind gradually increased substantially. Its noise became louder with each new gust. And with every new gust of wind, Katy and her father noticed that Robin was becoming increasingly anxious. To break the tension, Eric produced a bottle of whisky.

'You fancy a glass of Arran's finest?'

Robin politely shook his head.

'Thanks, but no. I can't. Logan might need me. I need to stay absolutely sober.'

Disappointed, Eric returned the unopened bottled to its cupboard.

'Maybe later,' smiled Robin. 'Once I know Logan's alright.'

'Do you know where he is?' asked Sandra.

Robin hesitated before answering.

'Not exactly. Although I think he's trying to get more information about what's going on.'

He didn't want to divulge more. He suspected that if he had told them what Logan was actually doing they would likely insist on getting additional help which could cause more problems.

After two hours, Logan switched his phone on to send a brief text to Robin, saying:

'*I'm good. Still doing things. I'll text again later. All OK with you?*'

Robin replied by text:

'*All OK here.*'

'*Good. Catch up later.*'

'Logan's doing good,' said Robin.

'What's he doing?'

Katy and her parents realised that Robin wasn't willing to give away too much information, so they spent the evening chatting about other things, until Sandra asked Robin:

'How long have you and Logan been friends?'

'We became friends in the army,' said Robin. 'We actually joined up at the same time and trained together at the same place. Normally after training, all the new recruits can expect to be sent anywhere, but we were sent to the same unit, so we spent most of our army days working together.'

'So, you've done a lot of travelling?' asked Sandra.

'Oh yes. We did plenty of that. Some nice places. Some not so great. The funny thing is, as a child I always wanted to travel the world, but now that I've done that, I've decided that the Scottish mountains are perfect. I've probably visited places which are equally as nice as Scotland, but never really found anywhere which I would say is nicer. Logan thinks the same, although he really likes Arran more than anywhere else.'

'Do you think he'd want to live here some day?' asked Katy.

'I know he would. But you know yourself, the job prospects aren't exactly fantastic here. I'm sure you've seen it yourself when people come to the island to start a business without realising just how much the island relies on summer tourism.'

'You're right about that,' said Eric. 'I've lost count of the times I've seen new businesses starting here. They usually thrive for about three months in summer and then fail by the autumn.'

The doorbell rang. Sandra went to answer it. Seconds later she returned to the kitchen, followed by Reynolds, no longer in police uniform.

'Hi Katy… Robin,' she said. 'I'm off duty but something's happened. I said I'd deal with it. I need to speak with Logan. I know it's a bad idea to call his phone, so I want to chat with him face-to-face. It's urgent.'

'Logan's out of touch just now,' said Robin. 'He's on the island somewhere but I don't think he's going to appear until either very late tonight or tomorrow morning.'

'What's wrong?' asked Katy. 'What's so urgent?'

'Can anyone tell me exactly where the little girl is? Logan said he'd taken her to Glasgow, but where exactly?'

'Logan took her to the police in Glasgow. They knew nothing about her, but they've taken her and they're keeping her safe somewhere, but I don't know where exactly.'

'How can you be sure he took her to the police?'

Katy glanced worryingly at Robin. He quietly nodded in agreement that Katy should tell the truth.

'Because… I was with him. I was with him when we went to Glasgow and handed her over.'

Katy's parents were surprised at this news. They had no idea that Katy had left the island.

'Katy's right,' said Robin. 'She and Logan took Heidi to safety. And she's in safe hands with the police in Glasgow. Exactly which police officer is guarding her now, we don't know. But she's safe. So, Heidi is not a priority just now.'

'Heidi's just become a priority,' said Reynolds in a slightly raised voice. 'This evening a man was taken to hospital with serious injuries from a fight he'd got into after a car chase by one of these people camping at Glen Sannox. He's being treated under anaesthetic right now. But before he went to theatre he said his daughter had been kidnapped and brought here.'

Katy and her parents looked surprised at this news. Robin sat there un-phased, gazing at his mug of tea as he said:

'Well, so much for these spirit idiots pretending to be full of peace, love and spiritual mindfulness or whatever it is they claim to preach. Maybe tomorrow when he wakes from the anaesthetic you can get more information from him. Did he mention his daughter's name? Logan was never sure if Heidi is the girl's actual name. So, if this guy's daughter has a different name, we can't be sure if his daughter is the same girl, or maybe there are more children being kidnapped. But we have more immediate problems on the island just now. A massive drugs problem. And I mean massive. And a dead body at the Punchbowl.'

Reynolds answered defiantly:

'We sent two officers to look for that body. They searched the exact area where Logan told them to look, and the only dead creature was a deer. So, to be honest, I'm starting to become suspicious at Logan's judgement here.'

'I can assure you there's nothing wrong with Logan's judgement on anything he deals with,' said Robin in a defensive tone. 'If Logan told me there were little green aliens landing from Mars, it would be because little green Martians had landed.'

Katy detected an awkwardness in this disagreement, sensing that it was perhaps about to turn into an unpleasant confrontation because she knew Robin and Logan were the best of friends with a high sense of loyalty to each other. In an effort to resume a calm atmosphere, she quickly changed the subject, asking Reynolds:

'What nationality is the man in hospital?'

'I don't know that yet,' said Reynolds. 'It was the hospital staff who notified us of what the man said. He had already been taken to theatre when we got the call.'

She sat down and gratefully accepted a mug of hot tea which Sandra had been brewing.

'Tomorrow will be an interesting day,' said Katy. 'I find it strange that I hadn't heard anything about the Spiritbeamer gathering until a few days ago.'

'Likewise,' replied Reynolds. 'I only heard about it at the weekend. Whoever organised it managed to keep it quiet.'

'I think I know how they managed that,' said Katy. 'I overheard people talking in the shop. Several events were planned in other areas. Some in Ayrshire. Any leaked information to police or rival dealers would make them look in these places instead of Arran. From what I heard, it seems that the organisers set up some private chatrooms on social media and managed to get hundreds of members to join each one. Then they were all told to go to different Spiritbeamer gatherings in different places on the mainland. Each gathering had its own organiser. It was only at the last minute, the organiser from each gathering got told to come here.'

'Why the sudden change of plan?' asked Sandra.

'I think I can explain that one,' said Robin. 'There's a big drugs haul already on the island. It's probably been here for several months or maybe years. Arran's wilderness makes it an easy place to hide drugs. But for selling these drugs, organising regular drug runs between here and the mainland would increase the risks of getting caught by police or by rival drug gangs. So, the dealers are better to sell as much as they can in one event organised at short notice to minimise police numbers and rival dealers.'

Katy added:

'While the police have been looking into the events planned for tonight on the mainland, they were being led to believe that the Spiritbeamer event on Arran was just going to be a small gathering which wouldn't require police priority, especially with a storm developing.

'How do you know all this?' asked Reynolds.

'Logan spoke with the Glasgow police in detail,' said Katy. 'His friend is a senior police officer there. Almost retired. We stayed at his house last night and the two of them spent hours talking, long after I'd gone to bed.'

Reynolds' face was clearly surprised at this news as she leaned forward and quietly asked:

'What? I mean, who is this senior police officer?'

'I don't know his actual rank,' said Katy. 'I think Detective Inspector or maybe Superintendent. Whatever he is, his name's Geordie Buchanan.'

Reynolds raised her eyebrows in recognition of that name. She sat back in her chair and took in a deep breath, partially relieved in her own surprise at this answer.

'You know him?' asked Katy.

'He was one of our trainers at police college. He's one of the most highly respected police officers in the area.'

'Most of these campers wouldn't have known there was going to be an event on Arran until yesterday or today,' said Katy. 'So, suddenly there could be as many as two thousand of them arriving here while the police across the water are already pre-occupied looking at the other mainland events being planned for tomorrow night... and also looking for grey squirrels.'

'Grey squirrels?' asked Eric. 'What?'

'Grey squirrels would devastate the wildlife if any breeding pair were to arrive on the island,' said Reynolds. 'Apparently, someone was trying to smuggle them here, but I don't know for what purpose. The mainland police have been checking the cars boarding the ferry at Ardrossan.'

'When did the mainland police notify you of this?' asked Eric.

'Saturday.'

'I don't know about any squirrels,' said Robin. 'But the organisers who have been here since before the weekend are now successfully preaching to their followers that it's their spiritual mission to convert Arran into Scotland's long-term drug-dealing capital. They're using the storm like a sort of one-way valve. The drugs, the addicts and the drug dealers have been able to come here, and nobody can remove them from the island until the storm eases. Police back-up can't get here, and rival drug gangs can't get here either. Nobody can escape the island until after the storm, so the dealers can apply as many persuasion techniques and threaten as much violence as they want to force trade on their buyers and on anyone who tries to stop them. And just to add some more excitement into the fiasco, they're also planning some sort of protest.'

'But they don't know what they want to protest about,' added Katy.

'What sort of drugs are being dealt?' asked Sandra.

'Various,' replied Robin. 'These Spritbeamer people who are here for the party are more interested in the less expensive stuff. They don't realise they're being used as a distraction to hide the more expensive drug deals.'

Reynolds, still holding her mug of tea nodded her head in her understanding of what she was hearing.

'Any particular reason why they chose Glen Sannox to set up camp?' she asked. 'Glen Rosa is nearer.'

'Maybe,' said Robin. 'But I think you should ask Logan that question. Tomorrow night in Brodick, the spirit people in Sannox will be sold cheap low-grade and deadly drugs from a boat which they already call Noah's Ark. It's all set up to make police and drug-dealer rivals think that the story ends there.'

'Do you know how much money's worth of drugs are being sold tomorrow?' asked Eric.

Robin answered:

'If Logan's prediction is correct about how much of each type of drug is already on this island, based on what he's already found, the main dealers will make millions of pounds tomorrow and never be seen again.'

'So, that Noah's Ark… will all the drugs will be on that boat?' asked Sandra.

'I'm not sure but I think there are more drugs coming in from elsewhere,' said Robin. 'Also, according to what Logan heard from the campers, and from what I heard last night, tomorrow it's going to be securely anchored off Brodick bay where it'll be inaccessible until the storm eases.'

He looked at a website page on his phone showing the weather synoptic chart. It displayed the isobars of the approaching cyclone. The website provided the feature allowing him to select future times of day and night, each time showing the forecast position of the storm.

'Look here,' he said, scrolling through the hours. 'The eye of the storm should reach here at about seven o'clock tomorrow evening. That should provide a break in the weather for about an hour. Only at that time will the water be calm enough for the Ark to be accessed by someone in a small boat or dinghy to bring the drugs to shore. My guess is that each party-goer will have already paid money and will have been given some sort of token to exchange for packages. Some of them will hide whatever they buy. Others will try to sell their stuff to local kids, and some will try to take it home with them.'

There were a few moments of silence while the others processed what Robin was telling them. Eventually, Sandra asked:

'But why have everything on a boat? Why not just have all their drugs in a big van or something? As you say, two thousand people very much out-number the police. Going to the trouble of using a boat seems pointless.'

‘I think it’s for extra protection against rival dealers,’ said Robin. ‘A boat in stormy seas is difficult or impossible to get to. One of my concerns is that some of these party goers might be crazy enough to try to swim out to it in the storm.’

‘Surely nobody would try to swim out to a boat in these waters, in these weather conditions,’ said Sandra.

Robin sighed as he looked at Sandra, momentarily letting his memory take him back to previous events he’d witnessed, telling her:

‘When drug addicts try to buy drugs, I don’t think there’s any limit to their desperation.’

He then showed them the website on his phone showing the tidal times.

‘If these people try swimming out to that boat or row out to it in a small dingy without an engine they’ll likely be swept out to sea because the tide will start to go out at almost the same time as the eye of the storm comes overhead. An outward tide and even a light westward wind blowing away from the shore will almost certainly cause people to drown.’

‘The drug dealers won’t care, will they?’ said Eric.

‘Correct,’ said Robin. ‘According to Logan, the dealers in Glen Sannox were determined to get the cash from their Spiritbeamer gathering by tonight at the latest. If these people manage to get their drugs off that boat tomorrow night, there will be chaos on the beach. That’ll cause a massive distraction from the other, bigger, multi-million-pound drug deal which we think has been planned. On the other hand, if people start getting swept out to sea, there will be just as much chaos.’

‘And some of the drugs we’ve analysed will guarantee deaths,’ added Reynolds.

'I know about the cyanide pills,' said Robin. 'so, it will either look like a successful drug deal involving the lesser expensive drugs being sold to a cult group with a few deaths due to cyanide, or it'll look like a failed attempt with drownings. Whatever happens, the police will struggle to cope with the mayhem in Brodick while the bigger drug deal will be happening somewhere else on the island. So, whether or not people will die tomorrow evening, either way it'll be a win-win situation for the big-time dealers who can do whatever they're planning elsewhere without being disturbed.'

'Geordie hasn't been in touch with you has he?' asked Katy.

'No,' replied Reynolds.

'That's because there's suspicion about the phone conversations being intercepted.'

'I know about that,' said Reynolds.'

'He'll be in touch,' said Katy.

'But not until tomorrow,' added Robin. 'It's already too late to get police back-up. But he'll be in touch. And when he does, he'll tell you to trust Logan.'

'How exactly do you know Geordie?' asked Reynolds.

'Logan introduced me to him. Geordie had been put in charge of a particularly complicated case a long time ago. Actually, two cases. Logan helped him with these and put himself at a lot of risk by doing so.'

He produced the tissue with the bullets rolled up in it, telling her:

'I think you should see this.'

He removed the bullets from the tissue and placed them on the table in front of her. He then picked up his mobile phone to scroll through the photographs. He showed the phone screen to Reynolds as he spoke again:

'This is the dead deer your police officers found. It was killed by these bullets.'

He scrolled to the next photograph.

'And hidden beneath that dead deer is this human body, very dead and very broken, exactly as Logan described. Judging by the condition of the body, both myself and Logan agree that the bloke fell from a great height onto these rocks.'

Reynolds looked closely at the pictures as Robin scrolled through them, showing the corpse from different angles.

'When did you find this?' she asked.

'This afternoon,' said Robin.

'Why didn't you notify us at the time?'

'Well, it was more like late afternoon, or early evening. I couldn't call you from the Punchbowl because there's no phone signal there, and of course I wouldn't have told you by phone because of the possibility of someone intercepting phone calls. And I only got back here about a couple of hours before you arrived.'

Looking over and smiling at Eric and Sandra, he added:

'These good people had a hot bath and a meal waiting for me so that took priority.'

Reynolds studied the pictures on Robin's phone. She noticed the spider's web tattoo on the left side of the dead man's neck and the dark-green jacket with the blue patch on its right sleeve.

Robin gave her the passport and the damaged sunglasses which he'd found, telling her:

'His name's Gerry Munro.'

'Gerry Munro? I've met him,' said Reynolds. 'I met him on Saturday.'

Robin could see that Reynolds was troubled by the dilemma of this situation. Robin knew he had to persuade her to not resort to any action without careful consideration, so he spoke slowly and quietly to her:

'Don't do anything about this just now. Think of it this way. For now, Heidi's father might be that the guy in hospital. Or Heidi's father might have been this dead guy who was found on a hillside, with a parachute ripcord, only a mile away from Heidi who was found with a parachute. And someone was in a rush to cover him. Literally.'

'It's all too weird,' said Katy.

'And it's all too stormy and getting dark soon,' added Robin. 'You're not going to get a forensics team to that body tonight, especially with the storm strengthening.'

Eric joined in, saying:

'Heidi's safe. The guy in hospital is asleep on anaesthetic. And there's nothing anyone can do to help a dead guy.'

'And Geordie will be in touch soon,' said Katy.

Sandra had been sitting quietly listening, eager to contribute to the conversation:

'Nothing like this has ever happened on Arran before. Perhaps you need to interview that man you say is in hospital before assuming anything. Or, like Robin says, maybe there's more than one kidnapped child.'

They spoke more for another two hours, having moved into the lounge for more comfort on the sofa and armchairs where they allowed the conversation to drift into different subjects. Looking at the clock, Reynolds eventually stood up to leave, saying:

'When you see Logan, please tell him to contact me.'

As she was about to leave the house, Robin quickly approached her from behind and quietly said:

'Joyce. Just a quick word… please.'

She turned to him, listening. He continued:

'Geordie will be in touch. Logan explained to him about the possibility of the phone lines being compromised. Of course, we're not sure about it but that's what we suspect. But anyway, please don't tell anyone what was discussed here tonight until Geordie contacts you. Logan's busy tonight. He'll be finished soon. Geordie will contact you.'

Reynolds quietly acknowledged with a slight nod, saying nothing as she left the house.

Eventually, Robin's phone received another text message from Logan. It read:

'*OK again. I'll be finished soon.*'

'He'll be finished soon,' said Robin.

'I'm getting tired, so I'll go home,' said Katy as she stood up to leave.

'I can give you a lift,' offered Robin.

'Thanks, but I'm just five minutes away. If Logan gets in touch with you, can you tell him I'll put my door key under the mat?'

She left the house to walk home. Robin continued chatting to her parents until eventually they went to their bed, leaving Robin sitting up waiting for news from Logan. Eventually at almost two o'clock in the morning, Logan sent Robin a text:

'*Anyone awake? All OK here.*'

Robin replied by text:

'*All gone to bed. Go to Katy's flat. Key under mat.*'

Logan went to Katy's apartment and let himself in quietly.

As he had done the previous night at Geordie's, he went to the bathroom from where he could see that Katy had gone to bed and was already sleeping. As quietly as possible, he made his way barefoot to the lounge sofa where he placed his small blue holdall next to him as he sat down. He tried browsing some pictures on his mobile phone, but he was exhausted and fell asleep in his upright seated position.

CHAPTER 7

Wednesday September 22nd Autumn Equinox

Logan awoke at seven o'clock in the morning. As had happened at Geordie's house, he was momentarily confused when he opened his eyes and was unable to immediately recognise his surroundings in daylight. A duvet had been placed over him during the night without waking him. Through the open lounge door, he could see Katy in the kitchen dressed in only a long T-shirt which hung down almost to her knees. He walked into the kitchen, his clothes filthy with mud and grass stains and two noticeable rips in his trousers.

'Sorry I got back later than I'd planned last night.'

'I knew you were busy,' she said as she handed him a large mug of coffee. 'I don't know what you were doing but I sort of expected you'd be very late.'

'After I finish this coffee, do you mind if I have a shower? I got a bit scruffy last night.'

Katy looked at him and the filthy condition of his clothes.

'Did you get into some trouble last night?'

'No. No trouble. Just a bit busy. I'll tell you about it later. And I have some fresh clothes to change into.'

Katy showed him to the bathroom where he enjoyed a hot shower and freshen-up. He returned to the lounge fully dressed in denim jeans, white trainers, a dark blue T-shirt and a lightweight brown leather jacket, all of which were brand new with the price tag still dangling from the jacket. Katy noticed him removing the price tag.

'Where did you buy the jacket?' she asked. 'I don't know any shops on Arran which sell that style.'

'I bought it when we were in Glasgow.'

'But you were empty handed when we came back from Glasgow.'

'Ah yes, I had it specially delivered,' he said as he held back a mischievous smile. 'Like I said, I'll tell you everything, but meantime, what are your plans for today? Are you working at the shop?'

'Yes, I have to work. And you have to go to the police station. Some guy's in hospital claiming to be the father of a little girl who's been kidnapped.'

The surprise element of that comment made Logan drop the price tag he'd detached from the jacket.

'Really? I mean, eh, okay. I'd better go there now.'

'Catch up later?' asked Katy.

'Yes, for sure. Come on. I'll give you a lift to the shop.'

'It's alright. I'll walk. I have a few things to do before going there. You go on. I'll see you later.'

Logan drove to Lamlash and parked outside the police station there. The wind had strengthened considerably since the previous evening. He sat in the car for a few minutes to gather his thoughts. If Heidi was somehow linked to all the other criminal action being planned, there was still a possibility that the man at the hospital could be a last-minute desperate attempt to locate her and use her as some sort of ransom. It could all be a coincidence, but why would her father suddenly appear on the scene four days after Logan had found her, and at a time which was only a few hours away from what could potentially become the biggest drug deal in British history? This wouldn't be a good time to trust anything or anyone suspicious, especially with the unsolved mystery of the dead man at the Punchbowl. Perhaps this could be some sort of trap. With that in mind, he entered the police station. As he walked in, one of the other officers was sitting behind the reception desk. Logan showed him his driving licence for identification.

'Hi, I'm Logan. PC Reynolds wants to talk with me.'

'Just one minute, Sir,' said the officer.

He stood up and went into the back room. Almost immediately Kyle appeared.

'Logan, thanks for coming. Come through to the back. We need to talk.'

Kyle led Logan to the back room where they both sat down.

'I heard there's a man in hospital claiming to be Heidi's dad,' said Logan.

'Well, yes, but he says her name's not Heidi. It's Karina.'

'Karina? If that's her name I wasn't even close. But are you sure about that? Is Karina her real name, or is Karina another missing child?'

'Her description fits,' said Kyle. 'But he didn't have any pictures of her to show us. Do you have any saved on your phone, so we could show him?'

Logan checked his pockets.

'Ah, sorry no. I changed my clothes this morning and I left my phone at Katy's. I can go get it. But, even if we show him pictures and he claims to recognise her from them, that doesn't prove anything. Did he show you any identification?'

Kyle became visibly uneasy at this question. He knew Logan was trying to help but it would be a breach of police confidentiality if too much was discussed between them.

'I can't…'

'Sorry,' said Logan. 'I'm not being nosey. Just getting carried away with myself.'

Logan remembered from the previous day, seeing a man running through Sannox while being chased by Sloucher.

'Well, in case it's of any use, I did see a man running, and, eh, no, forget that. It was probably nothing. Anyway, is there anything else about this situation that you're allowed to discuss with me?'

Kyle shook his head.

'No. I really can't say more.'

'If he could show me a picture of his daughter I'd be happy to help,' said Logan. 'And if I knew where she was I'd tell you, but only the police in Glasgow have that information. Meantime, I have a present for you.'

He produced a polythene bag from his pocket. It contained about two hundred white pills identical to the ones he'd found beside the body at the Punchbowl.

'I think I know where there are more, but I haven't been able to get to them yet. I'll go back to Brodick and get my phone. Give me about an hour. You have my number.'

He left the police station and noticed that the protest boat was still anchored offshore in the same position as before. Although the wind was strengthening, the sea was less rough in Lamlash bay than he had seen earlier in Brodick bay.

He drove to Brodick which had become even more stormy than it had been just half an hour earlier. The mini golf was closed. There were only four cars parked at the shop where Katy was working. He parked there and went into the shop. There were no customers except for two teenage boys sitting in the tea-room area, talking to each other. Katy was keeping herself busy reorganising some new stock.

'You went to the police station?' she asked.

'Yeah, but not much happening. The guy's still in hospital I think, but I don't know any more.'

He looked around the shop, commenting:

'No customers?'

'No. Almost none. The storm's keeping everyone indoors. And we're closing soon because of the weather. What are your plans?'

'Nothing immediate,' said Logan. 'Staying indoors might be a really great idea. I can wait for you to finish or I can come back and pick you up if you want.'

Katy looked at her watch.

'I don't have much to do. Just a few things to put away. And I brought your phone in. You'd left it on charge and forgotten to take it. I knew you'd need it.'

She gave him his phone as she pointed to the tearoom corner with her head.

'Go over there and have a snack. I'll come over when I finish.'

Logan went over to the tearoom area and sat at the table next to where the two teenage boys were sitting. There were two girls cleaning behind the counter to prepare for shop closure. The boys appeared to be in their late teens. One of them had short curly hair and was wearing a dark grey waterproof jacket. The other had thicker straight hair and was wearing a sheep-skin-lined denim jacket. Again, with Logan's habit of mentally nicknaming strangers, he decided on *Curly* and *Sheepskin* as suitable names for them. He overheard them talking to each other, mostly about cars. Curly had been looking at advertisements hoping to buy his first car. Logan invited himself into the conversation by calling over to their table:

'Hi lads. Sorry to interrupt, but what sort of car are you wanting to buy?'

Curly looked over to Logan, surprised but welcoming the attention.

'I don't know. Just an old cheap car that I can work on and do it up.'

'You're good at that?' asked Logan. 'Fixing old cars?'

'My dad had a garage in Kilmarnock,' said Curly. 'He used to let me help him work on cars there.'

'That's great,' said Logan. 'People who can fix cars can save themselves a lot of money. You have a driving licence?'

Curly grinned:

'I passed my driving test a few weeks ago. All I need is a car.'

'You have a job?' asked Logan. 'I'm not prying. It's just that cars tend to be expensive things to keep on the road.'

'Yeah I know. I'm an apprentice joiner, working for a company in Irvine.'

'Again, that's great because when you get your own house you'll save yourself a fortune if you buy something old and carry out your own repairs and renovations on the place. Unlike me. I can do joinery, but I'm crap when it comes to finesse like getting all the edges squared off.'

'That's the part I'm still learning,' said Curly.

Logan looked to Sheepskin, asking him:

'What about you? You have a car?'

'Yep. That's it there,' he said as he pointed out to the car park at an old red Vauxhall with what appeared to be partially repaired damage on the driver's door.

'Jamie here helped me to restore it. It was in a worse state when I got it.'

On that answer, Logan realised that Curly's real name was Jamie.

'Okay, so you're both car enthusiasts,' said Logan admiringly.

Looking out at the Vauxhall he added:

'And I see you like sensible cars. Too many guys of your age are only interested in buying the fastest thing they can find.'

Sheepskin agreed, replying:

'I lost a good friend a couple of years ago because he was driving too fast. I'm not interested in speeding.'

Logan raised his thumb in agreement with that comment.

'What car do you drive?' asked Jamie.

'I have that old Ford parked out there,' said Logan. 'It's an old car but it does the job.'

'Well, maybe it's an old car,' said Jamie, 'but it's better than not having one.'

'What are you guys doing here? Like me perhaps? Visiting and then getting stranded because of the storm?'

'Not exactly,' said Sheepskin. 'We're cousins and we're staying with our gran in Whiting Bay for a few days, so we were planning to be here anyway.'

'Ah yes. I like the Whiting Bay area. I like that walk towards the Glenashdale falls. And that Giant's Graves area near it.'

'Our gran stays just beside that walk,' said Jamie. 'That's her favourite walk so we go along that path all the time when we take her dog out.'

'So, you're regulars to the island then?'

'Yeah, we come here every few weeks. We're hoping to go mackerel fishing after this storm calms down. Our gran's neighbour has a small boat we sometimes use.'

'I used to go fishing in Lamlash Bay many years ago,' replied Logan. 'I used to borrow or hire a small boat until the bay became a no-fishing zone.'

'Yeah that's right,' said Jamie. 'So now we go over to Whiting Bay. But the last time we fished there we didn't catch anything.'

'We have a back-up plan' laughed Sheepskin. 'If we don't catch anything, we buy some fish from the butcher in Blackwaterfoot. Then we don't go back to Gran empty-handed.'

Jamie nodded and smiled, adding:

'And Gran thinks we've caught them. She says freshly caught fish tastes better than anything she can buy in the shops. But she can't tell the difference, so we don't tell her.'

Logan made a slight laugh at this while admiring the enthusiastic attitudes of the two teenagers.

'Yeah, it's good to have a back-up plan,' he said.

He was about to say more but he stopped speaking, immediately changing his facial expression to a more serious pensive look before hesitantly asking:

'Back-up plan? So, your original plan was to go fishing at Lamlash, but then your back-up plan was to go fishing at Whiting Bay, and so the butcher's shop is your… back-up… to… your back-up plan?'

The teenagers were cautious to talk as they noticed his serious look and change of voice tone.

Logan turned his head away from the boys and looked out the window at the rough sea. Deep in thought, he rested his mouth and chin into the palm of his hand as his elbow rested on the table.

'Did we say something wrong?' asked Jamie.

Logan continued looking out of the window for a few moments before jolting himself back into the conversation with the boys.

'Eh, no. No. You've just reminded me of something I hadn't thought about.'

He considered that perhaps these two boys could have noticed something unusual happening which he wasn't yet aware of. Trying to appear casual, Logan asked:

'One thing I like about Arran is that it doesn't change much as the years go by. Or maybe you can correct me on that. Have you noticed anything different since the last time you were on the island? I usually find the visitors are either mostly Scottish and English, but this week I'm noticing a lot of other accents.'

Sheepskin spoke:

'Nothing really. A few obnoxious people going about. Seems like they're not enjoying their holiday.'

'And that crappy boat anchored off Lamlash pier,' said Jamie. 'Apparently it's being used for some protest. But it looks like it's falling to bits. No idea where it came from or where it's going but it doesn't look seaworthy to me. And that weird guy on it is really creepy. He's been going about pestering the girls in Lamlash. I think he's a bit of a perv.'

'Actually, I saw that boat,' said Logan. 'I don't know much about boats, but I'll agree it looks like a floating heap of scrap.'

'I think it was towing a raft a couple of days ago,' said Jamie. 'They've anchored the raft in Whiting bay, but I don't know what anyone's going to do with it. And there was a helicopter a few days ago doing something around the Holy Isle. Not sure what that's all about. Maybe rich tourists.'

'I saw a helicopter on Saturday,' said Logan. 'A black one with a yellow stripe down the side.'

'Yeah that's it,' said Sheepskin. 'We saw it on Friday when we were out in our kayaks.'

'You said it was doing something on Holy Isle. Did you see where it landed?'

'It looked like it was hovering around the south end of Holy Isle. Not sure if it landed, but it looked like it was trying to.'

Logan pulled his mobile phone from his pocket and looked at his maps app. He zoomed into the south end of the Holy Isle and showed it to the two boys.

'Where do you reckon it would have landed?'

The boys looked at the screen picture. Sheepskin touched the screen at an area of coastline to the east of the Holy Isle's 'Inner Lighthouse'.

'There's an area of flat land there,' he said. 'And it's sheltered by that steep slope.'

Logan zoomed the picture out to see the wider area. Any helicopter parked in that area would be sheltered from the worst of the storm. It would also out of sight from anyone.

'When were you last in Whiting Bay?' he asked.

'This morning,' replied Sheepskin. 'But we weren't fishing.'

'And that raft was still there?'

'Yep. And another one was towed around the point and anchored in Lamlash bay.'

'How big is it?' asked Logan.

'I'd say the one in Lamlash is probably big enough to park four cars onto it. The one in Whiting Bay is a lot smaller.'

Again, Logan went silent as he looked out of the window, thinking deeply. He looked at his watch then stood up to leave.

'Nice talking to you guys. Maybe I'll see you around.'

He walked across the shop to speak with Katy.

'Something new just came along,' he said. 'I need to go somewhere. I'll call you when I can.'

He left the shop and started driving south towards Lamlash. He parked his car on the sea front and stopped the engine as he sat there looking out to sea. At the south end of the bay, about two hundred metres offshore was the raft, just as the boys had told him. He looked at it through his binoculars and could see that it was constructed from what appeared to be wooden boards strapped onto canoe-shaped flotation devices. Whatever this raft's purpose was, he knew there was nothing he could do about it at that moment.

Attached to one of its corners was a thin pole about a metre tall with streamers attached to the top which clearly indicated the wind direction.

He looked again at the satellite picture of Arran on his phone screen and zoomed into the area at the south east of the Holy Isle. Drawing a straight line on the screen with his phone app, the best place for him to actually see around the south end of the Holy Isle's coastline would be to follow Arran's coastal road south through Whiting Bay towards Largybeg, about half a mile north-east of Dippen on Arran's south coast.

He drove there and stopped in a lay-by on the stretch of road which was raised well above the coastline. From there he could easily see the south end of Holy Isle without his view being restricted by the rising sea spray. The cloud base was low, covering the top of the Holy Isle, but the visibility was good below the clouds, giving him a good view of its coastline, just over three miles offshore from where he stood. As he looked through his binoculars, the strong blustery wind was making it difficult to keep his binoculars steady. He stabilised his arms by resting his elbows on the car roof and focused on the south point of the Holy Isle. He had a limited view of its coastline, but he could see the area the boys had mentioned.

He closed his eyes for a few moments, allowing himself to remember some of his earlier hillwalking ventures during which times he had visited the Holy Isle. He enjoyed being surrounded in its natural habitat which has always been almost entirely undisturbed by humans. Eriskay ponies, Soay Sheep and Saanen goats are the most noticeable animals living there, living freely in their own natural habitat. It's believed that this species of goat has been living there for several centuries. There was a period of several decades when it had been traditional for these goats to have their horns painted orange. Then in nineteen ninety-two the ownership of the island was taken over by the Buddhists who preferred the more natural approach of leaving animals undisturbed.

A sudden gust of wind shook him from his dream state, reminding him that he was trying to fulfil a purpose with limited time available to do so. He focused his binoculars again on the coastline and noticed an object which he couldn't identify on the exact spot the boys had mentioned. He was looking for a helicopter, but what he could see was a dull coloured object in a place where he knew there was no building or structure of any sort. In the darkening overcast conditions it was difficult for him to accurately determine the colour of what he was looking at. Perhaps it was grey, green or brown. Whatever it was, something un-natural was there, sheltered from the west wind and out of sight from anywhere except from a few places along the Ayrshire mainland coast which was at least fourteen miles away. After ten minutes of closely watching, he sat back into his car.

His mobile phone started ringing.

'Logan?'

'Speaking.'

'It's PC Kyle here. Can you come for a talk?'

'Yeah sure. I'll be with you in a few minutes.'

Logan drove back to the police station at Lamlash. Kyle met him at the main door and asked:

'Kleo and Jasper are here. They're being, well, not the easiest people to reason with. Would you be prepared to speak to them?'

'Of course.'

He led Logan through into the interview room where the parachute had been laid out on the floor. Reynolds was already there with Kleo and Jasper.

'Lo... Logan?' asked Kleo. 'What's going on?'

Although reluctant to speak with her, he quietly replied:

'Actually, I'm not sure.'

Reynolds pointed to the parachute and asked Logan:

'Please can you help us identify this.'

'Sure. It's a twenty-eight-foot round emergency parachute with a three-pin ripcord.'

'No,' said Jasper. That's our tepee.'

Kleo agreed, adding:

'And he stole it when he took Karina.'

She then looked at Logan and asked him:

'Why are you here?'

Logan was confused. Knowing better than to interfere with police questioning, he said nothing, allowing Reynolds to do the talking.

'So, what exactly is this?' asked Reynolds. 'A tepee or a parachute? Because it looks like a parachute to me.'

'That's our tepee,' repeated Jasper. 'We… well, our friend… he put it up in Glen Sannox on Saturday morning. But in the afternoon, it had been stolen.'

Reynolds looked at Logan gesturing to him to say something.

'It's a parachute,' said Logan.

'No,' said Kleo. 'Stop talking nonsense. We acquired that last week for our group. It's a tepee. Look at the centre hole where the frame fits through.'

'It's a parachute,' repeated Logan calmly but firmly.

Kleo started to slowly shake her head in denial of what Logan was saying. She rolled her eyes in her pretentious belief that she knew best. She started arguing with him in her most sarcastic patronising tone of voice:

'I think you'll find that parachutes aren't shaped like that. I've seen them on television. They're shaped differently nowadays. More sort of rectangular. Not circular like our tepee…'

'It's a parachute,' repeated Logan confidently.

'Excuse me,' said Kleo. 'I hadn't finished talking yet. You interrupted me.'

Logan raised both his hands, signalling his agreement to stop talking. Kyle and Reynolds glanced at each other while facially acknowledging to each other their recognition of Kleo's patronising attitude. Logan stood quietly waiting for Kleo to continue but Jasper spoke in a sarcastic tone of voice:

'You've never seen a tepee, have you? This is a place where native Americans carry out their spiritual ceremonies. This is a sacred item.'

Logan shook his head. His attempt at staying quiet had become overwhelmed by the arrogance of Kleo and Jasper.

'No, I've never seen a tepee close-up,' he said calmly. 'I've never jumped out of an aeroplane wearing a tepee on my back. But I have jumped out of aeroplanes many times wearing a parachute. And I've lost count of the number of times I've inspected, repaired and packed parachutes. This is an old parachute. At least thirty years old.'

He picked up the end of one of the rigging lines.

'Look at this. Tents have guy ropes to secure them to pegs in the ground. Guy ropes are stitched into the hem. But these here are parachute rigging lines which are stitched all the way to the apex and continued down the opposite side. Each line is stressed to a hundred and fifty pounds breaking strain. And each line is sleeved.'

He pulled back the sleeve of one lines exposing the cord inside.

'Tents don't have guy ropes like that. And look closely. The fabric with the tiny squared pattern stitched into it is rip-stop nylon. Standard material for parachutes.'

He then unfolded the parachute more to reveal the harness. He could see that Kleo was upset at being defeated in her argument.

'Well it doesn't matter what it once was,' said Jasper as he tried to defend Kleo from embarrassment. 'It's now a tepee because that's why we have it.'

Logan turned to Reynolds.

‘Can we talk in private for a minute?’

Reynolds led him to a small back room.

‘Ask me anything you like,’ said Logan. ‘But right now, while you’re talking to them, I think I need to make myself scarce so there’s no breach of confidentiality. But whatever they think about a tent or tepee still doesn’t explain why Heidi was alone when I found her with it or explain a dead body at the Punchbowl with a ripcord.’

‘I saw the pictures last night,’ she said.

Logan was startled by that comment.

‘What pictures?’

‘I went around to Joyce and Eric’s house last night. Your friend, Robin, was there. Robin found the body you told me about. He showed me the pictures.’

‘Ah, good. He showed me the pictures yesterday, but I haven’t actually spoken to him yet this morning. I stayed at Katy’s last night. As soon as I woke up she told me you needed to speak to me, so I came straight here.’

‘She told me you went to see Geordie Buchanan?’

‘Yes. Has he been in touch yet?’

‘No,’ Said Reynolds. ‘But for now, you’re right. We need to interview these two in there. And the man in hospital woke from the anaesthetic so we managed to speak with him. It’s interesting. Can you stay nearby and come back in say, half an hour?’

‘Sure. I haven’t eaten breakfast yet. I’ll come back but I might need a bit more than half an hour. Meantime, if you interview Kleo and she becomes too annoying or you think she’s talking nonsense, just tell her she’s wrong. That’ll get her thoroughly flustered. I’ve see her style of behaviour so many times.’

Reynolds led Logan back through the hallway where Kleo and Jasper were still standing looking at the parachute and talking with Kyle who was taking notes. Reynolds spoke:

'Let's go into the interview room.'

Jasper refused, saying:

'No. This isn't going to be a formal interview here. We've done nothing wrong. Go and do your job and arrest Adam.'

Logan, on hearing that comment, stopped in his tracks before leaving the police station to listen to what was being said. Kyle was becoming increasingly frustrated at Kleo and Jasper's attitudes. He tried again to persuade them both to agree to come into the interview room, but Kleo became more defiant while being supported by Jasper.

'We have better things to do,' she said. 'Karina's missing. It's obvious that Adam took her. He's the one you need to speak to. Now go and do your job.'

Logan turned around and sighed, then asked:

'Everyone, please, not as a formal interview but just as an informal group chat, can I just clarify something?'

The four looked at him. Kyle and Reynolds were concerned about allowing him to enter into what should be a confidential discussion. Kleo didn't want to be questioned on anything. Jasper didn't want to talk either. Logan spoke quietly:

'I really don't want to get involved in something which is none of my business, but I think I'm, well, caught up in something here, so it's become my business.'

He looked at Kleo as he continued talking:

'Kleo, that little girl you're all talking about, the one who's missing. Karina. Do you a have picture of her? The reason I ask is because I think I might have seen her.'

Kleo initially hesitated before showing Logan her mobile phone. On it were a few pictures of Heidi wearing the same dress she'd been wearing when Logan found her.

'That's Karina?' asked Logan.

'Yes.'

'When and where did you last see her?'

'She was with us in Glen Sannox on Saturday until just after Lunchtime. But Adam took her away.'

'And who is Adam?' asked Logan.

'My sister's ex-husband.'

'And he's the girl's father?'

'Well, yes, but that doesn't give him any rights.'

'Let me get this absolutely clear,' interrupted Reynolds. 'Who is the girl's mother and where is she?'

'Her mother is my sister. Her name's Ingrid and she's away on holiday just now with her new partner.'

Kyle sternly told her:

'Adam said you took her from the nursery where she was playing on Friday afternoon. He said he went to collect her to take her home, but she was gone. He was told that it was her mother who had taken her. But he was unable to contact her mother. So, did you take her away and bring her to Arran without his permission?'

'But I'm her aunt,' said Kleo. 'I don't need to ask him. I don't even need to talk to him. He has no say in the matter.'

Logan sighed and opened his mouth to talk, prompting Kleo to hold her hand up, palm facing him, signalling that he should remain quiet. Jasper spoke directly to Kyle while pointing his finger at Logan.

'If he's not a police officer why is he even here? None of this is his concern so I don't have to answer his questions'.

'Does anyone here have a picture of Adam?' asked Logan.

'Why?' asked Kleo.

'It would really help us if you could show us a picture of him,' explained Reynolds. 'Because you've not been to visit him in hospital. So, we need to check that the man in hospital is the same man you're talking about. He doesn't have the child. And you don't know where she is. You've already told us to do our job, so here we are, doing our job by making sure we collect information rather than just accept assumptions.'

Sighing heavily, Kleo scrolled through her mobile phone picture album. She found a picture which she showed Reynolds. It was a picture of a group of people sitting around a table in a restaurant.

'This was taken over a year ago,' she said. 'It was Karina's birthday. That's Adam sitting there wearing the white shirt. And that's Ingrid sitting beside him.'

Reynolds took the phone from her and showed the picture to both Kyle and Logan. Logan nodded his head in recognition of Adam.

'Ingrid looks like you,' said Reynolds.

'Yes, we're twins.'

'So that would explain why the nursery thought you were Karina's mother, and why they told Adam that it was her mother who had taken her.'

'All the more reason why he had no right to come here to abduct her,' snapped Kleo.

'Adam didn't abduct her,' said Kyle.

'Is that what he told you?' asked Jasper. 'And you believe him?'

Logan produced his mobile phone and gave it to Reynolds, allowing her to present it to Kleo and Jasper. Kyle looked on from over Reynold's shoulder.

'Adam didn't take Heid… I mean Karina on Saturday,' said Logan. 'I'm the person who took her. And you should see the video on my phone.'

Reynolds showed the video of the little girl trapped in the small mining pit in Glen Sannox, desperately holding on to the parachute to prevent herself from sinking into the water. While they all watched the video, Logan spoke:

'That was about ten past twelve in the afternoon. 'She was alone in that pit and only about two minutes away from drowning because she was losing her grip. There was nobody else around. I was there. You weren't. Why…'

'Why was she alone?' interrupted Kyle.

'She wasn't alone,' answered Jasper abruptly. 'She was playing with her brother.'

Kyle looked at Logan, noticing his worried facial expression.

'What brother?' gasped Logan in his concern that another child may have also been there and drowned in the pit.

'My son,' answered Kleo. 'Jonathan.'

'Where's Jonathan?' asked Logan. 'Is he missing too?'

'You've met Jonathan,' said Kleo. 'You must have seen him when you were at the campsite with us. He was the boy with the football shirt.'

Logan immediately became more relaxed as he recalled seeing the young boy as she'd described.

'Ah yes I remember seeing a young boy there, about three years old I'd guess.'

'Four years,' said Kleo.

'Wait,' said Kyle with a baffled look on his face. 'So, you say that Jonathan is your son, and Karina is your sister's daughter. Your niece. But you say that Jonathan is Karina's bother, not cousin. Can you explain that?'

'We're all brothers and sisters within the Spiritbeamers,' said Jasper.

They then watched the video recording taken from Logan's drone that day from when he was searching the area surrounding the quarry pit.

'Like I said, there was nobody else there,' said Logan. 'No brother or cousin or any responsible adult. And that tepee or whatever you want to call it, is a parachute which wasn't attached to any type of tepee frame or even guy ropes. It wasn't secured to anything. And parachute material is lighter than tent material, so it's much more susceptible to getting blown away in windy conditions. The breeze that day was slowly dragging it further into that pit. You weren't there. Her father wasn't there because he wasn't even on the island yet. I know that because I saw him arriving here on the ferry yesterday.'

Kleo remained speechless as she watched the video. When it ended, Kyle took the phone from her and handed it back to Logan who then added:

'When I found her, I didn't understand what she was saying except that she sounded Russian, and so, I called a translator in Croatia who speaks several languages. She could only partially understand her, and she thought her name was Heidi.'

Jasper, in defiance of their now-proven lack of responsibility, spoke angrily to Logan:

'You've admitted you've abducted her. So, where is she now?'

'She's safe,' he replied. 'This is police work now. I shouldn't be here. But you absolutely need to adjust your attitudes and start speaking to these police officers.'

He walked outside, followed by Reynolds. By now the storm was battering the island.

'Katy told me that you've taken the girl to Geordie Buchanan?'

'Yes. she's in Glasgow. Being looked after by good people. But right now, I have something I need to do. Geordie will tell you more. He knows the situation and actually he knows better than me about exactly where the girl is. I don't know if his wife is looking after her or if perhaps they've taken her to someone else, but she's in good hands. I want you and Kyle to meet me later. I'll have a crime to report.'

He turned to walk away.

'Wait,' shouted Reynolds. 'What crime?'

'I haven't decided yet,' smiled Logan. 'Oh, these two idiots in there… you mustn't charge them with anything. At least not today. Maybe haul them in for questioning tomorrow. They're not going to run away anywhere because the ferries have already stopped for this storm. You can catch up with them tomorrow if you need to do that. But not today. If you charge them with anything, you'll spook the other event organisers by making them know you're giving them attention. Geordie will explain better.'

He drove away leaving Reynolds confused. He parked his car next to the Old Pier and switched off his engine. He sat there watching the sea with the Holy Isle barely visible in the low cloud. He phoned Robin.

'Wakey wakey rise and shine. How's things?' asked Logan.

'Ok here. I'm still at the house. Where are you?'

'Lamlash. I'll be back in Brodick soon.'

'Someone here wants to meet you,' said Robin.

'Shh!' said Logan. 'I know. Stay there. I'll be with you soon.'

Logan started his car and set off towards Brodick. He parked at the shop to meet with Katy who was closing up.

'Can you give me a lift home? I mean, to my parents? I don't really want to walk in in that weather. I think Robin's still there.'

'Of course.'

They drove round to Katy's parents. Robin was sitting at the kitchen table. Sitting with him were Katy's parents and Geordie. Logan sat at the table with them.

'How's your progress?' asked Logan.

'Good,' said Geordie. 'But we're a bit clueless about some of the details. I need to check the weather again. What do you think this storm is going to do?'

They both looked at Robin's phone screen as he opened the weather app to see the satellite images. Sandra left the kitchen.

'It looks like the storm won't be centred here,' said Robin. 'It should be at its quietest in about three hours, but only for an hour or so then it'll become lively again.'

Logan looked at his watch. It was almost midday.

'What are you thinking?' asked Robin.

'There's a big raft a couple of hundred metres offshore in Lamlash bay. I'm not sure why it's there but it's big enough to land a small helicopter on. And it has a pole and streamers indicating the wind direction which I've never seen on any raft before.'

The others sat listening in anticipation of Logan's theory.

'I think this is part of their plan, or maybe part of a collection of back-up plans.'

Sandra returned to the kitchen holding a large map she'd retrieved from the living room sideboard. She unfolded it and spread it out on top of the kitchen table.

'This is easier to see than all of us looking at your phone,' she said.

Logan pointed to the various positions on it as he spoke, starting with Glen Sannox.

'Firstly, let's start with the decoy. That's why these Spiritbeamer people are here and planning to have a big party on Brodick beach tonight or perhaps on Brodick green when the storm eases.'

He pointed at Brodick Bay saying:

'That small boat… the one they call 'Noah's Ark', is full of drugs. I think mostly cannabis, but there are a few other substances. For sure there's crack cocaine. Highly addictive and highly dangerous and being sold at a minimal price, hence the reason these Spiritbeamers think they're getting a bargain. And we already know there are some cyanide pills on it. The big-time criminals organising this want the police to think that all the action will happen in Brodick.'

He pointed at Lamlash.

'I think this is where the big plan is. This happens in two parts. The first part of the plan is to distribute the less expensive drugs to the Spiritbeamer party-goers. These drugs were hidden under the water in Sannox Bay, just beside Cod Rock which very few people know about. These drugs have been loaded onto Noah's Ark which is anchored now in Brodick bay.'

'Cod Rock?' asked Katy.

'Yes,' said Logan as he placed his finger on the map. 'It's

here, just off the sandy bay. When I was a boy I used to catch fish there… always cod. Not many people know where it is because it can't be seen.'

Logan turned to Geordie, telling him:

'Verhoeven knows exactly where it was. Because it was me who told him about it when I was twelve.'

He then placed his finger on the map at Lamlash bay, saying:

'I think the big drug deal will happen in Lamlash, almost next to the police station. That's the last place the police would expect a massive drug deal to take place. But I think they have a back-up plan. I'm not sure. I'm trying to figure out why there's a big raft floating in Lamlash and a smaller one in Whiting Bay. So, for now, while some of the drugs are hidden under the waves at North Sannox, and perhaps also at Cod Rock, I think we should accept the possibility of more being hidden elsewhere. Maybe on Holy Isle. Maybe on the rafts. When the storm starts to ease off, Whiting Bay, and especially Lamlash Bay, will be the best sheltered places. It won't take long for their speedboat to bring the drugs across from Sannox.'

'Speedboat?' asked Geordie.

'Yeah. With two engines.'

'Maybe they'll use the rafts as a trading place,' suggested Robin. 'That would minimise their chances of being caught instead of carrying out their business on land.'

'Maybe. Yes, maybe that's their plan, although the storm might force them to change that.'

He pointed to Brodick again.

'The Spiritbeamers will be going wild in Brodick and some of them will be dead because they'll have drowned or swallowed cyanide. So, the police will be so pre-occupied in Brodick that they won't be able to stop or even know about what'll be happening in Lamlash or Whiting Bay. Once the hard drugs have all been sold, the buyers will need time to hide them in various parts of the island. What they won't want is for additional police support to arrive from the mainland for at least forty-eight hours so that's why the organisers must have another back-up plan.'

He pointed at Lamlash Old Pier, with his voice becoming increasingly enthusiastic as he spoke, saying:

'The people I spoke to have told me that the protest will happen in Brodick. I reckon that protest boat is planning to sail round to Brodick's harbour and attach itself there. That would prevent any ferries from coming over when the storm eases. Nobody seems to know what the protest is about, but they want to take part in it regardless. So, there's going to be plenty of chaos at Brodick, thoroughly distracting the police from Lamlash. I wouldn't be surprised if the boat gets deliberately sunk where the ferry normally docks. That would block the terminal for several days and give the buyers plenty of time to hide their bulk purchases all over the island.'

'If drunk and spaced-out protesters are on that boat when it sinks while the sea's still rough, I don't want to know how many will drown,' said Eric.

'If that happens, even if the local police know there's been a major drug deal going on, their priority will be to deal with the carnage here in Brodick,' said Robin.

'But that would mean these people would be stuck on the island,' said Sandra. 'Why would they do that to themselves?'

'Think about it from a business point of view,' said Geordie. 'Imagine you run your own business. It doesn't matter if it's legal or illegal. You've accumulated goods to sell for maybe a few million pounds. You probably already have your customers waiting. It might take you a couple of years to sell it all. But in a couple of years you'll be obscenely wealthy. But there's the minimal inconvenience that you'll have to treat yourself to a few days holiday on Arran and pretend you enjoy hill-walking. It's not a huge burden.'

Sandra was fascinated at what she was hearing. She asked:

'But if they hide all their drugs here on Arran, what then? How will they get them off the island?'

'They won't,' said Robin. 'The drugs will stay here. The gangsters can sell them in small amounts by organising phone deals with addicts and other small-time dealers.'

'They don't deal with cash any more,' said Geordie. 'They get their buyers to buy cryptocurrency with a code so that their transactions can't be traced.'

Katy and her parents looked puzzled at this.

'Any new buyers will have to come to Arran,' said Logan. 'Let's imagine I'm the drug dealer and you're a desperate drug addict or maybe you're another drug dealer working small-time. I could be living anywhere in the world like maybe in a beach mansion in Barbados. I'm using an unregistered mobile phone. So, you call me. I tell you to go to Arran. I tell you to buy, let's say, a few hundred pounds or dollars or euros worth of cocaine. It takes only a couple of minutes for you to buy cryptocurrency and transfer it to the code I'd give you. It only takes me a few minutes to check that you've transferred the payment. Then I send you the information of exactly where to find the drugs to the value of what you've paid. I'd send you accurate GPS information so that you can find the exact rock-pool or rabbit hole where it's hidden. So, you go and dig up the drugs and do whatever you want with them. If you're not sure about trusting me with money you could start buying small amounts. Once you realise you're actually getting the drugs you've paid for, it would only take you a few more minutes to buy more cryptocurrency and for me to send you more GPS information for you to find the next stash I'd hidden. I wouldn't care if you'd get arrested when taking it back home on the ferry. If you would get arrested, I'd still have the cryptocurrency you'd paid for and I still couldn't be traced. I'd still have the rest of my drugs hidden in various places around the island which only I would know about and be able to sell to other buyers.'

'You'd need a lot of hiding places all over the island,' said Eric.

'Yes. And almost certainly these drug dealers have already been here many times to establish their hiding places. But of course, they'll still need time to split their bulk into small amounts and distribute them around the island without police watching them, hence why they'd want to create mayhem in Brodick to distract police and isolate the island for a few days to prevent additional police support from arriving.'

Katy and her parents paused to absorb what they were being told. After a few moments, Sandra looked inquisitively at Robin and Logan, hesitantly asking:

'How… how do you know all this?'

Robin looked at Logan. Logan looked on at Geordie. Sandra sensed that her question was one they'd rather not answer.

'Sorry, I shouldn't have asked.'

'It's okay,' interrupted Geordie. 'I've shared some of my

police work with these guys in the past. They were trained in the army in some aspects of police work. We've all seen drug dealers before and we sort of know how they work although it's always difficult to grasp how evil they tend to be.'

He gave Logan and Robin a questioning glance to which they both responded with a gentle nod of their heads, allowing Geordie to continue talking:

'We're fairly certain we know the people behind this plan. And we already had an idea some years ago that they were planning something similar to what's happening now. The main man is still in prison but he's due to be released soon.'

'Was that the guy you mentioned a few minutes ago… Verhoof…Verheffan…?' asked Eric.

'Verhoeven,' said Logan.

Geordie added:

'We knew that some preparation for this plan had been put in place before he was sent to prison. We expected him to activate the plan when he'd be released but we didn't expect things to develop to this level while he was still locked behind bars, and of course, we don't know all the details.'

Logan took a deep breath before speaking quietly:

'That man and his wife have a weird interest in the equinox dates. We already knew that his wife had set up a cult following of weirdos which she named Spiritbeamer to celebrate their drug-fuelled belief that they should celebrate the equinox. Today is the autumn equinox. The name Sannox happens to rhyme with the word equinox. I think that's one reason why Sannox was chosen for their Spiritbeamer gathering.'

'What about the Claonaig ferry at Lochranza?' asked Eric. 'How will they stop that one from sailing?'

'They have a few options which we're not sure about,' said Geordie. 'We have police already at Claonaig keeping an eye on that.'

On the Ordnance Survey map, Logan placed his forefinger on the south of Holy Isle.

'I was speaking with two lads. One's named Jamie and I don't know the other one's name. They're cousins. They saw a helicopter which I think has landed on the south part of the island. I think it's still there and parked between the jetty and Pillar Rock Point, out of sight from anywhere on Arran and too far away to be seen from the mainland, especially in these conditions with so much sea spray. It's also well sheltered there from the westerly wind. I'm guessing it's sitting there ready for the main dealers to leave the island after the dealing's finished. If it's the same one I saw on Saturday, it's a Bell Jetranger which can carry five people plus the pilot.'

Robin recognised Logan's enthusiasm.

'I have a feeling you have a plan already?'

'Yeah, well, some ideas. Not yet a plan. But we're running out of time. I'm not sure where that raft in Lamlash bay fits in. It's anchored quite far offshore. I'd say too far to be some sort of recreational thing for small boats. But I think our priorities now are to stop that protest boat from sailing to Brodick and stop that the helicopter from flying, assuming it's where I think it is. I'm not too concerned about the raft. Whatever it's doing, it isn't going anywhere on its own.'

Robin closed his eyes and bowed his head. He knew exactly what Logan was thinking.

'You can't do this alone,' he said.

Geordie sat silently for a few moments. He agreed with

Robin.

'It's too dangerous,' he said. 'I know what you're thinking, and… no.'

'If that protest boat sails to Brodick, people will die,' said Logan.

Katy became concerned at the sudden increase of seriousness between Logan, Robin and Geordie.

'How can you be sure that'll happen?' she asked. 'It's only your guess about that boat being sunk with people on board. But maybe there's some other reason for it being there. Maybe a more innocent reason.'

'What if we're right?' replied Logan. 'If we're right about all of this, people will drown. And if I'm right about that helicopter, it could be the one thing standing in the way between the police and their chance to catch some people who will continue to kill and destroy lives for many years.'

He turned to Robin, knowing the contents of his motorcycle toolkit, and told him:

'I'll need your adjustable spanners, wire cutter and pliers.' That comment confirmed his intentions to Robin. Knowing how he could never stop Logan from performing any task he was determined to do, he hesitantly told him:

'They're in the left pannier. It's not locked.'

'What else will you need?' asked Geordie.

'About three hours,' said Logan. 'And a police officer. PC Reynolds or Kyle. Nobody else. They know me. Katy can you call the police station and ask if either of them are there just now? Text me when you know. If they're not nearby I'll think of something else. And I'll need some sugary biscuits for an energy boost.'

Eric became alarmed at what he heard.

'Please tell me you're not going swimming in that sea in that weather out there.' he said.

'It'll be fun,' joked Logan. 'But seriously, I'm a strong swimmer and I have a good quality wetsuit which I bought when I went shopping with Geordie on Monday. It's in the back of my car. Geordie brought it over last night.'

'You arrived last night?' asked Katy.

Geordie smiled, nodding his head. Katy looked at Logan.

'You can't swim in that sea. These waves are crashing on each other.'

'I've been swimming in worse,' said Logan as he stood up to leave.

He picked up the previous morning's newspaper from the kitchen table.

'I need a photo,' he said as he handed his mobile phone to Sandra.

He posed side by side with Geordie next to the fireplace while holding the front page of the newspaper towards the phone. Sandra clicked the phone camera. She handed the phone back to him, puzzled as to why he wanted that picture. Talking to Robin, Logan said:

'I'll deal with the protest boat later. I'll call you to meet me at the Old Pier when I'm ready for that.'

Robin raised his thumb. Logan took the newspaper and grabbed a half-empty packet of biscuits as he left the house.

Robin then turned to Katy:

'Don't worry. He really is a strong swimmer.'

Then he jokingly added:

'He's shit at football, but he's strong in the water.'

Geordie agreed, saying:

'It's alright. I've seen him swim. He'll be fine.'

Minutes after leaving the house, Logan received a text message from Katy:

'*Kyle and Reynolds both there.*'

'Good,' sighed Logan to himself. 'One less problem to solve.'

Meanwhile in Brodick, Geordie faced Robin:

'What do you suggest we do now?'

'He knows what he's doing around aircraft,' said Robin. 'And he's a strong swimmer, so he'll deal with the helicopter. Meantime, I can't sit here being useless. I need to take a closer look at that protest boat.'

'I wish we'd bought two wetsuits last night,' said Geordie. 'Katy, you said your shop's closed, but do you have a key to get into it?'

'Yes, of course.'

'Do you have anything like a windsurfer's wetsuit in there?' asked Robin.

'Yes, but there are only four left. I know two of them won't fit you. The other two might. We can go now.'

Geordie drove them to the shop. The swimming gear was upstairs. All four windsurfing suits were too small for Robin.

'I have a friend on the island about the same size as you, who does windsurfing. He lives in Lochranza. I could take you to him,' she said.

Robin looked at the weather outside. He noticed that the wind strength seemed to be decreasing slightly.

'There's not enough time,' he said. 'The storm's easing slightly before it gets strong again. We only have a small window of opportunity and now's the time. I'll just have to get cold and wet.'

He grabbed a flotation vest, a pair of swimming goggles, a pair of dark grey sports trousers and a large grey sweatshirt from the display.

'I need to stay camouflaged in the water,' he said. 'I'll pay for these later.'

'Charge it to me,' said Geordie. 'It'll go on a police account.'

Katy placed the goods in one of the rucksacks from the wall display. The three of them walked out of the shop into Geordie's car then set off towards Lamlash, by which time Logan had already arrived at the police station. Both Kyle and Reynolds were there.

'I need one of you to follow me,' said Logan.

Reynolds and Kyle looked at him as they were waiting for him to explain what was going on. Logan glanced around the inside of the police station.

'You're both alone in here just now?' he asked.

Again, they looked at him blankly as Kyle gestured with his hands out for Logan to explain himself.

Logan put the newspaper on the wooden counter.

'That's yesterday's newspaper,' he said. 'It was delivered to the island yesterday morning.'

He showed them his phone screen.

'This is a picture of me about twenty minutes ago. You can see me holding yesterday's newspaper. Joyce, you'll recognise Sandra and Eric's living room. And you'll recognise Geordie standing there with me.'

Kyle and Reynolds looked at each other in surprise.

'What? Geordie's on Arran? What's going on here?' asked Reynolds.

'Geordie will contact you very shortly. But right now, we're running out of time. One of you needs to come with me. I'm not going far. Just into Whiting Bay.'

Reynolds agreed to follow him. He drove south through Whiting Bay and began looking at the houses to the south side of the village near Ashdale Bridge at the start of the Glenashdale forest walk. The last turning before the bridge would be the most likely place to find what he was looking for. He turned into Montrose Terrace: a small road with a few houses. Very quickly he recognised Jamie's red Vauxhall car with its partially repaired driver's door parked in front of a detached house. He parked in front of the house. Reynolds parked her police car behind him. They both approached the front door. On ringing the doorbell, Logan could hear the sound of a dog barking from inside. After a few moments a woman answered the door. Logan reckoned she was aged in her mid-seventies.

'Sorry to trouble you,' started Logan. 'I met two lads earlier today in Brodick. I think they're your grandsons. One was Jamie and I didn't ask the other lad's name. Are they in?'

The woman looked concerned.

'Is there a problem?' she asked. 'Are they in any trouble?'

'No. I need their help with something. When I spoke with them, we were talking about boating and kayaking. I need to ask them something about that.'

The woman shouted into the house.

'Jamie. Darren. There are two police officers at the door wishing to talk with you.'

'Darren,' though Logan quietly to himself. 'So, Sheepskin has a name now.'

Jamie and Darren both came to the door, both looking

concerned as to why the police would want to talk to them.

'Hi Guys,' said Logan. 'It's okay you're not in any trouble. And I'm not a police officer, but I brought PC Reynolds here to confirm that I'm genuine. Earlier today when we spoke, you mentioned kayaking. I didn't ask earlier but do you actually have a kayak? Or do you know where I can get one urgently?'

Darren looked out towards the shore then up at the overcast sky.

'You want to go kayaking in this weather?' he asked.

'Yes. And I'm running out of time.'

'Even a maniac wouldn't go out in this,' said Jamie.

'Yeah, I know,' replied Logan. 'But I'm a bit of a maniac. It was obvious to me today that you're both sensible guys, and I know you wouldn't be so irresponsible that you'd lend someone like me, a stranger, a kayak in these weather conditions.'

He pointed at Reynolds.

'But she can confirm that this is police work. If you have a kayak or a canoe, or you can access one right now, I really need one. Please.'

Darren shrugged his shoulders as he spoke:

'You're interested in that helicopter that we saw on Holy Isle, aren't you? You're going to try to take a kayak over, yeah?'

Logan sighed. He hadn't wanted to divulge such information, but Darren had figured out his intentions.

'Yes,' replied Logan. 'Also, I need a length of thin fishing line. Can you help me?'

'Yeah sure, but it's an inflatable kayak. Not made for rough seas like it is out there.'

'I've done this work before,' said Logan. 'And if anything happens to your Kayak I'll pay you.'

The boys led Logan and Reynolds to the back garden shed where they stored the kayak. It was deflated and rolled into its container.

'You'll need this pump as well,' said Jamie as he handed over a cardboard box and a reel of fishing line.

Logan placed the items on top of his damp wetsuit in the back of his car.

'What exactly am I doing here?' asked Reynolds.

'There's no way these guys would have given me that kayak if you hadn't been there to authenticate me. Thanks for doing that. I'm going kayaking now.'

'What was it you both said about a helicopter?'

'That's what I need to check out. Meantime if you're not busy, I'd suggest that you go to the Old Pier at Lamlash. I think you'll meet Geordie there in a few minutes.'

Logan drove off northwards out of Whiting Bay then made the sharp right turn into Sandbraes Road which led him towards King's Cross Point. He parked his car as close as he could to the point, then proceeded on foot along the coastline which leads towards Dun Cairn: an ancient Viking burial site dating back to the ninth century. The storm was easing but he knew he had limited time before the wind would increase again. He undressed himself and donned his wetsuit which was still cold and damp from its previous use.

He placed his dry clothes and an old towel into a polythene bag which he then wedged into a crack in a large rock. He forced himself to eat six of the sugary biscuits he'd brought for energy. He inflated the kayak and carried it to the shoreline where he waded into the water up to his knees before sitting in it. He wore a small waterproof pack strapped across his chest and a new rucksack which he wore back-to front so that it would rest on his lap. Although the storm was easing, the sea swell was still significant enough for him to be confident about using the waves to keep him out of sight while he paddled across the water.

Meantime, Geordie had driven Katy and Robin to Lamlash Old Pier. Due to the wind direction, the protest boat's bow was pointing slightly south of the pier.

'I reckon that's about fifty to seventy metres out,' said Geordie.

'How strong are you at swimming?' asked Katy.

'I'm okay. Not as good as Logan but I can swim the seventy metres to that boat there. That's just three lengths of the swimming pool I often use.'

'In rough weather and cold water though?' asked Katy. 'And besides, do you have a plan?'

'I'll have a plan in a few moments.'

He stepped out of the car and walked along the Old Pier towards its end. On either side of the pier was a slipway for launching small boats. The north side slipway had concrete steps leading down to the water. To the north side of the pier there was an area of ground where boats had been parked on their trailers. Strewn across the ground were several ropes attached to metal chains for securing boats. Robin could see a man on the protest boat. He was standing on deck and smoking a cigarette. Judging by the man's physical shape, Robin correctly assumed he was looking at the man nicknamed by Logan as Gremlin. After standing and looking around for just two minutes, Robin returned to the car.

'I have a plan,' he said. 'But I need a sharp knife and four small padlocks.'

'I know where to get them,' said Katy. 'Drive me to my friend's house. It's just two minutes away.'

Geordie drove them to the house. He and Robin stayed in the car while Katy went through the back garden. Within minutes she returned to the car with a small sharp kitchen knife and four small padlocks.

'Are these any use?'

'Perfect,' said Robin. 'You stay here. Two's company and three's a crowd. Crowds get noticed. It's best that it's just myself and Geordie do this. I shouldn't take long. Maybe twenty minutes. We can catch up with you later.'

Katy agreed. Geordie and Robin drove back to the Old Pier. Robin watched the boat carefully. The man on board couldn't be seen, presumably because he'd gone beneath the deck. Robin and Geordie carefully looked around the area to check that nobody else was watching them. Robin proceeded to use the knife to cut free one of the chains on the ground from its length of rope.

'Are you sure about this?' asked Geordie. 'That's cold water out there.'

'I'll be fine,' replied Robin as he carefully walked down the steps to the north slipway.

He put on his bright orange floatation vest and then pulled the extra-large dark grey sweatshirt over the top of it for camouflage in the water. He placed the four small padlocks into his lightweight sports trousers and then coiled up the chain. He entered the water.

'Shit!' he gasped. 'It's freezing!'

He hesitated for a few moments while he adjusted his

goggles. He then gasped some sharp breaths and collapsed his knees to plunge himself under the water for a few seconds before coming up for air. He remained in position for about a minute to allow himself to adjust to the temperature. Geordie was standing midway down the steps to keep himself out of sight from the boat. When Robin was ready to start swimming he looked up at Geordie.

'Still all clear?'

Geordie looked around again, and also checked the boat.

'All clear. Nobody's watching.'

Robin set off, swimming with one-handed front crawl towards the boat while his left hand was weighed down by the coiled chain he was holding. He allowed himself to drift southwards so that he was swimming directly in front of the boat's bow to make him less visible to Gremlin on board. As he reached the front bow he carefully swam around the starboard side to the north, keeping himself close to the boat's hull to stay out of sight.

About half way along the boat's hull, he found a rectangular section of fibreglass, partially submerged below the water. It measured almost the same size as a sheet of printer paper. On closer inspection, he could see and feel that there was a layer of rubber between this fibreglass panel and the boat's skin. It appeared to be attached by four loops of heavy duty strapping. He questioned his suspicion about this. If Logan's prediction was correct about the organisers planning to sink this boat, it looked like it had been set up so that the strapping was tensioned by ratchets which could easily be released from the inside. That would allow the fibreglass panel to fall away and cause the boat to flood rapidly. Robin could have cut this strapping from the outside, but he had left the sharp kitchen knife on the land. Also, he believed that any sabotage of the planned criminal activities should not be noticeable until the latest possible time, otherwise the criminals may decide to change their plans.

He continued swimming until he reached the propeller and rudder which were positioned beneath the hull such that they couldn't be seen from anywhere on deck. The propeller was submerged about a metre beneath the water surface. Robin submerged himself and started wrapping the chain around the propeller's axle. He then pulled one of the padlocks from his pocket and used it to secure the chain. He came up for air.

Meantime, Geordie walked back along the Old Pier towards his car when he noticed Reynolds walking towards him.

'Joyce?'

'Geordie.'

They greeted each other with a quick hug like old friends.

'So, how's Arran treating you?' asked Geordie.

'I like it here. I'm just a bit baffled at the last couple of days.'

Geordie pulled a green waterproof jacket from his car and gave it to her.

'Put this on to cover your uniform. I'll explain what I know.'

As they talked, Geordie noticed Katy walking down the south slipway. She was wearing a black wetsuit and carrying a paddleboard. Katy could see the surprised look on his face, so she gestured to him by placing her forefinger on her lips, whispering:

'Shh!'

Robin was preparing himself for submerging again when he heard Gremlin talking. He seemed to be having a telephone conversation in English although Robin couldn't make out what was being said. There was enough noise from waves splashing around the boat to enable Robin to make smaller splashing movements without being heard. He submerged himself again, this time using the attached chain to pull himself down to the propeller. He wrapped the chain diagonally through the three propeller blades and then again around the axle, securing it to itself with another small padlock.

When he surfaced for air he could still hear Gremlin on deck, talking. Robin repeated the process again and made sure the propeller was thoroughly secured by the chain before finally wrapping the remaining length of chain around the rudder. He left enough slack in the chain so that the rudder could still be moved. If the boat skipper had reason to move the rudder before starting the engine there would be no suspicion that anything had been tampered with. But when the engine would start, the propeller would immediately tighten the chain to the rudder and seize the engine. The only way to rectify the problem would be with a chain cutter which would be an unlikely tool to be on board the boat.

With the chain secured and all four padlocks used, he was ready to swim back to shore, but he could still hear Gremlin talking from the deck. Robin knew he'd be seen as soon as he'd start swimming away from the boat. The cold water was making him lose his strength. He knew he'd need to start swimming soon or his life would be in danger. He started to tread water at the boat's stern where he was more sheltered from the wind. After treading water for a few minutes, he heard a female voice calling. He moved himself to the port side of the boat where, to his surprise, he could see Katy in a wetsuit sitting astride a paddleboard. She was calling up to Gremlin.

'Hi there,' she shouted.

Robin could hear Gremlin respond:

'Well hi Babe.'

Katy replied:

'I heard about a protest happening later tonight. I'd like to take part. Can you tell me more?'

'Of course, Babe. It's happening at Brodick tonight. I'm sailing this boat there later today. As soon as you see this boat in Brodick you can come on board and bring your friends.'

She kept giving the man eye contact until he momentarily looked down at his feet to avoid tripping as he stepped closer towards the edge of the deck. Katy used that moment to glance over to Robin, signalling him to start swimming to shore. For the next two minutes, Katy engaged in conversation with Gremlin while discretely using her hands and feet to position the board to the south east of the boat. Geordie and Reynolds watched from the harbour.

'Brave girl,' commented Geordie.

Katy gradually unzipped the front of her wetsuit to show cleavage in an attempt to hold Gremlin's attention while Robin swam northwards and westwards back to shore. Gremlin continued shouting to Katy:

'You can come on board now Babe if you want. I'll give you special treatment before the protest starts.'

His appearance was particularly scruffy. His face was haggard such that it reminded her of some of the worst looking villains in an old Hollywood western movie. Her idea of being alone on a boat with him was horrendous. She wanted to turn her head around at that moment to check on Robin's progress but to do so would have activated Gremlin's curiosity as to what she was looking at. She pretended to lose her balance for a moment, giving her reason to splash herself then pretend she was shaking the water from her hair. This action was enough for her turn her head enough to see that Robin hadn't yet reached the shore.

'Sure,' said Katy. 'What drinks do you have on board?'

'Beer, Vodka, Whisky, Gin. Anything you want. And some stuff to smoke. Some special pills. We're having a party before the protest starts. Come on board now if you like. I'll take good care of you. And you can get out of that wetsuit.'

Katy again pretended to lose her balance to check on Robin. He still hadn't reached the shore.

'Ah, okay. I'm not very good at keeping my balance on this thing in these conditions. How do I get onto your boat?'

'I'll get the rope ladder,' said the man.

Katy needed him to stay in his position to keep looking at her. If he was to go and get a rope ladder he would possibly have to turn away, enabling him to see Robin swimming.

'No, wait,' shouted Katy as she unzipped her wetsuit more. 'I'm actually getting too hot in this wetsuit. I think I'm going to take it off now. Then I can throw it up to you. Can you catch it?'

Gremlin grinned in a sleazy way which Katy found disturbing.

'Of course, Babe. Take it off.'

Katy pretended to struggle with the zipper for a few moments, then slowly started to peel the wetsuit off to deliberately display more cleavage. Simultaneously, she continued pretending to struggle with her balance in order to prolong her actions to hold Gremlin's attention. Eventually she could see that Robin was now on shore on the slipway.

'Actually,' shouted Katy as she zipped up her wetsuit. 'I'll need go back to shore. If we're going to party, I'll need to get some, eh, condoms. I'll be back in about twenty minutes. Make mine a gin and tonic and… make your cabin cosy for me.'

Gremlin grinned in anticipation of his belief that she would return in twenty minutes. Katy paddled back to shore as quickly as she could. When she reached the south slipway, she picked up the paddleboard and walked towards the small childrens' play park next to the road. Robin, now wrapped in a towel walked around to meet her.

'That was an unexpected but welcome surprise,' he said.

Katy wiped her face on his towel.

'My friend who gave me the padlocks was telling me that she'd seen that guy in Lamlash. She said he's really creepy. He's already made a nuisance of himself with a few local women and been inviting them to come onto his boat. She can see the boat from her house and she noticed that he's almost always outside on deck. Even in the storm. Even in the pouring rain. When you'd started swimming out to it you must have caught him just going beneath deck for a couple of minutes. When she told me that, it was already too late for me to warn you that he'd be back on deck before you'd have been able to make it back to shore. He'd have seen you. One of her neighbours gave me this wetsuit and board. It was the only thing I could think of doing.'

During this time, Logan had been paddling the inflatable kayak. After several minutes of exhaustive paddling, he reached the shoreline of Holy Isle at the jetty on its south-west coastline. After looking around carefully to check that nobody could see him, he carried the kayak onto the seaweed-covered rocky beach. He turned it upside down and placed some rocks over it to secure its position. He then gathered several handfuls of seaweed to cover it as much as possible to keep it hidden.

He understood that if there would be any helicopter on the island, almost certainly there would be at least one person guarding it, and that person could be anywhere in the nearby vicinity. With that in mind, he decided to climb the land immediately west of his position rather than walk around the coastline. That would reduce the chances of him being seen. He had expected that any helicopter would be on the east coast of Holy Isle near Pillar Rock Point but to his surprise, he found himself looking down on it more closely to where he had come ashore, just around the south point. It had been parked facing a south-west heading.

The steep hillside sheltered the helicopter from the westerly wind. The aircraft had been almost entirely covered by a large brown awning.

There was no sign of any human. He suspected that whoever was guarding the area would likely be camping under the awning or perhaps be inside the helicopter.

He shuffled himself back from the grassy ridge and walked further north so that he could descend down to the helicopter from behind. The noise of the waves on the shoreline were loud enough to drown out any noise he might make. The awning had been pegged to the ground surrounding the helicopter in such a way as to leave a gap of about a metre above the ground on its left side facing the sea and almost touching the ground on its right side from where the wind was blowing down the steep slope.

He slowly walked towards the helicopter, eventually crawling on his belly to the aircraft's starboard side, looking at it from under the awning where it was almost touching the ground. He could see a man lying across the passenger seats wearing headphones. Perhaps he was sleeping, or perhaps he was listening to music, but either way, he was likely to be the pilot. Logan carefully slid himself beneath the awning towards the tail rotor where he could confidently stand without being seen. He knew he would need about three minutes to disable the aircraft.

From his waterpack, he removed Robin's tools. He cut the locking wire and unscrewed the two bolts which connected the first tail rotor control rod. He started removing the second control rod but he heard movement from inside the helicopter. Watching carefully, he saw the port side cabin door starting to open. In anticipation of the pilot stepping outside, Logan quickly picked up his rucksack and rushed to the helicopter's starboard side, diving to the ground to roll himself out from under the awning and out of sight.

He lay flat on the ground, gently lifting the awning from the ground just enough to look beneath it as he watched the feet and ankles of the pilot stepping out from the aircraft. The pilot then crouched down and went out from beneath the awning to the seaward side and made his way towards the water's edge.

Logan watched carefully, making sure that from his position he couldn't see more than the pilot's legs. If he couldn't see his eyes, the pilot wouldn't be able to see him. From the water's edge, the pilot strolled casually along the coastline towards the direction of the jetty near to where Logan had hidden the kayak. He watched until the pilot's legs were out of sight around the coastline.

'I just need a minute,' thought Logan. 'I can remove that second rod in one minute.'

Still holding his rucksack, he quickly slid beneath the awning and returned to the tail rotor. He looked beneath the awning to the seaward side to make sure the pilot wasn't returning before he unscrewed the last bolt as quickly as possible. He then placed both control rods into his rucksack. The helicopter would not be able to fly with these control rods as it would be impossible to stop the aircraft from spinning around as soon as the pilot would try to take-off. If any pilot failed to check the tail rotor before flight, the problem would become obvious before the helicopter could leave the ground, so although it was sabotage, nobody would be hurt as a result.

Now he had a new problem. He couldn't see the pilot, and therefore had no idea how far he'd gone for a walk or how soon he'd return. It would take Logan less than a minute to climb the steep slope and position himself out of sight, or it would take him just a few seconds to run to the shore and submerge himself into the sea. But whatever he would do, he would be visible in all directions if the pilot would return to the helicopter before he was out of sight. He had no idea as to whether or not the pilot was armed with a gun. The longer he thought about this dilemma the more risk there was of the pilot returning and seeing him, so he had to make a decision as quickly as possible.

He opted for walking backwards away from the tail of the helicopter to keep it and its awning directly in-line between himself and the coastal bend where he knew the man would be most likely to reappear from. This tactic would enable him to make some distance while keeping himself out of sight.

Within two minutes of moving backwards, he noticed the shoreline had a slightly raised line of rock running towards the water's edge. He was confident that he was far enough away from the helicopter and that the raised rock line was just high enough that he could hide behind it by crawling on his belly towards the water's edge. As he started to crawl, he saw the pilot returning from around the coastal bend. Logan was only partially hidden by the contour of the slightly raised rocks. The pilot hadn't seen him but any movement from Logan would almost certainly be noticed by the pilot's peripheral vision. Logan remained motionless, knowing that his shoulders, head and right arm were visibly exposed. When the pilot reached the helicopter, he stopped to light a cigarette. All Logan could do was watch him.

After four minutes, the pilot finished his cigarette and then went for another walk around the coastal bend where he'd been a few minutes earlier. As he walked out of sight, Logan continued crawling towards the shore. When he reached the water, he knew he was unable to retrieve the kayak without being seen. He removed his swim-fins and swimming mask from his rucksack and prepared himself for swimming back to King's Cross Point. He placed Robin's tools and the control rods into his waterproof pack which was still strapped across his body. The storm had eased considerably in the minutes since he had arrived on Holy Isle, but he was confident that there was still enough sea swell to keep him hidden from view while in the water.

From his position, his swimming distance back to Dun Cairn would now be twice that of the distance he'd paddled in the kayak. He knew it would be the approximate equivalent distance as fifty lengths of his local twenty-five-metre swimming pool. Taking into account the disadvantage of swimming in more turbulent sea water with the advantages of wearing fins and having extra buoyancy in the salty water, he knew he would be able to swim back in about thirty minutes.

The tide hadn't yet started going out, so there was minimal risk of a strong current sweeping him out to sea, so long as he started swimming immediately. He abandoned his rucksack and started swimming. Before long, he reached the shore where his bag of dry clothing and his dry towel awaited him, still wedged into the rock crack. He dried and dressed himself while eating some more sugary biscuits to keep his energy level maintained. He returned to his car and checked his mobile phone. There was a message on it from Robin:

'*The second part of your plan is done OK. How about you?*'

Logan replied by text:

'*Done OK here too. What next?*'

Robin replied:

'*Viewpoint then Katy.*'

Logan drove northwards towards Brodick with his car heating set to maximum. On the way to Brodick he stopped at the viewpoint parking area. The view of Goat Fell and the Sleeping Warrior mountain range was hidden by the low cloud. He sat in his car with the engine running for a few moments to gather his thoughts. After five minutes Geordie arrived and parked beside him. They both stepped out from their cars to talk.

'Robin said you'd be here,' said Geordie. 'He says you usually stop here to look at the view.'

'Yeah, but not much view of the hills today.'

'We got these junction boxes looked at,' said Geordie. 'You

were right in saying they'd been tampered with, but they've been checked as alright inside. Also, the ones in Lamlash. For sure someone's tried to get into them although I suspect it would be more for the purpose of cutting off communications rather than intercepting them. But as a precaution we've secured our own contact with the mainland.'

'Good,' replied Logan.

'Joyce… Reynolds told me you'd noticed that guy with the sunglasses. The journalist. Apparently, he told her that his name's Gerry Munro.'

'The dead guy?'

'Apparently so. But you said that you'd seed him at Reynold's house after you found the body.'

'Several hours later, yes.'

'When he spoke to Joyce he introduced himself as the son of an elderly neighbour. She believed him at first and invited him into her house. Once he was in there, he started telling her that he was a freelance journalist and was interested in the Spiritbeamers in Glen Sannox, but at that time she didn't know about any such gathering.'

'Why would a journalist ask police about a bunch of weirdos when he could just go and see them for himself?' asked Logan. 'Maybe he was trying to find out just how much the police know. What did he ask her about?'

'Seems he spent a couple of minutes asking what she knew about Spiritbeamers and told her that he was going to climb Coich na h'Oighe. Then he started annoying her by trying to ask her out on a date which she wasn't interested in. Then he couldn't keep his hands off her. Eventually she had to issue him a warning to leave her alone. I was told it was you who'd given

Kyle a note of his car registration.'

'That's right. That was when I was at the ferry terminal.'

'Well, we checked it, and yes it belongs to a guy named Gerry Munro.'

'... and...?'

'... and he has an interesting history. Let's just say he's not the most squeaky-clean character on the planet.'

'You reckon he was here as a journalist or did he come here as a criminal?' asked Logan.

'Not sure yet. But we have a living character saying he's Gerry Munro, and a dead body with Gerry Munro's passport. His Mercedes has been seen by one of our guys in Lamlash. Looks like he's been staying in a small guest house there. Either that or someone else is driving his car and pretending to be him. Please let me know if you see him again.'

'Any news on Heidi... I mean... Karina?'

'Yes, she's doing good. Her father is recovering in hospital. We checked him out. He's the genuine father. Karina is still with Janice. Kleopatra, or whatever her name is, had no permission to take her. I think she's going to be charged with abduction although we need to not disturb her just now until we see what she's up to later tonight.'

'So, what, I mean, how does she explain abandoning a little girl next to a quarry?'

'It seems that she and her waste-of-space partner were the first to arrive in the glen to organise the Spiritbeamer gathering. They'd been given that old parachute by someone. She was using it as a sort of tent, or tepee as she calls it. Karina was left alone playing with Kleo's son and were playing hide-and-seek. That's probably why you thought her name was Heidi.

I think she was telling your Croatian translator that she was hiding from her cousin, Jonathan. But being so young and half Polish, her speech hasn't yet developed. And I suppose the word 'hiding' sounds a bit like 'Heidi'.'

'Ahh, yes. Possibly,' said Logan.

'Meantime, Kleo and Jasper, trusted a three-year-old to play safely with a four-year-old next to a dangerous pit while they decided to leave the children and take a stroll. They then got themselves wasted on whatever it was they were smoking. Maybe also taking pills or something. Whatever it was they took, it was too powerful for them to handle so they went into a deep sleep, hidden in deep bracken near the small bridge there, leaving poor Karina to drown. And of course, you couldn't see them behind that bridge.'

'I didn't see Karina's cousin when I was there,' said Logan.

'Apparently he saw you and thought you were Karina's father. He'd never met her father but had only heard Kleo saying negative things about him, so he was scared and hid himself from you.'

'And the names Pyotr and Mikhail?'

'Janice says that Karina talks about Jonathan as 'My cool brother' which was what Kleo had been teaching her to say but being so young and with her half Scottish and half Polish accent it sounds a bit like 'Mikhail Pyotr', which, as you know, are Russian names.'

'So, there's no connection to that little kidnapped girl in Russia or her politician father?'

'No. Seems not.'

'Okay good. So, what's with the Russian writing on the parachute hem?'

'I don't know how to explain that,' said Geordie.

'Well, at least we know the girl's safe and her family's been identified so that's one less complication to worry about. Any update on a weather forecast for tonight? I think this wind's starting to pick up again.'

'It's going to get windy again, but it should calm down by about seven o'clock. But you don't have to worry about the protest boat. That's been dealt with.'

'Eh… yeah he sent me a text. But he didn't tell me everything. What did he do?'

'He swam out to it and wrapped a chain around the propeller.'

'That's a good… wait. He doesn't have a wetsuit. Does he?'

'No. He's back at Katy's place getting heated up. He's fine. I didn't want to ask this in front of Katy and her family, but how did you get on with the Noah's Ark last night?'

'Partially dealt with,' said Logan. 'Did you bring your tool kit?'

Geordie grinned.

'Toolkit and all the other bits you need are in the car, except I don't have the wire shirt hangers. Katy says she has some in her wardrobe.'

'Okay good. Let's go. I think Katy's expecting us.'

They both drove their cars to Katy's apartment. As they entered, Geordie brought in his toolkit from the back of his car.

Robin was sitting in the living room. The welcoming aroma of tomato soup drifted in from the kitchen.

'Katy's making soup and sandwiches,' said Robin.

Geordie sat beside Robin while Logan went into the kitchen to help Katy. On the way there, Logan could see that the bathroom door was open. He noticed the wetsuit draped over the bath rail. In the kitchen was Katy, standing at the cooker wearing her dressing gown. Her hair was still wet. On seeing her like that, he looked again at the wetsuit, realising it was too small for Robin. With a surprised facial expression and pointing at the wetsuit he hesitantly spoke:

'What? What happened?'

'I went for a swim,' said Katy. 'I had to borrow that wetsuit.'

Robin walked in at that moment.

'We both went swimming,' he said. 'The protest boat's disabled. Couldn't have done it without Katy.'

Katy added:

'And before you get annoyed at him, he didn't ask me. He didn't know I was in the water until I was, well, already in the water.'

Logan looked round as Geordie who was now standing in the kitchen doorway. He smiled and nodded his head.

'Both telling the truth,' he said.

Katy poured the hot soup into four bowls and invited them all to sit around her kitchen table where the sandwiches had already been placed.

'What needs to be done next?' she asked.

'I need to do some D.I.Y,' said Logan. 'I need two metal wire shirt hangers.'

Katy gave him two wire hangers. Geordie handed Logan a plastic carrier bag containing some items which had been bought in Glasgow. Using the pliers from the bag, Logan proceeded to cut the hangers into three straight lengths. He bent the lengths into hooked shapes and then, using the same pliers, twisted them together to make the shape of a three-point grappler hook with a handle. With more twisting of the metal, he made a loop at the end of the handle to which he tied a length of fishing line.

'Please can you get my drone?' he asked Katy.

She brought him his drone, now fully charged having been plugged in all morning. He tied the fishing line around the main body of the drone, carefully positioning and tightening the line so that it wouldn't tangle with its motors. He then taped a lightweight torch to its underside. He held it above his head to check that the grappler hook was dangling correctly.

'Will that cope with the strong winds?' asked Geordie.

'So long as the wind doesn't get much more than forty miles an hour,' replied Logan.

Katy was curious, eventually asking:

'What's that going to do?'

'I went for a swim last night to that Noah's Ark boat, but I knew I daren't finish the job until the timing is right.'

'Okay. Maybe I shouldn't ask what it is you're going to do.'

Logan smiled, telling her:

'You'll see later if this works.'

'You have a back-plan?' asked Robin.

'Yes, but it's a terrible one.'

He placed the drone into a cardboard box and looked at his watch.

'There's another issue we haven't dealt with,' he said. 'The Claonaig-Lochranza ferry. The organisers will almost certainly want to stop it from sailing for a few days.'

'Have you seen any rickety old boats up there which look ready for sinking?' asked Robin.

'No,' said Geordie.

'If you were to block that port, how do you think you'd do it?' asked Katy.

Logan thought for a moment.

'It's a slipway. All anyone has to do is drive a car or a van or maybe a lorry down the slipway. Then it's blocked until the local haulage company can pull it out. Then if the organisers need more time they just need to drive another van or lorry down there.'

'But they won't need to do that when they realise the Brodick ferry won't be blocked,' added Geordie.

'Let's hope not, but it might be a good idea to set up some sort of barricade in Lochranza when things kick off,' suggested Robin.

'I'll get someone onto that,' said Geordie. 'But we mustn't be seen doing anything until the action starts.'

'Wait. Am I missing something?' asked Katy. 'You said you'd get someone. How many more police did you bring with you?'

'Almost two hundred,' said Geordie. 'You didn't see them. But you might have seen a few big lorries you hadn't seen before. We came over on the Claonaig ferry last night.'

'Wow!'

'This is a big operation which we've been expecting for a long time,' he said. 'We expected it to happen around an equinox date, but we weren't expecting it this year because the main man is still behind bars where he belongs. And we only had a vague idea about how it would be organised and no clue whatsoever as to who else would be involved. Logan here stumbled on it by accident when he found that little girl.'

'Do we know for sure the beach party will be tonight?' she asked. 'Maybe the weather will get worse than forecast and force them to cancel.'

'It's the equinox today,' said Robin. 'It will certainly happen tonight.'

Katy looked at the three of them.

'I don't understand. Why equinox? You've told me a little bit, but I still haven't figured out the significance of equinox and all this other stuff that's going on.'

'The equinox happens twice each year,' said Logan. 'The exact time and date varies slightly, partly because of leap years, but it's usually the twentieth or twenty-first of March for the spring or vernal equinox, and then there's the autumnal equinox which happens on or near the twentieth of September. This year it's today, the twenty-first. It's the time when the Earth's equator is exactly in line with the centre of the Sun's disk as we see it. In other words, the Earth's poles aren't tilted towards or away from the Sun. That means that for these two days every year, the entire world has the approximate equal amount of daytime as it has night-time.'

'So, what's that got to do with drug dealing?' asked Katy.

'It's not connected to drug dealing,' said Logan. 'But it's connected to Paganism and a collection of other religions. Pagans call the autumn equinox: 'Mabon'. And there are some celebrations and rituals which go with it. So, the drug dealers are using these Spiritbeamer weirdos as decoys by persuading them to organise what they think is some sort of spiritual-get-in-touch-with-nature type of event. By attracting so many of these barking-mad idiots here to hold a party to create a distraction to the main drugs deal, this is the best day of the year to use. The spring equinox would usually be too cold. The midsummer solstice would normally be warmer but with too much daylight. These drug dealers need darkness to do what they're planning.'

'And it seems that the drug dealers are financing the Spiritbeamer event, to make sure it goes ahead,' said Geordie.

Katy look at Logan inquisitively.

I'll explain later,' said Logan. 'I've had some experience with this nonsense some years ago.'

'The dealers almost certainly didn't want stormy conditions,' added Robin. 'But they knew they'd have to make a plan and stick to it, so they will have prepared themselves for all weathers.'

'I think it's going to be a long late night,' said Geordie. 'I need to sort some things out. Maybe you three should catch some sleep to get some energy back after your swims.'

Geordie left the apartment. Robin, Katy and Logan sat around the table with their empty soup bowls.

'What now?' asked Robin.

'I think for now we just wait until it gets dark outside.'

Robin sensed that this would be the time when Logan was ready to talk to Katy about his childhood.

'Well, I'm going for a motorbike ride while it's not raining,' said Robin. 'I'll catch up with you both later. If I see anything interesting, I'll call you.'

He left the apartment to let Katy and Logan talk more. Logan and Katy stood up to move themselves to the more comfortable sofa but found themselves standing facing each other in the kitchen doorway. Katy said nothing as she looked down at the floor waiting for Logan to talk, confident to talk to him yet too shy to ask any awkward questions. After a few moments standing there, Logan asked her:

'You're curious about my background, aren't you?'

She looked at him and slowly nodded her head.

'Well, yes, but not if it's none of my business.'

'Having involved you in what's going on, I think it's become your business. I'll tell you about my life. Let's use your sofa for this. It's a sort of unusual story.'

They sat on her sofa. Logan took in a slow deep breath while thinking carefully before telling her:

'It's a bit of a long saga. Thirty-seven years ago, there was a baby girl born in Glasgow. She had Down's Syndrome and she was named Lorna. Her parents were Margaret and Clive Verhoeven. Margaret, was a weird woman who believed in all sorts of cultish and paranormal stuff like witchcraft. She had a few friends with similar mentality. Clive was a violent gangster. He was able to use Margaret's beliefs to manipulate her to comply with anything he wanted to do. All he had to do was tell her was that his actions were part of some sort of spiritual calling and she'd go along with it. He didn't want children, especially not a child with special needs, so he manipulated one of Margaret's weird spooky friends to persuade her that baby Lorna's condition was some sort of spiritual curse. So, just a few days after the birth, they murdered their baby girl and dumped her body. But people knew that Margaret had given birth to a girl, so to cover things up, they kidnapped a baby girl from Aberdeen and pretended that she was theirs. They named her Lorna after their murdered baby.'

'That's horrible,' remarked Katy.

'It gets worse. A year later, they had another baby. This time, a boy, by which time Margaret had already been persuaded by her friend that any child she'd ever give birth to would be cursed, so they killed the baby boy and dumped his body. Then again, to avoid suspicion, they kidnapped someone else's baby from Aberdeen to raise as their own. They named him Tommy.

And then about a year later, on the tenth of March, the same thing happened again. They had a third baby… another boy. Again, believing him to be some sort of curse, they killed him and dumped his body. I became the third child they kidnapped to cover up that murder.'

Katy's jaw dropped when she heard that, but she was compelled to say nothing as she listened.

'Like the others, I was born in Aberdeen. I was just a few days old when my real mother was knocked unconscious in the garden and I was taken. Because I had been born on the twenty-first of March, and my real parents hadn't yet fully decided on my name, the press decided to name me as the 'Equinox Baby'.'

'I've heard people talking about that… about you,' said Katy.

'I'd also heard about the equinox baby when I was growing up, but I didn't realise it was me. I believed that Clive Verhoeven was my dad. He went on a sort of power trip about the fact that he had kidnapped the now-famous equinox baby. Every time that term was mentioned in the press or by anyone, it seemed to give him a warped feeling of pride that he had the answer to a secret which was baffling the police. I think he regarded my kidnapping as some sort of achievement because of the attention the case attracted. And with his warped sense of satisfaction or whatever it was he had, it became a sort of bizarre obsession. It was as if I was some sort of trophy which he seemed to think made him the envy of all kidnappers.'

'That's beyond evil,' said Katy.

'Yeah. Well, Margaret adopted the same mentality. She kept mentioning things about the equinox, and planning house parties on the equinox dates. It was like they were both wanting to display their secret without actually telling anyone, giving themselves some sort of self-pride thing. They named me Steve and raised me. Except they didn't really raise me. They sort of just dragged me up in a family which was heavily involved in the criminal underworld. I actually believed they were my parents until I became a teenager when I found out the truth.'

'That must have been a shock when you found the truth.'

'It was more of a relief because I don't have any happy childhood memories. They'd sort of accepted the idea of having to raise two unwanted kidnapped children, but being the third, I was the most inconvenient and unwanted. Clive was regularly stirring up hatred between myself and Tommy to make us get into fights. He said it would make us tough, but I could never stand up to Tommy as he was a year older which made a big difference at that age. I kept running away from home. Lorna wasn't so bad I suppose but we didn't get on well. The Verhoevens raised us with hatred and contempt for each other. It wasn't a happy family situation.'

'Were they powerful in the criminal world?' asked Katy.

'Yes, and ironically it was because of me. Clive used to swear so much that people thought he had Tourette's syndrome. So, I did the same until I realised I was losing friends. As soon as I stopped swearing, my life at school got easier. My teachers and friends started to respect me more. They could hear the real me expressing myself rather than hear me copying what I'd been hearing. Clive noticed this, so he did the same, except with his evil attitude, people could better identify his cold, calculating and callous nature. By having more control of his speech, he was able to take more control over people, so he found himself rocketing his way up the criminal hierarchy.'

'You were raised in Glasgow?' asked Katy.

'East Kilbride. Because their first baby had Down's Syndrome and had been seen by neighbours in Glasgow, they had to move away from their Glasgow home to a place where nobody could recognise that the kidnapped baby was a different one. They chose to live in East Kilbride. That's where I lived until I was fourteen. I went to school there.'

Katy sat listening to Logan's story, horrified at what she was hearing. Logan continued:

'When I was five years old and learning to read and write, my teacher had encouraged my class to write a short news article every morning in our school jotters. Most of us would write stuff about what we did at home the previous evening. She wanted us to write on the bottom half of the page and use our crayons to draw a picture on the top half to illustrate what we were writing about. I don't remember much about what I ever wrote, but I remember most of my pictures would have green crayon scribbles for the grass and blue crayon for the sky. I think I always drew a yellow circle for the sun shining. I thought the sun was some sort of machine in the sky, so, I somehow figured that there must be people who would fly up to it and repair it when it broke down. I'd heard of the term 'sunbeam', so, somehow I believed that the people who repaired it were called 'sunbeamers', and that they wore yellow spacesuits.'

Katy smiled when she heard this.

'That's good imagination for a five-year-old.'

'My imagination wasn't bad, but my common sense hadn't developed, so I drew these yellow sunbeamers over my writing on the lower half of the page. My teacher gave me a telling-off for doing that. When I returned home after school, I told Margaret, the woman who I believed was my mum, about the sunbeamers I'd drawn. With her extravagant unusual beliefs in spirituality and superstition, she believed that I had actually seen some sort of yellow spirits flying about, and that I'd got the wording wrong. She decided that these sunbeamers would more likely have been called 'spiritbeamers'. And because she had heard of this from a child born on the spring equinox, she believed that these spiritbeamers would be more active during the spring and autumn equinox dates.'

'She must have been really screwed up,' remarked Katy.

'That's an understatement,' said Logan. 'Since then, she started performing her own unusual rituals on the equinox dates with a few of her friends, most of whom were brain-damaged drug addicts who bought their drugs from her. She quickly formed a small group of followers, and she named that group 'The Order of the Spiritbeamers', but I was too young to pay any attention to what she was doing.'

'So, do you think she's involved in what's happening here on Arran?'

'I'm sure of it. Twenty years ago, she was arrested and jailed at the same time as Clive. I haven't heard the word 'spiritbeamer' since then although I did hear that she was released from prison about two years ago. Almost certainly, Margaret will have been involved in setting up that Spiritbeamer nonsense on the island but that still leaves a few things unexplained.'

'Did she visit Arran?'

'Yes, because of me. One day when I was eight years old we were visiting somewhere in Kilmarnock. I'd got into a really bad fight with Tommy in the back of the car, and the violence was rapidly going out of control. Clive and Margaret started screaming at each other and at me. The situation escalated rapidly to a point which was unbearable. As soon as the car stopped at traffic lights I opened my door and ran away. I climbed into the back of a builder's truck which was parked on the first street I ran into. Nobody saw me do it. I knew that when I'd be found I'd be thoroughly beaten. So, I cowered under a tarpaulin in the back of the truck. I think maybe five minutes later, someone got into the truck and started driving. About maybe an hour later I dared myself to look out from beneath the tarpaulin and I was inside the ferry on my way to Arran.'

'That must have been confusing for you. Did you know you were inside a ferry?'

'No. I just knew I was inside a giant building made of metal with lots of cars around me. By that time, all the other cars' occupants had made their way to the upper decks, so nobody saw me climbing out from the back of the truck. I went to the upper decks and just walked off the ferry with the other passengers when we arrived at Brodick. Nobody noticed I was alone.'

'That must have been terrifying.'

'Actually, it wasn't. Seeing the view of Goat Fell and the Sleeping Warrior made me fall in love with the place as soon as I stepped off the ferry. It just felt peaceful. I was lost but somehow it felt right. I was lucky that it was summer and warm. I managed to find plenty of hiding places. I vaguely remember stealing some food from the grocery store at Brodick Green and raiding the bins for scraps of food. I found a couple of big towels drying on someone's front porch which I stole so I could use them as blankets at night. The ground was dry, so I slept in the rhodendron bushes just outside Brodick going towards Glen Rosa. Then a few days later I found someone's unlocked garden shed so I slept there. I managed to stay hidden for several weeks.'

'And, on your own at that age. Alone and scared.'

'Scared of being found, but I wasn't scared of Arran. My picture was all over the papers and eventually someone mentioned to the police that they'd seen me in Brodick. So, there was a police search on Arran and that search was joined by Clive. Quite honestly, he'd have been delighted if I'd never been found, or better still, if I'd been found dead. He hated me.'

Katy was awestruck at what she was hearing.

'When I was eventually found, he couldn't give me a beating because of all the publicity. He couldn't afford to have me going to school with any bruising. But actually, he was in a better mood than I'd expected because during the search for me, he had become familiar with Arran. That was his first visit to the island. He realised he could use the place to run some of his criminal exploits because he could easily hide things here and be isolated from the mainland. He started planning what he called a massive business deal to take place on the island. I'd overheard him talk about it a few times although I was too young to realise that it was a drug deal he was talking about. Much to my delight, he started to regularly visit Arran to make plans for drug dealing. Because of all the press publicity, he'd become known to some of the locals, so each time he came here he'd bring me so that he could pretend to be a devoted loving father taking his son hillwalking.'

'Did the woman, Margaret come too?'

'Sometimes.'

'So, this week's events were actually planned many years ago?'

'Yes. I remember him saying it would take several years to organise. But when I was fourteen, Clive and Margaret were arrested. I was reunited with my real family. I struggled to adjust for a while, and eventually I joined the army. Robin was in the same unit as me. He knows the full detailed story. We served a few years together in the army and travelled many places. I had to leave the army because of a knee injury from a parachute jump which landed badly. It usually doesn't bother me too much, but it restricted what I could do in the army, so I left to pursue a career in aviation. And I still love to come to Arran.'

'Glad to hear it,' smiled Katy.

'Maybe on another occasion I can tell you more. Much more. But for now, what's happening on the island is very close to some of the planning Clive was making more than twenty years ago before he went to prison. That's why I've been able to predict a few things. Although I admit that finding a little girl with a parachute really confused me. And the Russian writing on the parachute is still a mystery. Also, there's the unsolved mystery of a dead body at the Punchbowl. I don't know if Margaret's here but, as Geordie confirmed, Clive Verhoeven is still in prison so I'm not sure exactly how much involvement is his doing and how much is by other people.'

As he spoke, the comfort of the soup, the sandwiches and the warmth of Katy's apartment were making him sleepy, especially after his earlier activities. Katy saw his eyes slowly closing. She decided to stay quiet to let him fall asleep. As Geordie had said, some sleep might be a good idea for preparation towards what could be a late night. Logan slept while sitting leaning back on the sofa.

Meanwhile, Reynolds, Kyle and two other officers visited Sannox. Having parked their two police vans in the small parking area opposite the glen entrance, they walked into the glen. The flat area near the entrance was filled with campers. Most of them were adults. Reynolds could see Kleo standing next to her tent and talking to a group of ten people. On seeing the police arrive, many of the campers stopped whatever it was they were doing and carefully watched the officers approaching Kleo. As soon as Kleo saw them, she rolled her eyes, audibly saying:

'Oh, what do they want now?' then faking a smile to welcome them.

Kyle spoke:

'Kleo. It seems you have some influence here so please gather your friends round. This is important.'

'Is there a problem?' asked Kleo in a slightly patronising voice. 'This gathering is also important to us.'

Kyle produced a small clear plastic evidence packet containing two of the white pills which Logan had handed in.

'These pills are on the island,' he said. 'We think there will be somebody handing them out tonight at the beach party. But they're deadly.'

'Oh, stop talking nonsense,' interrupted Kleo. 'You're always talking nonsense. These pills have already been on this campsite. Our friends have taken them here already. Now stop trying to spoil our evening.'

'They've been mixed,' said Reynolds. 'We've been given a

batch which we ran tests on. About one in every ten contains a deadly dose of cyanide. Anyone swallowing one of these will die within seconds.'

'Stop trying to scaremonger us,' shouted one of the campers. 'You cops have nothing better to do than to try to scare us away. Go do your job and catch some criminals.'

'We're trying to save your lives,' said Kyle. 'These pills will kill you.'

'Well they haven't killed anyone here yet,' shouted Jasper. 'And we've been here for a few days. Why don't you take a pill and you'll find out for yourself rather than criticise them? Hypocrite.'

'We had them tested,' said Reynolds. 'And we had to double check the results. They've been mixed with identical pills containing cyanide.'

A crowd gathered round them, with various voices becoming more aggressive. Some of the crowd started shouting at the officers:

'Rubbish! Cops go home! Educate yourselves! Go and catch real criminals!'

The atmosphere rapidly became so hostile that the officers became concerned for their safety.

'These people have travelled from all over the country to be here for this celebration,' said Kleo. 'Just because you think you own the place doesn't mean that you do. They're not doing anything wrong and so you have no right to just come here and interfere.'

'It's discrimination,' said Jasper.

Another camper shouted:

'We'll be protesting against the Arran police tonight too.'

Two of the campers started pushing the officers.

'There are almost three hundred of us here, and four of you,' growled Jasper. 'What… I mean, really, what are you going to do? Do you really think that four of you can arrest three hundred of us?'

'We're not trying to arrest you,' said Kyle. 'We're trying to stop you from taking cyanide pills.'

Kleo became less patient at that remark, turning to walk away from them, finally shouting:

'Just stop talking your conspiracy nonsense.'

With tension mounting, and Kleo walking away, it became clear that the officers were only seconds away from being harmed by a few of the more aggressive members of the group. One of them lunged towards Kyle, prompting him to pull out his baton.

'We're going,' said Kyle as the four officers walked away.

In Lamlash, Gremlin began preparing to take the protest boat to Brodick harbour. He tried starting its engine, oblivious to the fact that its propeller had been chained to the rudder. He made three attempts, all of which failed, convincing him that it was the battery which was out of charge. He called Badger:

'I can't start the engine.'

'Can you fix it?' growled Badger.

'Maybe, but I'll need an hour.'

'Do what you can. And whatever you do, don't let our clients hear you struggling with it. They need to know you're going to sink it at Brodick and stop the ferry for a few days. If they think you can't do that, they'll call off the deal.'

'I'm on it,' said Gremlin.

Sloucher heard the conversation.

'Maybe if that English idiot had spent less time chasing the women here and spent more time actually checking that heap of floating shit, he would have been able to start the engine.'

'We'll improvise,' said Badger. 'We'll tell our clients that he's waiting for the sea to calm slightly. So long as they think he'll sink that boat before the next ferry arrives, they'll be happy.'

In Brodick, Logan awoke and looked at his watch. It was four o'clock. He'd been sleeping on the sofa for nearly two hours. Katy was also sleeping, sitting next to him, resting her head on his arm. It was still daylight outside. Sunset would be at twenty minutes after seven, but the thick clouds were already making the island dark. Gradually Katy awoke.

'I think some coffee's needed,' she said as she stood up and made her way to the kitchen.

Logan looked out of the window. The wind was still blowing strongly but there was no rain. Ten minutes later, Robin sent Logan a text message:

'*I'm at the putting green waiting for party to start. I think you should join me and keep me company.*'

Logan replied:

'*OK. Having coffee with Katy then will come.*'

Robin sent an immediate responding text:

'*No. I am VERY lonely! You should get here NOW!*'

'Something's going on,' said Logan. 'I need to see Robin immediately.'

'Do you need me to come?'

'Not sure. Maybe best you stay here. I'll come back when I can.'

He rushed outside to his car. Within two minutes he was at Brodick Green. He parked his car beside Robin's motorcycle.

Robin was sitting on one of the benches next to the putting green.

'What's happening?' asked Logan.

'I saw Gerry Munro's grey Mercedes just over an hour ago in Sannox. I followed him to Corrie harbour. He was wearing his beige jacket and shades on his face like you described. I think you were right about him carrying a gun. I watched him for a while. He climbed onto the sandstones and threw something into the sea there. I can't be sure, but from the distance it looked like a gun. Then he took off his beige jacket and sunglasses and threw them into the sea. Then he threw away another jacket.'

'Getting rid of evidence perhaps? Geordie's been checking on him. Apparently, he has a dodgy past, but I didn't get the details.'

'There's more,' said Robin. 'After he threw everything into the water he put on a red jacket and hat then started hitch-hiking. When he was out of sight I climbed over the rocks. He hadn't thrown the jackets very far. I had to go for another quick swim. I couldn't get the beige one. It had sunk too quickly, but I managed to pull out the other one. When I drove back here he was still hitchhiking only about a mile out of Corrie. I figured he'd either be going to Lamlash for whatever's happening there or come here to the green in preparation for tonight. I took a chance and came here and waited for him. He must have got a lift from someone because he arrived about fifteen minutes later. I wanted to talk to him. There was nobody else around, so it was easy to catch his attention for a few minutes. I made a point of apologising to him for riding past him without offering him a lift because I didn't have a spare crash helmet.'

'He was happy to speak with you?'

'Yeah. We had a brief chat. Nothing significant. He was keen to admire the motorbike. He said he's been staying at a guest house in Brodick.'

'That's strange. Geordie's officers were checking on him. They said he'd been staying at a guesthouse in Lamlash. And why would he leave his car in Corrie?'

'Good question. He started talking about other things like politics and news events. Just small talk stuff. Eventually he asked my name. I made up my name to be Bob. But when he told me his name, it wasn't Gerry Munro. He said his name's Alex Novic.'

Logan was startled at this information.

'Alex Novic? Or Gerry Munro? Maybe this guy uses different names according to the clothes he wears.'

'Ah, well, the jacket he was wearing… it's soaking in the back of my bike but it's identical to the jacket on the dead guy, including the blue circular patch with the bird logo on its sleeve. He seemed really nervous about something. Like he's scared. He's gone for a walk towards the golf course. I think he's making a call to someone. Maybe when he comes back you should take a look at him.'

Logan opened his mobile phone video files. He showed Robin the footage from when he had the drone camera pointed towards Reynold's house from above her garden.

'This is the moment when he puts his arm on her shoulder,' said Logan. 'If I zoom in, we'll be able to see his wristwatch. There it is.'

'I can't see what make it is,' said Robin.

'No, neither can I. But it's a metallic band with a light blue face. What was his accent when he spoke?'

'Scottish,' said Robin. 'I think he's from Glasgow.'

Robin and Logan sat chatting on the bench for the next twenty minutes. The Noah's Ark was still anchored in its same position in the bay. After about half an hour the same man appeared on the green. He was wearing the red jacket as Robin had mentioned and a tartan scarf.

'He's coming this way,' said Robin. 'So, is his name Novic or Munro?'

'I think I prefer calling him Shades,' said Logan.

Robin greeted the man as he approached the bench.

'Not the best weather for a walk,' said Robin.

'No,' replied Shades. 'I think it's time for me to just get back to the guest house and stay in for the evening.'

Both Robin and Logan were doing their best to discretely study his face without their actions being obvious.

'What time is it?' asked Logan.

The man looked at his watch, enabling Logan and Robin to see its metal wrist band and blue face.

'Ten past five,' said Shades as he walked away.

'I think it's him,' whispered Logan. 'But I don't see the spider's web tattoo on his neck. Where's he staying?'

'I'll follow him,' said Robin. 'You go back to Katy. When I'm done I'll go to her parents' house. The box you asked Geordie to bring from Glasgow is waiting for me. I'll take it to the golf course.'

Logan drove back to Katy's apartment. Robin discretely followed Shades on foot to a guest house in Brodick's Mid Mayish Road: a short walk uphill from the Post Office. He phoned Geordie:

'Hi Geordie. That journalist you say is Gerry Munro? Logan told me you'd checked him out and that he's not squeaky clean?'

'That's right. He has a bit of a problematic history.'

'You said that one of your officers has seen his car at a guest house in Lamlash?'

'That's right.'

'Well, it seems his name is also Alex Novic. He's staying at a guest house here in Brodick. I'll text you the address. Maybe when all the action's finished tonight you could get some forensics into both guest houses. I think you'll find out that the two guys are the same bloke. He's abandoned his Mercedes at Corrie.

'You're sure it's the same man?' asked Geordie.

'About ninety percent sure.'

'Okay thanks. I'll check it out.'

Robin strolled back towards the green. Several people had started occupying the green and the beach. Most were carrying various items in preparation for the event. Some were carrying blankets. Others had carrier bags filled with what looked like bottles and cans of various alcoholic drinks. Without talking to anyone, Robin slowly rode his motorcycle away from the green and set off to return to Katy's parents' house.

In Lamlash, Geordie was in the theatre at the academy where special permission had been given for his officers from Glasgow to use the facilities there as a temporary operational base. Approximately a hundred and fifty officers were there. The theatre had been accessed gradually over a period of several hours as officers entered the building on foot from different directions and also through the wooded area north of the school to avoid being noticed. Most of them had arrived in plain clothes. Another fifty plain clothed officers were discretely positioned throughout the village of Lamlash.

A large camper van, occupied by ten officers, was parked at the Old Clockhouse to the north of the Old Pier. The boat parking ground at the roadside had some old boats which had been placed there in a state of disrepair. Five officers were able to hide inside two of these boats. One of the officers phoned Geordie:

'Sir. That guy on that protest boat. He's rowed to shore in a small dinghy. We're watching him trying to break into a car here. Looks like he's trying to get into the engine for something. We could arrest him now, or would you rather we just observe?'

'Do nothing,' said Geordie. 'Just watch him and let me know what he's doing.'

Geordie phoned Logan:

'Everything good with you?'

'I'm almost ready,' said Logan. 'I'm sitting in my car across from the mini golf watching things. The beach area and the green are filling up with people. The locals don't seem to be getting involved. Maybe because of the weather.'

'Or because they're too sensible,' said Geordie.

Thirty minutes passed. Geordie received another call from the officer who was watching Gremlin:

'Sir. It looks like that boat guy has stolen the battery from the car he was tampering with. He's taken it onto the protest boat.'

'Good,' said Geordie. 'He thinks his boat has a battery problem. He hasn't realised… oh, anyway. Do nothing.'

Almost an hour passed. Daylight was fading, especially as the thick overcast clouds had already made the island dark. Logan received a call from Geordie:

'Logan. You're outside watching the action?'

'Yeah Geordie. I'm watching.'

'One of my officers is positioned in Sannox. He saw a speedboat travelling south from Sannox area about two minutes ago. He thinks the boat is full of these cases of drugs you found underwater.'

Logan looked out to sea and waited. After a few minutes he was able to see the silhouette of a speedboat on the horizon heading south. He called Geordie:

'That speedboat's passing Brodick now. At the speed it's travelling, I reckon it'll be in your area in about ten minutes.'

'Okay. Kyle and Reynolds will be in Brodick.'

'Do you know exactly where they'll be?'

'Not yet,' said Geordie. 'That will depend on what happens. But as soon as things start, we're sending all the local officers to Brodick. If that's what the dealers are planning, we need to keep to their plan so that they don't get spooked. Where will you be?'

'I'll go to Katy's to get my drone. I'll be back here in a few minutes.'

'Be careful,' said Geordie. 'Four officers confronted these idiots at Sannox to warn them to not take cyanide pills and it all turned nasty very quickly.'

'Doesn't surprise me,' said Logan. 'I'll be careful.'

He drove back to Katy's apartment and picked up the cardboard box containing his drone.

'Action time,' he said enthusiastically as he made his way out the front door.

'I'm coming with you,' said Katy as she grabbed her jacket.

Logan drove his car back to Shore Road. He phoned Robin.

'I'm almost ready. What about you?'

'I'm in position,' said Robin. 'I'm between the green and the golf course hidden in the trees across the stream behind the tennis court. I was able to listen to some of them talking. Apparently, the Noah's Ark is being towed to shore in about twenty-five minutes. Where are you?'

'We're parked in front of the mini golf.'

'I can see your car from here. You're too visible. Park yourself somewhere else.'

Logan took his advice and moved his car to Alma Road behind the mini-golf. Katy removed the box from the car and carried it as they walked towards the sandstone-walled picnic benches at the southernmost end of the grassy sea-front near the ferry terminal. From there Logan was confident that he and Katy were out of sight from anyone else in Brodick. He called Geordie:

'The party's started on the green. I see more people arriving. My guess is that I'll have to do this in about twenty minutes, but I'd rather wait for your call.'

'That'll work perfectly,' said Geordie. 'There's some movement happening here now. You do it when you think it's the right time.'

Logan placed the cardboard box on the ground beside the picnic bench on the seaward side of the small wall where it couldn't be seen. He opened the box. Watching the beach through his binoculars, he could see people with lights and a few small fires which had been started on the sand. He switched on the torch which he'd attached to the drone and then switched on the drone battery. Leaving the box at the bench, he and Katy started walking towards where two police vans were parked. He approached the first van. Reynolds and Kyle were sitting watching the event. He caught their attention. Kyle opened his window to talk to Logan:

'Geordie says you have a plan?'

'Yes.'

'What's the plan?'

'I'm going to stop the drugs on that boat from coming ashore.'

'And how will you do that?' asked Reynolds.

'Simple,' grinned Logan. 'I'm going to swim out to the boat and then tow it to that little harbour across the bay in front of the castle gardens. And then I'll call the police for you to come and seize the contents.'

'You're not serious,' said Kyle.

'Serious or not, that's the legal answer,' said Logan with a slight smile. 'But I did hear a rumour that there's going to be a fireworks display tonight. Maybe in about fifteen minutes or so. It would be a terrible shame if a spark went in the wrong direction. And if that happens, everyone on that beach will know that it wasn't the police who spoiled their party because they will see your vans sitting around here in plain view, nowhere near their boat.'

In Lamlash, Geordie was at the clock tower with one of his officers. His mobile phone rang. The voice told him:

'All vehicles are in position Sir.'

Geordie and his colleague could see Gremlin on the deck of the protest boat, oblivious to the fact that he was being watched. Just then, Geordie recognised Katy's father, Eric, walking along the road with his dog, Sheena.

'Eric? What are you doing here?'

'Robin mentioned you'd be here watching the Old Pier. I want to be useful, so I decided you'd look a lot less conspicuous if you're standing here talking to an old fart walking his dog.'

Geordie smiled with reluctant agreement.

'I can see who Katy takes after.'

Within minutes, the speedboat arrived from the north and headed towards the raft at the south end of Lamlash bay. Although it was difficult to see what was happening in the darkening conditions, the police could see it pulling alongside the raft. As they watched, they could see that the man on the speedboat was unloading large heavy objects onto the raft.

'I think these are the cases of drugs which were hidden underwater at North Sannox,' said Geordie to his colleague. 'And I think that's the guy who Logan named Badger,'

'What's he unloading?' asked Eric. 'Drugs or weapons?'

'Almost certainly hard drugs,' replied Geordie as he watched. 'And then when the deal's finished, we think they've planned for their helicopter to pick them up from Holy Isle and take them away somewhere.'

'Why would a helicopter pick them up from Holy Isle? Couldn't it just land somewhere around here like on the beach?'

'There's always the possibility that one or more of the drug buyers will turn against the sellers at the last minute,' said Geordie. 'If the sellers are going to be holding a few million pounds in cash, it would be much safer for them to get themselves offshore as quickly as possible after the dealing's finished.'

'But the helicopter's been… dealt with?' asked Eric.

'Apparently so,' said Geordie.

Earlobe and Sloucher were watching the speedboat from the grass area in front of the grocery store.

Earlobe called Badger:

'Plan A, B or C?'

'Plan A is no-go. The water's too rough to trade on the raft,' said Badger. 'Plan B can't happen because the water at Whiting Bay will be worse. Use plan C. Trade on land.'

'Understood,' said Earlobe.

Badger finished unloading the speedboat except for one case. He sat in the boat beside the raft with his hand-held radio. Nine cars arrived into Lamlash shore road. Six from the north and three from the south.

'Almost time,' said Earlobe. 'As soon as we see the police leaving Lamlash, we start.'

From the speedboat, Badger could see these cars on the road. He called Gremlin:

'Did you fix the boat?'

'It's fixed. It just needed a new battery. I'm ready.'

'Good. Take it to Brodick now and start a protest. I'll tell Kleo to start sending her idiots round to meet you. As soon as they're on the boat, pull the plug and get on that jet-ski.'

Gremlin acknowledged:

'On my way.'

He went below deck to start the boat's engine.

Earlobe spoke again into his radio:

'Noah's Ark… start now.'

In Brodick, Logan and Katy watched a car coming from the ferry terminal. It was pulling a jet-ski on a trailer. It parked at the small slipway opposite the mini golf. As they watched, they saw two men getting out of the car. Logan recognised one of the men as Flabby. The two men positioned the jet-ski to launch it, although it looked like it would only be Flabby who would be driving it. Logan phoned Geordie:

'There's a jet-ski being launched here. These things are fast. I need to do this now.'

'Okay, go for it,' said Geordie. 'I think it's action time here too.'

Geordie quickly walked around the shoreline towards the Old Pier. He could hear the protest boat engine starting but only for a few brief seconds. Then he could hear three more attempts at starting it, all of which failed. Gremlin was aware that something had seized, but he had no idea of the cause.

In Brodick, Logan and Katy quickly made their way along the shoreline and onto the narrow footpath leading towards the putting green. Near the end of that path was a hedged area where they were able to sit on the sloped grass out of view from anyone. Logan produced his drone controller from its pouch and switched it on. Looking though his monitor screen he could clearly see through the drone camera lens inside the box at the picnic bench. He called Robin:

'Light up the sky for me.'

Robin was hidden in the bushes to the west of the green with three boxes of fireworks which had been brought over by Geordie. Robin lit the fuse which would take a minute to set off the first firework, giving him a chance to flee the scene. That first firework would activate the other fireworks in sequence to give a full ten-minute display. Logan watched from where he was sitting. The first firework exploded in the sky and made a loud bang with a spectacular colourful display which thoroughly thrilled the crowd on the green. One-by-one the fireworks launched into the dark overcast sky.

While the crowd was looking at the fireworks display, Logan

seized the opportunity to launch his drone without it being seen by anyone. He initially hovered it, enabling him to see through its camera lens via his monitor at the view of Brodick Bay. He hovered it to a height just below the low cloud base and guided it towards Noah's Ark. The upper wind was strong, so he had to fly the small aircraft partially sideways to maintain its direction to the Ark. There was enough light reflection from streetlights, and helped by the fireworks display, to enable him to see Noah's Ark from where he was sitting.

He explained to Katy:

'This was what I was doing last night. I'd planned to swim out to it when it was anchored off Sannox, but it had been towed here. That makes it easier for me to sabotage it without being seen.'

'What did you do to it?'

'My original plan was to remove the contents by throwing them overboard, but I remember an operation from the army when a gang of drug smugglers had placed explosive devices in their drug stores to deter thieves. In these situations, the army usually prefers to destroy these findings with controlled explosions. When I got inside that tent thing on the Ark, I couldn't be sure if it had been rigged the same way. Part of my shopping spree with Geordie in Glasgow was to acquire a wetsuit and some equipment for this operation.'

'You've put explosives inside the boat?'

'Not explosives. But I made a simple little incendiary device. Crudely made with a few batteries, some wires, sticky tape, some fireworks and some petrol which is dripping out slowly from three deliberately pierced plastic containers. It shouldn't explode, but it should catch fire and burn quickly. If I'd destroyed the boat last night, I would have screwed up the whole operation, so I had to leave the electrical circuit open. But it has to be destroyed now.'

'So, what does that hook thing do?' asked Katy.

'Well, I would have preferred to use some sort of radio-controlled device so that I could simply press a button, but I didn't have anything radio-controlled except my drone, and its battery was empty, so I left a thin wire loop dangling at the back of the boat. What I have to do now is grab that loop with the grappler hook hanging from the drone. If I can do that, I can pull the wire loop which will close the electrical circuit in the boat and detonate the incendiary device so hopefully I can set fire to it before that jet-ski gets there. I only have to pull the wire loop a couple of centimetres.'

'You've done this before?'

'Eh, well, no. This is my first attempt.'

'So, what was your back-up plan? You said you had a back-up plan which was a terrible one.'

'Ah. Yes. Well, the terrible back-up plan was for me to swim out there and just grab the wire loop by hand and pull it, then swim back while the boat burns but there's no time for that now. I hadn't planned on them using a jet-ski. That'll get there in less than a minute.'

He flew the drone down to the top of the fabric cover. The torch he'd attached to the drone enabled him to see the exposed wire loop. The boat was rocking violently in the rough water with its bow pointing towards the beach. Logan hovered his drone above the wire loop at the stern. Although he could see through the drone lens, he couldn't see the position of the grappler hook dangling beneath. Having made several attempts to hook the loop, each time lifting his drone higher, and realising each attempt had failed, he became increasingly concerned about the jet-ski which was speeding towards the Ark. He estimated that the jet-ski would arrive there in less than twenty seconds. It would likely take about a minute for Flabby to raise the boat's anchor and then another minute to tow it to the shore.

In desperation, Logan hovered the drone to the stern, enabling him to again see the wire loop through the drone lens.

Flabby positioned the jet-ski next to the Ark. He saw the drone, but he didn't know why it was there and he could do nothing about it anyway. He positioned the jet-ski to the bow of the Ark to pull up its anchor. The rough sea was making his task difficult.

Meantime, Logan flew the drone down to the stern to make a low swoop as fast as possible. As soon as his monitor could no longer see the loop, he knew the drone would be almost directly over it. At that moment, he lifted the drone in a forward sweeping motion which made the grappler hook swing forward. In doing so, the grappler caught the loop and pulled it, successfully closing the electrical circuit. As the loop tensioned, the drone came to an abrupt halt in flight. For a few moments, Logan couldn't be sure if he'd pulled on the loop as planned, or if the grappler hook had snagged on something else, but there was nothing else he could do to free his drone from its position. He applied full power to its motors to try to lift it with as much force as possible, hoping that he was tensioning the loop.

Because of the way he'd set the main fireworks fuse, he knew it would take a few seconds for a small fire to ignite. He could see the jet-ski at the front of the Ark as Flabby was frantically trying to pull its anchor out of the water.

After what felt like too long, through his monitor, Logan could see a faint orange reflection in the drone lens. From where they were sitting, he and Katy could see the beginning of a small fire on the Ark.

'Come on, come on, light up a bit more,' he sighed to himself.

Twenty seconds later the flames blasted out from the top of the boat. Flabby had no option but to abandon his mission and steer his jet-ski away from the flames. Logan tried to fly his drone away from the flames, but he struggled to maintain control of it. The heat from the flames started to melt the drone's nylon rotor blades. After a few moments the drone spun around and crashed back onto the boat which had quickly become an inferno. Flabby stopped his jet-ski about fifty metres from the flames. He knew he could do nothing to stop the fire. The crowd on the green gasped and shouted in their stunned disappointment at what they were seeing. Some of them started crying. A few of them screamed.

Logan called Geordie with an enthusiastic satisfied tone to his voice:

'There's been a fireworks display here. Oh, and a small boat's on fire. And about two thousand people rather annoyed. Maybe you should send some police here.'

Geordie chuckled.

'Nice work guys. Now, go and get yourselves hidden.'

He called the police station.

'It's time,' he said. 'All local officers to Brodick now. Make it obvious. Use the sirens.'

Almost immediately, all the local officers on duty sped their vehicles towards Brodick with blue lights flashing and sirens blaring.

By now, Earlobe was parked in his van in the small carpark beside Lamlash's rockery memorial to the Arran Clearances. He watched the police cars speeding out of Lamlash. He looked at his watch as he spoke to Sloucher:

'Fifteen minutes sooner than planned. Good. That's the police gone. Let's get down to business.'

He called Badger who was still in the speedboat next to the raft:

'Let's do this.'

'Who gave the order for it to happen so early?' asked Badger nervously.

'Who cares?' said Earlobe. 'Two-thousand crazy people will keep the police busy there and they already have pills so maybe one of them got impatient and started early. And it's just going to keep getting crazier as the evening goes on. We're police free now for the next hour. Let's go. Call the first client.'

Earlobe, accompanied by Sloucher, drove their van the short distance from the car park to the Old Pier and parked on the ground immediately to its north to stay hidden from the road. As they arrived, one of the nine cars which had just arrived into the village was already parked on the same part of the harbour.

Sloucher pointed at the protest boat.

'Why is he still here?'

'Good question. But not urgent. The important thing is that he gets it over to Brodick before the ferry starts again and that won't be until morning.'

Just then, Gremlin called Earlobe's phone.

'Engine problems. I can't start it.'

Earlobe sighed in frustration at this news.

'How many times did you try to start it?'

'About four or five.'

'Did you try starting it when our client's car was here?' asked Earlobe.

'I don't know if he was here. I was below deck trying to start this heap of shit.'

'Can you fix it?'

'No. It's seized up.'

Badger was guiding the speedboat towards the north slipway. Sloucher walked down the steps to meet him.

'Why is that boat still here?' asked Badger.

'Engine problems,' said Sloucher. 'so, we have to tell them we're just waiting for calmer seas.'

'Okay, let's get this over with. We'll be out of here in less than an hour if we can get this right. Tell the jet-ski to change the plan. As soon as he's finished with the Ark, he needs to come straight here instead of the ferry terminal.'

The officers watched as Badger carried some bags from his speedboat. Two men from the first car entered the black van. One of them was carrying a briefcase. One of Geordie's colleagues could see this from the small fishing tackle shop on the pier. She called Geordie.

'I think the dealing's started,' she said. 'They're all inside that van.'

'Good,' said Geordie. 'I'm guessing there will be more cars and it looks like their plan is to trade with each car one at a time. We need to do nothing yet. These cars will need to be followed separately. Did anyone manage to count the number of items that guy unloaded from his speedboat onto the raft?'

'I wasn't able to count accurately,' said his colleague. 'But I think about a dozen or so.'

'I'm guessing one package per car, so let's expect about a dozen cars. I've counted nine so far.'

After just three minutes, the two men stepped out of the van. The one who had been carrying the briefcase was now carrying a large holdall. Both men got into their car and drove out from the pier area then turned left, southbound. Geordie spoke into his police radio:

'Team one, go.'

His command triggered two unmarked police vehicles to discretely follow the car.

Meanwhile Badger walked back to his speedboat, telling Earlobe:

'Call number two to be here in six minutes.'

Sloucher was visibly nervous.

'I just got a text,' he said. 'The Ark's caught fire. It didn't make it to the beach.'

'Call the next car anyway,' said Earlobe. 'Then call Gerry to find out what's happening. We can't stop now.'

Sloucher made the call. Gerry Munro answered. He was standing in his guest house bedroom and looking out of his window from where he could see Brodick beach.

'Are you at the beach?' asked Sloucher.

'Yes,' lied Munro calmly. 'I'm on the beach watching the chaos.'

'What happened to Noah's Ark?'

'I don't know,' said Munro. 'There was a fireworks display on the green and then the Ark caught fire.'

'Fireworks? What idiot organised fireworks? It's not part of the plan.'

'Well, it doesn't matter now. These people are going even more crazy because they're not getting their pills and weed. The place is crawling with police and it looks like they'll be here for enough time to stay out of your way.'

Meantime, Geordie and his colleagues continued watching from the shadows while Badger returned to the raft and loaded another bag onto the speedboat. Within six minutes from leaving the slipway, Badger returned the speedboat to the pier with another large bag. At the same moment, another car arrived and parked beside the van. This time there was just one occupant in the car. He was also carrying a briefcase as he entered the van. Within about three minutes, the same man stepped out from the van carrying a holdall instead of his briefcase. Like the first car, he drove away southbound through Lamlash.

Geordie called on his police radio:

'Team two. Go.'

In Brodick, Logan, Katy and Robin met up at Katy's parents' house.

'It's too wild out there for us,' joked Robin to Sandra. 'Eh, where's Eric?'

'He took Sheena for a walk,' said Sandra, oblivious to the fact that that he'd taken the dog to Lamlash.

In Lamlash, Geordie and his officers watched patiently as they eventually counted nine cars, each taking their turn at meeting with Earlobe and Sloucher in the van. On each occasion Badger would take his speedboat to the raft to collect another large bag. As the ninth car drove away, Badger, now standing at the van, having delivered his final package, made a call to the helicopter pilot on Holy Isle.

'It's time,' he said. 'We're on our way to you.'

'I'll be ready,' said the pilot.

He stepped out of the helicopter and started to remove the awning.

Sloucher, Earlobe and Badger walked to the speedboat, each carrying three briefcases. On seeing this, Geordie knew the drugs deal was over and that they were attempting to make their escape. He called on his radio:

'All teams block the roads. Make the arrests. Go.'

Twenty police officers stormed the slipway from the shadows behind the boats which had been parked on trailers beside the fishing tackle shop. One unmarked police car drove onto the slipway as the three men managed to get into the speedboat which was floating just a couple of metres offshore. Badger started its engines and was steering the craft away when the police driver accelerated the car as fast as it could go down the slipway and into the water, ramming the speedboat with enough force that it punched a large hole in the boat's starboard side while simultaneously pushing it further out to sea.

On seeing this, Gremlin threw his small partially-inflated dinghy overboard from the protest boat for his companions. Knowing that their speedboat was sinking, but with its engines still running, Badger was able to steer the now-crippled speedboat the short distance to the dinghy where all three men jumped into it from their sinking vessel. Gremlin, realising that he wasn't going to achieve his mission of steering the protest boat to Brodick, started climbing down the rope ladder as if to get into the dinghy, but Earlobe shouted at him:

'This dinghy isn't designed to take four of us. Stay where you are. The jet-ski will be here in a few minutes for you.'

Gremlin climbed back up the ladder. Sloucher took the oars of the dinghy. In the rough water, the waves were splashing against it and spilling inside it at a rate faster than the men could bale out the water with their cupped hands.

'Call the helicopter,' shouted Sloucher. 'Tell him to use our back-up plan and pick us up at the raft.'

'Can't you get us to Holy Isle before this thing sinks?' asked Badger.

'No,' shouted Sloucher. 'And if you keep asking stupid questions at a time like this, we won't even make it to the raft. So, stop talking and do what you can to keep the water out.'

On Holy Isle, the helicopter pilot had already partially removed the awning and was fully prepared for his expectation of the men arriving by speedboat and jet-ski. He received a call from Badger:

'Change of plan. Get airborne now and pick us up from the raft.'

'The raft, okay,' said the pilot. 'I'll be there in a few minutes.'

'Glad we have the raft as a back-up plan,' shouted Badger. 'But how did the police find out?'

'Bad time to ask that question,' replied Sloucher. 'Let's just concentrate on keeping afloat until the jet-ski gets here.'

Sloucher stopped rowing and helped the others to bale out the water with his cupped hands. They managed to hold onto the nine cash-filled briefcases throughout the event. To their relief, they saw the speeding jet-ski arriving from the north, still being driven by Flabby. Earlobe flashed his torch at the jet-ski, telling the others:

'We're going to be okay now. We'll be airborne long before the police can figure out how to catch us out here.'

Flabby threw his tow line to the dinghy and towed it to the raft while the three occupants continued baling out the water. When they reached the raft, Badger, Earlobe and Sloucher climbed onto it clumsily while keeping a firm hold of the briefcases. When they were all on the raft, the dinghy was quickly carried away with the wind.

Flabby drove the jet-ski to the protest boat to collect Gremlin who was already half way down his rope ladder.

'Why are you not in Brodick?' shouted Flabby.

Gremlin said nothing as he boarded the jet-ski. Flabby drove it to the raft. As he and Gremlin climbed onto it, a wave hit the jet-ski and pushed it out of reach. Gremlin, Badger, Earlobe, Sloucher and Flabby now sat helpless on the raft as they watched the jet-ski drift away. None of them were strong enough swimmers to venture into in such rough water to try to retrieve it. The raft was rocking violently in the rough sea, prompting Sloucher to say:

'This is a bad idea. This raft's like a roller coaster and none of us can swim.'

Badger looked at his watch.

'Our pilot said he'll be here in a few minutes. What's taking him so long?'

'Are you sure that helicopter can land on this?' asked Earlobe.

'He's an experienced pilot. But can he cope with this storm?'

'Relax men,' said Badger. 'We've made him an offer he can't refuse. He'll not chicken out.'

On Holy Isle, the helicopter pilot removed the last guy rope from the awning when he noticed it pulling on the thin fishing line which Logan had attached to where the control rods had been.

He called Badger:

'I've been sabotaged. I can't fly.'

Badger sat on the raft in disbelief at what he was hearing.

'Can you fix it?'

'No. The tail rotor's had its control rods removed.'

The men watched helplessly as the jet-ski kept drifting away. They didn't talk as they looked around them. After a few minutes, Badger saw a small boat coming towards them.

Meanwhile at the harbour in Lamlash, Geordie gave his binoculars to Eric. He grinned as he told him:

'We managed to bring our own speedboat on a trailer with the rest of our convoy.'

On the raft, Badger shouted at his colleagues:

'We have company. Almost certainly armed police.'

Sloucher pulled out his pistol and pointed it at the oncoming boat. Badger grabbed his wrist and pulled his arm down.

'We can't have a shoot-out,' he said. 'These guys will have body armour, rifles and night vision goggles. Guys throw your guns into the water now before you get us all killed.'

'What about the cash?' asked Sloucher.

'If they haven't arrested our clients, there's no proof that the money's a dirty. Hold onto it. We'll get a good lawyer.'

Outside Lamlash, police blockades were set up in various locations along the roads, and the nine cars belonging to the drug buyers had been pulled over by armed police.

In Brodick, the beach party was continuing while the local police watched from a safe distance. Katy, Robin and Logan were sitting in Katy's parents' house enjoying a casual conversation. Eric had returned home with Sheena.

The police had successfully arrested all the occupants of the nine cars. Sloucher, Gremlin, Earlobe, Flabby and Badger were arrested from the raft and taken back to shore where they were placed into custody at the police station. With all five men in custody, Geordie called Kyle on his mobile phone:

'How's life in Brodick?'

'We really need back-up,' said Kyle. 'The crowd are angry at the Ark being destroyed. Some of them are blaming it on local vigilantes. Others are blaming it on police. Most of them are drunk or under the influence of whatever drugs they've been taking. And they're too curious. They want to protest but that protest boat hasn't arrived so some of them are planning to go on the rampage through the streets of Brodick and they're determined to find out who destroyed the Ark. They're clashing with the local police here. We're outnumbered. We had no choice but to back off. There's going to be carnage here very soon if we don't get back-up.'

'We've already sent back-up' said Geordie. 'They'll be with you in less than five minutes. Another team will be with you in about ten minutes.'

As promised, Geordie sent Logan a text saying:

'*Lamlash Successful. Massive drug haul seized.*'

Within five minutes, Brodick's Shore Road rapidly filled with unmarked police cars and vans. Over a hundred officers rushed to the green and beach area. Police sirens could be heard from Katy's parents' house. Logan stood up from the sofa.

'I need to be there,' he said.

'I'm coming with you,' said Robin.

They strolled along to the green area from where they could see the chaos. There was a crowd of almost two thousand people. Some of them were dancing to loud music. Some were lying drunk on the ground. Some were crying due to being upset about Noah's Ark being destroyed and the money they'd lost in the process. A crowd had gathered on Shore Road beside the putting green to confront the police. Logan and Robin walked towards the police, who told them to stay back. Robin spoke to one of the officers:

'I'm Logan. This is Robin. We're friends of Geordie Buchanan. If you let us through we can help.'

Kyle saw them and walked over.

'Logan, this isn't the safest place to be right now. The crowd are furious about the boat fire and they think it was caused by some local vigilantes.'

'Who told them that?' asked Robin.

'The organisers,' said Kyle. 'They're preparing to cause mayhem around the town. There's going to be a lot of destruction in Brodick in the next few minutes if we don't stop these people. I think things are going to get violent. And we're still outnumbered. You've helped us, but really, you need to stay away just now.'

'Actually, I think you need me here,' replied Logan. 'We need to find Kleo and Jasper.'

Kyle nodded to the other officers to let them through.

'I'll need four of your plain clothed officers to come with us,' said Logan. 'Two for me and two for Robin.'

'I'll check the beach,' said Robin. 'You check the green.'

After searching through the crowd, Logan eventually saw Kleo and Jasper sitting on a blanket with a small group surrounding them at the north end of the Green. He and his two officers approached her. On seeing him, she turned her head away to indicate that she was ignoring him.

'We need your help,' said Logan.

'We?' asked Kleo aggressively.

The two officers showed their police identification to Kleo and Jasper.

'I don't think you have any business being here,' said Kleo. 'Look around you. People have come here from all over the country for a peaceful celebration of equinox. But the police wanted to antagonise us. And you're friends with the police. Now you want me to help you… to help them?'

'Yes. You and Jasper organised this event. Am I right is saying that?'

'Yes, we did,' said Jasper. 'A lot of people travelled a long way and invested a lot of money for what was on that boat out there, but some local arsonist destroyed it. And the locals must know who's responsible, so the locals owe these people a lot of money. And the police are siding with the locals. And you're friendly with police. So, tell me Mister Logan. Why should we help you?'

'If so many people have invested so much money to buy the drugs on that boat, and now the drugs are destroyed, then whoever took the money from you all would be the person who owes you money. So, who would that person be?'

'That's none of your business,' said Kleo.

'You're right. It's none of my business. I don't care about the money. But anyway, for what it's worth, it wasn't you who organised this event. You might think you did, but you were being used by an organised gang to create chaos and get people killed. It wasn't a local vigilante who set fire to that boat. And it wasn't the police. But in the next few minutes your crowd is planning to take revenge on the locals by destroying their property and clash with anyone who tries to stop them. These people think that you're the organisers, so they'll listen to you.'

'If it wasn't the locals or police who started the fire, who was it then?' asked Kleo.

'It was me,' said Logan. 'I set fire to the drugs. There! I said it. It wasn't the police or any local.'

'I don't believe you,' said Jasper. 'Why would you do that?'

Logan produced his mobile phone and showed them the video footage of his drone flying to the Noah's Ark, and the last few seconds of the flames before the drone was destroyed. He then showed the video footage of the dead man's body at the devil's Punchbowl.

'He's dead. That was the day I found Heidi… I mean Karina.'

Kleo and Jasper watched the video as it panned round to show Karina standing near the dead body.

'A major drugs bust happened in Lamlash tonight. You were set up as a distraction to assist a massive drug deal linked to attempted mass murder. You deliberately organised a drug-fuelled party on this beach area with illegal narcotics. Some of these pills contained cyanide. You carried out the abduction of a little girl last week. At least one man is dead. Now some of your followers are about to go on the rampage in the streets of Brodick to destroy property to avenge a local vigilante who doesn't exist.'

Logan showed her the various pictures and video clips on his phone.

'There's a sabotaged helicopter stranded on Holy Isle. And that protest boat was being planned to be sunk at the ferry terminal to prevent the ferry from arriving here for at least several days to stop police back-up coming. Think about it. A worn out old boat in a dreadful state of repair being sunk out there in rough cold water with a crowd of spaced-out drunk protesters without lifejackets. How many of you would have been able to survive that?'

Kleo was furious yet speechless.

'Both of you would have been blamed for the deaths while the main drug dealers would have flown away with the money, in a helicopter which I had to sabotage on Holy Isle.'

Kleo remained silent. Logan continued:

'Margaret Verhoeven was the founder of the Order of the Spiritbeamers. You must know that.'

Kleo and Jasper were surprised at hearing that name. Kleo, with her patronising voice told Logan:

'You know nothing about the Order of the Spir…'

'I started it,' interrupted Logan. 'When I was five years old. I was a kid living illegally in the same house as Margaret Verhoeven. I was kidnapped and raised by the Verhoevens. I was that kid named in the press as the 'equinox baby'. I invented the word 'sunbeamer' when I was five because I thought they were the men who could repair the sun when it broke down. Margaret Verhoeven turned that into 'spiritbeamer' and set up her own cult. She claimed to have some spiritual connection with the equinox, but it was just her weird way of hiding behind the fact that she was a ruthless killer and kidnapper living with another ruthless murderer. She spent eighteen years in prison and only got released about two years ago. A lot of people were going to die tonight, and you would have been left to face the charges and almost certainly a very long prison sentence.'

Kleo and Jasper stood silently as Logan continued:

'You're already in serious trouble. Abduction, accessory to attempted mass murder and drug dealing. Blocking the ferry would be regarded as terrorism. And now that you've been told all of this in the presence of these two police officers here, it'll be on record that either you've decided to keep your event peaceful, or deliberately chosen to ignore what we're saying and allow a rampage to take place, in which case you'll be encouraging violence against innocent locals. More terrorism. You're possibly already looking at prison time.'

Kleo started trembling. Her facial expression started to show that she was worried. Jasper removed the cigarette from his mouth and threw it to the ground while looking away from Logan as he tried to think of something to say. Logan continued:

'I've noticed how you like to form the same opinion as the majority of any gathering around you. And somehow, despite your arrogant stupidity, I don't think you like violence. So, instead of you forming the same opinion as the majority surrounding you, this is your chance to get the majority to form your opinion. They'll listen to you. You claim to have some sort of authority on all that peace and love stuff to make the world a better place. This is your chance to actually practice what you preach. Go to the police over there. Take their loudhailer and make the crowd calm down before someone gets killed. If you do that, you can reduce your chances of going to prison.'

Reluctantly, Kleo and Jasper made their way towards the police vans. Unknown to Logan, Robin had been watching from the beach. He approached Logan.

'She listened to me,' said Logan. 'But she's so spaced out on whatever she's been smoking, I'm not sure how much of what I said got absorbed into her pickled brain. I had to tell her it was me who started the fire. And as you know I don't trust people on drugs, so I don't know if she'll do what I suggested, or if she'll take that loudhailer and point me out to the crowd.'

'In that case it's time to make ourselves vanish,' said Robin.

'Good idea. Let's get out of here.'

CHAPTER 8

Thursday September 23rd

It was eight o'clock in the morning. Logan had again fallen asleep with exhaustion, finding himself waking on the sofa at Katy's parents' house. As before, Katy had fallen asleep next him, with her head resting on his shoulder. Robin had been given a bed in the spare room. Katy's parents were already awake and preparing a cooked breakfast in the kitchen. Gradually the morning unfolded peacefully as the five of them sat at the kitchen table.

'What are your plans for today?' asked Eric. 'The weather seems to have calmed down, and sunny spells are forecast for later.'

Robin had already noticed the golf clubs in the shed where he'd been allowed to shelter his motorbike.

'You fancy a game of golf?' asked Robin.

Eric grinned.

'I thought you'd never ask.'

Logan looked at Katy and Sandra.

'What are you two girls planning?'

'I offered to help set things up in preparation for the church jumble sale,' said Sandra. 'You two can do whatever you want.'

'You said one of your favourite places is the shop at Brodick Castle because it sells the best chocolate cake,' said Katy.

'Oh yes. Not quite as good as my gran's chocolate cake but… yes. Chocolate cake at the castle is like the eighth wonder of the world for me.'

'Okay then. I'm buying you chocolate cake at the castle.'

The rest of the day was pleasant and relaxed. Logan strolled with Katy around the castle grounds until they sat on the wooden bench surrounding the inside of the Bavarian Summer House at the east side of the garden.

'I once tried counting the pinecones in here,' he said. 'I got to several hundred and then fell asleep. I didn't try again.'

They sat there for over an hour as Logan told Katy more about his childhood. He showed her the tree just a few paces outside to the right of the path where the roots had picked up a large rock as it grew, trapping the rock inside the tree.

Meanwhile, Robin was enjoying his game of golf with Eric on the Sannox golf course while being surrounded by the mountainous scenery and the specific scent of fresh Arran wilderness. Across from the golf course, they could see the police talking to campers. Gradually, the campsite started to empty as tents were being taken down and campers packed their bags.

In Brodick, an extra ferry had been arranged to carry a convoy of police vans. Later in the evening, Logan and Robin met up again, this time at the Auchrannie Resort for a meal in the Eighteen-Sixty-Nine restaurant, named after the year when that part of the resort was built. They had invited Katy, her parents and Geordie to join them for a meal. When they arrived, Roz was already sitting at the reserved table with her sister, Lynn.

'I didn't fly this time,' she joked. 'I took the first ferry after the storm eased.'

Minutes later, Geordie arrived looking tired but satisfied. As they sat the table, he explained:

'The five men in Lamlash: The guy with the earring who you named Earlobe, and the dark haired bearded bloke who you named Badger, are brothers from Albania. They were the main guys in the operation. The scruffy one with the longer hair who you named Sloucher, is Hungarian. The bald-headed one on the protest boat who you called Gremlin, is from London. And the fat one…'

'Flabby,' joked Logan. 'That's what I named him.'

'Well, I think he's not a major player in any of this. Small time criminal and a bit arrogant but he's actually being quite helpful with some of the information he's giving us. We managed to catch twelve drug buyers. They were in nine cars. Each car was carrying nearly a million pounds worth of cocaine and crystal meth.'

'Nine million pounds worth of drugs in one operation?' asked Eric.

'Give or take a few thousand.'

'What about the crowd on the beach?' asked Sandra.

'That's more complicated. Some of them were carrying plenty of illegal substances. Many others weren't carrying any drugs because they were waiting for their supply to come to shore. Twenty of them had managed to get hold of cyanide pills but they didn't know what they were. Thankfully nobody swallowed any of them. We reckon a few hundred of these people would have been given them if Noah's Ark had made it to shore. Out of about two thousand Spiritbeamer followers, we made fifty-three arrests for various offences including assault.'

'You have enough space in the police station for so many people?' asked Katy.

'No, we haven't. All we could do was keep the more serious ones in custody. The rest we processed. They'll get taken back to the mainland in our police vans and further questioned there. There will be police monitoring everyone who uses that ferry until all fifty-three are picked up. For now, they're stuck on the island.'

'What about the helicopter pilot?' asked Logan.

'We got him too. His name's Jansa. A Slovenian guy. He was actually very helpful at explaining some things. Apparently, there was another pilot… some Russian guy… chosen for this event but there was a last-minute change of plan so Jansa got called to fly for them. He doesn't have a criminal record, but he was being paid a lot of money and also having his family threatened. He helped to explain a few things, including the mystery of Gerry Munro and Alex Novic.'

'Both the same person?' asked Robin.

'Yes and No. Starting with Gerry Munro. His name hasn't always been Munro. He'd changed it legally by deed pole about ten years ago. You'll recognise the name when I tell you.'

Robin and Logan sat in anticipation.

'Billy Macfarlane.'

Robin looked at Logan with eyes wide open. Logan looked equally surprised.

'Eh? I'd heard that Billy died about ten years ago,' said Logan.

Geordie shook his head.

'He'd faked his death because he was being threatened. People wanted to kill him, and others preferred to blackmail him. You'll remember.'

'I remember he wasn't popular,' said Logan. 'But I didn't recognise him this week. I remember Billy being a massive fat blob. I mean, obesely massive. When I was a kid I used to call him 'Mammoth', especially as he had long hair and a beard like candy floss. Are you sure it's the same guy?'

'Definitely him. He had long hair and a big beard ten years ago when he carried a lot of extra weight. And he had a crucifix tattooed to his forehead.'

'I remember that,' said Logan.

'When he was released from prison he faked his death, and emerged with a new identity, using the name Gerry Munro. Being freshly out of jail meant that he wasn't wanted by the police for anything, so we weren't watching him closely. He even had his crucifix tattoo removed by laser treatment. Having gone to all that effort, he didn't do himself any favours by returning to his criminal lifestyle and living in the same area where he already had a criminal reputation. And his size gave him away. He got too confident and got himself seen by the wrong people who still recognised him, so they continued to threaten and blackmail him to make him do anything they told him to do.'

'Blackmail him for what?' asked Logan.

'We're still trying to find that out. We think he committed some crimes before he went to prison. For now, he's refusing to say more until he speaks with a lawyer. But I can think of some unsolved crimes from years ago which sort of put Munro, or Macfarlane as he was named then, a prime candidate for a suspect. We think it was Verhoeven who was controlling him.'

'That bit doesn't surprise me,' commented Logan.

Geordie continued:

'I'm embarrassed to say, when we checked him from his car registration you gave me, I didn't immediately realise he used to be Billy Macfarlane. Anyway, he was ordered to come here to help Kleo and Jasper organise the Spiritbeamer event. He donated about two dozen tents to the Spiritbeamers. The original helicopter pilot… the Russian guy… had met with Munro a few days earlier. He had that old parachute in his attic which he knew he'd never use, so, thinking he was being helpful, he gave it to Munro to give to Kleo to use as a tepee.'

'That explains the Russian writing on its hem,' said Logan.

'Yes, maybe. Anyway, Munro hung it up on a tree for them, but they were already so wasted on drugs that they didn't notice its harness was still attached, otherwise they might have realised it was a parachute. Unknown to Kleo, Munro had also been ordered to retrieve a rucksack which had been buried, wrapped in waterproof sheeting, somewhere in a graveyard near Pirnmill.'

'Pirnmill?' asked Logan as he stared up at the ceiling.

'You have a memory about that?' asked Geordie.

'Y… yeah, actually… maybe. Is that the rucksack which I found at the Punchbowl?'

'Yep. In our estimate, it contained about half a million pounds worth of cocaine. It had been buried over twenty years ago in one of the war graves at Pirnmill.'

Logan sat back in his chair as if he'd realised something, thinking carefully about what he was hearing. He recognised that the others had noticed his reaction and were expecting him to say something, but he just sat pensively quiet, allowing Geordie to continue explaining:

'Anyway, Munro decided to take advantage of this venture to change his identity again. To do that he had to hire an assistant. He found a lonesome alcoholic named Alexander Novic from Glasgow.'

'The dead guy?' asked Robin.

'Yes. At least, that's what we think for now. Novic had moved here from Ukraine with his parents when he was a boy. He was a harmless and homeless guy with some mental health problems but with no criminal record, no job, not many friends and no immediate family who would miss him if he disappeared. He had similar build and appearance to Munro's new slim physique, but with his lifestyle, he had very few teeth, so he had no reliable dental records. Munro decided to kill him and steal his identity. To prepare for that, Munro started laser treatment to remove his own spider's web tattoo, but he kept drawing over it to keep it visible to anyone who knows him. Then just two weeks ago he paid for Novic to get an identical spider's web tattoo on his neck.'

'Presumably he was already planning to kill Novic so that his body would be found?' asked Katy.

'Yes. That's why he made sure Novic was wearing an identical dark-green jacket with the noticeable blue circular patch on the sleeve. Munro had been ordered to give the rucksack to the Albanians. He asked to borrow their helicopter, using the excuse that the rucksack was too heavy to carry from a remote hillside. So, when he located it from Pirnmill, he and Novic carried it all the way to Loch Tanna where the helicopter picked them up.'

'That's a long hike,' said Robin. 'Especially with a heavy rucksack.'

'All the better to persuade the Albanians to let him use the helicopter. If he'd told them he'd found it in Pirnmill they'd just have sent a car which wasn't part of Munro's plan. You see, once he was in the helicopter, he said he wanted to fly with the door slid back so he could see the view. They flew over Coich na h'Oighe. There was a lot of ground mist, so any hikers on the ground might have heard the helicopter but wouldn't have seen it. They certainly wouldn't have seen a body falling from it. According to the pilot, Munro had asked him to put the helicopter into a hover just above the cliff at the north side of the Punchbowl, so he could take photographs, but actually, Munro's plan was to push Novic out so that he'd land at the foot of the cliff.'

'Making it look like a climbing accident,' said Logan.

'Yes. That was his plan. He'd already told people that he was planning to climb Coich na h'Oighe. There have been several deaths from that cliff over the years so another one wouldn't look suspicious.'

'But that doesn't explain the ripcord or the rucksack being there,' said Logan.

'Munro knew there would be a struggle if he'd try to push Novic out of the helicopter without killing him first, but he didn't want to shoot him because he wanted the body to be found, but forensics would find the bullet, proving it wasn't a climbing accident. That's why Munro kept the ripcord from the parachute to use it as a strangulation device.'

'So, that guy… Novic… was dead before he fell?' asked Katy.

'No. Novic struggled much more than Munro had expected. Eventually, Munro managed to kick him out, but in desperation, Novic tried grabbing anything to stop himself falling. Unfortunately for Munro, he grabbed the rucksack. Munro tried holding onto it but with the weight of Novic dangling from it, Munro lost his grip, so the rucksack and ripcord fell with Novic.'

'And he misjudged his position,' added Robin. 'Novic hit the ground about two hundred metres away from the cliff.'

'That's because the pilot wasn't expecting a murder to take place in the back of his helicopter, so when he saw what was happening he stopped hovering in position and started to make his way back to the landing area at North Sannox. That's why Novic fell out further away from the cliff from where Munro wanted him to fall. The pilot landed at North Sannox and told Munro to get out. He wanted to go to the police, but the Albanians threatened him to say nothing if he wanted his family to stay alive.'

'I must have found the body by accident just after it happened,' said Logan.

'Novic fell on the Friday evening before you arrived. But it was getting dark. Then on Saturday morning it was misty, so nobody went looking for it at the time. Badger ordered Jansa to fly over the area when the mist was clearing to look for the rucksack. That was when you were on your way down from the Punchbowl with the little girl.'

'We were hiding in the birch trees,' said Logan.

Geordie continued:

'Actually, the pilot, Jansa, saw you. He could see that you were carrying something. He knew you'd be killed if they found you, so he steered the helicopter away from you. The guy, Badger as you call him, was looking out of its right side, so, Jansa turned the helicopter away from you by turning right so you wouldn't be seen.'

'I noticed he manoeuvred quite abruptly,' said Logan.

'It was Munro who hiked up there at sunset on Saturday evening and found the body. He was hoping it had landed as planned at the bottom of the cliff like a climbing accident so that it would eventually be found, once again enabling him to fake his death like he had done years earlier. But because his plan went wrong, he had to hide the body in case someone else would find it and call the police who would then start searching the area and perhaps find the rucksack before he could.'

'That would explain why the body was covered by a dead deer,' remarked Robin.

'Yes. He shot the deer and covered the body with it. Also, having lost the rucksack, the Albanians suspected Munro of deliberately losing it, perhaps so that he could retrieve it later and cash in for himself, so they threatened him to find it before they'd allow him to leave the island. That's why gangsters were posing as officials checking all the cars leaving the island.'

'So, originally he was just planning to walk away with a new identity?' asked Eric.

'That's right. He didn't care about the drugs. He just wanted to start a new life. But now he had to help find the rucksack. He was the one who had tampered with the junction boxes to try to listen into conversations which he hoped would have given him information about someone finding the rucksack, but he had no idea about what he was doing, so he didn't succeed at that other than to cause some slight superficial damage to some junction boxes and create some disruption to some local telephone connections.'

'And that would explain why I saw him staking out the police station in Lamlash and following the police in Brodick,' said Logan.

'Yes. But incognito. Not wearing the dark-green jacket with the circular bird patch. He followed Reynolds to her home. He was hoping to use his charm to somehow seduce her into giving him police information. His seduction method failed. She wouldn't have been interested in him if he was the last man on the planet. Besides that, she didn't have any information about the rucksack at that time, and she wouldn't have told him anyway. He started making a nuisance of himself so that she'd mention him to other officers to guarantee his description was well noted by others as Gerry Munro with the dark-green jacket, blue circular sleeve patch, sunglasses and a spider tattoo. When he was with her, he still believed that Novic's body was at the foot of the cliff as he'd planned, so he even made a point of telling Reynolds that he was going to climb Coich na h'Oighe in a couple of days.'

Geordie's talk was interrupted by the waitress taking their order for food. After giving their requests, Geordie added:

'I'll just finish this talk quickly then we can enjoy our meal together.'

'We checked out Karina's father. His name's Adam. He had created a scene in Glen Sannox and told Kleo that he was going to the police to report her for abducting his daughter. The last thing they wanted was police attention, so that guy you named Sloucher chased after him to silence him. That became a car chase which ended with two bashed cars and a nasty fight just outside the sawmill. Initially it was believed to have been a road rage incident. Adam was discharged from hospital this morning and was able to travel back on the afternoon ferry although he'll need more hospital treatment. He was reunited with Karina in Glasgow.'

'What about her mother?' asked Katy.

'Her mother is apparently in agreement with Adam that Kleo had not received permission to take her away. But that's now another legal matter which I don't have any control over. One thing's certain Logan. You saved that little girl's life.'

He then looked at everyone at the table.

'All of you helped Logan. All of you have saved a lot of lives here this week.'

'Excuse me for one minute,' said Logan as he stood up. 'There's someone I want you to meet.'

He walked out of the restaurant, then walked back in with two teenagers.

'Meet the two young men here I met in Brodick. I nick-named them Curly and Sheepskin but now I know their names are Jamie and Darren.'

He pulled out two chairs for the boys to join them for the meal.

'These are the two guys who gave me their kayak.'

'That, eh, would that be the kayak you left behind on Holy Isle?' asked Robin with a half-smile.

'Ah, eh, well, yes.'

He turned to Jamie and Darren.

'I promised you I'd somehow replace your kayak if anything happened to it.'

'It's not a problem,' said Jamie. 'It was an old one. And it wasn't one of the expensive ones. And we understand what you needed it for.'

'Well, I like to keep my promise, so you can expect a new kayak to delivered to your gran's house in a few days, but meantime I want you to take this envelope.'

Logan pulled an envelope from his inside jacket pocket and told them:

'This isn't one of the expensive ones either, and I understand what you need it for.'

He handed the envelope over to the boys containing keys.

'I bought a Ford car last week from an elderly couple on Arran, but I didn't complete the registration into my name. It's yours now.'

For the next two hours they all sat and enjoyed their meal together, laughing and joking as if the entire events of the last few days hadn't happened.

'Does anyone have any plans for tomorrow?' asked Katy.

'I should get back home,' said Robin. 'I have a waggy-tailed dog waiting for me. But before I go I have a present for Logan here.'

He handed Logan a small box which Logan opened. Inside it was a pair of dark-rimmed glasses.

'I reckon you'll need these,' he said. 'Extra strong lenses.'

Logan grinned.

'Thanks. They'll be useful.'

Katy looked baffled. Logan turned to her saying:

'You've not actually seen me wearing glasses before. I don't normally wear them. They're just for a special, eh, art project.'

'I need to get back to Glasgow,' said Geordie. 'I have a lot of work to do because of all this.'

'I also need to get back home,' said Roz. 'Too many things to do.'

Katy and Logan looked at each other. After a momentary pause, Logan suddenly sat up straight and announced:

'War graves at Pirnmill… war gr… war stuff.'

The others look at him, baffled at what he was thinking. Logan closed his eyes to concentrate. After a few moments he announced:

'War… second world war… Rudolph Hess.'

The others sat and watched as he searched into his memory.

'Rudolph Hess was the high-ranking Nazi,' he said. 'I think he was second in command of the Nazi Party. Second in command to Hitler. He flew to Scotland in the early stages of the war and crashed his aircraft. I think it was in nineteen forty-one.'

The others continued looking at him with baffled faces.

'Verhoeven kept talking about him even though he never showed any other interest in war history other than having a worrying admiration for Nazis. So why would he want to keep mentioning Rudolph Hess?'

The others looked at him curiously. After a few moments, Logan turned to Geordie with an excited tone of voice:

'I need to take a look at that graveyard in Pirnmill where Munro dug up that rucksack. Today.'

He then turned to Katy with a more relaxed tone of voice and told her:

'Then tomorrow I want to buy more chocolate cake at the castle, then again the next day, and the day after that as well, and just maybe some more later on.'

CHAPTER 9

Three months later. December.

It was a clear but cloudy mid-December day. Logan sat in his artist's studio near the village of Kenmore at the edge of Loch Tay. His oil paintings surrounded him. He was working on one large canvas which was perched on an old table and leaning against the back wall. He had already given the upper half of the canvas a light blue background as he'd done with most of the other paintings there. His left arm was in plaster and held in a sling around his neck with various signatures and messages of *Get well soon* scribbled on the plaster. His left hand was heavily bandaged such that his fingers were completely covered.

Using only his right hand, he painted curved lines of green paint on the lower part of the canvas. A yellow circle had been crudely painted on the upper left corner. He had been trying to replicate his memory of his childhood drawing on his school jotter from the day when he had been reprimanded by his teacher for drawing sunbeamers over his writing.

Hanging on one of the walls were three unfinished paintings of what looked like an owl perched on a rock, painted from different angles. Above the window was a small shelf with a stuffed owl perched on a lump of wood. Around the room were some framed photographs of Logan with a woman of similar age, smiling, with two girls aged approximately seven years old.

All the photographs looked like happy family holiday pictures.

Surrounding the room were various types of colourful hand-painted signs. *Beware of the dog*, *Close the door*, *No Parking*, and *Caution Jet Blast* were just four of the many signs. Some of them were only partly painted. Others appeared to have had paint accidentally spilled on them. One was covered by coffee stains due to it being used as a placemat with a partially-filled mug of coffee on it.

The room was messy. Its floor had been crudely tiled by an amateur builder. It looked like it hadn't been mopped or swept for months. Bread crusts could be seen in one corner. A mousetrap sat in another corner with a mouldy lump of cheese on it, untouched by any mouse. Logan's appearance was scruffy due to his clothing being stained by multiple colours of paint splashes. He was wearing the thick dark-rimmed glasses which Robin had given him on Arran.

Outside the room in the adjoining kitchen was a metal bucket which was overflowing with empty beer cans. On the window ledge stood an empty vodka bottle. Beside the painting he was working on was a wall mounted mirror on which were various reminder notes stuck to its cracked glass. He had a small music system playing an Elton John album. He enjoyed the music until it stopped suddenly while half way through *Rocket Man*.

Logan sighed, muttering:

'Ugh, power cut,' as he looked over at the electric socket in the corner.

He put his brush down on an old plate and turned around to move towards the kitchen where the mains fuse box was situated. When he opened the kitchen door he stopped and froze in position when he saw three people standing staring at him. Clive and Margaret Verhoeven were standing together. Clive's brother, Donnie, stood immediately behind them. They were all wearing black leather gloves. Donnie still had one hand on the electricity fuse box having switched off the mains electricity supply to the house. In his other hand he was holding a double-barrelled twenty-bore shotgun. They had entered through the back-door and were now slowly making their way into the living room. Logan stared at them in silence for several seconds as they stared back. Behind them he could see the shadow of another man who was standing outside the back door. Logan took a deep breath as he stared back at them while trying to avoid showing any facial expression of surprise. He slowly walked backwards into the living room, back to the same spot where he'd been standing painting just seconds earlier. He spoke, almost jokingly, saying:

'Well, I guess there's no point in me inviting you in because here you are. So, the least I can do is offer you a drink. I have, eh…'

He looked through the door into the kitchen.

'… I have beer. And beer. And actually, I have more beer. Help yourselves.'

'It's been a long time,' growled Donnie. 'Twenty years and nine months. Tommy told us you'd become a fat bastard, but you're a lot fatter than I expected.'

'I like chocolate cake,' replied Logan. 'I'd offer you some, but I ate it all.'

Clive walked into the living room, followed closely by Margaret and Donnie. They stood in the room in such a position that Logan was now trapped with his back to the wall.

He stayed calm and composed while pointing to five wooden chairs placed around the old wooden table in the middle of the room. There was an unwashed dinner plate on the table with the remains of a hamburger and some chips on it. The dirty knife and fork sat together on the plate. Next to the plate was a salt shaker and an empty unwashed beer glass.

'You might as well sit down,' said Logan as he fixed his gaze on the shotgun.

Clive, Margaret and Donnie sat on one side of the table with the kitchen door behind them. Donnie kept a firm grip on the shotgun, keeping it pointed towards the ceiling. Logan sat on a three-legged wooden stool at the opposite side of the table from where he faced them while fixing his gaze on the shotgun.

Donnie opened the gun then slowly and menacingly loaded two orange-coloured cartridges into its barrels. He closed the gun abruptly, proudly demonstrating to Logan that it was now loaded. The other man entered the room and slowly walked around the table to the same side where Logan was sitting. He pulled the chair next to Logan further out from where it was so that he could sit diagonally behind him. Logan didn't look at him although he could see enough with his peripheral vision that the man wasn't wearing gloves.

'How did you find me?' asked Logan.

'I'm smarter than you,' said Clive. 'You thought you could go into a witness protection scheme and change your name to Pete and never be found, didn't you? Pete O'Head? What sort of stupid Irish name is that?'

'I liked the name,' said Logan while keeping his gaze fixed on the shotgun.

'Aren't you going to say hello to your brother here?' asked

Margaret.

'I don't have a brother.'

'That's a very upsetting thing to say about your poor upset bother Tommy,' said Clive. 'And what about your sister, Lorna? Have you forgotten her?'

'I never had a sister,' said Logan defiantly.

'Well, that's a poor excuse for screwing up their futures so that you could go to another family and have a useless retard for a brother instead. What was his name? Oh yeah. I remember. Leigh. But he's dead now.'

'Best thing for him,' added Margaret in her typical callous tone.

'Well, say hello to your brother Tommy here,' said Clive. 'He's been looking out for you for the last twenty years and nine months making sure you're alright. Isn't that nice of him?'

'Very touching,' commented Logan with more sarcasm in his voice.

'Because of Tommy here, we knew where to find you when we came out of prison. And here we are. It's very rude of you to not say hello to him.'

'I don't have a brother,' repeated Logan.

'You could at least turn and look at him,' said Donnie.

'I'd rather not,' said Logan while still staring at the shotgun.

Calmly, Clive picked up one of the framed family photographs from the table and began trying to tease Logan with a slow patronising tone:

'Your wife looks good. What's her name? Oh yes, I heard about her. It's Sonya. The beautiful model from Ireland. Where is she now? And where are your kids?'

Then, looking at the single unwashed dinner plate on the

table, he sarcastically added:

'Oh, you're living alone. How sad. Your beautiful wife could get any man she wanted, but she got you. A fat alcoholic who threw away his chance at being a millionaire. She left you because you're a loser. She couldn't put up with you being an alcoholic. And an obese one at that. Have you actually looked at yourself in that mirror over there?'

'You're proud of yourself, are you?' asked Margaret as she looked around at the paintings. 'We've been in prison for years and here you are making stupid paintings.'

Again, Logan said nothing as he could see Clive preparing himself to say more.

'We would have been multi-millionaires by now if it wasn't for you. We would have been rich. Have you never heard of the saying that only a stupid dog would bite the hand that feeds it?'

'I was a baby when you kidnapped me,' said Logan calmly. 'I didn't bite off the hands of my parents… my real parents, who would have raised me through my childhood better than you ever did. And they wouldn't have had to deal in crime to do it. And they never hated, hurt or killed anyone.'

'Oh, these wonderful parents,' said Donnie. 'You think we don't know about them? That story was all over the news. You found yourself in some pathetic family with a retarded brother and you stayed with them for what, four years? As soon the retard died you walked out on them too. You even tried to have that woman…'

'My mother,' interrupted Logan.

'You tried to have her arrested on the day you left home. You haven't spoken to them for what, sixteen years now?'

'You could have been rich,' said Margaret. 'You were living

in our family and we would have been worth millions by now if it wasn't for you.'

'At the expense of how many more lives being killed or destroyed?' asked Logan.

'Worthless lives,' said Donnie.

'I'll tell you about worth,' said Logan. 'The three of you are murderous drug dealers. Killers. Vermin. Well, the remains of last night's meal which I flushed down the toilet this morning was worth more to this world than any murderous drug dealer.'

'Yet here you are, bankrupt,' said Clive. 'Yes, I know about that too. You're in big debt which makes you worth even less than anything going down any toilet. And now, here you are in this filthy shit-hole of a studio. Painting these… what are these pictures anyway?'

'Modern art of a specialised nature,' said Logan. 'But I don't expect you to understand, so there's no need for you to concern yourself.'

'They look like shit to me,' said Margaret. 'You're a hopeless artist.'

'I told you I was going to kill you, didn't I?' said Clive.

'Yeah but I don't think…'

'You didn't believe me, did you?'

'No,' said Logan. 'But I do believe you want to tell me what you think of me because you've hated me all my life and especially so in the last twenty years while you've been festering behind bars being used as a punch-bag and a sex toy by the prisoners who were tougher than you. So, if you don't mind, I'll sit here and pretend I care while you tell me exactly what you want to say to me. Then we'll all feel much better and then maybe I can offer you a beer. And if you're really nice, I'll give you some of my paintings to take away because one day they might actually be worth quite a lot of money.'

Margaret looked at the paintings of the owl, saying:

'You really expect us to believe these paintings are worth anything?'

'Eh, well, yeah for sure. Once… if… when I become famous.'

Donnie forced an exaggerated fake smile while shaking his head.

'Famous?' asked Margaret. 'At painting this rubbish?'

'You're a born loser,' said Donnie. 'You've failed at every job you ever had.'

'How do you know anything about any of my jobs? You've been in prison for twenty years with your brother Clive here.'

'Twenty years and nine months,' growled Clive.

'Your brother Tommy here has been updating us,' said Margaret.

'You sent him to spy on me?' asked Logan.

'Aren't you going to say hello to him? He's been looking forward to meeting you.'

'Tommy's loyal,' said Donnie. 'He visited us as much as he could for the last twenty years. When we got arrested, you actually thought he'd want to go back to these people just because they're…'

'His real family,' interrupted Logan.

'Real? He knows what's good for him. We did him a favour when we took him away from them. He knows that. And he kept us updated on you and your attempt at being all goody-goody while you became a fat alcoholic so-called painter.'

Logan refused to look at Tommy.

Donnie looked out of the window. He looked at Clive and

Margaret. The three of them nodded in agreement. Donnie turned away as if to walk out of the room then turned around and pointed the gun at Logan.

'You're not going to shoot me,' said Logan. "Think about it. You've been out of jail for how long? Maybe a few weeks? The police know you hate me. So, if I get killed you'll be the first suspects.'

'Being a suspect isn't a crime,' said Clive. 'We know where we're going to dump your body where nobody will find it, so don't you worry about us. We won't get arrested.'

Clive then spoke to Tommy:

'Best you go outside and check there's nobody passing by.'

Tommy stood up. He spat on Logan and kicked him on the chest with enough force to send Logan tumbling to the floor and banging into the wall with a loud thud. As Logan lay there, Tommy kicked him repeatedly on the chest and into his groin.

'I've practiced that,' said Tommy as he walked out. 'But now I'm leaving you to your Mum, your Dad and Uncle Donnie here. Goodbye Loser.'

He walked out of the room and made his way towards some trees at the far end of the rough track near the roadside.

Logan slowly picked himself off the floor and looked out of the window. Gasping for breath, he asked:

'Is that Tommy's car out there?'

Nobody answered.

'So, what next?' asked Logan.

He picked himself off the floor and trembled as he sat back on the wooden stool.

'You kill me, then what? You've been in prison for twenty

years…'

'And nine months,' added Clive.

'Whatever. Anyway, do you have a job? Or any qualifications in anything? Savings? You have no credibility. You've never done an honest day's work in your life. Or will you go to college and spend time studying for something which you could have been doing in prison? Or wave a magic wand and become rich and successful?'

'We have our plans already made,' said Clive. 'We have our investment waiting for us. And it's been making us interest for twenty years… and nine months.'

'Humour me,' said Logan. 'You've got money saved away in a piggy-bank?'

'Arran,' smiled Clive smugly. 'Your favourite place. What a pity you're never going back there.'

'Oh yeah, Arran. That place where you wanted to plan the perfect crime. I remember that. So, eh, how did that work out? Funny thing is, on the news about three months ago, there was a major drugs bust there. Seems that someone stole your idea. I did think of you at the time. But I knew it couldn't be you because you were in prison.'

'That was disappointing,' said Clive. 'But we still have our investment hidden there. But you don't need to worry about that.'

'Ah okay. Retirement. That's for the three of you. Or is it for the three of you plus Tommy, your beloved son. The arrogant bastard who couldn't do anything without getting into a fight. The thick idiot who failed everything at school. And your beloved daughter Lorna who wasn't quite so bad and probably would have turned out alright if she hadn't been trained to be so arrogant. And like Tommy, she kept failing every exam at school. You tried telling the teachers that she was dyslexic, but actually she was just as thick as two short planks because you kept faking her illnesses so that she wouldn't go to school in case she'd start telling people about her home life.'

Clive kept looking out of the window. He could see Tommy standing at the roadside. After a pause, Logan continued:

'You sent Tommy out of the house before you told me about your hidden investment. So, I reckon you've never told him anything about whatever your plans are. And you don't want him to know. So, you've been using him for twenty years… and nine months… to keep a watchful eye on me, but you've no intention of sharing any family fortune with him.'

'It's not your concern,' said Donnie.

'Even if you don't kill me, the very fact that you're here threatening me with a shotgun is enough to get you sent back to prison. The only road leading to here has several police cameras and you came here in his car, didn't you? So, if anything happens to me, he'll take the fall. So much for family loyalty. And when Tommy finds out you've betrayed him, I reckon he'll turn on you like a rabid dog.'

'Tommy won't turn on us,' said Margaret.

'How do you figure that?'

'Tommy hates you too much,' said Clive. 'That's why he supplied us with this shotgun. I must say, I'd have preferred a twelve-bore, but this'll do the job nicely. And the orange cartridges. My favourite colour. But he didn't want to shoot you. That's too much for him to stomach. I have to say I'm disappointed in him. But he's made it loud and clear to a lot of people that he wants you dead.'

'I see you're already wearing gloves, said Logan. 'I… I don't think Tommy was, so let me guess... his prints are all over that gun, aren't they?'

Clive shrugged his shoulders.

Donnie looked at the barrel.

'Oh yes. Look at that,' he said. 'He's right. Fingerprints are on the barrel.'

'But that's not your problem,' said Margaret.

Logan took a long deep nervous gasp of air, quietly saying:

'So, once you eh, kill me, and then go to Arran and collect your stash of whatever it is, you're not going to share it with Tommy. Or Lorna. So, all this family stuff you preach means nothing to you. It never did. You're planning to collect whatever you've hidden and then vanish to another part of the world leaving poor Tommy penniless and in prison, framed for a murder he didn't commit.'

'It's not my fault my children were cursed,' said Margaret. 'I wasn't meant to have children. The spirits made this happen. So now it's time for us to move on with our lives without any of you.'

'Did your imaginary spirits tell you that bullshit, or did Clive tell you that?' asked Logan as he calmly started painting more green paint onto his partially-painted canvas.

Clive looked out of the window and waved at Tommy who raised his thumb.

'Now's a good time,' he said.

Donnie spoke to Logan:

'Two of us will fire the non-fatal shots and your daddy here will fire the fatal shot after we've watched you suffer for a while. But don't worry. It'll all be over in less than an hour.'

'And you'll all be back in prison,' said Logan.

Clive looked over at Donnie and told him:

'Let's do this.'

'This one won't kill you,' said Donnie. 'We're saving that for your daddy.'

He pointed the shotgun at Logan's groin and pulled the trigger. Logan could feel the blast from the shotgun into his groin. He immediately doubled over and fell to the floor, clutching his groin with his right hand. Clive was thrilled when he saw the wall and floor turning red. Lying on his side on the floor, Logan looked up at them with a sad begging facial expression, gasping rapidly, hyperventilating, and shaking all over. Donnie passed the shotgun to Margaret.

'This is for my eighteen years,' she said as she pointed the gun at his right knee and pulled the trigger.

Again, Logan could feel the blast hitting his leg. More of the floor turned red.

'Look at that blood,' laughed Clive. 'Red. What a surprise. I was almost expecting it to be yellow.'

With Logan's right hand clutching his groin and his left arm still tied into a sling, he continued to lie on his side, writhing and trembling. Clive walked over to him and wiped his finger on the wet floor. He then licked his finger before spitting it out.

'Your blood tastes weak,' he said.

Gasping the air and panting heavily, Logan spoke:

'H… how… how many… have… you… killed?'

'About a dozen,' said Clive proudly.

'You… you killed the Livingstones… didn't y…?

'Clive sneered:

'The Livingstone family. You won't remember them. They

were about to report myself and your Uncle Donnie here to the cops because they saw something they shouldn't have seen. You were friendly with their kids Freda and Liam when you were three years old.'

'These were interesting times,' said Donnie.

'Yeah sure were. But we had to kill them.'

Logan trembled more, and his voice faded as he looked up at Donnie.

'Yes,' said Donnie. 'Your good old uncle Donnie helped your mum and dad here to kill the Livingstone family to stop them screwing up our futures. I killed your little girlfriend, Freda. And I popped off your little friend, Liam. Your mum and dad here killed her parents, and Billy… you remember Billy Macfarlane? He filled in the grave for us. All that effort so that we could become rich instead of getting arrested. All these lives wasted. They died in vain because you wanted to have a pathetic life with a pathetic family.'

Logan lay there in the same position. He didn't try to move. His breathing became quieter.

'This is great,' said Margaret. 'He's suffering like we did in prison and now we can stand here and watch him.'

Clive knelt down beside him and spoke quietly into his ear:

'I think you're in so much agony that you just want me to put you out of your misery, don't you?'

Logan hesitated and nodded with his eyes tight shut.

'But I'm not going to finish you off just yet,' said Clive. 'We've got all day to enjoy watching you like this.'

Margaret, Clive and Donnie each calmly sipped though a can of beer each while Logan continued lying on the floor. His trembling lessened. His breathing became quieter. After ten minutes Margaret told Clive:

'I think he's dying. Maybe you should take your shot while you can.'

Clive agreed and put two more cartridges into the shotgun. He told Logan:

'We agreed that I get to make the fatal shot.'

He looked out of the window again to check on Tommy who was still standing guard at the roadside. He then pointed the shotgun at Logan's chest.

'Goodbye Equinox bastard,' he said as he pulled both triggers.

At the sound of the two simultaneous shots, the entire floor corner turned red as Logan's body became instantly limp, lying sideways and motionless with his clothes now soaked red.

'Done,' said Clive. 'Now I can sleep peacefully for the first time in over twenty years.'

Clive put the shotgun on the window ledge and then produced two large cigars from his inside jacket pocket. He gave one to Donnie. Margaret smoked a cigarette. After five minutes, Tommy returned and hesitantly walked into the living room.

'It's over?' he asked.

Clive just smiled at him. Tommy looked at Logan's body on the red floor and wall immediately behind him. The wooden stool lay on its side. Donnie took the shotgun from the window ledge and unloaded the two empty cartridges from it. Tommy sat at the table opposite Clive, Margaret and Donnie and looked down at Logan's limp body. Nothing was said until Clive and Donnie finished smoking their cigars.

Looking at Logan, Tommy quietly said:

'I thought I saw him moving just now.'

'Muscle reflex,' said Donnie. 'It happens.'

Logan slowly rolled over from his position.

'He's still alive,' gasped Margaret.

Clive watched Logan's movements, uncertain of what he was witnessing. Donnie looked on, speechless, as Logan stood up and smiled, saying:

'I hope you enjoyed the cigars. Congratulations. You all passed your job interview.'

Tommy looked as surprised as everyone else. Logan picked up the stool again sat on it next to Tommy. He started removing the plaster and bandaging from his arm. Beneath the thick bandaging, he was holding a small electronic device attached to some thin wiring which led up his arm inside the fake plaster and into the jacket he'd been wearing. As he removed his jacket, they could see that his overweight appearance was the result of his abnormal clothing.

'Special effects,' he said. 'Just like the movies. Whenever you fired the shotgun I pressed one of the buttons inside my glove which activated a small cartridge in my clothes. Makes it look like I was being shot. I even have several buttons to press so that it looked like I was being shot wherever I saw the gun pointing at. Leg, torso, groin or wherever. I have a really great friend named Roz. She knows people in the film industry. She helped to organise the special effects equipment. Except the movies use some sort of red dye stuff. Instead, I got some strained onion soup, put lots of salt in it and some red cordial which I thickened with cornflour. I made it specially for you so that if any splatterings landed on your faces it wouldn't taste of dye. I have to say, I didn't expect you to actually dip your finger into it to taste it.'

He removed his glasses.

'I don't wear glasses,' he said. 'But even a blank shotgun cartridge can damage the eyes at close range. And all this padding I'm wearing which makes me look fat is just to hide the equipment I'm wearing. That's why I made myself look fat and wore glasses when I went to visit you in prison earlier this year.'

He pointed to the family photographs they'd been ridiculing.

'I don't have a family. I've never been married, and I don't have kids. These are pictures I downloaded from the internet. That woman in the picture is some professional model I found on an American website. And the two young girls are actually the same woman when she was a child. I had to use a bit of computer wizardry to make them look like holiday pictures with me placed in there too.'

Donnie stood up aggressively.

'Please sit down,' said Logan. 'I need to explain to you about the job I mentioned.'

Donnie looked at Clive.

Stunned at what was happening, Clive quietly said:

'Sit down Donnie. Let's hear what he has to say.'

Logan opened a small drawer beneath the table. From it he produced an envelope. He opened it and removed some photographs.

'I'll show you these pictures, but before I do that, I should explain a few things. Let me ask you. What do you think my name is? Anyone?'

The others sat in silence.

'Alright, well, as you know, I thought my name was Steve Verhoeven. When I discovered the truth about you murdering the real Steve and the real Tommy and Lorna when they were innocent babies, and kidnapped the three of us to replace them, I woke up to a nicer type of reality. I must admit I still don't fully understand why you had so much obsession about the equinox every year just because of a name the press had given me. That obsession was a bit weird. But anyway, I discovered that my real name was Craig Lockhart. But you knew that already.'

'Stop pretending you found a loving home with these people,' said Donnie. 'You fell out with them after four years and you haven't spoken to them since.'

'Actually, I didn't ever fall out with them,' said Logan. 'I knew I wanted to leave school and get a career, but I had my brother… my real brother, Leigh. You know about him. His Down's Syndrome and a few other medical problems gave him a limited life expectancy. He was a fantastic guy and I wanted to spend as much time as I could with him until he died. During that time, I used the name Craig.'

'Then you went into a pathetic cowardly witness protection scheme,' said Donnie. 'We knew about that.'

'No, I didn't. The police knew that you had an obsession to get revenge on me. They also knew that Billy Macfarlane, the mammoth, still lived in the area and had been watching me for you.'

Margaret started looking out of the window nervously.

'Relax,' said Logan. 'There's nobody out there. As I was saying, the police offered me a witness protection scheme, but I refused because I was happy with my real family and my new friends. Also, we suspected that you'd killed the Livingstone family. We knew that one day you'd get out of prison and return to your old style of destroying people's lives again. So, I agreed to help them by becoming bait. But I needed to protect my parents in case you managed to get some of your crooked friends to harm them to avenge me for getting you jailed, so I orchestrated events to make it look like I hated my parents. I agreed with the police to fake an arrest at a time and place where we knew Macfarlane would be. We even got the arrest publicised in the local *Press and Journal*. Then I made it look like I'd accepted witness protection and changed my name to Pete O'Head. Because we knew Macfarlane was watching me, it was easy to make him find out what I wanted him to tell you. Thereafter it was easy to start the occasional rumour about me being some sort of alcoholic loser who couldn't hold onto a job.'

Margaret, with a confused look on her face, asked:

'So, who was Pete O'Head?'

'Pete O'Head was my little joke. You've always known I liked aeroplanes. It's part of an aeroplane. It's a small hollow tube which sticks forward into the airflow to supply air pressure to the air speed indicator. It's spelled P-I-T-O-T. And its tip is called the pitot-head. Didn't expect you to understand my sense of humour though.'

Clive stared at Tommy. Tommy stared back at him while Logan continued:

'I knew that Tommy was visiting you in prison, so he was being supplied all sorts of false information about me to relay to you.'

'I'd like to hear what Tommy has to say,' said Donnie. 'And what's this job interview that we've all passed?'

'Oh yes. The job. Let me finish the explanation first. Then I can give you the good news about the job.'

Logan started looking through the photographs he'd removed from the envelope and announced:

'A few months ago, when I went to visit you in prison you told me that Tommy here is a better man than I ever was. Actually, I'll agree with you on that.'

Tommy was visibly startled at that remark. He looked at Logan in surprised anticipation as to why he had said that. Logan continued:

'You see, I never really changed. You were already incapable of loving two children which you kidnapped to cover up the murders of two babies which you never wanted in the first place. But then having a third kid was much more inconvenient for you, so you treated me like shit. So much more than you did with Tommy and Lorna. So, I spent my entire childhood despising you. I never had any respect for you and I never had any doubt or confusion about that. Tommy however, being a bit older and being your second kidnapped kid, got better treatment from you while you indoctrinated him into your way of thinking. You trained him to mimic your behaviour and attitude. You trained him to be arrogant and violent. You punished him if he didn't stoop down to your level. He was taught how to hate good people. But when he was reunited with his real family… a really fantastic family, he realised he wanted to change.'

Clive, Margaret and Donnie stared aggressively at Tommy, while Logan continued talking:

'After only a few weeks of adjusting to his new life, he came to talk with me. I think it was the first time we actually spoke to each other without any feeling of hatred. We talked, and talked, and talked. He blamed himself for all the fights we had as kids, but none of that behaviour was ever his fault. And because our real families still lived quite near each other in the Aberdeen area, myself and Tommy became friends. Except his name's not Tommy Verhoeven. It's William Blyth. He…'

'Stop,' growled Clive. 'Tommy, it's your turn to talk now.'

'Logan's right.' he said. 'My name's not Tommy. You already know I'm William Blyth. Actually, I'm William Robin Blyth. People call me Robin nowadays. You kidnapped us as babies and took away what would have been very happy childhoods with wonderful families. And I took on a massive guilt trip because of the way you made me bully Logan relentlessly when we were kids. You were turning me into a monster like yourself. What I thought was normal behaviour isn't anything near normal. But I didn't know that until I met my real family.'

'All the stories you'd heard about me losing jobs and being a drop-out alcoholic were all fake,' said Logan. 'I joined the army when I was eighteen. By that time, myself and Tommy, real name William, had become such good friends with so many common interests, that we joined the army together and were lucky enough to serve in the same unit. But in case any of you would ever find out about that, I started using my middle name, Logan. The press never mentioned my middle name when I was kidnapped, and my parents never told anyone, so you could never have known about it. And Tommy, here, real name William, started using his middle name, Robin.'

Logan spread the photographs onto the table and started pointing at them one at a time as he described:

'That's the two of us in the army training camp. Then this picture here is from when we were in Syria together. Then here we are together in the Falkland Islands training with the local Falkland Islands Defence Force.'

Robin added:

'I couldn't let my younger, eh, brother, join the army alone. When I lived with my real family, I realised the difference between the person I really was, and the person you had been trying to make me become. I became horrified at myself and at the way I'd been treating Logan all through his childhood. You had been teaching me that by bullying the kid who I believed was my younger brother, it would somehow make me a better son for you to boast about. You told me that kicking and punching him was helping him to build his character. It didn't take me long to realise that all I wanted to do was look out for him and protect him. That's what older brothers should do to their younger brothers. That's something you told me to never do. But it turned out to be the best thing I ever did. It's just tragic that I had to find out that he wasn't my brother before I changed my attitude.'

Just then, Roz walked into the room from the kitchen. She sat on the chair at Logan's left side.

Margaret was the first to recognise her.

'Lorna?' she asked.

'Happy families,' said Logan as he smiled. 'Here we are all together for the first time in just over twenty years.'

'And Lorna sitting here isn't Lorna,' said Robin.

'You stole my childhood too,' she said. 'My name's Lynn. Lynn Kinnaird. But you always knew that. After you kidnapped me, my parents adopted another child. A baby girl. Thinking they'd never see me again, they named her Lynn after me. So, when I was reunited with them and the step-sister I'd never met, it seemed a bit strange having two sisters with the same name, so I became Rosalyn, but people just call me Roz.'

Logan put his left arm around Roz's shoulders and his right arm around Robin's shoulders, giving each one a kiss on the temple.

'Sorry for saying you were thick as two short planks,' said Logan. 'I'd forgotten the speech we'd rehearsed.'

'No offence taken,' smiled Roz.

She glared at Margaret and told her:

'We're more like a family now than we were back in the days when we thought we were a family. Also, Logan's not an alcoholic and he doesn't paint pictures for a living.'

'I never have,' said Logan. 'You're right Margaret. I'm a terrible painter. I know nothing about art. These efforts you see here and on my website were painted specially to make you believe that this was my full-time occupation. I never tried selling any paintings. I doubt if anybody would buy them.'

Clive started to stand up with an aggressive posture.

'Oh, sit down,' said Logan. 'In a few minutes we'll all be out of here and you'll know about the job we have lined up for you. And to be extra nice, we'll help you find out about the drugs you buried on Arran all these years ago.'

Clive sat down, thoroughly bewildered at what was going on. Donnie started looking out of the window nervously and picked up the shotgun.

'There's no point in doing anything with that,' said Roz. 'We were concerned that you might have brought some of your own twelve-bore cartridges. We know you like twelve-bore, so we supplied a twenty-bore gun so that none of your cartridges would fit.

'Anyway, let's talk about the retirement plan.' said Logan.

'The one you didn't want me to know about,' said Robin.

'The one Billy Macfarlane lost,' said Roz.

Clive and Donnie were startled at that remark. Donnie started to ask:

'How did you know…'

'Shut up and let him speak,' interrupted Roz.

Robin continued:

'You'd planned a massive drug deal since before you went to prison over twenty years ago. We knew that you were planning something big to happen and we knew it would almost certainly be on Arran. I can confess that we only suspected, but didn't know for sure, that you already had drugs hidden on the island.'

Logan then removed a small calendar which had been hanging on the wall. He pointed at the months of March and September.

'Because of your obsession for attaching things to the subject of equinox, I was ninety percent certain that for whatever year you'd planned anything, you'd plan for it to happen on either the spring or autumn equinox. For that reason, I made a point of visiting Arran every spring and autumn around equinox to look out for anything suspicious in case you ever managed to organise anything from prison. Of course, my other reason for visiting Arran is simply because I love the place.'

'I'd go with him on many occasions,' added Robin. 'As the years went on, it started to make more sense that you'd try to do something as soon as you'd be released. And most likely it would be the first equinox after your release date. That's why we wanted to let you plan something, then at the last minute we'd find something to keep you in prison a bit longer so that your plan would go ahead but without you being there.'

'I found the evidence which extended your sentence,' said Logan. 'The blood-stained crowbar. By staying quiet about that crowbar until just a few weeks before your planned release date, I could be certain that it would keep you in prison for a few more months.'

'We know how impatient drugs cartels are,' said Roz. 'The consequences of cancelling such a massive drug operation would have caused you a lot of problems. You had four of the country's most dangerous drug dealers going to a lot of trouble and expense for your operation. You wouldn't dare let them down. They'd come after you. So, having had your prison sentence extended through the planned date for your drug deal, you still had to make it happen even though you were behind bars.'

'So, you got Billy Macfarlane,' said Robin. 'In previous years he'd have done anything you told him to do because he was scared of you and scared of what you might tell the police about his past. Having changed his name to Gerry Munro, he stood in for you because he knew you trusted him. I admit I'd heard that he'd died, but we figured you'd have found some other fool to work for you.'

'You liked to hide things in graveyards,' said Logan. 'You said that graveyards are the most unlikely places for anyone to want to dig. And I remember you once telling us how graves which have been already dug and filled in tend to have had any awkward large stones removed, making them easy to dig. You buried your rucksack full of cocaine in a graveyard at Pirnmill on Arran's west coast over twenty years ago. You ordered Munro to unearth that rucksack three months ago.'

Clive sat speechless. Logan continued:

'You told him to dig up the drugs and give them to the Albanians to sell them on your behalf. But he was tired of being scared of you, so on this occasion, with your absence from the scene, he planned to run away with a new identity.'

'He failed,' said Roz.

'Having met him,' I'm actually amazed that you ever trusted him at all,' said Robin.

'He lost the rucksack,' said Logan. 'I found it.'

Logan showed Clive a printed photograph of the rucksack, adding:

'When I found out about this, I decided to visit Pirnmill war graves to see which grave he'd dug into. I found the disturbed grave of a man who died on the spring equinox some years earlier. I hadn't realised that your weird obsession for equinox dates had been extended to include grave digging on graves with equinox dates. That was when I started looking at equinox dates on headstones. We went into the records to find any other graves on Arran which had anyone dying on or near an equinox date.'

Clive, Margaret and Donnie all fidgeted nervously in their chairs, dreading to hear what Logan would say next. Logan continued:

'The one I found was in the graveyard at Sannox. Ebenezer Kent. Died on the twenty-first of March many years ago. Equinox. And his initials 'EK' are an anagram for East Kilbride: that town which you called home. One spade later we found this padlocked box in that grave buried just two feet down.'

Logan showed Clive a picture of the box which had been wrapped in waterproof packaging.

'When I was fourteen, just weeks before you were arrested,

when I was already suspicious about you. It was during the last time you took me to Arran for another false display of devoted father-and-son stuff when I saw you hiding three keys in a small bag and placing them into your jacket pocket. I didn't know what they were for, but I figured you were up to something bad. So, I stole the keys and wrapped them in a plastic bag then hid them in the hollow part of a tree beside that Bavarian summer house in Brodick Castle gardens. When I found that box with three padlocks in Kent's grave, I instantly knew where to find the keys. I think that's the retirement plan you were talking about.'

'But don't worry about your retirement plan,' said Roz. 'We have a job for you. And as Logan told you, you all passed the interview.'

'That's true,' said Logan. 'Here's the situation. We need you to do something for us.'

'And if we do this we'll get our stash?' asked Margaret.

'Much better,' said Logan. 'We need you to go back to prison for a while. I have a job for you in there.'

Donnie stood up in a mild panic at the thought of prison.

'Let's shut him up now,' he shouted.

'You're going to arrest us?' asked Clive aggressively. 'Do you think the three of you…'

'We're not going to arrest you,' interrupted Roz. 'Just listen.'

Logan spoke to Clive:

'The thing is Clive. Since I was very young. Four years old. I've been getting these horrible flashback memory things. They only last a few seconds. I remember being in a graveyard somewhere and I was terrified. I remember cowering behind a gravestone, watching the three of you killing people and burying them. For years I didn't know if it was just a bad dream or an actual memory, or maybe from a movie I'd seen. But after you were arrested, the police told me about how, about ten years earlier, the Livingstone family had gone missing. There was plenty of evidence against you. But they couldn't convict any of you without the bodies being found. Then nine months ago, I went to visit you in prison...'

'At your request,' added Robin.

'... yes, at your request. Well, sort of. You see, I went to a hypnotist to try to extract the memory, but he suggested to me that perhaps the most effective way to unlock bad memories from so far back would be to actually meet with you again. That's why Robin here, acting as your faithful loyal son Tommy, tricked you into requesting a visit from me. He knew you wanted to kill me, so he played with your mind to trick you into thinking that if you'd tell me you were planning to kill me I'd assume that it would be such a crazy idea that I wouldn't believe you and so I'd let my guard down. So, you made the call wanting to meet with me.'

Robin explained to Clive:

'I'd been visiting you for twenty years pretending that I still wanted to be your son, Tommy, instead of wanting to be with my real family. Each time I visited you I was astounded at how evil you really are. I couldn't bring myself to call you 'Dad' anymore, so I started calling you 'Boss'. You thought I was being respectful, but I wasn't. Perhaps you never realised it, but your way of thinking is amazingly predictable for someone who continually boasts about being smarter than everyone else. Especially with your obsession about doing things on the equinox dates. By the time you agreed to meet with Logan, I knew almost exactly what you were going to say to him, especially as I partially suggested to you what to say.'

'We knew you were going to try to kill Logan,' said Roz. 'So, we helped him set the scene here so that he'd be ready for you.'

'Complete with terrible paintings,' smiled Logan. 'That's why I said these paintings are modern art of a specialised nature. They were specially painted to set this scene. Just for you. Hopefully you all feel special now.'

'So, we rehearsed that prison meeting,' said Robin. 'The three of us sat facing each other across a table night after night, predicting what you'd say, and rehearsing it.'

Clive glared at Robin, not knowing what to say. Logan told him:

'That prison meeting was the first time I'd seen your face and heard your voice in twenty years. I'd forgotten that sensation of actually experiencing the vile evil hatred that spews out of your mouth.'

He rotated his fingers to either side of his own head, saying:

'That just got the old brain cells activated again and so many old memories suddenly came flooding back. Just like the hypnotherapist suggested to me. And since finding out about the war graves in Pirnmill and Sannox, and the way you kept mentioning the equinox, I remembered how you had a weird fascination about war stuff and that Nazi guy, Rudolph Hess, similar to the way you would talk about the equinox.'

'I remember you telling us about Eaglesham when we were kids,' said Roz. 'But all you had to say about the place is that it was where Rudolph Hess landed during the war.'

'It felt like you were trying to boast about something,'

said Robin. 'Just like you kept trying to secretly boast about the equinox, it seemed strange that you often mentioned Eaglesham to us, but you didn't seem to know anything about the place.'

'So, I went to Eaglesham cemetery,' said Logan. 'And, like magic, the memory came flooding back. I found the gravestone I was hiding behind while you were killing and burying the Livingstone family in that other grave where its occupant had died on an equinox date from years earlier. A whole family crammed into one grave just a few feet underground. I even remembered you telling me to wait in the car, but I got bored, so I went to explore the area and I saw what happened. There was another man there. That big bearded hairy guy Billy Macfarlane… the mammoth.'

'You threatened to frame him for killing that family unless he'd let you take control of his life and be your errand boy while you were in prison,' said Robin. 'He's changed his appearance, so we didn't recognise him when we met him on Arran.'

Logan showed them some pictures of the graveyard in Eaglesham. He told them:

'The police have found the bodies of the Livingstones. Forensics are dealing with their identification. You were wanting to get your retirement sorted. Well, we've sorted it for you. We have a job for you. You need to do that job from inside prison though.'

Donnie opened his mouth to speak but Clive raised his hand to signal to Donnie to stay quiet.

'Exactly… what do you expect us to do in prison?' asked Clive.

Logan looked at Roz and Robin who both shrugged their shoulders.

'Oh, nothing particular,' said Logan. 'Just staying there for the rest of your lives would be enough.'

'Let's get out of here,' said Margaret as she panicked and stood up.

'Actually, we're just about to leave,' said Roz. 'You can stay longer if you want.'

'Look at the signs,' said Robin. 'All these hand-painted signs on the walls here saying things like *Beware of the dog* and so on. If you look around, you'll see there are some signs clearly saying that this place is being monitored by CCTV recording equipment. I decided to display these signs just to make sure your lawyer doesn't try saying anything silly about you being illegally recorded.'

He pointed to the owl.

'Look at the stuffed owl on the shelf up there. Its right eye is a hidden camera. There's a microphone under its feathers. Everything in this room is being recorded. The three of you committed attempted murder here today and confessed to a mass murder from years ago. We needed to get that recorded and witnessed just in case the evidence of the buried bodies doesn't hold up.'

Roz stood up and opened the door at the back of the room. Six uniformed police officers walked into the living room. Simultaneously, another six officers walked in from the kitchen. Robin pointed to a mirror on the wall.

'That's a two-way mirror,' he said. 'So, these officers have been watching, listening and recording everything here.'

'We've had twenty years to prepare for this,' said Roz. 'It took us a couple of years to renovate this old woodshed and make it look like a small house. It's also a pleasant little holiday cottage for us.'

'Sorry for the smell of dog pee,' joked Robin. 'I accidentally locked Chino in here last week and his bladder was full.'

Margaret sat still, holding back tears, and bowing her head. Clive and Donnie desperately looked for a way to escape but they were surrounded by twelve police officers. They knew they couldn't fight them.

'You're going to prison for the rest of your lives,' said Roz.

'And I won't be visiting you any more,' said Robin. 'No more calling you 'Boss'.'

Logan, Roz and Robin walked out of the house, leaving the police officers to make the arrests.

'Sorry I spat at you and kicked you in there,' said Robin.

Logan jokingly replied:

'Your motorbike body armour was a good idea. And the groin guard. But more importantly, like me, you'd be a lousy footballer with these kicks.'

They stood outside until all the police vehicles had driven off, leaving only Geordie talking to them. He looked at the name plaque on the front door and smiled.

'Chocolate Cake Cottage'. I like it.'

'Especially Arran chocolate cake,' joked Robin. 'I wanted a silly name for the place.'

'Oh, changing subject… I found out about the squirrels,' said Geordie.

'Squirr…? Oh yeah, I forgot about that.'

'It was Verhoeven's idea. Someone anonymously lied to the police about a foreign animal rights activist planning to smuggle a large cage of grey squirrels on the back of a foreign registered vehicle. The organisers welcomed the idea of having police checking vehicles boarding the ferry because it would deter rival dealers from attempting to visit the island. The Spiritbeamer followers were told about possible police searches and advised to not bring drugs onto the ferry. That might explain why you saw some of them thoroughly spaced out on the ferry. They'd taken their fix before boarding. And of course, during these searches, the police didn't find any drugs so there was no suspicion of drug dealing going on until you informed us.'

'I'm still baffled about the Russian writing on that parachute,' said Logan. 'You said that it was the original helicopter pilot who gave it to Munro, who then gave it to the Spiritbeamers. But we don't know who or where that helicopter pilot is? Old parachutes are easy to find, but why Russian? Are we missing something here?'

Geordie nodded his head and sighed.

'I'm thinking the same. I think there's more going on. We have a lot more questions to ask.'

Roz sent a text. After two minutes, Logan's car approached the driveway. The car stopped and out stepped Katy from the driver's seat. She opened the back door to let Chino run towards Robin.

'All good?' she asked.

'Never better,' said Logan.

'For sure they'll be in prison for their rest of their lives,' said Geordie. 'What are your plans for the rest of the day?'

Roz, Logan and Robin all looked at each other in bewilderment. Roz became noticeably emotional, as she looked around at the beautiful scenery surrounding Loch Tay. Robin looked at Logan, not knowing what to say. Logan looked somewhat lost in his thoughts.

‘Did I just say something wrong?’ asked Geordie.

The three of them shook their heads. Katy was concerned at their sudden change of mood.

‘What’s wrong?’

Logan inhaled a deep breath of the cold fresh December air.

‘Nothing’s wrong,’ he said. ‘It’s just that this is the first time in our lives that we don’t have any plans because we’re not worrying about what these people will do any more.’

‘We can put the past away now,’ said Roz.

‘And never have to look back,’ said Robin.

Geordie looked at Chino.

‘Seems to me he’s planning to take you on a long walk.’

Geordie drove away. Logan, Robin Roz and Katy went for a walk with Chino. They didn’t look back.

CHAPTER 10

March 21st the following year. Spring equinox.

Robin, Roz, Logan and Katy were walking along the grass along Shore Road in Lamlash. The weather was cold but dry. There was a slight wind but the sea water in Lamlash Bay was well sheltered. Chino and Sheena followed them, wagging their tails. Today was Logan's birthday. They had all been for a meal.

We've been keeping a secret from you,' said Robin. 'Myself, Roz and Geordie decided we actually like Arran as much as you do, so we decided to buy something together for all of us. And Katy here organised and paid for the paintwork.

Logan looked at Katy. She smiled back at him.

'We've been keeping it a secret from you for a while,' she said.

They walked the short distance to the Old Pier. Secured there was a white yacht, moored beside the steps which led down to the water. Its stern was facing the shore. Geordie and his wife Janice were sitting on deck which was heavily decorated with bunting and a large sheet saying: 'Happy Birthday Logan'. Sitting beside them were Logan's parents.

'Step in,' said Geordie. 'You always said you liked boats. Well, this one belongs to all of us. And I'm going to give you sailing lessons this week, starting from now.'

Robin handed Logan his camouflaged bush hat.

‘I went to look for it last week. It was still crumpled up blocking that wasps’ nest at North Sannox.’

‘I washed it,’ said Katy. ‘You can wear it again.’

They cast off and sailed around the Holy Isle. After two thoroughly enjoyable hours they returned to Lamlash. Logan was the first to step out onto the pier to tie the boat to its mooring. After securing it, Roz shouted up to him:

‘Take a look at the bow.’

Logan stepped a few paces forward to look down at the bow. In large letters, printed in gold paint, he could see the yacht’s name: *EQUINOX.*

THE END